The Day Trader

The DAY

Stephen Frey

TRADER

Ballantine Books / New York

www.ballantinebooks.com

LIBRARY OF CONGRESS CATALOGING-IN-PUBLICATION DATA
is available upon request from the publisher.
ISBN 0-345-44324-1

Text design Mary A. Wirth

Manufactured in the United States of America
First Edition: January 2002

10   9   8   7   6   5   4   3

For Lil, Christy, and Ash.
I love you.

ACKNOWLEDGMENTS

———————— ⟨∞⟩ ————————

So much help from so many.

Cynthia Manson, Peter Borland, and Gina Centrello.

Stephen Watson, Kevin and Nancy Erdman, Andy and Chris Brusman, Gordon and Shannon Eadon, Bob and Allison Wieczorek, Matt and Kristin Malone, Scott Andrews, Marvin Bush, Pat and Terry Lynch, Baron Stewart, Bob Flanagan, Tony Brazley, Mark Tavani, Mike Pocalyko, Walter Frey, Alex Fisher, Jack Wallace, Stephen Palmer, Bart Begley, Marc Shaener, Monty Davison, Chris Tesoriero, Barbara Fertig, Mike Attara, Alex Bushman, Drexel, and Cody.

The Day Trader

CHAPTER

1

I'm not a religious man, but I make the sign of the cross over my heart just in case. The way I do every time I start. After all, the next few seconds could change my life forever.

Employees aren't supposed to use company Internet access for personal reasons, but lots of us violate the policy and no one's ever been fired for it. Jesus, they only pay me thirty-nine thousand dollars a year to be an assistant sales rep for retail paper products in the mid-Atlantic region. So the way I see it, I deserve a perk or two along the way. I've dedicated eleven years to this company, but my wife and I still live paycheck to paycheck, even though she has a full-time job too.

Images flash across my computer screen, and I quickly reach the home page of the on-line brokerage firm I use to trade my small stock portfolio. As I enter the information required to access my account, adrenaline surges through me, like it always does when I get to this point. It's as if I've bought a lotto ticket with a fifty-million-dollar jackpot, and I have that lucky feeling tingling in my veins.

NAME: **Augustus McKnight**
PASSWORD: **Cardinal**
ACCOUNT NUMBER: **YTP1699**

My fingertips race across the keyboard as I close in on my target, and I pause for a sip of coffee and a deep breath. The deal is only a few screens away, and I'm addicted to the anticipation—so I prolong it. It's one of the few things I look forward to these days. This morning, as I guided my rusting Toyota through bumper-to-bumper northern Virginia traffic and thick summer humidity, I had a premonition that today would be different. That something was going to interrupt my daily grind. But I've had that feeling before.

There's a sharp knock and my eyes shift to the office doorway. Standing there is my boss, Russell Lake, vice president of all paper product sales. Russell is a slender man with thinning brown hair, a full mustache, and a pasty complexion. He leans into my cramped office, one hand on the doorknob, peering at me over wire-rimmed glasses. And I stare back like a boy caught digging in the cookie jar just before dinner.

"Good morning, Augustus."

I can tell by the intensity in Russell's eyes that he's trying to figure out what I'm doing on my computer, but I've positioned it so someone standing at the door can't see the screen. "Hello," I say warily. You never know what he's up to.

"Up with the eagles this morning?"

"What do you mean by that?"

"It's only eight o'clock," he says sarcastically, tapping the cracked crystal face of the same Timex he wore the day he interviewed me more than a decade ago. He's always been sarcastic. That's just the way he is. "Aren't you usually crawling out of bed about now?"

I'm in by seven thirty almost every morning, sometimes earlier, but there's no point in arguing. Like most bosses, Russell has a convenient memory.

"What are you working on?" he asks.

"Cold fusion."

"Very funny," he says, moving into the office. "Tell me the truth."

I'm tempted to flick off the computer, but that would be a dead giveaway I'm doing something wrong. "I'm updating a sales report for central Virginia," I say, hoping he doesn't walk around to my side of the desk. "Nothing exciting."

"Checking your stock portfolio again?"

Russell blurs before me. "What?"

He settles into a chair on the other side of my desk, an annoying smile tickling the corners of his mouth. "I know all about your day trading." He snickers. "You're on that computer at least two hours a day doing research, checking quotes, and placing orders." Russell removes his glasses and cleans the dirty lenses with his striped polyester tie. "I'm willing to look the other way at a little indiscretion, but sales in your region are way down. A couple of weeks ago senior management wanted to know what was going on. I defended you as basically a good employee, but I had to tell them about your stock market addiction."

"Dammit, Russell! Why'd you screw me like that?"

"Don't blame me, Augustus," he replies coldly, replacing the lenses on his face. "You've got to start accepting accountability for your actions if you want to get anywhere around here. That's always been a problem for you."

"How do you know what I'm doing on my computer?"

"I monitor the network."

"So you've been spying on me?"

"Spying is such a nasty way to put it," Russell says. "I prefer 'monitoring.' "

"You've been watching me without me knowing. That's what it boils down to."

He raises his eyebrows and grins smugly. "Now you know."

"That sucks."

"You shouldn't be using company property for personal reasons," he retorts.

"Lots of other people do."

"Other people get their work done on time. Besides, the company has a right to protect its assets."

"And I have a right to protect my privacy."

"Last year, you and everybody else around here signed a waiver permitting us to monitor your Internet activity," Russell reminds me, "including e-mails. This shouldn't come as any surprise."

Now that he says something, I do remember signing that waiver. It didn't seem like a big deal at the time, but it's come back to haunt me.

"Are you day trading right now?" Russell wants to know.

I hear a different tone in his voice. There's curiosity as opposed to warning, with a hint of goodwill too. But Russell is skilled at convincing people he's reaching out when he's really digging, so I have to be careful.

"Come on," he urges when I don't respond right away. "I'm interested."

I've been caught red-handed, but if I'm cooperative, maybe he'll cut me a break. "I'm not actually day trading," I say cautiously. "Real day traders execute hundreds of buy and sell orders every day. I'm not doing that."

"What *are* you doing?"

"I'm buying a few shares here and there and holding them for the long term." My entire portfolio is worth less than a thousand bucks. I won't be retiring on it, but I get a kick out of knowing that when prices go up I've made money without lifting a finger. "Once in a while I get in and out within a couple of days," I add. "But not very often."

"So give me an example. Like what are you doing right now?" he asks, gesturing at the screen.

"Checking my account. Last night I e-mailed my on-line brokerage firm about an IPO they're involved in."

"An IPO?"

"An initial public offering," I say deliberately. Russell knows almost nothing about the stock market. He's told me he puts most of his money in a bank account earning a boring four percent a year. He hates it when the market goes up and loves it when it dives. "The company's stock is scheduled to begin trading on the Nasdaq at nine thirty this morning. I was checking my account to see if I had won any of its shares in a lottery my firm was running yesterday."

"What do you mean, lottery?"

I've spent a lot of time over the past few years learning all I can about financial markets by reading the *Wall Street Journal*, studying business school textbooks I've borrowed from my local public library, and doing research on the Internet. It feels good to show off a little of what I've learned. "The big brokerage houses sell shares of going-public companies to their preferred clients," I explain. "Clients like insurance companies, mutual funds, pension funds, and a few rich individuals."

"The haves," Russell sniffs. He's from a working-class family, like me.

"Brokers sell shares to those preferred clients at a price they think will rise during the first day's trading," I continue, ignoring Russell's resentment.

"Ensuring their clients a profit."

"Right. The brokerage houses want to make sure the preferred clients are always happy so they can count on them for the next deal, and the next and so on."

"It's a stacked deck," Russell mutters. "An insider's game you and I will never get to play."

"That's mostly true," I agree. "In the past, small share lots were around, but you had to know somebody at the company or the brokerage house to get your hands on them. You really did have to be an insider. Now there's a chance for me to get them too."

"How?"

"That's where the lottery comes in. Because of all the Internet trading, the big Wall Street firms that lead IPOs have recruited on-line brokerage firms to help them sell shares to the general public. On-line brokers serve regular people who, individually, may have only a small amount of money to invest, but, when added together, control a lot of cash. Like big firms, the on-line firms give their best customers first crack at most of the shares they have. But as a marketing gimmick, they make a small part of their allocation available to all their customers by running a lottery. The lottery gets lots of people interested.

Even if they don't win any shares in the lottery, the little guys do their best to get them in the after-market as fast as they can."

"Which helps drive the price up on the first day of trading," Russell reasons, "just like the big Wall Street firms want."

"Exactly."

Russell leans forward in his chair and rotates the monitor so he can see the screen too. "And you participate in these lotteries?"

"Sure. As long as you have an account," I explain, nodding at the screen, "and money in the account to cover the share purchase if you win, you can play."

"How long have you been doing this?"

I can tell Russell isn't asking questions to build a case against me. He could do that simply by tracking my network activity. He wants to learn how to play the game. "Six months."

"Ever won?"

"No," I admit. "They don't make many shares available in the lottery. Like I said, it's mostly a marketing gimmick designed to spark interest in the stock."

"Ever *heard* of anyone winning?"

"No."

Russell laughs harshly. "No one like you ever wins at this game, Augustus. It's all a big con. They're trying to make you think they care about your business. But they really don't."

That thought has occurred to me before.

"Well?" he asks.

"Well what?"

"Aren't you going to check to see if you won?" He wants to see my disappointment because he's the kind of man who finds comfort in the despair of others. "Go on."

I move the mouse so the flashing white arrow is on the appropriate spot and click to my personal page. Instantly a summary of my account—a detailed description of the few shares I own—appears on the screen, but at the bottom of the page is a blinking message I've never seen before. A message instructing me to click on it. The text is surrounded by exclamation points and turns rapidly from red to white to blue with firework graphics exploding all around it. Usually this message is a dull black and white. Usually it informs me that I haven't won any shares—again.

Russell leans across the desk and points. "What does all of that mean?"

"I don't know," I admit, unable to hide my grin. "Looks good, though, doesn't it?"

"Click on it," he orders, an edge in his voice. As much as he takes pleasure in another's disappointment, he hates his own envy.

I glance at the ceiling, cross my heart one more time, then guide the flashing arrow down to the message and click.

Suddenly the entire screen is exploding, and in the middle of the chaos is a box with words congratulating me on winning five hundred Unicom shares. It informs me that the IPO price will be $20 a share and that my account has already been debited ten thousand dollars, plus commissions.

"My God," Russell exclaims. "Where did you get ten grand?"

According to Wall Street's experts, Unicom could finish today's trading at $100 a share, maybe even $200. The era of every dot-com IPO soaring into the stratosphere right away is long gone, but Unicom has been tagged a can't-miss kid by the Street's All-American analysts. It has developed an amazing, next-generation wireless technology, and the huge telecommunications firms are pounding on its Silicon Valley door to steal a peak inside the kimono.

Elation rushes through my body. In a few hours my ten thousand could be worth fifty thousand, maybe even a hundred thousand.

"Augustus, I asked where you got ten thousand dollars," Russell demands, irritated.

"Calm down. I haven't saved that kind of money working at this place." I know that's what he's worried about. "It's my inheritance."

On her deathbed last Christmas my mother instructed me to dig in the backyard beside the porch. There I would find something help-ful, she said. I was skeptical because during her last few years my mother's brain was ravaged by Alzheimer's. But in the fading light of a cold December dusk I followed her instructions, and a few inches down into the icy soil, my shovel struck metal. Inside a shoe-box-sized container lay neat stacks of hundred-dollar bills, flat and crisp, as though she'd individually ironed each one. I stood there in the cold for a long time, gazing at the money in the rays of a dim flashlight, overwhelmed. Apart from the money in the tin box, my mother had little else. The equity in the house barely covered her funeral.

My mother's last request was that I not tell my wife what I found in the yard. That I use the "something helpful" for myself. Mother never liked Melanie.

I've kept this money in a very safe savings account since I dug it up, afraid that if I invested it in anything else I might lose it. I earned almost nothing in interest, which was frustrating, but now it looks like my patience has paid off.

"What does Unicom do?" Russell asks impatiently.

"It has developed a state-of-the-art wireless application," I explain, eager to show how thoroughly I've done my research. I've tried to talk to Melanie about the market many times, but she doesn't share my passion for it. In fact, she doesn't share my passion for much of anything anymore. These days most of our conversations seem to dissolve into a predictable set of questions and answers. "And they've invented a codec, a compression-decompression device, that brings real-time interactive television to desktop computers regardless of a user's hard drive capacity or Internet connection. Now people won't need a server the size of a living room or a T-3 hookup to make two-way desktop television work. It's revolutionary."

Russell airmails me an irritated look. I know it annoys the hell out of him to think that I'm up to speed on concepts like byte compression, hard drive capacity, and bandwidth connections. Things he knows little about.

"You need to focus on why paper towel sales are down at the big supermarket chains in Maryland," he warns, standing up. "Not on technologies that have nothing to do with your job." He turns back when he reaches the door. "Listen and listen to me good, Augustus. I want half of everything you make on that Unicom stock today, and I want it in cash by the end of the week. Otherwise you're out of here."

———— ⟨⟩ ————

When I get home Melanie is waiting for me in the small foyer of our cookie-cutter three-bedroom ranch house, arms folded tightly across her ample chest, one shoe tapping an impatient rhythm on the scuffed wooden floor.

"Where have you been?" she demands before I've even shut the door.

"The Arthur Murray school of dancing. I know how you've always wanted to learn that ballroom stuff, and I was going to surprise you for your birthday, but—"

"Augustus!"

My attempt at humor isn't going over well. "Mel, I—"

"Dammit, Augustus, it's late and I'm in no mood for this."

At thirty-three—the same age as me—my wife remains a beautiful creature. The same long-legged blonde I fell for in eleventh grade. The same girl I followed to Roanoke College and married a month after graduation with a few family members and friends looking on. To me, she's still every bit as pretty as she was the day of our wedding. "Something came up at the last minute." I smile mysteriously, but she doesn't seem to notice.

"I can't count on you anymore, Augustus. You tell me you're going to do one thing, but then you do something else. You told me you'd be home by six and here it is after eleven."

"You said you had to stay late at the office again tonight, so I thought you wouldn't care if I went out." My smile fades. "And you've been working later and later over the past few months. I wasn't sure you'd come home tonight at all."

"I don't appreciate that," she snaps.

Melanie is an executive assistant for a Washington, D.C., divorce attorney named Frank Taylor, and I've always suspected that he has more than just a professional interest in her. During the past few months she's been wearing lots of perfume—sometimes heavier when she gets home at night than when she leaves in the morning. She's been dressing more provocatively too and working late several nights a week, sometimes until one or two in the morning. Even a few Friday and Saturday nights recently. I finally tried talking to her about it last week, but she flew into a rage right away, then accused me of silly macho jealousy and stalked off. But it occurred to me later that she never actually denied anything.

Melanie won't look at me. "I have to talk to you."

Her eyes are puffy, as though she's been crying. "What about, sweetheart?" I move forward to comfort her but she takes a quick step back and buries her face in her hands. "What is it, Mel?"

"Oh, Augustus," she murmurs sadly.

I wrap my arms around her and hold on tightly, even as she struggles to turn away. I work out almost every day in the makeshift gym I've set up in our basement, and at six-four and over two hundred twenty pounds, I easily control her slender frame. "Easy, honey."

"Let me go, Augustus."

"Not until you tell me what's wrong."

"Let me go!" she yells, her arms starting to flail.

Suddenly her fingernails rake the side of my neck. I've never seen her like this before. "Calm down, Mel."

"Get your hands off of me!"

"Stop it."

"You don't understand me!"

"Of course I do. You've had a long day and you're exhausted," I say sympathetically, controlling my anger despite the fact that my neck feels like it's on fire where she scratched me. "And you're sick of me telling you that we can't afford anything."

"You've been drinking," she says, her tantrum easing. "I smell scotch on your breath."

"I had a few drinks with a friend. That's all."

"A female friend, I'm sure."

Melanie has never accused me of cheating before. In fact, I didn't think she cared anymore. "I was with Vincent." Vincent Carlucci and I have been friends since I was ten years old.

"I've seen how women look at you, Augustus," she says, wiping tears and smudged mascara from her face, "and how you look back."

"I've always been faithful to you, Melanie."

She slumps against me like a rag doll, arms dangling at her sides, face pressed to my chest. "I can't do this anymore," she sobs.

"You're right. You can't keep up this pace," I agree, slipping my palms against her soft, damp cheeks and tilting her head back until she's looking up at me. I smile down at her confidently, feeling better than I have in years. I've scored big in the stock market and she's going to be impressed. "I want you to stop working, Melanie. I want you to sleep late in the mornings and pamper yourself."

"What are you talking about?" she asks, grimacing as she glances at my neck.

"You don't have to work any longer. It's as simple as that."

"We can barely make ends meet as it is. From what you've told me, sometimes we don't. How could we possibly survive without my salary?"

"You let me worry about that."

She stares at me for a few moments, then closes her eyes and shakes her head. "Did you think I was talking about my job when I said I couldn't do 'this' anymore?" she asks softly.

"Of course." In that awful moment I understand what she really needed to talk to me about tonight. "Wasn't it?"

"No."

"Then what did you mean?" My voice is hollow, almost inaudible.

She covers her mouth with her hand. She says nothing, but she doesn't have to. The look in her eyes says it all.

The first few moments of lost love are terrible. I gaze at her helplessly, and it's crushing to see how sorry she feels for me—pity is such a useless emotion, only making matters worse for both of us. Melanie wants to be with someone else. Over the years I've heard the whispers from her family and friends that I'm a disappointment to her. Now she's finally listened to those whispers and given in to her desire to be with another. "Melanie?"

"We don't have any children, Augustus," she sobs, "and so little money. It won't be hard to split things up."

"It's your boss, isn't it?" My rage erupts. An awful, mind-numbing fury that spreads like wildfire from my brain to my eyes to my chest.

I've tried to be understanding about the late hours, the new wardrobe full of short dresses and lacy blouses, the matchbooks from expensive Washington restaurants on her dresser, even the hang-up telephone calls I endure on weekends. Her indifference to me. But no more. "It's Frank Taylor!" I shout. "You're having an affair with your goddamn boss. I knew it! Taylor's made you all kinds of ridiculous promises and you've decided to take a chance."

"This has nothing to do with Frank!" she shouts back. "It has to do with me. I need a fresh start, Augustus. I'm drowning in our life. I have to save myself. If I don't do it now, I never will."

"He's tempting you with houses, cars, and jewelry. I know it."

"Wouldn't that be awful if he was?" she snaps.

"You bi—"

"It's not true!" she snaps. "But do you blame me for wanting those things?"

"Melanie, come to your senses," I beg, swallowing my pride. "It's going to be much better for us from now on. I promise."

"You've been saying that for eleven years. I'm not willing to wait any longer." Tears stream down her face, but they are tears of rage, not sadness or compassion. "I'm sick and tired of being married to a man who accepts being ordinary," she says, gesturing angrily over her shoulder at the inside of our modest home. "I want someone who needs success as much as I do."

"Let's not kid ourselves. You want money. That's all you've ever wanted."

Her eyes fill with tears again. "How can you say that to me?"

"Because it's true, and you know it."

She drops her face into her hands. "Let's just end it," she pleads pitifully. "Please."

I stare at her, wishing I could take back those words, even if they are true. "Mel, come on."

"I'm sorry, Augustus. I'm so sorry, but I want a divorce."

"This is crazy," I say, taking her gently by the arms. "Stop it."

"Let me go."

My heart sinks as I realize that this is not a passing drama. She's serious. "Oh, God," I mutter, looking down. Both of Melanie's wrists are marked by painful-looking purple bruises. "What have you done to yourself?" I murmur, looking up into her beautiful, anguished face.

She yanks her arms from my grasp and runs away down the short hall without answering.

"Wait, Mel. I hit it big today in the—" But the slam of our bedroom door cuts me off.

For five minutes I stand in our foyer, unable to comprehend what has just happened, my emotions ricocheting from dejection to rage. Finally I stumble to the kitchen and ease into a chair at the scarred wooden table where Melanie and I have eaten so many meals together. My eyes come to rest on a notepad lying beside the sugar bowl and a stack of unpaid bills. In Melanie's looping script I see that Russell Lake has telephoned four times this evening. I'm supposed to call him back no matter how late it is.

I touch my neck where Melanie scratched me, then bring my hand in front of my face. My fingertips are stained with blood.

CHAPTER

2

I'm not a greedy man, so my decision to sell is an easy one.

At four o'clock yesterday afternoon Unicom closed its first trading session on the Nasdaq at $139 a share, up $119 from the $20 IPO price. In the overnight "casino" market it spiked another $36, to $175 a share, where it opened this morning. So, after plowing my entire inheritance into this one investment, my ten thousand dollars has turned into nearly ninety thousand. I've made almost two years' salary in less than twenty-four hours. That, in a nutshell, is the allure of the stock market.

As I stare at my computer screen, I can't help wondering how Melanie would react if she knew about this. I never got a chance to tell her last night. Never got a chance to explain how we could afford to let her quit working. And she had already left this morning when I woke up on the living room sofa, cradling an empty scotch bottle.

A soft knock on my office door distracts me from some very ugly thoughts. "Who is it?"

"Russell."

I expected to see him as soon as I walked in this morning, but it's after ten and this is his first appearance.

"Open up," he demands.

He couldn't sneak up on me today because I closed and locked my door when I got in. "What do you want?" I ask, grudgingly allowing him to enter.

"Don't sound so happy to see me," he says, checking out the dark red marks on my neck. "God, you look awful."

"I didn't get much sleep last night," I admit, easing back into my desk chair with a loud groan.

"What happened?"

Russell should have been a CIA agent instead of a midlevel manager buried in corporate America. Ultimately he unearths everything, as he surely will in this case if I don't tell him. There will be plenty of clues. I'll have to change my address because Melanie wants me out of the house as soon as possible—she left that pleasant request in a short, unsigned note I found on my dresser this morning. Russell will be given that new address by the human resources department. And there will be a steady stream of e-mails bouncing back and forth between Melanie, the attorneys, and me as the divorce proceeds. E-mails Russell could read because he monitors the network. So it's better to be up-front with him about what's going on, rather than endure his nasty comments about being kept in the dark later on.

"Melanie wants a divorce."

"That's terrible." For a moment Russell looks as if he truly feels sorry for me, but his tone lacks compassion. It's as if he thought my divorce was inevitable and timing was the only question. "What was her reason?" he asks. Like most men who know Melanie, Russell is fascinated by her.

"I'd rather not discuss it."

"Did she find someone else?"

"Russell."

"Sometimes it helps to talk about these things."

"Sometimes it doesn't."

As usual, Russell relaxes into the chair on the other side of my desk without being asked. "What will you do about living arrangements? Will you stay in the house with her until the divorce is final?"

A familiar lump builds in my throat as I think about how I'm being evicted from my own home. Frank Taylor has stolen my wife. Worse, she has let him. "No, I'm going to look for an apartment at lunch." Melanie never admitted that Taylor was really driving all of this, but I know the truth.

"Close to the office?"

"Yes."

"Do you need some time off?"

"No." That would give me more time to brood, and nothing good would come of that. Besides, Russell might use my time away from the company as an excuse to demote me.

"So Melanie will get the house to herself."

"Yes." I stare at him, wondering what perverted things are on his mind.

After a long pause he says, "I was on a conference call with senior management this morning. The June numbers are in."

"So?"

"I'm sorry to have to tell you this, especially at such a tough time, but sales in your region were down again last month. Senior management is very concerned, particularly in light of the fact that sales in other areas of the country are doing so well."

"We've been over this a hundred times, Russell," I remind him, exasperated. "The major competitors in my region are running big discount programs right now. There's nothing I can do to jump-start sales until we lower prices. But you won't let me do that."

"Senior management doesn't want excuses."

"Screw senior management."

There's another long pause. "Unicom did very well yesterday," Russell finally says.

"Let's talk about that later. I've got calls to make."

"I checked the share price on the Internet before I came in here," he continues. "It's up to almost a hundred and eighty bucks."

"I sold everything this morning at one seventy-five."

"That's fine," he says, head bobbing as he stands up and moves toward the door. "I agree with that strategy. There's no need for us to be greedy in our first venture together." He hesitates, hand on the doorknob. "Now get on that computer and get us into another lottery. Do you hear me?"

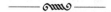

This afternoon, with her blond hair falling seductively down onto her shoulders to frame her angelic face, Melanie looks as pretty to me as she ever has. She wears a short dress and high heels, accentuating her long, perfect legs. From the beginning our friends said we made an appealing contrast. Melanie blond, me dark. Her eyes light blue, mine dark green. As she stands before me in the secluded courtyard of a small park a few miles from my office, her hands clasped in front of her, I'm overcome by her beauty. We're cut off from the world here, surrounded by tall hedges on all sides, and, suddenly, all I want to do is kiss her.

"What do you want?" she asks quietly.

"Thanks for coming," I say, not answering. I pleaded with her an hour ago on the phone to meet me here, not knowing what I'd say if she agreed to come because I didn't think she would. On the short drive over I planned my speech, but now, as I look at her, I'm finding it hard to focus. "Thanks," I mumble again.

She takes a step closer. "I know this whole thing is a shock to you, Augustus, and I'm sorry about that. I don't feel good about myself right now. I'm hurting too."

"Somehow I have a hard time believing that." Her expression turns grim, and I wish I hadn't said that. "We can work things out, Mel. I know we can." Her gaze drops to the gray slate beneath us. "We can't give up on each other," I continue, my voice intensifying. "We're too good together." Her perfume drifts to my nostrils, and it drives me crazy to think she might be wearing it for Frank Taylor. Perhaps he even bought it for her. But I can get past all the jealousy and rage if she'll just come back. I could even get past the bruises on her wrists. "We've been together so long. We can't let it end like this." Tears build in her eyes and I press, sensing that this might be my best chance to change her mind. "We promised ourselves we'd never let this happen. Remember?"

"Yes," she whispers.

"We need to rededicate ourselves to each other and to our relationship. We need to work at this thing." I take another deep breath and nod solemnly, implying that I am accepting my share of the blame. "I've been paying too much attention to all of my stock charts lately, and not enough attention to you. I apologize for that. I promise not to take you or us for granted ever again."

"Sometimes I think you care more about the *Wall Street Journal* than you do about me."

"I need to work harder at our marriage," I agree firmly. "Nothing can be more important."

She lets her head fall back slowly and looks to the sky, our future balanced precariously on her next words. "Augustus, I just can't. . . ."

"Give it time, Mel." I heard an awful finality creeping into her tone. "For God's sake, give it time."

She drops her head and catches a tear on her finger. "I've made my decision," she says, her voice raspy.

But I hear a tiny bit of indecision. Like there might still be a sliver of a chance. "Mel, you've got to reconsider."

"Don't do this," she pleads. "Don't make it more difficult than it already is."

"I can't lose you, Mel. I can't be without you." I take her hand and she doesn't pull away, which must be a good sign. I'm saying all the right things, despite how hard it is. After all, she's the one asking for the divorce. "You're the only woman I've—" Emotion suddenly strangles my words, and the brutal honesty causes her to glance up. "You're the only woman I've ever made love to, Mel. I've never said that to you before, but it's true." I had chances, before and after we were married, but I've never strayed. And that night so long ago, in the fall of our senior year in high school, when she surrendered to me in the back of my parents' old Chevy, was my first experience. "You're the only woman I've ever *wanted* to make love to."

A tear rolls down her cheek as she glances at my neck. "I know," she whispers. "Maybe that's part of the problem."

"What?"

"Frank has volunteered to help me with my side of the divorce," she announces, her demeanor turning professional. "Which is very nice of him. He says you need to retain an attorney right away, and he has several recommendations of people who can help if you don't know anyone."

"Does he now?" I ask, really feeling for the first time that the end of my marriage is at hand. My thoughts flash to a knife lying in the trunk of my Toyota. A knife I keep stashed in the folds of a red woolen hunting vest in case of trouble on the road.

"We have to move on, Augustus. I thought I made myself clear last night."

I swallow several times, unable to believe what I'm thinking. "Are you? . . ." My voice trails off.

"What, Augustus?" she snaps, anticipating my question. But she's going to make me say the words. "Am I what?"

Blood pounds in my brain and tiny spots flash before me. Iridescent spots that shoot across my retinas. I'm not certain I want to know the answer, but I can't help myself. "Are you screwing Frank Taylor?"

For a long time she says nothing, then her eyes narrow. "Do you really care?"

"Yes," I answer evenly. "I do."

"Is everything all right, Melanie?"

Together, she and I look toward a narrow stone archway—the only entrance to the courtyard. Frank Taylor is standing there dressed in a gray suit and red tie.

"You okay?" he asks suspiciously, giving me a warning look.

She hurries to him and comfortably slips her arm into his, as though she's done it many times before. "I'm fine, Frank."

"Hello, Augustus," he calls out in a trial-lawyer tone, like he's about to cross-examine a hostile witness.

I've met Taylor several times at the Christmas parties he hosts for his employees and their spouses at his offices. Each year we've had nothing to say to each other after mumbling hello. It always irritated me the way he smiled at Melanie across the party every few minutes, even when he was talking to someone else.

"I told Augustus that he needs to hire an attorney," Melanie informs him obediently.

Taylor pats her hand gently. "That's right, Augustus," he says, "get yourself a good lawyer. You'll need one."

"I made almost eighty thousand dollars in the stock market this morning," I mutter, the lump in my throat suffocating my words.

They don't hear me because they're already walking away and my voice is so low. As I watch, Taylor's hand comes to rest on the small of Melanie's back, then slips lower just as they turn the corner and disappear.

"I thought you'd gone home."

I look at Russell vacantly. I've been sitting at my desk for the last hour, staring at the wall, thinking about Frank Taylor's hand on Melanie. The image is seared into my mind, and I'm still seething.

"I'm glad you're still here."

"What do you want?"

"I want my money," Russell says calmly. "My share of the Unicom profits. The gain was almost eighty thousand, which means my share is forty grand."

"Forget it."

Russell steps into my office and slams the door. "I wasn't kidding yesterday morning," he hisses. "You pay me or I fire you. It's as simple as that. You made that money using company assets on company time. You owe it to me."

After taxes, my net proceeds from the Unicom trade should be about sixty thousand dollars, assuming I don't hit it big on anything else this year and get pushed into a higher tax bracket. That's a healthy chunk of change, and the thought of giving away so much of it makes me want to puke. I worked hard for that money, and now, like a hyena, he's trying to scavenge my kill. "I'm not giving you one cent."

"You damn well better!"

"Go to hell, you asshole." God, that felt good. I've wanted to say that to him for so long.

If steam could actually rise from a man's ears, it would be spewing from Russell's as though from a hole in a high-pressure pipe. I'm sure he expected me to roll over on this thing to save my job. In fact, in his mind he's probably already spent the money. But I'm not going to let him take advantage of me.

"I protected you this morning on that conference call with senior management!" he shouts. "Those pricks wanted to fire your ass, but I stuck up for you. If it wasn't for me, you'd be out of a job right now." He wags a finger at me. "Don't be stupid, Augustus. Give me the money."

I rise from my chair and move to where he stands, towering over him. I'm tempted to pick him up and throw him against the wall. It would be so easy and feel so good. "I quit," I snarl, somehow keeping my clenched fists at my side.

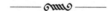

I'm sitting at my kitchen table in just boxer shorts and a T-shirt. The windows are wide open to the darkness, but even now, at midnight, the heat is still brutal. The air conditioner was broken when I finally made it home. I tried to get a breeze circulating through the house, but July in Washington is hot and stiflingly humid, and opening all the windows hasn't helped much.

One more time I check the charts and graphs spread out all over the kitchen table. I'm trying to decide what to do with the money I made off Unicom, but it's hard to concentrate with the heat and everything that's happened today. Finally I head into the living room to stretch out on the sofa. I've had enough day trading for one night.

The knock at the front door startles me from a fitful sleep on the sofa. An old movie is playing quietly on the television, and for a second I wonder if the knock was real or part of the film. I turned the television on to distract myself from thoughts of Melanie and Frank Taylor. I couldn't stop wondering how far she had gone for him. I couldn't stop wondering about his red silk tie and those purple bruises on her wrists.

The knock comes again. It's more urgent this time and I sit up and rub my eyes. Definitely not part of the movie. I check my watch in the glare from the television. It's almost two in the morning.

Standing on the front stoop are two men wearing plain slacks and sport coats, the top buttons of their shirts undone and their ties pulled down. Both of them are sweating in the intense heat, and one mops his forehead with a white handkerchief.

"Augustus McKnight?" the nearer one asks, pulling a gold badge from his jacket and flashing it at me. He's the older of the two, and he has a look in his eyes like he's incapable of being surprised by anything.

"Yes." I gaze at the badge. "That's me."

"I'm Detective Reggie Dorsey of the Washington, D.C., police department. I'm sorry to inform you," he says without emotion, "but your wife is dead."

CHAPTER

3

Melanie's body was discovered facedown in a trash-strewn alley in a crime-ridden section of Washington less than a mile from the Capitol. Her pocketbook lay a few feet away containing several hundred dollars and all of her credit cards, so Detective Reggie Dorsey ruled out robbery as a motive for her murder right away.

Despite having already matched the photograph on her driver's license to her blood-spattered face, Reggie requested that I come downtown with him immediately to make a positive identification. He said he had to have it at some point, and that I might as well get it over with as soon as possible. He said the longer I waited, the harder it would be. I figured he knew what he was talking about, so I agreed.

So here I stand beside the stainless steel gurney supporting my wife's naked body. I'm shivering in the morgue's cold, the odors of formaldehyde and death filling my nostrils. The images of toe tags and ashen fingers dangling from beneath sheets are fresh in my mind after I walked all the way through the place to get to this room. As I watch, an elderly man dressed in a long white lab coat slowly pulls one end of the shroud covering Melanie's body down from her forehead to her chin. He holds it tightly to the pale skin of her cheeks with latex-encased fingers so I won't see the horror of the hastily sutured ear-to-ear throat wound that, Reggie thoughtfully informed me, almost decapitated her. When I can no longer bear to look at Melanie's face, I nod at Reggie and bow my head. Then I cry. As an adult I've never cried in front of anyone, but I can't help it now. The thought that Melanie is gone forever overwhelms me—and I crumble.

During the drive downtown in Reggie's unmarked cruiser it didn't sink in that Melanie was actually dead. I had no reason to doubt Reggie's information, delivered on my front stoop with all the tact of an infantry assault. I assumed he wouldn't have told me that way if he wasn't certain of her identity. However, the events of the past thirty-six hours had anesthetized me. I hadn't yet fully grasped the notion that Melanie was divorcing me, so the idea of her death seemed even further from reality.

But seeing her stiff form sprawled on the silver gurney makes it sickeningly real. I realize there will be no divorce; no Frank Taylor invading the sanctity of my home. Now I face something much more terrible. The woman I always believed I would grow old with is dead.

I fleetingly touch Melanie's cold fingers—hanging from beneath the sheet—then Reggie takes me to a small office where he leaves me alone to face my grief. It takes me thirty minutes to get myself together. When my mother died last Christmas I shed a few silent tears after her breathing stopped and I gently closed her eyelids. But by the time a nurse entered the room a few minutes later, I was back in control. Death seemed natural in my mother's case, almost comforting. Not in Melanie's.

An hour later Reggie and I are heading south back to my house in Springfield.

Reggie is a barrel-chested black man of about fifty who projects a no-nonsense, confident attitude. At five-ten he's of average height, but he's still a mammoth and forceful presence, weighing well over two hundred pounds. His beige sports jacket and plain blue shirt stretch tightly across his broad chest, his fingers are thick and stubby, and he has almost no neck. But his most intimidating feature is his head. It's immense, like a bull's, exuding power. His expansive forehead, with its receding hairline, juts far out over his eyes. His wide nostrils flare when he breathes, and his deeply set dark brown eyes seem to be in constant motion, taking in and cataloging everything around him.

"You okay, Augustus?" he asks after we've driven a few dark blocks in silence. It's four in the morning and the city is still asleep.

"Yeah," I mutter, taking a deep breath. "I just want to find the person who did this to Melanie. I want to see them get what they deserve."

"Of course you do." Reggie tries to use a comforting tone, but I can tell that's tough for him because his voice and manner are naturally gruff. "We all do." He hesitates. "And we will. Make no mistake," he assures me confidently. "Justice will be served."

I shake my head and close my eyes. "I can't believe she's gone. Why would someone do this?"

Melanie's pocketbook sits on the seat between us, full of cash and credit cards. "Not for money," Reggie says, tapping it. "That's obvious."

We lapse into silence until we reach I-395, a three-lane expressway that leads out of downtown. "Where was Melanie supposed to be last night?" Reggie asks, taking the exit ramp and accelerating onto the almost empty highway.

"Work. She'd been putting in a lot of overtime lately. Sometimes it was hard for us to make ends meet."

"I can understand that. Times are tough. Where did she work?"

"At a law firm downtown," I answer quietly, taking a quick glance at the speedometer. The posted limit here is fifty-five and there are no other cars on the road, but he isn't even doing fifty. Reggie wants to talk. "The managing partner is a guy named Frank Taylor. Melanie was his executive assistant. Taylor does mostly divorce work."

"Yeah, sure. That firm is over on Farragut Square. Never met Taylor, but I've heard about him. A real pit bull, people tell me."

"Uh-huh."

"What time was Melanie supposed to be home last night?"

"She didn't give me a specific time." I speak deliberately so Reggie is certain to hear the growing irritation in my voice. I shouldn't have to go through this right now. "She stayed at the office until one or two in the morning sometimes. It wasn't something I was worried about, if that's what you're getting at."

"Okay," he says, as if he's already thinking two or three questions ahead. "Had she called you to tell you what time she would be home?"

"No," I answer curtly.

"Did she usually call when she was staying at work late?"

"Usually."

He starts to ask another question but seems to think better of it. We say no more until the signs for Springfield appear and I give him directions through my neighborhood.

Reggie eases the car to a stop in front of my house. "There's something I want you to understand, Augustus."

Suddenly I'm exhausted. All I want to do is crawl into bed and try to escape the horror of what's happened. Most of all, I don't want to listen to this, but I feel like I have no choice. I don't want him thinking I'm uncooperative. "What's that?"

"My job is to solve murder cases. To find the guilty party."

"Of course it is."

"By using any means necessary. Any at all."

"Uh-huh."

"During that process I don't allow myself to get close to any of the people involved. I've been around too long for that. I learned early on in my career that I have to remain completely objective to be as effective as possible."

"I'm not sure what you're driving at."

"In thirty years on the force I've seen plenty, Augustus. People I thought were as gentle as lambs turned out to be ax murderers. People I could have sworn were guilty as sin were innocent. Maintaining a certain distance allows me to see things for what they really are. To see people for who they really are." He hesitates. "We'll be talking a lot over the next few weeks, and I don't want you to think I don't appreciate what you're going through. I do."

I stare at him for a few moments through the gathering dawn, wondering what initial impressions he's already formed of me. "What does that mean?"

"I may ask questions that make you uncomfortable or that you find offensive. I want you to remember that I'm just doing my job the best way I know how. Like you said, we all just want to find your wife's killer."

As the sun's rays crawl over the horizon, I stagger up the short stone walkway to my house—clutching Melanie's pocketbook—aware that Reggie hasn't driven away. Aware that he's watching me and that he's already begun his investigation.

Melanie's memorial service is a private affair, just as our wedding was. I had her body cremated, and now I've arranged this brief ceremony at a funeral home a few minutes from our house. The only people who attend are Melanie's parents, her sister, an aunt who lives in south-western Virginia, one of Melanie's coworkers, and my friend Vincent Carlucci. No one from my family comes because there isn't anyone. I'm an only child, both of my parents are dead, and my mother's two sisters live in Atlanta. Too far for them to travel. Besides, like my mother, they never cared for Melanie. And I never knew any of my father's relatives, so there wasn't anyone from his side to invite.

Melanie attended early Sunday services at a Catholic church near our house almost every week while I slept late. She'd been going for years, but suddenly stopped a few months ago. She never told me why. I would have held the memorial service at the church, but, in a way, I was afraid to talk to Father Dale, the priest there. She'd made such an abrupt break with her faith I was worried I'd find out something bad. So I held the service at the funeral home where I felt I would receive compassion from the proprietor, not judgment by association.

I stand behind the lectern, a framed photograph of Melanie resting on an easel beside me. It was taken when she was in high school, and it's amazing how little she'd changed. Her parents brought it today. It was the only one we had.

I try hard to control my emotions as I prepare to say a few words to the mourners. In the hushed room, I try to think of anything *but* the good times we shared in the first few years of our marriage. It's just too painful to remember those days. I think about my own father. It's strange where the mind takes you sometimes.

I've never known much about my father. I don't know about his childhood, if he had brothers and sisters, or even where he originally came from. I tried to talk to him about all that once when I was twelve, but he told me to stop bothering him. He told me he just wanted to read his evening paper. He was a damn cold man who would leave home for two or three days every few months without even saying good-bye. My mother explained he had to travel for his job, but I have my doubts. He worked on an assembly line and I've never heard of any other factory workers who have to travel for their jobs. I finally asked Mother about all of that one Thanksgiving when I was home from college and we were alone in the kitchen together, but she had no answers. None she was willing to share with me anyway.

It was clear to me at a very early age that my father didn't have much interest in my life. I tried hard to get his attention, but nothing ever worked. I played high school football, played it pretty well in fact, but he never came to a single game. He never even asked me how my team was doing. He'd sit at the dinner table and stare at his plate while Mom asked me questions. The moment he finished eating he would rise from the table without a word and go back to his bedroom, shoulders stooped, slippers shuffling across our bare hardwood floors. I say "his" bedroom because from the time I was eleven, my mother and father slept in separate rooms. They thought I didn't understand, but I did, and that's hard on a kid. Hard to think that they didn't really care about each other anymore. That maybe everything was somehow my fault. I promised myself that my marriage would never come to be like that—but it did.

My father died in his sleep last October of a heart attack, and I never had a chance to say good-bye to him. I always held out hope that we'd connect with each other someday, but it didn't work out that way. I guess we were destined never to know each other.

I look up from the lectern and see Melanie's coworker sitting to my left, a vacant chair between her and Melanie's family. She gazes at me sadly, tears in her eyes. I don't know her name—she just showed up at the funeral. I don't remember her from any of Frank Taylor's Christmas parties, but what was I going to say? She seems nice—and genuinely grieving. I'm not going to deprive her of her chance to say a final good-bye to Melanie.

My eyes flicker to Melanie's parents. Her mother is sobbing softly while her father sits stoically, his lips forming a tight, straight line. They were always kind to me and they helped us financially whenever they could. But, like my parents, they didn't have much to give.

I'm not an eloquent man. When I'm speaking in front of people, my breathing quickly becomes choppy and loud, making the audience as uncomfortable as I am. So today I keep my remarks short. I tell them how wonderful Melanie was. How she always took care of me. How much I'll miss her. How shocked I am at the terrible act of violence that stole her from the world, and how some things just don't make sense. And I tell them that she's gone to a better place because there is no way a woman as sweet as she could be kept from the glory of heaven. As I look out at their honest, sympathetic faces, it occurs to me that these people have no clue that Melanie asked me for a divorce the night before her death, and I won't tell them. There's no last word to be had here, no victory to be won. She's gone and the only important thing now is that Melanie's mother and father are left with fond memories of their daughter. When I'm finished, I bow my head and whisper, "Good-bye, Mel."

CHAPTER

4

In the days following Melanie's memorial service I remain mostly inside the house—except for one solitary day trip to the mountains—occasionally making halfhearted attempts at packing her things into brown cardboard boxes. The same boxes I might have used to pack *my* possessions. I don't get very far though, managing only to remove some of the clothes from her closet.

One afternoon Father Dale stops by unexpectedly to offer words of encouragement. He's a small man with thinning white hair, ruddy cheeks, dark eyes, and a compassionate manner. He says that he always liked seeing Melanie at Mass, and that I'm welcome to drop by his church anytime to talk. His visit lasts only a few minutes and, thankfully, he doesn't bring up the fact that she stopped attending his Sunday services so abruptly.

The second Monday following the funeral is different. I wake up

early, shower, shave, and dress in business casual—not the old jeans
and T-shirts I've been living in for the past ten days. Over a full breakfast of coffee, eggs, and bacon I read the *Washington Post* from cover
to cover for the first time in weeks.

Then, at nine sharp, I drive to the day trading firm of Bedford &
Associates. It's located in McLean, Virginia, fifteen miles west of downtown Washington and about a thirty-minute drive from my house.
McLean is the center of the technology boom that has gripped northern Virginia since the mid-nineties.

Over the past six months I researched several of these day trading
firms, and from what I could tell, Bedford offered exactly what I was
looking for—the best research systems for the buck. And the firm has
been extremely proactive about marketing to me, mailing me promotional information almost every week.

"Good morning. Welcome to Bedford and Associates," Bedford's
receptionist says cordially. The nameplate in front of her reads Anna
Ferrer. Anna has long black hair, honey-hued skin, and huge brown
eyes. She's a work of art and I feel a pang of guilt for noticing. I guess I
should still be in mourning.

"Hello." My voice sounds strange to me after weeks of not using it
very much.

"What can I do for you?" she asks with a trace of a Spanish accent.

"I want to rent a desk here."

"What's your name, sir?"

"Augustus McKnight."

"Please have a seat, Mr. McKnight." She motions across the lobby
toward a comfortable-looking sofa. "Someone will be with you in a
moment."

I'm sure I could have kept my old sales job if I'd gone to the human resources department and told them about Russell's attempt to
steal half my Unicom profits. But I realized that I was sick of doing
what I *had* to do. It was time to do what I *wanted*. Of course, day trading is one of the riskiest things I could want to do—most people fail
miserably in the first few months—but I know I'll kick myself forever if
I don't give it a shot. I have no one to worry about now but myself, and
I've saved up a decent amount of cash with my Unicom investment.

However, that ninety thousand is a drop in the bucket compared to the million dollars I should receive in the next few weeks as the beneficiary of Melanie's life insurance policy. It'll all be tax free too.

A few minutes later I glance up from the issue of *Forbes* I've been leafing through and am met by what looks like a cherub in suspenders. The young man has a freshly scrubbed appearance with short strawberry blond hair and a freckled face barely out of peach fuzz. His tiny eyeglasses have lenses so thin they appear to be just decorative, and he's dressed in a shirt, tie, and suit that probably cost more than everything in my closet put together. Despite his apparent youth, his confident expression suggests to me that he understands every rule, regulation, and by-law the Securities and Exchange Commission has ever approved, which is good. From everything I've read, day trading is a rough-and-tumble game, so I want the environment to be as controlled as possible, at least initially.

"I'm Michael Seaver," the young man says in a southern drawl, sitting down beside me on the sofa and shaking my hand firmly.

"Augustus McKnight."

"Good to meet you, Augustus. I'm the owner of Bedford. I understand you want to rent a desk from me."

"That's right."

Seaver pauses to inspect another man entering Bedford's glass doors. Tall, with a mop of dark, unkempt hair, a closely cropped beard, and sloping shoulders, the guy reminds me of what the Beatles looked like in those old black-and-white film clips when they were first getting famous in the early sixties.

"We run a very tight ship at Bedford," Seaver says. I can tell he's keeping one ear tuned to what Anna and the bearded guy are saying. "I personally interview everyone who takes a desk here. The press and the public's perception of most day trading firms is pretty sleazy, and I won't have Bedford and Associates thrown into that pool. I make certain everyone who rents a desk from me has the wherewithal and experience to handle the stress." He leans forward and clasps his hands together like he's praying. "You understand I can't guarantee success, Mr. McKnight. Success depends on your research, your system of buying and selling stocks, and a little bit of luck." He chuckles, like luck is a much bigger factor than he's letting on. "What I do guarantee is a business environment where SEC regulations are strictly adhered to, and where you can trust your co-traders."

"Mr. Seaver."

"Yes, Anna?" he asks, looking back over his shoulder at the receptionist.

"Sorry to interrupt, but this gentleman wants to rent a desk as well," she says, pointing at the bearded guy. "I thought maybe you'd want to see him now too."

Seaver smiles with the satisfaction of a man who knows he'll make money even if both of us go bankrupt. "Let's all go in the conference room," he suggests, gesturing at a door across the lobby.

"Augustus McKnight." I offer my hand to the other applicant as we sit down beside each other at the conference room table, but he ignores my gesture.

"Roger," he mutters into his shirt, stroking the hair on his chin instead of shaking my hand. A burgundy golf shirt and faded jeans hang loosely on his gaunt frame.

"Let's get started," Seaver says, taking a seat on the other side of the table. "As I was telling Mr. McKnight, I run a very tight operation here. For a thousand dollars a month I'll set both of you up with an eight-by-eight cubicle, a desk, a chair, a phone, a computer, two screens, and Trader One."

Trader One is a software package that provides real-time quotes from major financial markets worldwide and makes reams of research information available. I've read about it in all of the trading publications. "Which version?" I ask, trying to make it clear I'm no pigeon.

"Seven-point-oh. It's fully loaded," Seaver snaps. Like I've insulted him. "You get Merrill Lynch and Morgan Stanley research analysis, Bloomberg, Hoover's, Yahoo!, and most important, real-time quotes. Most of the time you'll actually see dealer quotes so you'll know which way the market is really going. And all of the information is piped straight to your desk over T-1 lines with multiple generators backing up the network so summer thunderstorms can't nuke you in the middle of a hectic day in the markets. It's a sweet deal here at Bedford. For a thousand bucks a month and the requirement that you run all of your trades through me, I give you the tools to make millions. It costs a little more than the bare-bone shops, but believe me, it's worth it. Plus, the higher cost of admission keeps out the riff-raff. It's the difference between a doorman high-rise and a walk-up tenement. Now, I ask you, where would *you* rather live?"

I glance over at Roger and he has a blank expression on his face. Like he can't believe he's getting himself into this.

"How much does each trade cost?" I ask, feeling my competitive juices start to flow. It's going up against suckers like Roger that will make it much easier for me to win at this game.

"As low as ten bucks."

According to my research that's not a bad price, but I want to be sure of what I'm really getting. "On the in *and* the out?"

"Pardon?"

"You mean it will cost me ten dollars when I buy shares *and* ten dollars when I sell them?" I ask slowly, making myself as clear as possible. Day traders work on very thin margins where every dime counts.

"Of course."

"But it could be higher than that." I've heard about these guys who own day trading firms. You have to dig to find out what the real deal is.

Seaver groans, like I'm being a real pain in his ass, but I don't care. These are all legitimate questions, and I'm not one to back down.

"It could be, right?" I push. "Higher than ten dollars a trade, I mean."

"If my clearing firm has to go to several sources to buy shares for you quickly, the price of a trade could go up," he admits.

"How much?"

Seaver gives me a nasty look. "Say you put in a purchase order for five hundred shares and we have to buy two fifty from one shop and two fifty from another because nobody can fill the whole five-hundred-share order fast," he explains. "Then you've got to pay twice. In that case you pay twenty bucks, but you get the trade executed right away, before the market can move against you. That's the most important thing."

"How will I know if you really had to go to two sources or you just double-charged me?"

"You won't," Seaver replies evenly. "You'll just have to trust me."

There's an uncomfortable pause.

"Do you offer a training program?" I ask.

"No. I assume you know what you're doing when you get here."

"What about the new pattern day trading rules the big exchanges have suggested?"

"What about them?"

"Do you enforce them?"

Seaver studies his cuticles for a moment. "We do our best to comply with all the exchange rules."

"How about margin lending?" I remember Seaver bragging at the beginning of the conversation about how he personally makes certain each person who rents a desk from him can handle the stress of the situation. "Does Bedford offer that?"

Day trading firms often lend money to people renting space from them, using shares of stock as collateral. Exactly like banks lend against the value of someone's house with a mortgage.

"I'll lend you fifty cents on the dollar," Seaver informs me. "Marked to market at the end of every day," he adds.

Marked to market at the end of every day means that if the shares I own fall in value between the opening and closing bells, and I'm borrowing on margin, I'll owe Seaver fifty percent of the stock price's decline before I can go home for the night. If I can't pay him, he'll take my shares and sell them to cover the shortfall.

Margin lending took me some time to understand, but now I get it. If I want to buy a share of stock that costs ten dollars, fifty percent margin means I have to put up five dollars of my own money and Seaver will lend me the other five—fifty percent of the stock's market value. Borrowing the five dollars gives me the opportunity to purchase and control more shares—and gives Seaver the opportunity to make more money. Not only do I pay him rent for the cubicle and interest on the margin loan, but I also pay him that fee for each trade because he acts as my broker. He becomes my lifeline to the market instead of some on-line trading firm like the one I purchased the Unicom shares from. Seaver wants me to spin my account fast because the more volume I do, the more cash he makes. For him, it doesn't matter whether I'm buying or selling. The margin loan doubles my opportunity to spin the account and therefore his opportunity to earn brokerage commissions.

That's all fine if the price of that stock I bought for ten dollars keeps rising. I'm paying a smidgen of interest on the five dollars I borrowed and guzzling champagne as the price goes up. But if the price drops, it's a different story. Say the share price decreases from ten to eight by the end of the first day's trading. Then I would owe Seaver fifty percent of the two-dollar loss—one dollar—because after the adjustment he'd still be lending me fifty percent of the market value of the stock: a four-dollar loan against an eight-dollar stock. Doesn't sound too bad when it's one dollar I owe him. But if I'd bought ten thousand dollars' worth of stock, then I'd owe Seaver a thousand dollars. And if I'd used every last dollar I had for my original five-thousand-dollar half of the purchase, I'd have to sell some shares to repay him. And I'd have to sell them exactly when I didn't want to—when the price was down. That's when day trading turns nasty. Bottom line, margin lending exaggerates your profits—and your losses.

"Fifty percent?"

"Fifty percent," Seaver confirms. "You may have heard that some day trading firms will lend more, but I won't because that would be irresponsible. The last thing I want to have to do is grab your stock certificates and sell them." He glances at Roger, who is still stroking his beard with a measured cadence. "How much money are you guys starting with?"

"Over a million," I answer immediately. That won't be true until the insurance check clears, but I want Seaver to think of me as a player right away.

Roger shrugs. "About half that," he mumbles.

Seaver nods gravely, as though he's made a momentous decision. "I require a six-month security deposit for the cubicle and the equipment, and rent is due by the twenty-fifth of the preceding month. That's seven thousand dollars from each of you. If you agree to the terms, you can make out a check for that amount before you leave and be free to trade when the U.S. markets open tomorrow morning at nine thirty. Just give the check to Anna. She keeps our books."

So Anna is more than just a hood ornament.

"Mr. Seaver, the promotional information I received from Bedford said that if I rented a desk from you by August first, I'd be eligible for an introductory discount on the monthly fee. Twenty-five percent off the first six months. Today is July twenty-second."

Seaver's face scrunches up so it looks like he's shitting razor blades. "You must have gotten dated material, Augustus. We haven't offered discounts for over a year. Demand for my desks has been strong, even with the choppy market. I haven't had to cut my fee," he says proudly.

I was ready for this. The older I get, the more I realize that every transaction in life is negotiable, even if the price is clearly marked on the item. Making money is a zero-sum game. If you get it then the other guy doesn't, so he's going to fight you as hard as he can for every dollar. Some people are smoother at it than others, but I don't let anybody fool me. I know everyone's trying to pick my pocket.

"I'd be happy to show you the information I received," I say. "The offer is very clear. In fact, the discount kept rising. It started at ten percent back in the spring, then went to—"

"Twenty-five percent?" he asks incredulously, glancing at Roger, who is looking away, trying to stay out of the discussion.

"Yes."

"How much did you say you'd be trading with?" he asks.

"Over a million."

Seaver purses his lips, then finally nods. "All right, I'll make an exception, but I can't offer *you* the same discount, Roger," Seaver says quickly, pointing at the bearded guy.

"That's fine," Roger mumbles. It's obvious to me he's not big on confrontation or conflict, which doesn't bode well for his ability to get ahead in the day trading game. "I never got that promotional stuff," he adds.

"Then it's settled," Seaver says flatly. "You both are in."

Anticipation surges through me. I'm thirty-three years old, and I'm finally setting out on a path I have chosen for myself. A path that offers huge upside but no security whatsoever. My million could turn into ten million—or zero.

"I'll be happy to show you to your cubicles," Seaver offers, glancing at his watch. "Then I've got to go to a meeting downtown."

"I agree to the terms," Roger announces, standing up, "but I've got to be somewhere in a few minutes. I don't plan to start trading until next Monday anyway, so I'll come back this afternoon and look around."

"Okay." Seaver turns to me. "What about you?"

"I'd like to see mine now."

A few moments later Seaver leads me through a pair of swinging doors and onto Bedford's large trading floor. Over the constant hum of conversation there are occasional shouts of elation or frustration, as well as the sound of fists pounding on desks. Seaver leads me down a long carpeted aisle past four-foot-high cubicle walls. Inside the cubes, casually dressed people are speaking into phones, tapping impatiently at keyboards, scrawling figures on notepads, and studying charts on their computer screens. Arranged in groups of five, the cubicles seem to reflect the lives and personalities of their tenants. Some walls are decorated with childrens' drawings, others with inspirational quotes, while some are bare. There are about a hundred people working on the floor alltogether.

"Here it is." Seaver points to an unoccupied cubicle at the very end of the aisle, and it's just as he promised. A plain desk supporting two large computer screens, a keyboard, and a processor from which thick wires disappear down one side of the desk into the floor. All surrounded by gray temporary partitions.

"Hey, pal."

Leaning back in his chair, a man appears out of the cubicle beside mine. He has a crew cut and small, intense eyes. "You going to be joining us?"

"Yes."

"I'm Max Frasier. Good to meet you."

"Augustus McKnight."

Max stretches and shakes my hand with a grip like a vise, then stands up and leans over his desk, resting his palms on the four-foot-high partition. "Hey, come here," he says, motioning to someone I can't see.

"I've got to go," Seaver announces, giving me a friendly pat on the back. "Slammer will take care of you," he says, pointing to Max as he hurries away. "See you in the morning, Augustus."

"Okay." I nod good-bye to Seaver as Max saunters over to where I'm standing. "Why did Seaver call you Slammer?" I ask.

"I'm ex-military," Max replies, as though that explains it. "Special forces. I served with the Army Rangers for ten years. Did most of my tour down in Central America." He rolls up one sleeve and shows me an ugly scar and a tattoo of an angry devil on his upper arm. "Shot up pretty good in Nicaragua back in 'eighty-seven, but it was worth it," he says. "I love my country."

Max is short, no more than five-six, but he's built like a Sherman tank. "Yeah, but why did Seaver call you Slammer?"

Before he can answer, a woman with sandy blond hair sidles up beside me. "Hello, I'm Mary Segal," she says.

The first thing I notice about Mary is that she's wearing lots of expensive-looking jewelry. I mean, it's dripping off her. "I'm Augustus, it's nice to meet—"

"We call her Sassy around here," Max interrupts. "We keep her around for her sex appeal. Dresses up the place."

"Stop it, Slammer." Mary reaches over and pats the ex-military man on his scrub-brushy head. She's an inch or two taller than he is. Despite her protest, I can tell she enjoys his teasing. Though not beautiful, she's still striking and she was probably accustomed to being the center of attention in her younger days.

"And I call this guy Freak Show." Max laughs loudly as a young man wearing an earring in his left lobe, a ring in his eyebrow, and sagging, baggy jeans appears beside Mary. He has shoulder-length hair dyed a dark purple, and I take an obvious second look. "Freak Show is our rebel without a cause," Slammer adds with a smirk.

"Daniel Jenkins," the young man says loudly, clearly pissed off at

Max for assigning the nickname. Despite all of the decoration he has a serious demeanor about him.

"Hi, Daniel."

"Freak Show still has some maturing left to do," Slammer says arrogantly, "but I'll teach him what's right and what's wrong."

"Shut up, you—"

"Easy, boys," Mary says, placing a hand on each man's chest. "Lord, Augustus will get the idea we don't get along." She smiles at me when Daniel stalks off. "When will you be starting, Augustus?"

"Tomorrow."

"Good," Slammer says gruffly, giving Daniel the finger behind his back. "We can use some new blood around here. We lost two people in our group last week."

"Lost?"

"They went bankrupt. Lost everything they had," he explains with a chuckle. "It happens all the time."

"How long have you been here?" I ask.

"Six months," Slammer replies. "The longest of the three of us. Sassy came in the spring and Freak Show joined a few weeks ago. It's churn and burn at Bedford, Gus. Seaver has no mercy if you can't pay your bill. He seems nice and all at first, but he's a prick about being paid on time. You eat what you kill, and that's the bottom line."

Slammer's rapid-fire voice fades as I move slowly into my cubicle, sit down in the chair, and gaze at the dark computer screens. This is it. Suddenly it's up to me and me alone to make it happen. No more events I can't control, like pricing discounts by big competitors, getting in my way. The only thing that matters from here on out is what my scoreboard says at the end of every day. Up or down. And that's totally up to me. Bedford is everything I hoped it would be, and it already feels like I belong.

CHAPTER

5

The Grand is a pricey steakhouse located on the ground floor of the same office tower that's home to Bedford & Associates. Dimly lit and tastefully furnished, it has all the extras one would expect of a hangout for movers and shakers or those who want to be. There are always tables—and even waiters—reserved for regulars, magnum bottles of wine and champagne, and a cigar menu fit for Jack Kennedy. The walls are covered by caricatures of national and local celebrities who frequent the place—professional sports team owners, politicians, and prominent venture capitalists who've led the area's technology explosion.

The Grand also has a large bar, even more dimly lit than the restaurant, where people wait for tables or simply their next martini. I've read about this place in the *Washington Post* but never had the money to afford the menu. Until today I've been a midlevel, old-economy sales assistant with a negative net worth. But now things are different. Now I'm a day trader with a bankroll.

Vincent Carlucci stands with his back to the Grand's dark wood bar, nursing his standard gin and tonic. Dressed in a blue warm-up suit and white Reeboks, a thin gold chain hanging from his neck, Vincent looks out of place in the middle of the business suits all around him. There's disdain for him in the expressions of some as they glance his way, but he doesn't care. We've been friends for a long time and so I know he's never cared what others think. It's a trait I've always admired.

A wide grin lights up his broad, olive-skinned face when he sees me. "You're looking good, pal," he says as we shake hands. "As always."

"Thanks." Years ago Vincent and I were teammates on our high school football team. After we won the state championship our senior year, he went to the University of Virginia on a full scholarship and played pro ball for two years, while I rode the Roanoke bench and then went to work for Russell in paper sales. But Vincent always stayed in touch with me and visited whenever he could. When he moved from New York City to D.C. five years ago, we started getting together regularly. "You look good too."

"Hey, Joe." Vincent motions to the nearest bartender, who interrupts the order he's about to take from another guy. It's after seven and the place is packed with people trying to get a drink, but Vincent is served right away. It's always been easy for him to get attention. "My buddy needs a scotch and water."

After so many years, Vincent knows that scotch is my drink of choice, and a moment later I'm holding a glass of Dewar's.

"Good to see you, Augustus," he says, gently tapping his glass against mine. "I'm glad you could make it tonight."

"This place turned out to be really convenient." Vincent called me at home yesterday to arrange dinner this evening. "And it was time for me to start getting out again," I add softly.

His expression turns somber. "I'm sorry about Melanie."

"Thanks, and thanks again for coming to her memorial service. I needed you there."

"Sure." He takes a sip from his nearly empty glass of gin. "Are you holding up okay?"

"Some days are better than others." I take a couple of large gulps to catch up. God, the scotch tastes good. I can feel it relaxing me immediately. "I'm doing all right for the most part, but it's been tough."

"Sure it has." He shakes his head sadly. "Melanie was a wonderful woman."

"Yes, she was. I miss her." I want to tell Vincent how Melanie asked me for a divorce the night before her murder, and how she let Frank Taylor fondle her as she walked away from me for the last time. But I don't. Saying those things might make him think I'm bitter, or change his memories of Melanie, and I don't want that. "She was so beautiful too," is all I say.

He nods several times. "She was a stunner all right. I always said that if you hadn't married her first, I would have."

Vincent has told me that many times, but I don't buy it. I doubt he'll ever get married. His wavy jet black hair, gray eyes, boyish grin, and football player's physique allow him to captivate many women with just a lock of the eyes. He uses his looks relentlessly to get women into bed. I noticed him even trying to pick up Melanie's coworker after the memorial service, the redhead who showed up without an invitation. Vincent's told me on several occasions that the thrill of the chase is what makes life worth living for him, and I don't think any woman will ever be able to change that.

"I just want to get the monster who killed her," I say grimly.

"Right," Vincent agrees, elbowing aside a small man to make room for me at the bar. "Any progress in the case?"

"Nothing yet." Detective Dorsey stopped by the house twice last week. He told me that he and his men were following up on several leads and said he was confident they would solve the case. "A guy named Reggie Dorsey is the lead detective, and he seems capable. He'll figure out what happened."

"What do you think Melanie was doing in that part of the city so late at night?" Vincent asks, swirling the ice cubes in his glass. "That's a pretty rough neighborhood."

"I don't know." I take another large swallow of scotch. "It's crazy, isn't it?"

"Yes, it is." Vincent finishes what's left in his glass and motions to the bartender that we need another round. "Have you been involved in the investigation?"

"No, I've stayed out of it and let the police handle everything."

"That's probably best." I can tell Vincent has more questions, probably about how Melanie and I were doing near the end—Melanie's father subtly asked me the same thing at the funeral home—but Vincent doesn't push. "They can't let the trail get cold. You've got to stay on them."

"I intend to," I say, finishing my scotch as the bartender hands us two more.

"It's eerie the way you and Melanie took out those insurance policies on each other just a few months ago," he says out of nowhere. "And now this."

I look up and Vincent's eyes dart away, apparently diverted by a tall brunette across the room. I told him about the million-dollar policies when Melanie first mentioned that she wanted them. I wanted to gauge his reaction to see if he found the whole thing as strange as I did. "I never understood why she did that," I answer.

"I didn't either," Vincent agrees, still focused on the brunette. In the midst of the noisy bar there's an uncomfortable pause between us. "It was all Melanie's idea. Isn't that what you told me?"

"Yeah."

He picks the lime up off the rim of his fresh glass and squeezes it into the gin and tonic, then runs it around the rim. "So, now that you've only got yourself to support, when are you going to take that plunge into day trading you've been talking about for so long?"

I know he asked the question just to be polite and expects the same answer he's always gotten. "As a matter of fact, I took it today."

Vincent's eyes flash back to mine. "Are you serious?"

"Yup." A smile I can't repress plays across my face. "The firm is on the ninth floor of this building. It's called Bedford and Associates."

"You quit your job of eleven years to be a day trader?" he asks, astonished.

"Yes." Vincent's amazement only makes me more proud of my decision. He's teased me for years about being too risk-averse and it's satisfying to see newfound respect in his expression. You don't surprise a friend of more than twenty years very often.

"That's incredible. Congratulations."

"Thanks."

"But don't you need money to—" He interrupts himself and a dark cloud drifts across his face.

Vincent knows that Melanie and I lived paycheck to paycheck, and he's assuming I'm going to use the insurance proceeds to fund my day trading adventure. Worse, as he bites his lower lip—the way he always does when he's uneasy—I sense that down deep he's worried I might have had a plan.

"A couple of weeks ago I made a bunch of money on a stock market investment," I explain. "On a company called Unicom. I used some cash Mom left me when she died to buy the shares. In one day I made almost eighty grand on a ten-thousand-dollar investment." If I had been able to invest the insurance proceeds from Melanie's policy in Unicom's IPO, I'd have grossed almost eight million dollars. I couldn't resist doing that math last night.

"Wow." His expression brightens. He seems relieved by my explanation.

"You should stop by Bedford sometime," I suggest. "People are crazy, yelling and shouting all day on the trading floor. It's capitalism at its—"

"Can you do it again?" he interrupts.

"Do what?"

"Can you keep making money fast like that in the stock market?"

"Sure."

"Do you have a system or something?"

"Yeah," I say hesitantly, "a system." So far my "system" consists of one lucky roll of Internet dice, but I'll never tell Vincent that. Besides, now that I have some money banked I think I can do pretty well. You have to have money to make money in this racket, and I've learned a few tricks with all the studying I've done.

"How did you figure out all that stock market stuff?" he asks.

Like Russell, Vincent considers the stock markets—numbers in general, really—a mystery. He's always claimed that it's because they bore him, but I know the truth. They *terrify* him. I've never seen Vincent physically frightened of anything. I've seen him take on three men his own size at the same time and crush them—he has a volcanic temper that can explode without warning due in part to the steroids he takes to maintain his muscles. But numbers are a different story. He almost wasn't accepted into the University of Virginia because his math SAT scores were so low. I tutored him every night for a week before the fourth and last time he took the test, and he finally got a decent score.

"I studied everything I could get my hands on, and I've been running a ghost portfolio for the last twelve months," I explain, swallowing more scotch.

"What do you mean, a ghost portfolio?"

"I gave myself a hundred thousand dollars of Monopoly money to play with, then pretended to buy and sell stocks with it. I would spend hours every night figuring out which stocks to add and which ones to dump." It's occurred to me maybe that's one of the reasons Melanie started working late. "I kept precise records, even charging myself brokerage commissions when I made believe I had bought or sold shares."

"How'd you do?"

"I quadrupled my money in a year." The portfolio's performance was really closer to a three-bagger—I almost tripled its value—but one of the things I've learned about the financial world is that everyone exaggerates. Performance inflation is standard operating procedure. If you don't juice your results, you're only shortchanging yourself because you better believe everybody else is stretching the truth.

His eyes widen. "Quadrupled? Really?"

"Yup."

He takes a slow sip of gin, eyes fixed on mine. "And you think you'll have the same kind of performance with real money."

"Absolutely. Maybe even better," I answer confidently. Suddenly I've never been more certain of anything in my life and I can tell the scotch is starting to affect me. I've always been guilty of gaining confidence by the glass. "I earned almost eight times my money on Unicom, and that was in one day." Vincent has no idea that I'd tried to win IPO lotteries for six months before finally hitting with Unicom. No idea that it might be six more months before I win another one. That I might *never* win another one. And he wouldn't get it even if I did take the next hour to explain it all. Sometimes you have to keep things simple for Vincent. "I have you to thank, by the way."

"For what?"

"You're the one who got me to seriously consider day trading as a career. I wouldn't have quit without you pushing me."

His posture stiffens. "Hey, I don't want to be blamed if things don't turn out okay at Bedford."

"Don't worry," I assure him, placing one hand on his shoulder, a little surprised that he remembered the name of the firm right away. His attention to details isn't usually that good. "It's the best thing that could happen to me. If I had to go back to my old job now, given everything that's happened, it would be terrible. Too many memories there. This is good for me right now, even if it doesn't work out in the long run."

"You sure?"

"Yeah."

"Okay then. Hey, I might even know some people who would invest with you," he says, lowering his voice. "Maybe you could charge them a fee for managing their money."

The idea of managing money for other people never occurred to me before, but as I start to think about his suggestion, it seems like a natural. The more money you control, the better your access to transactions. The better your access, the better your odds of success. Suddenly you're one of those preferred clients the brokerage houses cater to, and people pay big fees if you deliver good returns. "Who are these people?" I ask.

"Friends."

Since dropping out of professional football nine years ago after a career-ending knee injury, Vincent's working life has been a mystery to me. At different times he's claimed to run a sports agency, own an event marketing firm, and provide bodyguard services to celebrities. However, he's never had a physical office that I know of, and he's never been specific about the athletes he represented, concerts he promoted, or celebrities he protected. But he's always had a wad of big bills in his sterling silver money clip, always paid for everything when we've gotten together, and always driven a late model sports car.

His pals call him "Vinnie the ticket guy" for his ability to find tickets to any important event in the world—from Wimbledon to the Democratic National Convention—within twenty-four hours. From what he's told me he charges outrageous prices, but his clientele is wealthy enough not to care.

"Can you be a little more specific about who these people are?"

The brunette Vincent has been checking out has now spied him, and he's enjoying the attention. "Don't worry, you'll meet them," he says absentmindedly.

I notice that the brunette's companion, a petite blonde with blue eyes, is smiling at me. My gaze stays on her a moment longer than it should, and suddenly I get the guilts. Like I did this morning when I checked out Anna sitting behind Bedford's reception desk.

"She's cute, Augustus."

"Who is?" I ask, looking away and taking another long guzzle of scotch.

"The blonde over there. I saw her smile at you. You saw it too."

"I did not," I say defiantly.

"There's no reason to feel guilty," he says, patting me on the back.

"I don't."

"Yes, you do," he says. "I can tell. Look, I'm just trying to help get you back into the swing of things."

"By picking up women a few weeks after I buried Melanie?"

"Hey, this is a bar. That's what you're supposed to do here."

"At least I wouldn't try it at a memorial service," I mutter.

Vincent gives me a strange look. "What do you mean by that?"

"I saw you talking to that redhead in the parking lot after Melanie's service. You and she were getting pretty chummy."

"I was comforting her." He grins. "Who was she anyway?"

"You mean you didn't get her phone number?"

"Nah, the Carlucci charm failed me. First time in a long time too."

"You must be losing your touch. Or maybe she just had too much class."

Vincent shakes his head like the whole thing is a mystery. "Weddings are such good opportunities to get numbers from chicks. All that emotion really gets to them. So I thought Melanie's thing would be a good place too. Everybody being so sad and . . ." His voice trails off. "Sorry, Augustus. I didn't mean to make light of what's happened."

"It's all right." Sometimes Vincent ought to think before he speaks. But that's just not his style. He's always been impulsive. "I—"

"Hey, Jack. Over here." Vincent waves at a young guy wearing a sharp sports jacket and pleated khakis who's threading his way toward us through the crowd.

Finally the guy makes it to where we're standing. "Hey, Vinnie. How are you?"

"Good."

"Thanks for those Oriole tickets you got me the other night. Christ, they were right behind the Birds' dugout."

"No problem." Vincent nods at me. "Jack Trainer, this is a good friend of mine, Augustus McKnight."

Trainer is an inch or two shy of six feet with light brown hair that falls below his collar in the back. He's got a slim, tennis player's body, and his Brooks Brothers clothes fit him perfectly. His shaggy hair seems like a hint of rebellion in his otherwise preppy good looks.

"Jack owns an Internet company that he's selling to one of the big boys," Vincent explains loudly over the hum of conversation. "He's about to cash in on the American dream."

"Keep it down," Jack warns. "The deal isn't done yet. You'll jinx it." He turns to me. "What do you do?"

"He's a day trader," Vincent answers, stealing my thunder.

"Oh."

I can tell by Jack's expression he isn't impressed by my new career. He probably knows how few people succeed. "What kind of Internet company do you own?" I ask.

Without thanking him, Jack grabs the drink Vincent ordered for him. "It's an Internet service provider."

"Which one?"

"PlanetLink."

Jack can tell I'm impressed. "I just read an article about your company in *Washtech*. It said you had signed up almost a million customers in less than two years. That's tremendous."

"Thanks." Jack gulps the drink down, showing no appreciation for my praise of his company. "How long have you been day trading?"

"Just a few—"

"Augustus made big money on a company called Unicom," Vincent interrupts.

"Really?" Jack moves a tiny step closer, worried that he might have underestimated me. "Did you get in on their IPO a couple of weeks ago?"

"Yes."

"How the hell did you do that? I have a pretty big account over at Morgan Stanley and I couldn't pry any shares out of them."

"I—"

"Jack's pretty connected in the technology world, Augustus," Vincent says. "Not only here in northern Virginia, but out in California as well. Silicon Alley in Manhattan too. I don't know much about this technology revolution, but I bet he could help you identify some interesting companies to invest in."

I'm relieved not to have to answer Jack's question. He would understand that I'm no mover and shaker if he found out how I got my Unicom shares.

"Couldn't you, Jack?"

"Maybe." But Jack doesn't offer any immediate tips.

"Well, I'm going to chase some tail," Vincent says. "Be back in a while." He heads off toward the brunette and the blonde, who have worked their way closer to us through the crowd.

People automatically move aside as Vincent heads toward the brunette. I wonder if he knows more about the technology revolution than he's letting on. He knew the difference between Silicon Alley and Silicon Valley. Anyone who pays attention would be aware of the difference, but I didn't think Vincent paid attention to much of anything except women.

"How did you meet Vinnie?" Jack asks.

The blonde glances in my direction as Vincent corners the brunette. "We lived on the same street in Richmond from the time we were in fourth grade," I answer, watching her watch me. "How do you know him?"

"I met him one night a few months ago at a club downtown," Jack explains, reaching into his shirt pocket and handing me a business card. "I've got a dinner reservation, so I need to get going. Give me a call sometime." He turns to leave, then hesitates. "So you want a hot tip?"

My attention snaps away from the blonde. "Sure."

"Buy shares of Teletekk. The company designs and produces next-generation regenerators for fiber-optic networks."

I raise one eyebrow and nod as if I'm intimately familiar with next-generation whatevers. "Sure."

Jack leans closer. "The company is based out in the Valley and the CEO is a good friend of mine. He told me confidentially that in the next few weeks Teletekk will announce its first product with applications in the satellite arena. The fiberoptic business has stalled lately, but the satellite stuff is the sizzle. The stock's trading at around twenty right now, but he thinks the price will triple after the announcement." He pauses. "But don't hold it long. Don't try to ride the pop to the top. Take a quick profit and run. Remember, buy on rumor, sell on fact. You'll never get better advice."

I commit the name Teletekk to memory as Jack heads toward the dining room. My new coworkers—Slammer, Mary, Daniel, and Roger—will be impressed if I score big during my first few days at Bedford. The question is, do I share the tip with them, or do I keep it to myself? And how much of my Unicom profits do I risk on Teletekk? After all, I just met Jack Trainer. How do I know if I can trust him?

"Hi, I'm Laura."

It's the blonde. "Hi." I try not to seem interested. Laura's attractive but I still feel like I'm married. Like Melanie's watching me from across the room.

"What's your name?" she asks.

"Augustus."

"That's an interesting name."

"Mmm." I notice that Laura seems suddenly distracted by something behind me, so I turn around. And there's Frank Taylor, Melanie's old boss, right in front of me. He's not a small man—six feet and maybe a hundred and ninety pounds—but he'd be no match for me in a fight. I'm sure of that.

Taylor glances at Laura, then back at me, his eyes narrowing as he comes to his mistaken conclusion. "My God, Augustus, you just said good-bye to Melanie forever and here you are, already out chasing women."

"You're wrong," I snap.

"Couldn't take it, could you?"

"What are you talking about?"

"You couldn't take the thought of Melanie and me together," he says, "so you killed her."

"I'm warning you, Taylor."

"I was tempted to ask to speak to Melanie all those times you picked up the phone on weekends, but I didn't. I hung up like she asked, but now I wish I hadn't listened to her. You didn't deserve her consideration. You didn't deserve her."

"Get out of here!" I shout, my anger spiraling out of control.

"You killed her before she could sign her will, didn't you? Now you get the insurance money instead of her parents. She wanted them to have it." Taylor glances past me at Laura, whose mouth has fallen open. "Two weeks ago this man killed his wife, then dumped her body in an alley downtown," he says to her. "You sure you want to get involved with him? You never know, he might do the same thing to you."

The room turns crimson as my fist splits Taylor's upper lip and smashes his nose. But before I can hoist him up to hit him again, I'm wrestled to the floor by two huge men. All I hear are people shouting and screaming, then I'm lifted to my feet roughly, my left wrist wrenched up my back almost to my neck, sending searing pain through my shoulder. The two men hustle me past astonished patrons and into the building's lobby, then out the front door and into the summer heat.

"Don't ever come back here!" one of them yells as they hurl me down on the pavement. They stand guard at the door until I've made it back to my feet and staggered away toward the parking garage connected to the building.

The cashier eyes me from inside her glass-enclosed booth like I'm O.J. as I slip around the end of the flimsy yellow-and-black-striped gate. I head toward the stairs in a far corner of the building and walk to the third floor, where I parked my Toyota. As I make it up the last flight of steps and come through the door, I spot my heap at the other end of the garage.

I'm halfway to it when I hear the screech of tires and the whine of an engine. I stop and instinctively turn toward the noise. Racing around a pillar close to where I came out of the stairway door is a sleek silver Mercedes with darkly tinted windows. As I watch in disbelief, the car fishtails around the pillar, straightens out, then swerves so it's coming directly at me.

The alcohol has made me light-headed and unsteady, and the parked vehicles I sprint toward don't seem to get any closer. I hear the Mercedes's high-performance engine growing louder as the car quickly closes the gap. There isn't much time.

I put my head down, sprint the last few yards, and hurl myself desperately at the first vehicle in line—a huge Suburban—sliding across its dark blue metal hood and tumbling onto the cement floor between it and the next vehicle in line, jamming one wrist as I hold out my arms and try to cushion my fall. A split second later the silver Mercedes roars past, grazing the Suburban's front bumper.

I hear the squeal of tires as the Mercedes makes another 180-degree turn, then disappears down into the parking garage's next level. As the whine of the engine fades, I'm left to wonder if there are any more surprises waiting for me out there in the eerie silence—pierced only by the sound of my pounding heart and terrified breath. Left to wonder if that five-thousand-dollar emergency loan Vincent arranged for me a while ago from some "friends" has anything to do with what just happened.

CHAPTER

6

"Look at this stock price. It's falling off a cliff and I'm getting massacred. The shorts are screwing me. This is bullshit!"

Now I understand why people at Bedford call Max Frasier "Slammer." He pounds his desk and curses constantly as he rides the stock market roller coaster. "You all right, Slammer?" I ask, rubbing my wrist as I stand up to stretch. It's Monday morning, a week since I started at Bedford, but my arm is still sore from my tumble off the Suburban's hood.

"The shorts are baking me on this penny stock I bought Friday afternoon," Max gripes, banging out a message on the stock's Yahoo! chat board as he watches its price tick down another few basis points. On the chat board Max can complain to other traders out there in cyberspace about the early morning dive in the price and speculate with them about the cause of the sudden dip. "I knew I shouldn't have held this thing over the weekend. Jesus Christ, look at this!" he shouts, pointing at the spot on his screen where the ticker blinks its bad news. He sends out another quick message. "I knew this was a mistake," he bitches, slamming his desk hard. "Damn the shorts."

"By shorts, you mean the people who want that company's stock price to go down, right?" I observe tentatively, trying to learn whenever I can.

To really grasp the equity markets, it's important to understand that not everyone out there wants to see a stock's price go up. Not everyone is a bull. It may seem strange, but some investors—those who believe the outlook for a company is poor—expect to see the price go down, and so they invest that way.

To execute this bearish strategy, shorts borrow a block of shares from a market maker—usually an investment bank—then sell the borrowed shares to someone like you or me through a broker, get the proceeds from the sale, and invest that cash in other opportunities. At some point in the near future they'll have to get the shares back to the market maker to satisfy the loan so, in essence, while they're borrowers, they are "short" the shares. The shorts are hoping that the price of the borrowed shares will drop quickly so they can purchase other shares more cheaply in the open market and deliver those newly purchased shares back to the market maker to satisfy the original loan. When the loan is satisfied, the shorts' profit is measured by the amount the price dropped while they were borrowing the shares.

"Isn't that what you mean, Slammer?" I ask again when he doesn't respond.

Of course, if the shorts are wrong and the price rises after they've borrowed the shares, they're screwed because ultimately they'll have to buy a new block of shares at a higher price, losing the difference between that price and the price where they originally sold the borrowed shares. Plus they'll have to pay interest.

Selling short is a risky strategy because there's no limit to an investor's risk. The price of the borrowed shares could go way up while they're short. But the rewards can be substantial too. The neat thing is that, as a day trader, you can be active whether the market is going up or down, or the price of a particular stock is going up or down. So you can make money no matter what the economy is doing, or what a particular stock is doing.

"Slammer?"

Max's frantically moving hands finally pause for a moment over his keyboard, his fingertips trembling slightly. He looks up at me, teeth clenched. "Of course that's what I mean, you idiot. And don't call me Slammer again. I hate that name. You hear me, *Gus*?"

From where I'm standing I have a clear view over the chest-high walls of everyone in our five-cubicle group, and I see Mary glance up from her computer screen and roll her eyes.

"Be nice, Slammer," she chides delicately. "Let's all just try to get along. There's enough stress in here as it is without us being mean to each other."

"Shut up, Sassy," Max snarls, pounding on his keyboard again. "I'm gonna double down," he says loudly. "I'll teach the shorts not to screw with me. And if they keep doing this, I'll find out where the fuckers live, and then they'll be sorry."

"Keep it down, Slammer," Daniel warns, staring at his screen. Daniel is the most intense trader in our group—what they call a "banger"—executing a new transaction every few minutes. He rarely leaves his desk all day, methodically buying and selling from the opening bell to the close. "I'm trying to concentrate."

Slammer jumps out of his seat and points angrily past Mary at the younger man. "You say one more thing like that to me, Freak Show, and I'll come over there and teach you a lesson. I'll dye that purple hair of yours bloodred, and I'll yank that damn piece of jewelry out of your eyebrow. Then we'll see how big and bad you are."

Daniel mutters something I can't hear and continues to trade.

"What did you say, you little coward?" Slammer demands. "Hey, maybe I ought to show you what we did to people like you down in Nicaragua." Slammer glances at me. "What the hell are you staring at, asshole?"

My temper flares instantly, but kicking Slammer's ass right here on the trading floor probably wouldn't be a good idea, even though I know most of the people in the immediate area would love to see it.

"Easy, Max," Mary says soothingly, standing up and patting Slammer's hand. "There's no need to get upset. I'm sorry that position you took over the weekend isn't working out, but it'll come back. You know it will. Your instincts are always so good."

"Yeah, I guess you're right." Slammer glances down at Mary's hand. "Lunch today?" he asks.

She shakes her head. "Can't."

"Why not?"

"I have some errands to run, but why don't we get a drink after work? Just you and me."

Slammer takes a deep breath and nods. "Okay, yeah, that's a good idea." At the prospect of drinks with Mary he eases back into his chair and begins trading again as if nothing happened.

I mouth the words "thank you" to her, grateful that she defused the situation. She smiles up at me sweetly as she sits back down, pointing at Max through the cubicle wall and shaking her head as if to say, "Don't worry about him. That's just the way he is."

She's taken an early liking to me, helping me learn my way around last week and asking me to lunch later on today—the real reason she couldn't accept Slammer's invitation. She's nice, but her watchful eyes and the lines around the corners of her mouth suggest that her life hasn't always been easy. She has a hunted look about her, constantly raising her head up and looking around as if she's expecting to see someone or something pursuing her.

A gentle tap on my shoulder surprises me. "Could I have a word with you?"

It's Roger, the bearded guy who sat with me in the conference room last Monday while Seaver sold us on Bedford. Today is Roger's first day, and Seaver has assigned him to the last vacant cubicle in our group. "Okay," I agree hesitantly.

"Let's take a walk," he suggests in his soft voice, stroking his whiskers and glancing furtively past me.

I nod, wondering what this is about.

Roger leads me to an unoccupied conference room on the other side of the the trading floor. The conference room is at the corner of the building, and I take a seat at the table. From here I have a panoramic view of northern Virginia and downtown Washington in the distance.

"What's on your mind?" I ask. Roger seems troubled, but then I've already noticed that's his natural expression.

He sits silently for a moment before starting. "I thought maybe we should get to know each other," he finally says. "We're both new kids on the block here. We ought to stick together."

I don't know how to respond. I spent most of last week getting my bearings and so far have made only a few small investments, much less begun to day trade the way Daniel and Slammer do. I'm impatient to put the lion's share of my Unicom proceeds to work, and I have to make a decision on whether to follow through on the Teletekk tip. The announcement about the satellite application could come at any moment, and if I miss out I'll feel like a fool. Roger and I will have plenty of time to get to know each other later. "Look I—"

"I don't understand much about investing, Augustus," he admits quickly as I make a move to leave. "I'm nervous about this whole thing."

Roger arrived at eight o'clock this morning, a half hour after I did, and I noticed that he simply stared at his Trader One introductory page for the better part of ninety minutes before the stock markets opened. By this time on my first day last week, I had completely personalized my software. "Then what the heck are you doing here?" I ask, easing back into my chair. I need to get to work, but I want to find out why this guy would throw himself headlong into something he has no training for. "Day trading is difficult enough for people who know what they're doing."

"I understand that now," he admits, looking depressed.

"Roger, I'm kind of busy and—"

"I was at the Department of Energy for the last ten years, doing budget work." Roger's voice is so soft I can barely hear him. "It was terrible. In at nine, gone by five. It was a total grind. I always took orders from other people. I got a steady paycheck, but it was never enough. Four percent raises a year and no bonus." He lets out a frustrated

breath. "I thought joining Bedford would make me seem more exciting, especially to my wife. She's never said anything, but I don't think
she has much respect for me anymore." He pauses and swallows hard.
"I'm worried that she'll, well, that she'll . . ."

He doesn't finish, but I understand what he's trying to say and the
words hit home.

"But now that I'm here, I'm petrified I'm going to lose everything
I've ever saved," he continues.

And he could too. An inexperienced day trader can get caught in a
whirlpool and drown before he even realizes he's wet. "You were able
to save half a million dollars working for the federal government over
the last ten years?" I ask, remembering the discussion we had with
Seaver about our initial capital.

Roger grimaces. "I exaggerated a little. Well, actually a lot."

"How much are you really starting with?"

"Less than fifty thousand. It's everything my wife and I have."

"And she's okay with this? Risking your entire savings on day trading, even when you don't know what you're doing? Just for the sake of
being exciting?"

Roger leans back and looks up at the ceiling. "She doesn't know
I'm here," he admits quietly. "She thinks I'm still at the DOE."

"Oh, man," I groan.

Roger's taking a drastic step to try to solve his midlife crisis, but
he'll only end up making matters worse for himself. Then who knows
what will happen? A shooting spree at a fast-food joint or a school? A
suicide attempt from the Chesapeake Bay Bridge? Roger could become that next headline we all see flash across our portal page when
he finally loses every cent he has and dives into debt to support a habit
that people say can be more addictive than crack. And Roger *will* lose
everything if he doesn't get very smart very fast. The capital markets
are brutally efficient, constantly chewing up and spitting out the weak
and the naive.

"I figured I'd make a bunch of money here and surprise my wife
with the cash. Then she wouldn't care when I told her I had quit the
DOE and made the money day trading."

"Day trading is tough, Roger," I say firmly, as though I'm an expert.

"What made you think you could be successful right away without any experience?"

"I've got this neighbor who's spent the past two years bragging about how much money he's made investing in all of these dot-coms. My wife lit up every time he started talking about how he's into this stock or that one, and the guy has been buying new furniture and flashy cars. Even a boat. He's no rocket scientist so I figured I could do the same thing." Roger shakes his head. "But get this. Last night he and I were in the backyard watching our kids chase fireflies while it was getting dark, and he lets on that he hasn't really made much money in the stock market after all. In fact, he's lost a lot lately. He's bought all of the new stuff on credit, and now the bill collectors are closing in on him. He actually asked me for a loan. He almost broke down in tears, and it shook me. When I came in here this morning I was paralyzed thinking about how he's going to lose everything. I had a couple of stocks I wanted to buy, opportunities he told me about, but I couldn't pull the trigger. I was worried I'd end up like him. I mean, who is he to make recommendations anyway?" Roger stops stroking his beard. "Will you help me, Augustus?" he pleads. "It seems like you know what you're doing. I could tell Seaver was impressed with you." Roger hesitates. "I guess that Slammer guy knows what he's doing too, but frankly, he's a prick. I doubt he'd be very helpful."

The last thing I need right now is a pupil. I've gotten off to a good start with Unicom, but I don't know how I'll react when things go against me the first time—which they inevitably will. Everybody hits a slump sooner or later.

"I'm losing my wife, Augustus. I can feel it."

I lean forward and rub my eyes. This is no good.

"I'll pay you," he offers desperately. "I'll give you a share of my profits."

"You don't have to do that."

Roger looks up. He's heard a friendly tone. "I don't?"

I don't need a second shadow, but I feel Roger's pain, and down deep I like to help people. I don't want to see him lose everything, nor do I want him coming into the office one day brandishing a loaded twelve-gauge shotgun like some deranged postal worker who's finally realized he can't ever get ahead because the mail will never stop coming. "I can't work with you right now, but if you stick around after the markets close today, I'll help you personalize your Trader One and we'll go over a couple of basics." He breaks into a wide grin. It's the first time I've seen him smile, and that makes me feel good. "But promise me this," I say gravely, pointing at him. "Don't execute a single trade until we talk."

"I won't. Thanks, thanks a lot," he says graciously. "I'll let you get back to work. I won't take any more of your—"

I hold up my hand to indicate that our conversation is over, and suddenly I feel like Don Corleone. Roger nods obediently and slips out the doorway into the trading room. I know I've just committed a cardinal sin in the day trading game. Never take on another person's problems because ultimately you'll have enough of your own. But what the hell, he seems nice enough, and I understand where he's coming from.

Anna comes into the conference room after Roger leaves. She isn't the blue-eyed blond type I'm typically attracted to, but her sexy body, provocative wardrobe, and Spanish accent make her incredibly seductive.

"Good morning, Augustus."

"Hi."

"This came for you a few minutes ago." She hands me a Federal Express package that's already been opened.

"Thanks."

"Talk to you later," she says with a quick smile.

Inside the FedEx package is a letter-size envelope, and the return address is that of the Great Western Insurance Company. The letter inside makes my mouth run dry. It explains that Great Western has received my claim and that "once a routine investigation is completed without exception, the payee, Augustus McKnight, shall receive $1,000,000." The amount is typed in bold.

The letter shakes as I hold it up and stare at the bold type. A million dollars. I often paid bills months late—only when I thought creditors were about to cut off a utility or send a collector to our door to repossess something—because Melanie and I literally had no money in our account. Now, a few weeks after bouncing a four-hundred-dollar check, I'm about to bank over a million. If Melanie and I could have had this kind of money, our lives would have been so much better, I think to myself, choking up as I flash on the image of her body lying on that silver gurney.

"Augustus." It's Anna again.

I quickly push the tips of my thumb and forefinger to the corners of my eyes to conceal my emotion. "Yes?"

"I'm sorry if I'm bothering you."

"It's okay. What's up?"

"There's a man in the lobby to see you."

I glance up into her huge brown eyes. "Who is it?"

"He says he's a detective with the Washington, D.C., police department."

I follow Anna's catwalk stride back through the trading floor and out into the lobby, wondering what Reggie wants. Perhaps there's been a break in the case, but how in the hell did he find me here? The buzz of voices fades as the doors swing shut behind me and I see Reggie Dorsey relaxing on the couch.

"Hello, Augustus," he says pleasantly, rising to meet me in front of Anna's desk.

I can tell she's listening closely to what we're saying even as she pretends to focus on sorting mail. "Good morning, Reggie. Let's go in there," I suggest, taking him by the elbow and guiding him away from her prying ears toward the conference room off the lobby where Seaver, Roger, and I met last week.

"How have you been?" he asks, sitting down in the chair at the head of the table.

"All right. Still hurting."

"Started a new job, I see."

"Yes." I haven't spoken to Reggie since he stopped by the house more than a week and a half ago. "How did you know I was here? I don't remember telling you I was coming to Bedford."

"We'll get to that," he replies, brushing aside my question. "I need to ask you a few things first."

I'm suddenly aware that the Great Western envelope is sticking out of my shirt pocket. I can't remember how I slid it in there—with the return address visible or not. His eyes flicker down to my chest, but I can't read anything in his glance. I want to look down, want to hide the envelope because he might get the wrong idea, but, of course, I can't do that now.

Reggie crosses his arms and his sports jacket rides up, exposing thick forearms. "How were you and Melanie getting along in the months before her death?"

He's never started a conversation like this before, and I'm on the defensive immediately. "I don't understand." I clasp my hands together tightly beneath the table and feel cool perspiration between my fingers.

"Any arguments or fights?"

"Nothing out of the ordinary," I say. "What's going on here, Reggie?"

"What was ordinary?"

He pays no attention to my request for an explanation. "We argued once in a while."

"About what?"

"Fall fashions, usually."

"Come on, Augustus."

"Oh, I see. I answer you, but you ignore me."

"Augustus."

"We didn't have much money, which was difficult." I shouldn't have to endure this kind of questioning. "Our financial situation was frustrating for both of us. We couldn't buy things we wanted or take nice vacations. We saw lots of people our age enjoying the good life, and we felt we were missing out. That caused problems. I told you all this the last time you stopped by the house. I've been very honest with you."

"Do you have any reason not to be honest with me?"

"Of course not." I think back to the speech Reggie delivered in his car after giving me a ride home from the morgue. The one about asking me questions that might upset me. About how he would just be doing his job. This is what he was talking about. He's given me a few days to recover, and now he's treating me like a suspect. There won't be any sympathy for me from now on because, as he warned me, he doesn't care about my feelings. He only cares about finding Melanie's killer.

Reggie leans forward, elbows on the table. "So you fought over money." He opens his hands, palms up like a minister, and his voice takes on a compassionate quality. "Most couples do. I bet Melanie was the one who wanted to spend all the money, and you wouldn't let her. Weren't you the one who managed the finances?" He shakes his head. "That's a tough job. I know. I manage the money in my household."

I've been to this movie before. The cop whose manner is typically brusque turns sympathetic when he wants something. Russell Lake and Reggie Dorsey are alike in this way. "I was the one who paid the bills," I confirm calmly. "I knew how little money we had. Melanie didn't want to know."

"She wanted all those nice clothes and jewelry, like any woman does. She probably went to that Body Beautiful shop in the strip mall near your house for a manicure once a week. Damn, there's thirty bucks up in smoke." He chuckles without a hint of a smile. "My wife does the same thing. But those things are important to women and we men have to realize that."

"True." Reggie's right. Melanie had to have her nails done every Wednesday or she was miserable. Like some people have to have coffee first thing in the morning or they turn into the creature from the black lagoon. And it was *thirty-five* dollars for each visit to Body Beautiful, not thirty. I wonder what else Reggie knows about our life together.

"Money is a problem for almost every couple. Ever argue about anything else?" he asks.

I feel like I ought to tell Reggie I need a lawyer present, but I don't want to take the conversation to that level. He probably knows that. He's got experience in these matters and I'm naive. "Little stuff. Everyday things. Nothing important."

Reggie's eyes narrow as they pan down again, then flicker back to mine. "Did the arguments ever become violent?"

I take a deep breath, thinking through my answer. I want to be very careful here. "Melanie had a temper. Her friends will tell you that."

"They already have, Augustus."

I can feel his eyes boring into me, and after a few moments of silence I feel compelled to say something. "She would . . ." I hesitate, uncertain of how much I should reveal.

"What, Augustus? She would what?"

"She would become physical once in a while when we argued. You know, throw a lamp or something. Nothing really bad, though. And I never did anything to her," I add quickly.

"Nothing?"

"Nothing."

"Never pushed her down or restrained her to protect yourself?"

I press my lips tightly together. "I might have pushed her away once or twice, when she'd get in my face and start yelling. But, as you said, it was simply to protect myself. I'm a big man but she could have hurt me if she wanted to. Some people might not understand that, but it's true."

"She was tall and in excellent physical condition according to the coroner's report. I'm sure she could get your attention," Reggie agrees. "I've seen tiny women beat the hell out of men bigger than you."

We're back at the movie. Second scene.

Reggie removes a pack of smokes from his jacket and puts one in his mouth, then takes out a lighter and holds the flame several inches from the end of the cigarette. Finally he extinguishes the flame without lighting the cigarette and stows the lighter back in his jacket with a groan. "It's a real pain in the ass trying to quit," he mutters.

"I can imagine."

"But I want to watch my grandchildren grow up, you know? I want to be around to see them graduate from college."

I nod, hoping we're done with the interrogation. "How many do you have?"

"Four."

"How old are they?"

"Seven, five, three, and two," he says proudly with a wide smile. I've noticed that he doesn't smile a whole lot.

"That's nice."

"Yeah, it is." He takes a long whiff of the unlit tobacco, then looks up at me. "Did you and your wife have a normal sex life?"

The interrogation isn't over. "What kind of question is that? Jesus!" Right away I wish I could take back my outburst, but I'm being co-operative. I don't think my sex life is any business of the Washington police.

"You've been so helpful up until now, Augustus," Reggie says re-gretfully, as if I've let him down. Then he just looks at me, waiting.

"We had sex a few times a month," I say after a long pause. God, I hate dead air. "Maybe once a week. We were married for eleven years. I'll be honest, it wasn't new and different after all that time."

"Of course it wasn't. You both probably needed to use your imagi-nations to get things going. Who usually initiated it during the last year?"

"Sometimes me, sometimes Melanie." I look away. Actually, I was always the one asking for it near the end.

Reggie taps the table. "Did she ever discuss her sexual fantasies with you?"

"That's none of your damn business! Give me a break, Reggie."

"Did she ever perform for you?" he asks, ignoring my plea.

"Perform?"

"You know, striptease in the bedroom or the living room before getting to the sex. Did she ever do anything like that?"

"No, of course not."

"How about bondage?"

I freeze. "Bondage? Jesus Christ! How can you ask me that?"

"The autopsy report indicated that Melanie's wrists and ankles were bruised, like someone had tied her up and she had struggled. But the coroner determined that the marks were made well before her murder. As much as a day before." He looks down. "And she'd had sex just a few hours before she was murdered. Rough sex. She had inter-nal bruises and scratches."

"Oh, no," I whisper.

"But there were no fluids. Nothing to trace."

"God."

"Did you and Melanie have intercourse the night or morning be-fore her murder?"

I put my face in my hands. "No."

"In your eleven years of marriage, did she have an affair?"

Reggie is relentless. I hate that about him. "Not that I'm aware of," I answer, my voice low. "But how can you ever really be sure?"

He replaces the cigarette in its pack. "I met with Frank Taylor late last week."

My eyes flash to Reggie's.

"He told me that Melanie asked you for a divorce the day before she was murdered. Is that true?"

"Taylor's an asshole."

"Maybe, but that's not an answer to my question."

I take a deep breath. "Yeah, she asked me for a divorce. But she would never have followed through."

"Why do you say that?"

"Taylor was filling her head with all kinds of ridiculous ideas. Mel would have come to her senses sooner or later."

Reggie pauses. "Was Mel *your* nickname for her?"

"Yes."

"When did you give it to her?"

"A few years ago."

"Did she use it? Did she introduce herself that way to others?"

"I don't think so. Why?"

"Taylor referred to her that way while I was talking to him."

I take a deep breath and I'm sure my jealousy is obvious.

"Do you think Melanie and Taylor were having an affair?"

"I don't know," I answer grimly, rubbing my forehead with both hands.

"Taylor's face was pretty banged up when I met with him last week. Do you know anything about that?"

"I told you. He's an asshole. I'm sure there are lots of people who would like to take a swing at him. After all, he's a divorce attorney."

Reggie goes quiet for a few moments, but this time he gets nothing out of me. "All right, Augustus. Well, I appreciate your help. Sorry to have put you through all of that."

I don't respond. He's not sorry at all.

"Oh, just one more question."

"There's always one more question, isn't there, Reggie?"

"Were there any insurance policies on Melanie's life?" he asks, paying no attention to my sarcasm.

I meet Reggie's eyes. Frank Taylor mentioned the policy at the Grand last week. That must be where Reggie got his information. "Yes."

"How much was the death benefit?"

"A million dollars. There is a policy on me for the same amount. It was all Melanie's idea. She filled out the paperwork for both of us. You can check that out. Except for the signature on mine, it was all her handwriting on both applications."

"When were the policies put into effect?"

I know how this will sound to Reggie, but facts are facts and it's better for me to be honest. "Several months ago."

"Who was the beneficiary of her policy?" he asks, his face expressionless. I'm sure he already knows all about this and is just testing me to see if I'll be honest with him.

"I was, of course."

"And who was second behind you?"

"I'm not sure," I answer slowly. "I think she said it was her mother, but I never looked at that part of the application. All I did was sign it, and then she grabbed it and took off."

Reggie nods. "I appreciate your honesty. Some people might have lied to me, for obvious reasons. Look, I need you to give us a blood sample," he says, glancing at the fading scabs on my neck.

"Why?"

"Routine," he says, standing up. "Why don't you come down tomorrow? Just tell the person at the front desk who you are. They'll know what to do."

He's almost to the door when I speak up. I try to resist, but I can't help myself. "Reggie."

"Yes?"

"How did you find me here? I never told you I was coming to Bedford. Are you having me followed?"

"Trust me, we don't have the budget for that kind of thing."

"How then?"

"I seem to have a source," he says. "At least I think I do."

"I don't understand."

"This morning, someone left an anonymous phone message for me at the precinct's front desk informing me of the fact that you're working here. Somebody wanted me to know how to find you."

CHAPTER

7

"Will this be all right?" The maitre d' turns and gestures to a secluded booth in the back of the Capital Grill. The restaurant is buried in the first level of the sprawling three-story Tysons Two Mall, which is connected to our office building. It serves decent food, though nothing as delicious as the Grand's steaks. But its prices are much more reasonable. Despite the money I've come into I'm not going to change my spending habits much. No big home or fast car—not yet, anyway.

"This will be fine," I answer, as Mary slips onto the bench seat.

The maitre d' places two menus down on the table, and I slide onto the seat across from Mary. He probably thinks this lunch is a prelude to a tryst because she wears a wedding band and a huge diamond engagement ring on her left hand, while the fingers of my left hand are bare. I took my wedding band off before I started at Bedford.

"This is a nice place for lunch," Mary says, leaning across the table and touching my forearm for the umpteenth time since we left the office under Anna's watchful eye. Probably another reason the maitre d' gave me that knowing smile. Mary was standing very close to me, even leaning against me at one point as we waited for our table. I'm sure she means nothing by all of this, though. That's just the way she is. A physical kind of person.

The Capital Grill was Mary's suggestion. I've never been in this mall before. Its upscale stores sell items that were way too expensive for Melanie and me, so we never bothered coming to it.

"I like your name," Mary says, toying with a long strand of pearls hanging from her neck, causing the diamond of her engagement ring to shimmer. "It's so unusual."

"Thanks." I chuckle, thinking about how Slammer called me Gus. "Slammer doesn't like it much."

"What do you mean?"

"Oh, nothing."

"Don't worry about Max," Mary says. "Don't take anything he says personally. He's just very intense."

"Maybe he's just never been able to let go of the military thing," I say. "I've never been in the armed forces, so I can only imagine what it must have been like. And he was in special forces. Army Rangers, I think he said. That must have been tough." I know for sure I'll never like the guy, but I'm being polite for Mary's benefit. Who knows, maybe she and Slammer are close. I haven't been at Bedford long enough to be able to tell.

Mary leans back and runs a hand through her shoulder-length sandy blond hair. Her long nails—painted a stark bloodred—move slowly through the strands so that the boulder on her finger doesn't become entangled. She's an attractive woman with delicate features, a deep tan, and lots of freckles. But she's a little older than I first thought. Daniel Jenkins—the one Slammer calls Freak Show—told me last week that Mary is in her mid-forties.

"Slammer has a vivid imagination," Mary says. "I wouldn't be surprised if he exaggerates a fact or two along the way."

"Really?"

"Oh, sure. You know that beat-up old briefcase he keeps on his desk beside his computer?"

"The tan one he seems to take with him everywhere he goes? Even to the bathroom?"

"That's the one. And he doesn't *seem* to take it with him everywhere he goes. He *does*."

"What's so special about it?"

"Well, he says he keeps a loaded revolver in it." She puts a finger on her cheek and her expression turns serious, like she's trying hard to remember something. "A forty-four Magnum, I think he said once. But I don't know much about guns."

Normally I would dismiss a piece of information like this as ridiculous, just office gossip, but Slammer seems like the type who might do something crazy. I don't know how else to explain it, but he gets that right-on-the-verge-of-going-ballistic look in his eyes sometimes. And last week I thought I heard him talking about ammunition while he was on the phone. "Has anybody ever said anything to Michael Seaver about the possibility of a gun in the office?"

"I don't know."

"Don't you think Seaver should be aware of something like that?"

Mary laughs. "Max doesn't really keep a gun in his briefcase. It's all about image with him. He wants us to think he's tough so he can convince himself he is. Beneath all of that bravado is a pussycat. I bet he wasn't even in the military. Like I said, I've caught him exaggerating before. When we first met he told me he drove a Porsche and owned a four-story town house in Georgetown. Turns out he drives a used Honda and rents a basement apartment from an old lady out in the country."

"Are you sure there's no gun in his briefcase? Have you ever looked?"

"I don't have to. I know his type. All bark and no bite. He's harmless."

Our waiter arrives. I order a Coke and Mary has a glass of white wine. I suspected that she wasn't very serious about day trading, and now I'm certain. No serious trader would let her judgment be clouded by alcohol during market hours.

"What are you doing at Bedford?" I ask when the waiter leaves. Usually I'm not so blunt, but the word on the floor is that Mary has a sugar daddy who keeps her in the expensive clothes and diamonds. That she doesn't really have to work, and that the day trading gig is simply a diversion.

"You mean, why don't I just sit at home watching soaps and eating bonbons?"

"That's not what I mean at all."

"Yes, it is," she says confidently, reaching across the table once more. "I know what you think. It's in your smile."

"I'm not smiling."

"The smile's in your green eyes and your thoughts." As Mary's fingers slide from my arm, her nails gently rake my skin and it gives me chills. The good kind. God, it's been so long since a woman touched me that way. "I can read your mind," she whispers.

I roll my eyes and chuckle.

"I'm serious, Augustus."

I chuckle again. I don't give much credence to the paranormal.

"You don't believe me." Mary pouts. "I can tell."

"Maybe I just don't have much experience."

"I'm a very spiritual person. I believe in astrology, extrasensory perception, and reincarnation. It only makes sense that those things should exist when you stop and think about it. So many advanced cultures down through history have believed in them."

I believe those things are simply ways of explaining coincidence, or are tools used to manipulate, but I don't tell Mary that. It wouldn't do either of us any good to talk about it because we're not going to change each other's mind.

"I'm not a psychic," she continues. "I can't constantly sense people's thoughts the way those who have the gift can. But sometimes I really believe I can tell what people are thinking. Like just now with you."

"Uh-huh." She seems to sincerely believe what she's saying, and I catch myself smiling at her. She isn't at all who I expected.

As the waiter delivers our drinks, I glimpse a hulking figure pass a far-off window of the restaurant, and I'm almost certain it's Detective

Dorsey. I strain to catch another look as the guy passes the next window, but I can't tell for certain whether it's him and then he's gone. As I ease back onto my seat Mary's expression turns to one of sharp interest.

"What did you see out there?" she asks, picking up her wine glass. "My God, your face went white as a sheet."

I smile lamely, trying to act as though my electric reaction was no big deal. "A woman I thought I recognized." I doubt Mary will want to dwell on that. "An old friend."

"Oh."

The thought of Reggie's presence shakes me. I don't know whether to believe him that this morning's Q&A was just standard procedure, or when he said he wasn't having me watched. I don't want to have to explain to him that there's nothing going on here, that this is simply an innocent lunch between two coworkers. I don't want to have to explain anything to Reggie because my impression of him is that he's the kind of man who draws significance from subtleties, and rarely changes his mind once he's reached a conclusion.

"Are you all right?" Mary asks, taking another swallow of wine.

"I'm fine," I answer quickly. "You were going to tell me when you first came to Bedford."

"Actually, you wanted to know what I was doing at Bedford," she corrects.

"Well, I—"

"My husband died seven months ago. On Christmas Eve."

I glance up. That was the night my mother passed away. It was the first time Melanie didn't accompany me to the hospital after my mother had been admitted the week before, so I had to drive those lonely miles home by myself after watching Mom die. "I'm sorry for your loss," I murmur.

"Thank you."

She looks down and it's my turn to reach across the table to comfort her. I hate seeing genuine sadness.

"My husband, Jacob, was a good deal older than me," Mary explains, her voice starting to tremble slightly. "He was in his mid-sixties, but he was so full of life. He acted much younger than his age. He made lots of money in the nineties as a commercial real estate developer here in Washington, so we were very comfortable. He owned a large house in McLean, but we were almost never there because we traveled all the time." Her eyes take on a distant look. "We went to exotic places like Tahiti, Africa, and the Amazon. He shared everything with me, and taught me a great deal along the way. He hired me as his executive assistant two years ago, and a week later we were inseparable. I had to divorce my husband at the time so Jacob and I could be together, but I knew the moment I laid eyes on him we would be married. I'm like that. I know when it's right, and when I get that feeling nothing stops me. Jacob said I was crazy when I first told him we would be together. He admitted how wrong he'd been after we made love the first time.

"Jacob's children weren't very happy about our marriage," she continues, "but ours was a match made in heaven. The age difference was never an issue." Her expression turns steely. "People accused me of marrying Jacob for his money, but that wasn't the case. I didn't have much when I met him, but Jacob's money had nothing to do with my feelings for him. Money can make people do strange things, even me sometimes, I'll admit. But it had absolutely nothing to do with my love for Jacob."

I stare steadily at Mary, thinking about what she just said and wondering if she's telling me the truth. Wondering if Reggie told me the truth this morning. Mary seems sincere. So did Reggie.

"When Jacob died of a heart attack last Christmas, he left me two million dollars," Mary says, swallowing more wine, "and the house. He left the rest of the money to the children. The house is huge, and I found myself lost in it. There were pictures of the two of us everywhere, mostly of us on our trips, and I couldn't take the constant reminders and the loneliness. I've thought about selling the thing, but I haven't gotten around to it. Anyway, one Sunday morning a few weeks after his death I saw an article in the *Post* about day trading. On a whim I decided to try it. Now I'm hooked."

"Just on a whim?"

"Yup, that's me. Impulsive to a fault."

I shake my head and smile. I wish I could be like that, but I'm a deliberate man. It took me years to pull the trigger on day trading.

"Augustus?"

"Yeah?"

"I haven't told anyone else in the office what I just told you. About Jacob and me, I mean. About the fact that he died. So please keep it to yourself."

"Why haven't you told anyone?"

"I want people thinking I'm married. Men think single women are vulnerable, which is why I still wear these," she says, flashing her jewels. "You know it would be more complicated if they thought I was available." She finishes her wine. "Not that being married keeps men completely away, but it helps."

"Why did you tell me about Jacob?"

"Because you seem like a nice man." She looks away, and the sadness I saw before passes over her face once more. "It's been hard these last seven months without him."

"I'm sure it has," I say quietly, thinking about the loneliness I've felt over the last few weeks.

"And it feels good to talk about it with someone," she says, reaching for my hand. "I've kept it bottled up inside and that's been hard."

"I'm glad you felt like you could open up to me."

"I told you, I had a strong feeling about you when Seaver brought you out to meet us last week. It was immediate for me."

I smile at her. Mary has a nice way about her.

"Don't worry about Slammer," she says, changing the subject as she reaches for her empty wineglass.

"I'm not worried about him," I answer defensively. "I could take him with one arm tied behind my back."

"I'm sure you could," she agrees, grinning at my reaction, "but that isn't what I was talking about."

"Oh."

"I meant that you shouldn't think anything of the fact that he and I are going out for drinks tonight. He's just a friend."

"That's none of my business."

"He's one of the reasons I wear these rings. I'm sure he'd like to get to know me better, but my diamonds will keep him away."

"Don't count on it," I mutter. I'm about to explain to her how some men are undeterred by a woman's marital status—men like Vincent—but the waiter returns. Mary orders a Caesar salad and another glass of wine, I order a club sandwich, and then the young man is off, striding purposefully back toward the kitchen.

"So you've been at Bedford now for a few months," I say, trying to distract her. The melancholy look in her eyes tells me that she's dwelling on Jacob's death, and I've had enough of death. "How's the trading going?"

She grimaces. "Not very well. It's not as easy to make money in the stock market as I thought it would be."

It's exactly as all of the magazines warn. Most people who get into the day trading game lose. "What do you mean, not very well? How bad has it been?"

She sighs. "In four months I've lost a million dollars."

A million dollars. I'm only just beginning to understand what it might be like to *have* a million dollars, let alone to *lose* it.

"Pretty sad, huh?" Mary picks up the second glass of wine the waiter placed on our table a few moments ago. "But I've still got plenty left, and things will turn around," she says optimistically. "Fortunately I've got the capital to ride out this bad streak."

She sounds like an amateur gambler who naively believes that if she can just stay at the table long enough, the odds will turn in her favor and she'll win back everything she's lost. Which is exactly what the casino wants her to believe.

"Jacob taught me all about riding out downturns," she continues. "He lost almost everything he had in the late eighties when the Washington real estate market crashed. But he had staying power and when the market came back in the mid-nineties, he made tens of millions. The same thing will happen to me," she predicts confidently. "He tells me all the time not to worry."

I notice her use of the present tense, but say nothing. I'm not going to be drawn into a discussion about being able to contact loved ones on the other side. "Did you have any experience analyzing stocks before you came to Bedford?" I'm still amazed at the size and speed of her losses.

"No."

"What kinds of stocks have you bought?"

"Mostly high-tech companies."

"But how did you—"

"I invested a lot of my money in a company named MicroPlan right at its peak," she explains, anticipating my question. "This past April. I'm sure you heard about what happened there."

"Yes, I did."

"That was a tough lesson."

"I'll bet."

Several months ago MicroPlan was a white-hot northern Virginia–based data-mining software company whose arrogant twenty-something CEO had become a national celebrity thanks to his multibillion-dollar net worth and his penchant for throwing outrageous jet-set parties. The stock rose to over three hundred dollars a share with all of Wall Street shouting that even at such a stratospheric price the company's shares were still a bargain. MicroPlan's software enabled large and small companies alike to effectively scour their networks for data concerning customers and suppliers, making them incredibly efficient like no other software could. Everyone would buy the product, the Street argued, because if they didn't, they'd be at a severe competitive disadvantage. In a few years MicroPlan would be as important as Microsoft, so investors needed to get in now if they expected to reap the huge returns later on.

But in late April the story broke that the company had overstated revenue for the previous year, and in the blink of an eye the net income printed in MicroPlan's glossy annual report turned into a huge loss after the accounting storm troopers sent in by the regulators crashed the corporate offices and revved up their calculators. Worse, customers began to complain to the press that the software wasn't all it was cracked up to be. That there were bugs. Within two weeks the share price had tumbled below ten and the brash, wunderkind CEO was under investigation for fraud.

"I read tons of reports written by people who were supposed to be experts," Mary fumes. "Wall Street analysts who, in the end, didn't understand the company any better than I did. Snakes," she mutters.

I happened to see MicroPlan's price this morning. It was trading at five dollars and fifty cents a share. A bloodbath for most investors. "Where did you get in?"

"Almost right at the top. At three hundred and nineteen dollars a share," she answers grimly. "Before I could react, the stock had dropped to a hundred and fifty."

"You should have ditched then," I say automatically, quoting what I've read in all of the financial textbooks.

"Of course I should have," Mary snaps. "But hindsight is always twenty-twenty. At that point I'd lost close to half a million dollars, and people on the trading floor were saying that it was a great buying opportunity. That the market was just overreacting to bad news like it always does. Max told me I'd be crazy to get out at that point. So I bought more shares to average down the cost of my position. That's the last time I'll ever listen to him," she says bitterly. "And if I had ditched the stock at that point and the price had gone back up, I'd have felt like a fool. Though not as big of one as I feel like now."

I lean forward over the table. "Teletekk," I whisper.

"Here you are," the waiter announces, placing Mary's salad and my club sandwich down on the table. "Will there be anything else?"

I flinch at the sound of his voice. I had no idea he was there. I don't want anyone hearing me give Mary this tip. Regulations regarding insider trading are ridiculously strict. From what I understand the authorities can come after you even if you don't know the information you're giving someone else is privileged. The laws are too severe, but brutally enforced, so it's best to be careful.

"I'm fine," I answer quickly. "Do you need anything else, Mary?"

"No."

The waiter darts off.

"So what's Teletekk?" she asks loudly.

I grin nervously, looking around to see who might have heard her. "I think we ought to keep our voices down. You never know who's listening, and I'd hate for this information to get out and the price shoot up before you've had a chance to take advantage of it."

"Right," she agrees, pushing her salad to one side and leaning over the table. "So what's Teletekk?" she asks, her voice a whisper.

"It's a company that makes advanced telecommunications equipment. Cutting-edge laser stuff. I bought a thousand shares this morning. It's trading around twenty-one bucks right now, but I think it'll run to sixty very soon. The company is about to announce an initiative into the satellite arena."

The market is so damn fickle. I finally bought a thousand shares of Teletekk this morning at $21.25, right after Reggie left. By the time Mary and I headed out for lunch the price had dropped to $19.75. So I lost fifteen hundred dollars in a little over an hour. But you have to be able to take the good with the bad in this game, or you'll end up like Slammer—on the brink.

It's crazy. I risked twenty-one grand on a thirty-second recommendation from a guy I'd never met before on a company I knew very little about. All because Trainer *seemed* credible. Suddenly I can't wait to get back to my cubicle to see how the stock is doing, and here is the sinister nature of the business. Sooner or later it consumes you. Sooner or later you become addicted to your computer screen—you might as well be chained to it—constantly checking and rechecking prices of stocks you've bought.

"How do you know all of this?" Mary asks.

I don't answer.

"What's wrong?" she wants to know, searching my expression.

I gaze at her without answering. Now I'm recommending Teletekk to this poor woman, and I wonder if I'm doing so because I'm trying to help her, or because I'm just trying to convince myself that I've made a good move buying it. "Nothing. Look, maybe you shouldn't—"

"How much money are you playing with?" she interrupts.

"What do you mean?"

"I heard a rumor on the floor that you're a real player. That your roll is well over seven figures."

"Roll" is short for bankroll on the trading floor. "Well, I . . ." My voice trails off. After the insurance money comes in I'll have over a million, but *well over* sounds much better, and I like the fact that she seems impressed.

"Is that true?" she asks. "Are you really trading with that much?"

"Yeah," I mumble, picking up my sandwich. Hoping she doesn't ask how I got the money.

She smiles at me. "You know, I thought it would be that way with most of the men at Bedford when I started, but it really isn't. Most of the guys are spinning less than fifty thousand." She leans forward. "Not like you."

I like the way she's looking at me. Like I'm powerful because of my brain and my bank account. I can't recall a woman ever doing that.

"Tell me about yourself, Augustus," Mary says, moving the salad back in front of her and picking up her fork. "Are you married?"

"No," I answer cautiously, uneasy about the sudden turn in the conversation.

"Ever been married?" she asks.

I hesitate. "No."

"Oh."

Mary turns strangely quiet, and though I try hard to nudge her into conversation on several different topics, she won't engage. As she picks at her salad, she gives only abbreviated answers to my questions and refuses to look up.

"What's wrong?" I finally ask.

"Nothing."

"Come on." She's almost finished her second glass of wine so I ought to be able to get her to talk. "Tell me."

"Why did you lie to me?"

I almost choke on a bite of my sandwich. "What are you talking about?" I manage, swallowing a big gulp of Coke to wash down the food.

"You said you'd never been married, but I know that's not true."

"Huh?"

"I know you were married to that poor woman the police found murdered near the Capitol a few weeks ago."

I stare at Mary, an eerie feeling crawling up my spine, and Reggie's admission about someone anonymously providing him information echoing in my ears.

"How did you find out about my wife?"

"Max did a search on the Internet and you showed up as the woman's husband in a bunch of articles."

My shoulders sag. Of course. Information is so easy to come by these days. "You're right, I should have told you," I agree. "It's just that Melanie's death is still so recent. I guess I'm doing my best not to think about it. I miss her very much," I say, my gaze dropping to the table. I feel Mary's warm fingers on mine. "Sorry."

"It's okay," she says softly. "I shouldn't have asked a question I already knew the answer to. That wasn't fair. It's just that I want you to trust me. I'll be here if you ever need someone to talk to." She hesitates. "I realize that's a forward thing to say, but I was attracted to you the moment I saw you. I told you, I'm a very intuitive person." She smiles. "It's almost as if I knew you before you came to Bedford."

I stare at her, wondering what that means.

Her smiles grows wider. "I just know we're going to be great friends."

CHAPTER

———— 〇ⅢⅨ ————

8

Vincent is standing in Bedford's lobby when Mary and I get back from lunch, and he's exactly where I'd expect him to be. Leaning way over Anna's reception desk, making time.

He smiles broadly when he sees me, as he always does. "Hi, Augustus." He's dressed in his typical loose-fitting warm-up suit, Reeboks, and gold chain. He must buy a pair of those Reeboks every week because they always look brand-new.

"Hello, Vincent."

I introduce Vincent and Mary, then she excuses herself with a parting smile. "What are you doing here?" I ask, watching her move through the swinging doors and disappear into the trading room. In the time it took us to have lunch, she has intrigued me, I have to admit.

"I was in the neighborhood so I thought I'd stop by, champ," Vincent replies, chuckling. "I wanted to see if you'd been back to the Grand to kick anybody else's ass."

Anna glances up from her desk.

"Why don't you come inside?" I ask quickly.

"Let's go for a walk instead," he says, gesturing toward the glass door.

Vincent wants something. I can always tell by the tone of his voice. "Let me check out something on my computer first."

"Fine. I'll wait for you out here." He smiles at Anna. "The scenery is so nice."

I jog down the aisle to my cubicle, eyeing Slammer's briefcase sitting in its customary position on his desk beside his computer. As usual, he's banging away on his keyboard, complaining about something to someone out there in cyberspace.

Mary smiles at me from her chair when I go into my cubicle, and I give her a quick return smile as I sit down and tap out my password to unlock my computer and access everything behind the colorful picture of a Yosemite waterfall I've chosen as my screen saver.

I'm quickly through to my portfolio page. I've bought only ten stocks after a week at Bedford, and I don't intend to sell them anytime soon. In the week it's taken me to execute ten trades, Slammer and Daniel have bought and sold thousands of times. I'll be doing the same thing, but I'm being cautious for now. According to everything I've heard, the kind of churn and burn strategy Slammer and Daniel employ can consume a lot of cash in a hurry if you don't know exactly what you're doing. Sometimes, even if you do.

I scan down the page and curse under my breath at the latest Teletekk quote. Since I left for lunch the damn thing has fallen two more points to $17.75. In a few hours I've lost almost thirty-five hundred dollars on this dog. The Lord giveth and the Lord taketh away, and Jack Trainer is a no-good son of a bitch.

Mary slinks into my cubicle. "I did what you told me," she says.

"Did what?"

"I bought Teletekk," she whispers, kneeling down and squeezing my hand.

"How much did you buy?"

"You said it was going to go to sixty. I didn't want to make the same mistake I made with MicroPlan by putting too much into one stock, but I didn't want to miss out on a sure thing either."

"How much?" I repeat impatiently.

"Fifty-five hundred shares."

"Jesus, that's almost a hundred thousand dollars' worth." I roll my eyes until my gaze meets Daniel's. He's standing up behind his desk, staring down at me. His eyes move slowly to Mary's hand in mine, then back up as he toys with the ring protruding from his eyebrow. "That's a lot of money," I say after he sits down.

"I trust you, Augustus," she says anxiously. "You wouldn't give me bad advice."

"Go, baby, go!" Slammer shouts. "Up another five points this hour. Christ, I'm gonna make a killing on this one." Slammer's luck has clearly changed this afternoon, and he's going to make certain the entire trading floor knows about it. He appears over the partition and breaks into a sly grin. "Whatcha doing down there, Sassy?" He snickers. "You two seem to have gotten friendly pretty quick. A long lunch the second week Gus is here and now you're about to crawl under his desk. Very interesting," he says snidely.

I've come to quickly realize that there are very few secrets on a trading floor. Even though Mary and I met out by the elevators to go to lunch—her suggestion—someone must have seen us together and told Slammer.

"Guess you got your errands done faster than you anticipated," Slammer says. "Or maybe Gus was your errand."

"Shut up, Max," Mary snaps, standing up and walking toward the ladies' room.

"Way to go, Gus," Slammer continues. "Sassy must like the tall, dark types. And I bet she's ready to give it to someone real good too because I hear that sugar daddy she's got at home is a wrinkled old man. Just a prune waiting for the grim reaper to come for him. Looks like you're going to have yourself some fun here at Bedford." He pauses and smiles. "Unless I get to the honey hole first."

I stand up slowly and move to where Max is smirking, towering over him. "Don't ever talk about Mary that way again." I can see Roger watching us out of my peripheral vision. "One more remark like that, and I'll pull your head backward through your ass. You understand me, Slammer?"

Max steps slowly back from the partition until his hand comes to rest on his briefcase. "Don't threaten me, Gus," he warns. "I don't take kindly to intimidation. In fact, I don't take to it at all," he says, patting the briefcase. "I do something about it."

I lean over the partition and point at him. "My name is Augustus, and that's what you'll call me. Got it?"

"And if I don't, what are you going to do? Slice my neck with a knife?"

I stare at Max, blood pounding in my brain, wishing I could.

"Augustus." Anna's voice crackles through the intercom on my desk. "Your friend is getting impatient out here."

I give Max one more warning look, then head for the lobby. When I get there, Vincent is still flirting with Anna. No wonder she called me. "Come on," I growl, irritated that I have to work next to an asshole like Slammer. "Let's go."

"See you, kitten," he calls over his shoulder as we walk toward the glass door.

When we're in the elevator and headed down, I ask Vincent, "Why did you call our receptionist 'kitten'?" I could have sworn Anna reacted strangely when he said it. As if Vincent had said something she *really* didn't like.

He shrugs. "I don't know. I call lots of girls that. So what? What's her real name?"

"Anna."

Vincent shrugs again as the elevator slows down. "She looks more like a Kitten to me than an Anna." He laughs as the door opens. "She thinks you're cute by the way."

"Shut up." I put my hand to my face as we cross the marble-floored lobby. The entrance to the Grand is off to the right, and I don't want to run into the two guys who threw me out last week.

"No, I'm serious," he says, trying hard to convince me as we push through the front door and hit the intense heat and humidity of the July afternoon. "She likes that little dimple on your chin. She thinks you're a hunk. She said you have rugged good looks."

"Yeah, yeah." Vincent finds it amusing to jerk my chain about how a woman we've just been around thinks I'm attractive. But he's been doing that for years, and I don't fall for it anymore. Not as much as I used to anyway.

"How's that guy Frank Taylor?" he asks, jerking a thumb back over his shoulder at the Grand. "The one you almost killed in the bar. Has he come back for more?"

"No." The morning after the fight Vincent called me to get details on what had happened. I told him a little bit, but not everything.

"Who did you tell me he was again?"

I glance up. There are ominous clouds building in the sky off to the west. "That lawyer Melanie worked for."

"Oh, right."

We jog across the street in front of my office building, then head down a long stairway into a quiet park, thunder rumbling in the distance.

"So why did you pop him?" Vincent asks as we walk slowly beside a small pond. "You never did tell me that."

"He broke down and admitted to Melanie that I was trying to re-tain him."

Vincent gives me an odd look. "Huh?"

"Nothing." Like I said, sometimes you have to keep things simple for Vincent.

"No, no, I get it. Ha, ha. Very funny. Now tell me the truth."

"It's not important."

"Come on, this is Vincent. Like we've always said. I tell you every-thing, you tell me—"

"He said he was having an affair with Melanie," I interrupt. I really don't want to listen to Vincent go on and on about no secrets, and I'm already pissed off about Teletekk. God, that was a stupid investment to make. "He bragged about it right there in the bar."

Vincent stops dead in his tracks. "An affair?" he asks, grabbing my arm and pulling me to a stop too. "You're kidding. Really?"

I nod curtly.

"Do you believe the guy?"

I take a deep breath. "Yes."

Vincent seems stunned, as if this news hits him almost as hard as it did me. But, as difficult as this is for me to admit, his show of concern could all be part of an Oscar-winning performance. Melanie was always fascinated with Vincent—and he with her.

"I'm sorry, Augustus."

"I appreciate that."

"I'm shocked Melanie would do something like that. Absolutely shocked."

"I guess you never really know anybody," I say quietly.

"Did you know about the affair before she was murdered?"

"I suspected."

"Did you ever confront her about it?"

"I confronted her about having an affair with *someone*. I wasn't sure who it was at the time." My pulse is suddenly racing. I've wanted to say this to Vincent for a long time. "I know this sounds crazy, but at one point I actually thought it might have been you."

He gazes at me steadily for several moments, expressionless, then finally bites his lower lip. "You can't be serious, pal. I would never—"

"She always liked you, Vincent. She fantasized about you even while we were in high school."

"I don't believe that."

"Believe it. She liked thinking you found her attractive."

"You're making this up."

"You thought she was beautiful. You always said so."

"Sure, and she was. But I didn't mean anything by it. I didn't think you'd be offended. I thought you'd like hearing that your wife was attractive."

"It excited Melanie to think that you looked at her in that way."

Vincent holds up his hands. "I don't want to hear this, Augustus."

"Remember last September when we went away for that long weekend in the Shenandoah Mountains? You rented that cabin in the woods and invited Mel and me along. You brought your flavor of the month. What was her name?"

"I don't remember," Vincent mutters. He wants no part of this conversation.

"I think her name was Beth."

"Whatever."

"You and Mel got up early Sunday morning and went for a walk in the woods together. You were both gone for a few hours, and Beth was convinced that you were going for it out there. She swore there was a blanket missing from one of the bedroom closets. Maybe she was a little paranoid, but it got me thinking, I have to admit. I told Beth over and over that you two were just good friends, but . . ."

"Nothing happened," Vincent says flatly as my voice trails off. "We talked and that was all." Vincent kicks at a pebble on the sidewalk. "It's been a tough few weeks for you, Augustus, and I think the stress has finally caught up with you. Despite what this Taylor guy claims he and Melanie did, she loved you very much."

"Melanie was an incredibly sexual woman, Vincent."

"You've told me that before."

"I haven't told you half of it."

Vincent looks up. He doesn't say anything, but I can see in his expression that he wants to hear more. He's unable to restrain his curiosity.

"When we were first together she wanted to make love all the time. She loved the power she had over me in bed, and when we weren't she loved how she could manipulate me with promises of what she would do for me later. She would call me at work and whisper in detail what she was going to do with me that night. If we'd meet for lunch at a restaurant, she'd be wearing nothing under her coat. She'd grab my hand under the table and beg me to touch her. She told me once that she wanted me to see her naked in front of other men so I could see how much they wanted her, too." I swallow hard. "One night when she was making love to me she told me she wanted me to watch her with someone else. She said she thought that would be so wild. I told her it was a wild fantasy all right. But I told her it would never happen. Not in my lifetime anyway."

Vincent shakes his head and lets out a long breath. "God damn."

"She was relentless, Vincent. I honestly believe that for Melanie the most intense pleasure came from her ability to control me, and not from the physical feeling itself. As time went by, she kept pushing the limits."

"How?" he asks, his voice raspy.

"She understood how to tease me and how to prolong the feeling until I thought I couldn't keep from letting go. Then, at the last second, she'd pull me back from the brink, then a few seconds later start all over again. It was incredible. It was like she was inside my body and could feel what I was feeling." Thunder rumbles off to the west, definitely closer than it was a few minutes ago. The storm is moving in fast. "When I told her I wasn't willing to watch her with someone else, that I wasn't willing to push things any further than we already had, she pulled away. She never said anything, but it was never the same."

"You could have been imagining things."

"I wasn't imagining anything."

"You think she went looking for someone who would play along?" Vincent asks. "Is that what you're saying?"

"Maybe." I close my eyes and shake my head. "It drove me crazy to think she might be giving herself to someone else. Doing the things for another man that she did for me. I'd become physically addicted to her, Vincent, and I knew that if she worked her magic on another lover, the same thing could happen to him as easily as it happened to me."

"Man, she really did a number on you," he mumbles, looking down.

I stare at him, staying silent until he glances up from the sidewalk. "I was addicted to her, Vincent, but I didn't kill her. You need to understand that."

The thunder rumbles again, closer still. "I never said you did," he replies, looking me in the eye. "I don't believe you're capable of that. You're a decent man."

For a few moments the only sound is the rustle of leaves as the wind swirls through the trees. "Why did you come by Bedford today?" I ask. "What did you want?"

Vincent checks the dark clouds rolling in, squinting against the breeze that's growing stronger by the minute. He takes a deep breath, as if the conversation we just finished has drained him. "Remember I told you the other night I have friends who might want to invest with you?" he says, his voice subdued. "People who would pay you to manage a piece of their money and let you keep some of the upside if you scored big?"

"Sure, I remember."

"I told them how successful you've been recently with your investing, and they were enthusiastic about partnering up. They may want to talk to you first, you know, meet face-to-face and do the sniff test before they give you some money. But I think there's a good chance something could work out."

We start heading back the way we came as a flash of lightning knifes through the sky. "How much would it be?" I ask.

"A little bit at the beginning. A few hundred thousand. But if you do well, there would be much more."

"How much more?"

"Five million, maybe ten. Who knows? It's a wealthy crew."

Five to ten million. I could charge them one or two percent a year as a commission and earn a damn nice living on just that. "Who are these people?"

"I told you before," he says, annoyed. "They're friends of mine. You'll meet them."

The trees surrounding the park sway violently against a sudden gust. "Vincent, I'd really need to understand who these people are before I—"

"I have tickets to a Baltimore Orioles home game this Thursday night," he says loudly as we climb back up the long stairway we came down only a few minutes ago. "Great box seats at Camden Yards. I'm going to be taking several of them to the game. Why don't you join us? It would be a great opportunity for everyone to meet."

"I don't know."

"Come on," he urges as we reach the top step. "One of the people will be Jack Trainer. The guy you met last week at the Grand. He's a good guy, right?"

A helluva good guy who gave me a stock tip that's cost me over thirty-five hundred dollars—so far. Probably chump change for him, but still a meaningful amount to me. At least until the insurance money gets here.

"So will you come?"

"I'll think about it."

"Well, think about this too," he says, reaching into his pocket as we jog across the street in front of my building. He pulls out an envelope and shoves it in my hand just as the raindrops begin to fall. "There's a check in there for three hundred thousand dollars, made out to you. This is the test case. Make that money hum, then we'll really talk."

Ten minutes later I'm walking back down the aisle toward my cubicle. I notice that Slammer is gone, apparently for the day, because his computer screen is dark and his briefcase is gone. Then I notice Mary standing up behind her desk, smiling at me, mouthing the words "thank you" over and over, hands to her heart. I enter my password, wondering what in the world she's talking about. I dive quickly to my portfolio page and there I find the answer. While Vincent and I were out, Teletekk popped to $57 a share. That quickly, instead of being down thirty-five hundred on my position, I'm up thirty-five *thousand*. For the second time in two weeks I've earned more in a day than a lot of people do in a year. Suddenly I'm making money hand over fist, and it's intoxicating.

Roger is staring at me. He's been waiting patiently since this morning for me to teach him how to day trade, but suddenly there's nothing I feel less like doing. I want a drink to celebrate—and to forget—but I've made a commitment and I won't renege on it.

"I'll be over there in a minute, Roger," I call as I enter a sell order on the entire Teletekk position. There's no reason to be greedy. Thirty-five grand is plenty on this one.

I check quickly for news stories about Teletekk and sure enough there's an announcement concerning the company's decision to enter the satellite market with an incredible new product that's just passed its beta tests. Jack Trainer was right on the money after all.

I pull out the envelope Vincent gave me a few minutes ago and glance at the amount on the check. Three hundred thousand dollars. I stash the envelope in my desk drawer. I'll set up a special account for it tomorrow, separate from my funds.

Three hundred grand. And if I pass the test, there could be so much more. I smile to myself. I know exactly how I'm going to make this money hum.

CHAPTER

9

"Thanks for all the help, pal," Roger says, checking his watch. "Hey, you know what, it's after eight o'clock." He cranes his long neck and scans the deserted trading floor. "This place is a ghost town. Everybody's gone." He slaps my back and laughs loudly. "But you didn't have anything better to do tonight anyway, right?"

I've been sitting with Roger in his cubicle for the last three hours, showing him how to use his Trader One software. It should have taken less than an hour, but he kept pestering me with questions about "the game," as he's started to call day trading. As though suddenly he's a player.

"No, nothing at all," I answer sarcastically. "Besides, I like spending my evenings showing *other* people how to get rich."

"Yeah, right." Roger snickers, then grabs the computer mouse and begins pushing it around the pad, clicking rapidly as he races through the software menu. He's like a little kid who's just learned to ride a bike. An hour ago he was tentative, as if each time I told him to enter something into the computer, the whole place might blow up. Now he's working the mouse like he's known how to use this software for years.

"No, it's true, Roger," I say solemnly. "I just want to serve my fellow man."

"I feel good," he says, ignoring me. "Like I belong in the game now."

"Don't get cocky," I warn. "Read any of the business magazines. The articles about trading always tell you that when you get cocky, you crash and burn."

"Now that I know how to use this software," he says eagerly, paying absolutely no attention to me at all, "I'm sitting fat. I wish tomorrow morning were here already. I'm gonna do great. I can feel it."

I was afraid of this. Roger's gotten a small taste of what technology can do for him and he's feeling invincible. What he's forgetting is that every other serious trader out there has all the same tools. The difference is that most of them have infinitely more experience than he does—which is what really matters. But Roger doesn't get that. He'll dive into the market tomorrow morning thinking he'll make a million bucks his first day, and in a week or maybe a month he'll have lost half his net worth. Just like Mary. It's so predictable and so sad, but nothing I say will make a difference. For my words to have any effect he'll have to experience that helpless feeling of watching his money vaporize in front of his eyes as a stock price ticks down and down.

"This software is really slick," he continues. "I can get to tons of research, see all of the trading ranges, and analyze option prices to see if they're in line with the stocks. It's awesome. No wonder people around here do so well."

Roger has no idea what it means for option prices to be in line with stocks. He's heard me say it, that's all. "Not everyone around here does that well." Mary's a perfect example, though she's a lot better off tonight after taking my advice on Teletekk. I'm glad for her, even if she did make almost one hundred forty thousand dollars more than I did on the trade. She needed a break, and I'm glad I could help her. "Re-

member, Roger, people constantly exaggerate their wins, but rarely admit their losses. Be careful."

"Ah, I'll be fine. Give me some credit."

"What about those stocks your neighbor recommended? How are
they doing?"

Roger strokes his beard. He does that when he's tense. "Not very
well," he concedes.

"And what are you going to buy now that you're so all fired up
about getting in here tomorrow morning at the crack of dawn?"

"Christ, who are you, my mother?"

"Nope. She has no idea how risky day trading is. If she did, she'd
send you to your room."

"Yeah, yeah."

I stand up and roll my chair back into my cubicle, reminded by the
thought of Roger's bankrupt neighbor that I need to make the payment that's been hanging over my head like a guillotine for a year: the
five-thousand-dollar loan from Vincent's friend I got when *I* was broke.
I never told Melanie about what Vincent arranged because I didn't
want to scare her, but we had no choice. We were about to lose our
house after bouncing three mortgage payments in a row.

I guess we had one choice. I guess I could have used the money
my mother gave me to repay the loan. The cash I dug up in the backyard last December. And I would have if Vincent hadn't come through.
But that wouldn't have been right. Mom wanted me to use that money
for myself alone. Now I understand why she never liked Melanie.
Somehow she anticipated her betrayal.

Vincent asked me about the loan this afternoon before saying
good-bye in the lobby. I told him I'd repay it Thursday night when we
go to the baseball game. I don't think the guy who gave me the cash
was a real loan shark. I doubt he would have shot me in the kneecaps
or anything if I hadn't made a payment, but I don't know for sure. I
never met him. Vincent seemed pretty relieved when I told him I'd be
repaying the principal and an outrageous amount of interest. I can't
help but wonder if the incident in the parking garage with the silver
Mercedes wasn't somehow related to the loan.

"What are you going to tell your wife about tonight, Roger?" I ask, glancing over the cubicle wall at him.

"Nothing."

"Aren't you usually home by now? I thought all you government workers left your offices by three thirty, and that was why the Beltway turned into a parking lot by four."

"I told you before, I usually didn't leave my office at the DOE until five."

"Well, it's after eight now."

Roger shrugs. "So what? I'm allowed to come home late without her permission," he says, annoyed.

I shake my head. "Roger, you should tell your wife what you're doing here at Bedford. It's not right to hide it from her. It's her money too." The woman needs to know that her husband is dealing with his midlife crisis by taking a huge risk that could ruin both of them.

"Ignorance is bliss," he says absentmindedly, not taking his eyes off his computer monitor. "Hey, how about some dinner?"

I was going to stop by the grocery store on the way home and pick up a frozen dinner to eat in front of the television while I watched a baseball game. With that and a six-pack I'd celebrate the Teletekk win.

"Tell you what. I'll even take you to the Grand," Roger continues, still fascinated by what I've shown him. "I know it's expensive down there, but you've gone way beyond the call of duty staying late with me tonight, Gus."

"What did you call me?"

"Gus," he says hesitantly, looking up from his computer for the first time since I rolled my chair out of his cubicle. "Was that wrong?"

Slammer's nickname is beginning to stick, and I need to stop the momentum. Once a nickname catches on, you practically have to start a new life to get rid of it. "Call me Augustus."

"Sorry," he says insincerely, rolling his eyes. "So how about dinner?"

My first reaction is to say no, but, after all, I have given him a ton of free advice and three hours of my time. "All right, but forget the Grand. Let's go to a place I know over in the mall." I appreciate Roger's offer, but I doubt they'd let me back in the Grand anyway. And I don't want that story getting back up to the trading floor. We shut down his computer and head for the door.

As we walk through the mall I notice that Roger is almost as tall as I am—about six-four—but he's much thinner. His rugby shirt sways loosely about his gaunt torso as he moves along in his uncoordinated gait, and his legs appear pencil thin inside his poorly fitting jeans.

"I actually never got your last name, Roger."

He hesitates. "It's Smith," he says, grimacing. "Now I ask you, how bland is that? Roger Smith. When I was growing up I always wanted to change Smith to something more interesting. Like Van Horn. Then people would call me Dutch, you know, and right away I'd have a hook." He shrugs. "But I guess I'm a pretty boring guy, so maybe the name fits. At least, I've been boring up until now."

Sitting in the conference room a week ago with Seaver, Roger struck me as the dark, brooding type who wouldn't ever have anything interesting to say, a person I wouldn't want to hang with. But as he chattered away in front of the computer tonight, I came to find that one-on-one he's basically a pretty good guy. He's brutally honest—especially about himself—but he doesn't constantly talk about himself the way most people do. Maybe he's just shy at first. I can understand that.

As I think back on it, I realize that it took three hours to set up Roger's software because besides his questions about the market, he got me to talk about my senior year of high school football—the season Vincent and I led our team to an undefeated record and the Virginia state championship. When I'm honest with myself I have to admit that nothing else I've done in life has ever come close to giving me the same high I felt that night we won everything. Sometimes, after a few drinks, I try to reminisce with Vincent about those days, but he never wants to talk about them. He went on to bigger and better things in his football career, so I guess he considers a high school championship small potatoes. I wish I did.

Roger seemed sincerely interested in hearing about that season. It wasn't as if he were asking the questions just to keep me helping him. At least, it didn't seem like he did. "Are you from around here, Roger?"

"I've been in the Washington area since college."

"Where did you grow up?"

"Um, Indianapolis."

"So, where'd you go to college?"

"The University of Maryland. College Park over on the east side of town."

"Why Maryland if you're from Indiana?"

"My older cousin went and liked it. And I'd always been interested in seeing the East Coast."

"What year did you graduate? I had some friends who went to Maryland."

Roger ignores my question because he's focused on an attractive Asian woman wearing tight leather pants and spike heels who's walking ahead of us. She's carrying a small Victoria's Secret bag. "Did you get a load of Anna today in that short little skirt and tight top? She didn't leave much to the imagination."

"Anna usually doesn't," I say, chuckling. When Anna walks through the swinging doors to deliver a package, action on the trading floor just about comes to a standstill. Most of the traders at Bedford are men, and they all try to get a look.

Roger sighs. "She's so beautiful."

"In an exotic way."

He snaps his fingers. "Right, exotic. Like an island girl. She's got that incredible body too. Nice firm chest, shapely ass, long legs, and tight, tight abs."

"In your dreams," I say, laughing louder.

He hesitates ever so slightly. "What do you mean by that?"

"Her abs must be in your dreams. Somehow, I don't think you got to see that much of her. I mean, this is your first day at Bedford."

"Oh, right." Roger grins. "No, no. One of the guys on the trading floor was talking about her this afternoon while you were out. He said he saw her jogging around here at lunch last week, and she was wearing a cutoff tank top and biking shorts. He said her stomach was really tight, Gus. I mean, *Augustus.*"

The Asian woman strolls into a boutique and my eyes follow. "Do you have a good relationship with your wife?" I ask hesitantly.

Vincent is the only person I talk to about things that really matter, but he's never been married so he can't relate to what it feels like to wake up beside the same person every day of his life. He's usually seeing at least three women at the same time. One he's just started to date, another who probably considers herself his girlfriend, and the third who he's in the process of dumping—even if she doesn't realize it. Vincent goes through women like most people go through bread, so he has no idea what commitment means. No idea how I could take Melanie, and our relationship, for granted. But Roger might.

"What kind of question is that?" he asks defensively, his mood darkening. "I have a very good relationship with my wife."

"Sorry, I didn't mean to offend you."

"What *did* you mean?"

This afternoon, while Vincent and I were talking about Melanie, it tore me up to think she'd had sex with Frank Taylor. But I wonder if I was actually mistaking jealousy for love. In fact, I wonder if that was all I ever did. Did I break down at the morgue because I'd lost my soul mate, or because experiencing the death of someone I had been so close to served to remind me of my own mortality? We got together so young. Melanie always said that would turn out to be a problem. "Do you ever think about other women?"

"In what way?"

"Being with them physically."

"Of course, I do. That's just part of being a man. That's the way we're programmed when we drop out of the womb."

"Have you ever—"

"No," he says curtly.

"Ever come close?"

He lets out a long breath. "Once or twice."

"But you didn't?"

"No," he says firmly.

"You think Anna's beautiful, don't you?"

"She's one of the most beautiful women I've ever seen," he says honestly, his eyes focusing on something far away. "She could be in magazines. *Cosmo* or *Penthouse*. Clothes on, clothes off. Either way, the issue would sell a million copies."

"If you had the chance to be with her, would you take it?"

"We both know that isn't going to happen."

We walk in silence for a few moments. "Do you and your wife have children?" I ask.

"Yes. A boy, five, and a girl, three. Roger Junior and Alice. They're good kids. I'm very proud of them."

That's nice and all, but what I want is an answer to my question about Anna. "Let's just say an opportunity with Anna, or someone like Anna, presented itself. What would you do?" I'm ready for another guarded answer, but that isn't what I get. Like I said, Roger's a pretty straightforward guy.

"I don't know, Augustus. I was with only a couple of women before I met my wife, and they weren't much to look at." He glances down as we walk. "My wife's a wonderful person, but . . . well, I doubt anyone would put her in Anna's league physically."

"There aren't many women in that league." Not even Melanie.

He grimaces. "I'd like to think I could resist, but given the right situation, I don't know that for sure. She's an incredibly beautiful woman." He looks over at me. "Are you happy now? Is that what you wanted to hear?"

I thought it was, but now that he's admitted it, I don't feel any better. I point at the Capital Grill. "There's the place."

"Did you come here with Mary for lunch today?" he asks. "Is that how you knew about this place?"

"Yes."

"Did she ask you or was it the other way around?"

I'm a little uncomfortable answering because I know what he'll think. "She asked me," I reply quietly.

"You dog," he says, slapping me on the back. "You just better hope that old man I hear she has at home doesn't find out and hire some goons to come looking for you. I bet he's possessive as hell. I know I would be if I were eighty years old and I were married to someone as pretty as Mary."

"She was being nice," I say firmly as we walk into the restaurant. "I'm just starting out at Bedford, and she wanted to make me feel welcome. That was the extent of it."

Roger holds up two fingers to the same maître d' who was working the floor this afternoon. "I'm just starting out at Bedford too, and
she hasn't asked me to lunch."

"She will."

"Sure she will." Roger laughs as we follow the maître d' through
the restaurant.

When we're settled at a table with our drinks, Roger picks up his
beer. "Here's to you, Augustus. Thanks again for the help tonight," he
says, wiping his mouth with the back of his hand after gulping down
half the glass's contents. "So, are you married?"

"No," I answer, shifting uncomfortably in my seat.

"Girlfriend?"

"Nope. I'm unattached."

"Lone wolf, huh? Guess that's why you were asking about Anna.
Got your eye on her, don't you?"

"I don't dip my pen in the company ink. That wouldn't be a good
idea."

"Bullshit. You'd do the same thing I would if you got the chance."

He's probably right.

Roger takes another long swallow of beer and relaxes into his seat.
"I'm going to take your advice about the trading, Augustus. I'm going
to be very careful."

"You just need to ease into it." I'm glad Roger doesn't push too far
into my personal life. I'll tell him what happened to Melanie at some
point, but I don't feel like talking about it now. "Don't fall into the
churn-and-burn mentality. You do that and you're only making money
for Michael Seaver."

"I know. I may be new to the game, but I know what his angle is."
Roger looks out over the restaurant. "You're a golfer, right?" he asks,
changing the subject.

My eyes flash to his. "Yeah, but how did you know?"

"Didn't I see a putter leaning against the wall in one corner of your
cubicle?"

I smile. "Yes, that's right." Sometimes I practice putting on the carpet in my cubicle. I did the same thing before and it irritated the hell
out of Russell, but I didn't care because it really helped ease stress.

"Do you play a lot?" he asks.

"I did a few years ago, but it costs so much and the public courses are always crowded." Plus my clubs are ancient—I got them at a garage sale right after Melanie and I were first married—and after a while I got tired of the disparaging looks I got from other people on the first tee. "How about you, Roger?"

"I play every once in a while. Maybe we should go out sometime."

"Yeah, sure."

Roger chuckles. "It'll be interesting to see if we ever do."

"What do you mean?"

"Ideas hatched over a drink always seem good at the time, but people don't usually follow up. It'll be interesting to see if we do."

Roger is a candid guy. I'll say that for him.

"What are you investing in?" Roger asks after the waiter has served us our second round.

His question reminds me that I made thirty-five grand today—thanks to Jack Trainer, the same guy I was cursing at lunch. I'm suddenly worth more than a hundred thousand dollars, with the big check still to come. It's overwhelming.

"You all right, Augustus?"

"Yeah, fine." I can tell Roger wants to know what I was thinking about so intently, but he doesn't push.

"What are you investing in?" he asks again.

"Psychiatric practices and gun manufacturers," I answer immediately, doing my best to keep a straight face.

"Really?"

Roger doesn't know whether to take me seriously or not. Vincent would take one look at my expression and realize I was kidding, but Roger hasn't known me long enough. "Absolutely."

"Why?"

"Last time I checked more people were getting divorced, more people were shooting up schools and workplaces, and more people were committing suicide. Which means more business for those kinds of companies all the time."

"Okay," he says, holding up one hand, "I'll give you all that, but gun manufacturers? The government's trying to put them out of business, for Christ's sake."

"Which will only make people want to buy guns more in the short term. The market really only cares about a company's next quarter results." I pick up my scotch. "Shouldn't be that way, but it's true."

Roger nods. "I thought maybe you were bullshitting me, but it all makes sense."

"I *was* bullshitting you, Roger."

"Oh," he says, glancing away.

"I've bought a few stocks to hold for the long term. I haven't actually started to day trade yet, but I will soon."

"Care to be a little more specific about those stocks you bought? That sure would be helpful."

I hesitate. I don't want to be giving out recommendations all over the place. Helping Roger personalize his software was one thing, but taking him completely under my wing would be quite another. "Well, I really don't want to—"

"Oh, I see," Roger interrupts, suddenly sounding annoyed. "No sharing tips with the guy buying you dinner."

"I just don't think I ought to be—"

"You'll give Mary a killer tip," he blurts out, "but not good old Roger."

I freeze. "Mary?"

"Mary told me all about the tip you gave her. She wouldn't tell me the name of the company, but she said she almost tripled her money this afternoon. I guess you and she had a pretty cozy lunch after all."

"She told you about a tip I gave her?" I ask incredulously.

"She told all of us. Bragged about putting a bunch of money into a satellite company or something you told her about, and how an hour later it went through the roof. You were out when she jumped out of her seat and started yelling. Christ, I thought she had won Lotto. Slammer looked like he was going to strangle her when he found out what was really going on. He, Daniel, and Mary have an informal agreement to share hot information with one another. But she said you told her to keep it quiet, so she couldn't say much."

"But when it hit, she—"

"She shouted all about it," Roger says, angry. "Slammer was about to throw his computer at her. He actually picked it up for a second, but then he put it back down, grabbed his briefcase, and took off. He was mumbling to himself about how you couldn't have possibly known the stock would go up that much in such a short time without some kind of inside information. He yelled across the floor that he was going to sic the Justice Department on you. Then he called Mary some pretty awful names."

"Christ," I mutter. "She hasn't done very well in the market lately and I was just trying to help. That's all. It was just one little tip."

"*Little?* Jesus, she bragged about making almost two hundred thousand bucks on the trade." He extends his right hand across the table as if he wants to shake mine. "Good to know you, pal. I like a man who thinks of two hundred grand as 'little.' "

"Like I said, I was just trying to help a friend. There's nothing between us."

He pulls his hand back and smiles. "I don't care why you gave Mary the tip. What I care about is that you didn't give it to me. I want to make certain you understand that if you give *me* a tip like that, I won't tell a soul."

"I didn't have any inside information, Roger."

He shrugs. "Hey, I'm not at Bedford to make ethical judgments. I'm just here to make as much money as I can any way I can. I figure everybody out there knows the stock market is a tough sandbox to play in, and that things go on in it that aren't always visible to the naked eye. And I'm not saying that's what happened in this case," he adds quickly. "All I'm saying is that I don't give a damn either way."

I'm still trying to figure out why Mary would tell everyone about Teletekk. Given how secretive I was being at lunch, she had to realize I wouldn't want it getting around.

"What were you doing before Bedford?" Roger asks.

"Paper sales."

Roger leans back in his chair, a perplexed expression on his thin face. "I thought you had been a trader for a long time."

"No."

"Then how do you know about all that stuff we talked about tonight?" It's as if he suddenly feels cheated. As if his newfound confidence at Bedford was based entirely on the fact that I was some kind of expert with years of experience under my belt. Now that he's found out I'm not, he's questioning his own confidence because my advice might not be as valuable as he assumed.

I pick up a piece of bread and begin buttering it. "I've been studying hard for two years. I was ready."

"But you have no real experience."

I enjoy the fact that I've quickly become the star of our group. As much as I hate that Mary blabbed to everyone about Teletekk, in a way I'm sure it gave me credibility. Now my cover's blown. "I ran a ghost portfolio that grew three hundred percent in one year."

"Big deal, so did I."

"And I made seventy-seven grand on my first major trade a couple of weeks ago."

Roger glances up, a glint of a smile creeping back into his expression. "On how much of an investment?"

"Ten thousand."

He whistles softly. "Damn, that *is* good. And I assume you put some of that money into the tip you gave Mary."

"Of course." Day trading is now my career, and I'm proud of it. Suddenly I picture myself as one of those guys at Salomon Brothers in New York who yells into the telephone about reaching down throats and ripping out hearts. A god of the market. I've never wanted anything so bad in my life. The high I've experienced with my Unicom and Teletekk wins rivals what I felt that night we won the state football championship—I'd resigned myself to never experiencing that kind of rush again—and I want more. "I made another thirty-five grand today on that investment."

"You really do know what you're doing." Roger is back to being impressed. "Can you keep your winning streak alive?" he asks.

"Absolutely." As I look more closely I see that beneath his beard are bad acne scars.

"And if I'm remembering correctly, you told Seaver you were starting with over a million bucks last week. Right?"

"That's right," I say slowly. Maybe that's how Mary found out. Maybe Roger told her.

"How in the world did you save a million bucks selling paper?"

I hesitate. "I didn't. My mother died recently. There was a million-dollar insurance policy on her life and it turned out I was the beneficiary. I had no clue I was going to get all of that money until the will was read." I don't feel guilty at all about making up this story. It's none of his business how I really got my money. "It was quite a shock."

"I bet. I'm sorry for your loss, but that's a nice way to ease the pain," he says, sliding to the end of the bench seat and standing up. "I've got to go to the men's room. I'll be right back."

As he stands up to go, a worn brown wallet tumbles from the back pocket of his jeans onto the floor. He walks away without realizing it, so I lean down and pick it up, curious to see what's inside.

CHAPTER

10

I live in a quiet, middle class area of northern Virginia just outside the Beltway in a bedroom community called Springfield. South of downtown by twenty miles, Springfield is a mix of nineteen sixties ranches and split-levels. It might have been a very desirable neighborhood back then, but now it's occupied mostly by first-home, blue-collar couples who both have to work, and the elderly who can't afford to move to Florida or a decent retirement home. Washington's newly rich high-tech population lives west of the city along the Potomac River. And the *very* wealthy live in Middleburg, an hour farther·west near the Shenandoah Mountains.

Melanie and I drove out to Middleburg one Sunday afternoon a few years ago to take in the beautiful Thoroughbred horse country. We were silent most of the way home, each painfully aware of what the other was thinking. That we'd never be able to afford even the smallest of the picturesque farms we'd driven past. That we'd never be able to afford a single horse let alone the herds that dotted the vast green fields rolling down in front of the stone mansions perched on hills far back from the country road.

My neighborhood is forty years old and the oak trees are tall and full. Their roots push up sidewalk sections in many spots to form natural jumps for the young children on their bicycles. We don't have street lamps and the thick green summer canopy easily blocks out the faint light of the moon and the stars, so the neighborhood is dark after midnight, when most people have turned in for the evening.

I didn't plan on being out this late so I didn't flip on the stoop light when I left for Bedford this morning. Without it, the stone path to my house is all but invisible.

I come to a quick stop a few feet from the steps leading up to my door and peer into the gloom, startled because I thought I saw something move. I squint into the darkness and it almost looks like there's someone standing by the hedge in front of the house. Just when I decide it's probably the alcohol playing tricks on me, the figure begins to move slowly toward me and I take a step back. As the person draws near, I recognize Frank Taylor.

"What do you want?" I ask angrily. "What are you doing here?" Roger and I stayed at the Capital Grill drinking until eleven thirty, but suddenly I'm stone-cold sober. "Don't come any closer," I warn.

"Don't screw with me, Augustus."

Taylor is slurring his words, which could be the result of my fist to his face last week—he's now standing close enough for me to see that his upper lip is still terribly swollen. But he's swaying and his movements seem impaired, like he's in slow motion. He's clearly been drinking too, and a lot more than I have.

"You started it last week, Taylor. You were looking for a fight. You followed me to the Grand."

"Fuck you!"

"What are you doing here?"

"Getting ready to kick your ass."

"Try anything, Taylor, and that punch I hit you with last week will seem like you were grazed by a cotton ball. There isn't anyone around to protect you this time, and you're trespassing. I could kill you and the law would be on my side."

Taylor staggers a step closer, ignoring my warning. "I want to know what you think you're doing sending the police after me," he says.

"What are you talking about?"

"You know exactly what I'm talking about. A detective named Reggie Dorsey showed up at my office this afternoon, asking me all kinds of questions about my relationship with Melanie and exactly where I was on the night of her murder. It was the second time in a week he dropped by without an appointment. He even asked for a blood sample today." Taylor sways well to one side and stumbles trying to keep his balance. "Dorsey wanted to know about this," he says, pointing at his lip. "I think it's fair to say that he was fascinated to find out you were responsible."

"You asked for it."

Taylor leans forward, and the smell of liquor on his breath hits me. "You're so desperate to throw Dorsey off your own trail, you're trying to make him think I killed Melanie."

"Maybe you did."

"I loved Melanie," Taylor says, his voice turning wistful. "I could never have hurt her." He taps me on the chest with his finger, then jerks a thumb over his shoulder, pointing at the house. "What did you do? Kill her in there, then dump her in that alley downtown? It must have been a helluva stressful drive with her body in the trunk."

"I'm warning you, Taylor!"

"Did Mel ever tell you that I made love to her in your house, Augustus?" Taylor breaks into a punch-drunk grin as he wavers back and forth. "In your bed one Saturday afternoon while you were gone. Did she ever tell you that? Did she tell you that it was the best sex of her life? Because it was."

The world turns red and my fist slams Taylor's jaw for the second time in a week. He tumbles backward onto the ground, and I'm on him before he can stand up. He struggles to crawl away, but I roll him over, throw him onto his back, and pin him to the ground with the weight of my body, a knee to his chest and one hand wrapped tightly around his throat. My adrenaline and his intoxication make the fight no contest. He grabs my forearm, desperately trying to pry my hand from his throat.

"You gonna kill me too?" he gasps, perspiration pouring from his face.

"You asshole." I squeeze harder, the urge to cause pain taking over. "What makes you think you can steal a man's wife?" In the background I'm vaguely aware of a door slamming. "What makes you think you can play with people's lives?"

"Melanie came after me." He takes a feeble swing at me, but I easily block his punch with the arm I'm not using to suffocate him. "Let me go!"

"I should kill you." I made believe I did so many nights when I was waiting for Melanie to come home. "No one would miss you."

For the first time he realizes that he may have pushed me too far. That I may have no intention of releasing my grip on his throat until he's dead. He panics, twisting and turning violently beneath me, so I lift up and drop a knee into his chest, knocking the air from his lungs. He lets out a sharp groan and goes limp beneath me, and I drop another knee into his solar plexus. This time I hear a faint crack.

Some people say revenge isn't sweet. I say those people have never been wronged. We're humans and we're ruled by emotions. I want to see Frank Taylor suffer. An eye for an eye.

Taylor's eyelids flicker and his mouth slowly opens. He grasps my forearms again but there's little strength left in his hands.

"Mr. McKnight!"

Suddenly a blinding beam of light is shining directly into my face. I pull my hand from Taylor's throat and stand up, blinking in the rays of what I realize is a flashlight. Taylor rolls on his side, contracts into a fetal position, and begins coughing violently.

"Mrs. Friedman." Behind the flashlight is the tiny form of my seventy-four-year-old neighbor.

"My God, I thought the world was coming to an end," she declares in her squeaky voice. In the glow of the flashlight she now aims at Taylor, I see that she's dressed in a flower-print cotton robe and fuzzy pink slippers.

"I caught this man trying to break into my home, Mrs. Friedman," I explain as calmly as I can. "But I've got everything under control."

Taylor can't deny my story because he can't speak. His only concern right now is being able to suck down his next breath.

"Should I call the police?" she asks, wide-eyed.

"No, no. I'll take care of it. You get back inside. Go on," I urge.

But she doesn't budge. She's staring at Taylor as he writhes on the ground. "He doesn't look like a—"

"In case there are others out here!"

With that she turns and hustles back across the lawn to her house, the flashlight beam bouncing in front of her. When I hear her front door slam, I grab Taylor by the collar and lift him to his feet. "Come on." He's beginning to regain his breath, but it's all he can do to stand up. "Where's your damn car?" I demand. It occurs to me that I don't know what kind of car Taylor drives. I want to make certain it isn't a silver Mercedes with darkly tinted windows. That would be appropriate for a snake like him who doesn't want to be seen. For a divorce lawyer who makes his money off of others' pain.

"Down the street," he mumbles, pointing toward the end of my cul-de-sac.

When we reach the car whose locks open with the keys I grab from his sweaty palm, I see that he drives an old Volvo that looks like it was built during the Nixon administration. Even my Toyota is worth more than this piece of crap. "What's your other car?"

"I don't have another car."

"God help me, Taylor," I snarl, "I'll put you down again and choke the life out of you for good this time. What's your other car?"

"This is all I've got. I can't afford another car." He leans over, blood dripping from his nose. "My law practice is failing. I'm going broke."

"Son, son."

I pry open my eyes to the dawn and a priest kneeling over me, shaking my arm. He's wearing his black suit and white collar, and there's a small silver cross dangling from his neck.

"Are you all right?"

"Father Dale?" I ask, rubbing my eyes and straining to pull myself to a sitting position on the church's front steps where I've been sprawled for the past few hours.

"Yes, son. It's me."

"I'm Augustus McKnight."

"I know, Augustus. I recognize you from my visit to your house last week." He raises one eyebrow. "You seem to have had a rough night." His expression turns grim. "I'm so sorry about Melanie's death."

When I finished with Taylor I went back to the house and drank what was left of a bottle of scotch I had received as a birthday present a few months ago. Then, around two o'clock, I drove to this small Gothic church only a few minutes from the house. It's the church Melanie used to come to every Sunday morning while I stayed in bed.

"I've been here for a couple of hours," I explain. Through the gray light I notice my Toyota parked in front of the church at an odd angle, driver-side door still open. I vaguely remember stumbling out of it and crawling to the steps.

"How can I help you?" he asks kindly.

"I'm not Catholic."

"That's all right," he replies reassuringly. "God doesn't discriminate. Neither do I."

"Oh. Well, thank you."

"Do you want to talk about your wife? Is that why you're here?"

My eyes flash to his, and for a moment I consider asking him if he knows why she stopped coming to his services so suddenly. "No," I finally murmur. "It's not."

"Then what is this about?"

"I understand that you support a local shelter for battered women and children." Melanie told me about the shelter one Sunday after Father Dale had mentioned it in his sermon. "That you personally take great interest in it."

Father Dale nods. "Yes, I do. It's in the heart of downtown and run by a woman named Betty Griswold. Betty has dedicated her life to assisting abused women and children. She runs the center on a wing and a prayer with the help of a few very dedicated volunteers."

"Melanie said the shelter was in financial trouble."

The priest sighs. "It's always in trouble. We do what we can for Betty, but as with most charitable causes, money is constantly in short supply."

I reach into my shirt pocket, pull out the check I scrawled a few hours ago, and gaze at it intently for a moment. The only line not filled in is "pay to the order of." "Would you give this to Ms. Griswold for me, Father?" I ask, handing him the check. "You'll have to fill out the name of the shelter."

Father Dale stares at my sloppy handwriting and shakes his head. "Son, this check is made out for ten thousand dollars. It's an incredibly generous gesture, but are you sure about this? Why don't you go home and think about it for a while?" he suggests, holding the check out toward me. "I'll be here tomorrow if you want to come back."

All I want right now is a tall glass of water. I'm so damn dehydrated. I make it to my feet with a groan. "I'm certain, Father," I answer, gazing at the Toyota, embarrassed by how decrepit it looks. I sure would like something nicer. "And you can tell Ms. Griswold that there will be more coming. Much more."

CHAPTER

11

I'm not a weak man. In fact, I'm pretty strong, both physically and emotionally. I've always worked hard to keep myself in good shape, and I can't respect those who don't. Life is an incredible gift, and it seems to me it's our obligation to develop what we've been given to the fullest.

Being strong means I'm able to recover quickly from a long night of drinking—which cuts both ways. I don't suffer from bad hangovers, but I don't slow down once I've started drinking either because I don't fear the aftereffects. Unfortunately, I'm still prone to saying and doing the same stupid things as everyone does while I'm under the influence.

Two hours ago I handed Father Dale a ten-thousand-dollar check for Betty Griswold and her shelter—which I don't regret at all. I'm glad to finally be able to help someone in a meaningful way. What bothers me is that I'm not certain *why* I gave the priest ten percent of my newfound wealth. Maybe I went to him with the gift as atonement for almost killing Frank Taylor on my front lawn. If Mrs. Friedman hadn't put on her pink slippers and come running out of her house with the flashlight, there's no telling what might have happened. Or maybe I handed Father Dale the check because of Melanie. She was devoted to that church for so long. Maybe I felt like that was what she would have wanted, and by making the gesture I would finally be able to say good-bye to her. Maybe the check should have been for more.

"Good morning."

Mary's fingers curl around my shoulders from behind, gently kneading my shoulders and neck. I know it's her by her voice. "Hi."

"How are you?" she asks.

"Fine." It's seven o'clock and we're the only people on the trading floor so I'm not worried about her public display of affection. "My God, where did you learn to do that?" She's only been rubbing my shoulders for thirty seconds, but I'm already drifting into that state of physical satisfaction where you feel like you can't keep your eyes open. "That's amazing."

"Someday I'll tell you all about my secret past," she says, her deft fingers continuing to work. "It hasn't always been a bed of roses, but I managed to take away a few good things from the bad times." Her fingertips rub my temples softly, and I feel myself starting to drift off. "Some not so good things too."

For a few seconds I'm not certain if her hands are still there, or if I'm even awake. Finally, I'm able to pry open my eyes and she's standing in her cubicle, smiling down at me while she turns on her computer. Her hair is up in a bun this morning—the first time she's worn it like that since I started at Bedford—and it's a completely new look for her. The transformation is startling. She hardly looks like the same woman.

Melanie had that same chameleon ability, and I found it incredibly alluring. It was as if I were making love to a different woman when she would come to bed with her long blond hair pulled back by a leather ribbon. As she entered the room she'd make a big production out of taking off her wedding ring and leaving it on the dresser, as if I wasn't her husband and she didn't want to be fettered by it during the encounter. Her back to me, she'd slip seductively out of a red silk robe she wore only on these occasions, then turn slowly around and stand before me, hands and arms covering what I most wanted to see until I pulled them away and dragged her onto the bed. She became a woman I didn't know but desperately wanted. She knew exactly how her game affected me, and she loved it. She loved that power.

Melanie never performed an actual striptease for me with music and lights and all—as Reggie Dorsey asked. But one time she led me by the hand down to our basement, where no one outside the house could possibly see, had me sit on an old sofa in one corner near my free weights and punching bag, and slowly took off all of her clothes. Right down to a new lacy white thong she bought for her performance. Seemed like that thing could have fit in a thimble. The whole show was incredibly erotic.

When she had slipped out of the thong and was completely naked, she knelt down on the couch and straddled me, kissing me deeply while she begged me to touch her all over. She kept whispering that she wanted me to watch her disrobe for a room full of strangers, how incredible that would be for both of us. When she finally took me deep inside her, I agreed with a moan.

Later, when we were upstairs, I reassured her that I hadn't been serious about wanting to watch her undress in front of other men. That I'd just been caught up in the heat of the moment, as I assumed she had been too. She smiled and kissed me, and I never heard another word about it.

She did other things for me too. Things that are hard to think about now that she's gone.

"Why are you here so early?" I ask, trying to distract myself from the memory of that last performance. "It's only seven o'clock."

"I wanted to make certain I got to thank you right away for the Teletekk tip," she explains gratefully, "and I had a few companies I wanted to look over as possible investments before I go visit my psychic." She winks at me. "Thanks to you I have quite a bit more money to invest today, and I wanted to put it to work as soon as possible. I hate leaving my money in cash. That's so boring." She stops rooting through her purse and looks up. "I sold out of Teletekk yesterday before I left. I would have died if the price had cratered overnight and I'd left so much money on the table. I hope you don't mind," she says apologetically, as if because I told her when to buy Teletekk, I ought to tell her when to sell it too.

"It's none of my business what you do with your portfolio. That's between you and your psychic. But it did go up another four bucks a share in the overnight market. I'm surprised your psychic didn't tell you that was going to happen."

Mary sticks her tongue out at me playfully. "I've learned my lesson about being greedy," she says, moving to the cubicle partition and leaning into my space. "I don't know how you got your information about Teletekk, and I guess I don't care. I do know that it was nice to enjoy a big win for a change. My confidence needed that. Thanks."

"You're welcome, and I got my information the old-fashioned way. I did my research." I don't want her thinking I've got some kind of intelligence network out there that's going to slide her that kind of tip every day. "One thing, Mary."

"Yes?"

"I heard you got pretty excited when the stock popped yesterday."

"What do you mean?" Her voice instantly takes on the same cool quality it did when I told her at lunch yesterday that she should have dumped MicroPlan as soon as its price started to tank.

"I heard you were jumping up and down at your desk, celebrating." I laugh a little and try to make light of something I'm obviously not happy about. "I heard the judges gave you a perfect ten for your cartwheels."

"Who told you that?" she snaps.

"A couple of people."

"It was Roger, wasn't it?"

"Doesn't matter who it was. I just don't want Slammer going nuclear on me because I didn't give him the same tip. That guy's a nutcase. I bet he really does have a gun in that damn briefcase of his."

Mary gives me a withering look, then turns away and sits down so I can't see her anymore.

"I'm not angry," I say contritely, standing up and moving to my side of the partition so I can see her. "It's just that I made it very clear at lunch yesterday that I wanted to keep it quiet."

"Why did you want to keep it so quiet?" She's typing, her carefully manicured fingertips working the keyboard the way they worked my shoulders a few minutes ago. I wish they were still there. "Should I be worried after all?"

"About what?"

"That the SEC might take a keen interest in how I knew to buy the stock just a few minutes before it popped."

"Of course not. That was just coincidence."

"Then what's the problem?"

Mary's voice is turning colder by the second, and I hate it. I want her to like me—more and more all the time. I admire the way she goes after what she wants, and I want to find out about that past she mentioned. "I was hoping that the information would stay just between the two of us. I don't want everybody pestering me. That's all."

"Mmm." Mary's fingers pause as she stops to inspect something on her computer screen.

"Come on, don't be angry with me." I spot Slammer coming through the swinging doors at the far end of the trading floor, brief-case in hand. "Please."

"Why not?" She looks up and I can see that we're friends again by the sparkle in her eyes. "You yelled at me." She pouts. "I hate being yelled at."

"I'm sorry." Slammer is staring at me as he strides down the aisle. I can tell he's still pissed off about yesterday. About my giving the Teletekk tip only to Mary. "How can I make it up to you?" I want this conversation to be done by the time he gets to his desk.

Mary looks at me coyly for a few seconds. "Okay, I'll tell you what you can do."

"What?"

"Come with me while I visit my psychic," she says excitedly. "That would make me happy. Her place is only a few miles away, over in Vienna. We'll be back by nine o'clock. A half hour before the opening bell in New York. You won't miss a minute of trading."

"Good morning, Mary," Slammer says in an uncharacteristically cordial tone as he places the tan briefcase in its customary position beside his computer monitor. He turns and glares at me. "Hey, dickhead." Then he sits down and turns on his computer.

When I'm sure he's not looking, I glance back at Mary and nod silently. This ought to be interesting.

Mary and I meet twenty minutes later in front of the shuttered entrance to the Grand. I don't want Slammer seeing us walk out of the trading floor together. I slipped out into the empty Bedford lobby, called Mary from Anna's desk, and told her to meet me downstairs. Meeting in front of the elevators didn't work yesterday at lunch, so I was extra careful today. She didn't seem to have a problem with that.

A few minutes later we're in my Toyota, heading to the town of Vienna, which is a few miles south of McLean on Route 123. Mary had to take a taxi to Bedford this morning because the Jaguar she says Jacob left her when he died is having engine problems and had to go into the shop for repairs. I didn't want to drive because I'm embarrassed about the Toyota's torn seats and its bad muffler, but she doesn't say anything.

I've got to buy a new car. There's no reason now for me to be driving around in this piece of junk, and if Vincent can make Thursday night work out, I'm going to be managing wealthy people's money. I'll need to project the appropriate image. Nothing could be worse than for his friends to see me driving around northern Virginia in this heap after they've given me a pile of their money to invest. You get the warm and fuzzies about your banker or broker if you see a lot of dark wood, expensive furniture, and elegant antiques when you walk in to see them. All of that opulence translates into a feeling of stability and solid performance, and gives you comfort that decisions about your money are being made with prudence and wisdom. Not for one minute does it occur to you that all of those expensive items are being paid for by the interest or the fees your banker or broker is charging you.

I won't feel at all guilty about using a portion of the insurance proceeds to purchase a nice ride.

"How long have you been visiting this woman?" I ask over the din of the Toyota's rusted muffler.

"Since Christmas. Since Jacob died."

"What's her name?"

"Sasha."

Mary seems anxious. Her hands are folded tightly in her lap and she leans forward, carefully keeping track of where we are. It's as if she's ticking off landmarks. Nodding to herself as we pass a 7-Eleven, then again as we go by a bank. "Do you really believe the dead can be contacted?" I ask at a red light.

She turns slowly in the seat and stares at me until the light turns green. "Absolutely."

We don't say anything else during the rest of the ten-minute drive. Our destination turns out to be a tiny basement room behind a door beneath a sign with an open human palm and the word "Tarot" painted on it. Mary gazes up at the sign for a moment, then leads me down the stairs.

"I hope you don't mind, Sasha," Mary says to a woman sitting behind a small desk in one corner of the basement room, "but I brought a friend along. This is Augustus."

"Hello," Sasha says in a husky voice, standing up and coming out from behind the desk.

She isn't at all what I expected. She's tall and thin with light brown hair, and she's dressed in a white button-down blouse and linen pants that fit her figure so snugly they border on provocative. I had foolishly assumed that she'd be short and pudgy, with a red bandanna covering wild black hair and a string of colorful beads hanging around her neck. But as we were driving over, Mary told me that Sasha's upscale clients include venture capitalists and attorneys, as well as the rock star twenty-somethings driving the technology mania of the area. I should have assumed she would dress appropriately for her upscale clientele.

"It's nice to meet you," I say. Sasha stares back at me with her large dark eyes, and I wonder what she's thinking. I can't explain it, but I instantly distrust this woman. And I can't be certain, but the feeling seems mutual.

Sasha motions toward a circular table in the middle of the room. When we're all seated around it, she reaches across the gray felt tablecloth and takes one of Mary's hands in both of hers. There are no tarot cards—as the sign above the stairs led me to believe there would be. Simply silence as Sasha closes her eyes and concentrates. Finally her thin lips curl into an omniscient smile, and I see for the first time that she would have benefitted from braces as a child.

"This is very strange," she finally says.

"What is?" Mary demands breathlessly.

"You aren't focused on Jacob today." She turns her head to the side without opening her eyes. "Are you, Mary?"

"No."

"You want to talk about someone else," Sasha says.

Mary looks down.

"Don't you?"

"Yes."

"And we will." Sasha opens her eyes only long enough to glance quickly at Mary. "But first let's discuss the money you've come into."

My eyes race to Sasha, then to Mary, who breaks into a nervous smile. "Money?"

Sasha raises both eyebrows. "A great deal of money. Someone was very kind to you. Someone helped you make all of that money. Someone gave you information, didn't he?"

"Yes, he did."

"He's someone you care about."

Mary nods.

"You must be careful with this money," Sasha warns. "Be wise with it, not foolish as you've been in the past."

"I will be, I promise."

"Jacob is still watching out for you, but you must learn to look out for yourself."

"I know," Mary agrees meekly.

Sasha goes silent again for several minutes. "Let's talk about that someone you've found, Mary," she finally suggests. "It's someone you were attracted to right away. That's why you didn't need to contact Jacob today. You're finally coming out of the darkness that has surrounded you since his death."

"Like you said I would when I was here last time," Mary replies, glancing at me, then back at Sasha. "Is Jacob upset with me?" she asks timidly.

"No. He wants this for you."

"Does this person care about me?" Mary asks anxiously. "Or will he reject me?"

"I believe he does care about you," Sasha answers, opening her eyes to look at me. "He's a strong man. A man who can take care of you."

"But can I depend on him?" she persists.

"I can't tell yet," Sasha says after a pause during which her face contorts into expressions of mild anguish several times, as if she is trying to see down a dark hallway. "The images aren't clear." She hesitates. "The answer must wait for our next session," she finally declares.

It's absurd for Mary to listen to Sasha. She's got nothing but money on her mind and can't be trusted. I want to reach across the gray felt and wrench their hands apart. This is costing Mary a hundred bucks, and it's obvious what Sasha is doing. She's speaking in high-level platitudes about which she has a fifty-fifty shot at being right, maybe even higher on the gooey stuff because Mary wants so desperately to believe every word she's being told. Like an irresponsible psychiatrist, Sasha has made Mary dependent on these visits, and ensures herself successive paydays by telling her poor client that the future isn't clear at this time and that another visit is required. I can't believe Mary falls for it.

Ten minutes later Sasha announces that the brief session is over because all has gone dark in front of her and she will be able to see no more today. Mary gushes her thanks despite the fact that no meaningful revelations have surfaced and that Sasha was dead wrong about a telephone call she claimed had been made to Mary last week by a relative or an old friend. Sasha covered herself when Mary said that no such call had occurred by convincing Mary that the call must have come while she was out and that the person didn't leave a message on her answering machine. Sasha stated with conviction that the person would call again, and Mary bought the entire load of crap—hook, line, and sinker.

When their hands part, Sasha turns toward me and gives me a look of disdain. It's as if she's seen every roll of my eyes and smirk of disgust I made during the session despite the fact that her eyes were closed most of the time.

"Why don't you give him a few minutes?" Mary suggests, pointing at me.

"No, no," I respond quickly. I have no desire to be part of this charade. I only came here to appease Mary, not to be involved.

Sasha shakes her head. "People must be willing to believe, Mary. Augustus doesn't believe. He thinks what I do here is fraud. That I might as well be stealing from you."

"Not at all," I say unconvincingly. Sasha is playing the probabilities again. She knows men are less likely to believe in all of this than women and probably sensed my attitude as the session unfolded. "You seem quite talented."

"Please, Sasha," Mary begs.

"Mary, I don't think I—"

"You have to do this for me, Augustus," Mary breaks in. "You can't come all the way over here and not experience it," she says, taking her wallet from her purse and handing Sasha five twenty-dollar bills. "Please, Sasha."

Sasha snatches the money and stuffs it into her pocket like a child from a poor family who learns to eat her dinner quickly so her siblings won't steal it. "I'll try but I can't promise anything."

"That's all right," Mary says triumphantly, apparently convinced that something earth-shattering will come out of this nonsense. "Go on."

Sasha looks at me steadily. "Give me your hand and close your eyes."

I feel sheepish, but I place my left hand on the gray felt anyway. The cloth feels strangely comforting, as do Sasha's hands as they close around mine. They're warm and soft.

Sasha says nothing for several minutes and it's pin-drop quiet in the room. I can hear Mary's breathing and the occasional faint sound of a car on the street. "You've recently experienced a terrible loss," Sasha finally says, her voice subdued. "I feel such sadness inside you."

"My God!" Mary blurts out. "Augustus, your wi—"

"Quiet," Sasha orders, and Mary obeys.

Again, Sasha could be playing the odds. A "terrible loss" could mean almost anything, and "recently" could cover the last decade. But I have to admit her words sent a light-speed chill up my spine. Suddenly I'm trying to rid my mind of all conscious thought on the off chance that the government really is keeping little green men at Area 51, that the sun revolves around the earth, and that Sasha can read my mind.

I might not believe Sasha has a "gift." But the problem is that now she has credibility with Mary thanks to the "terrible loss" revelation. And if Sasha is as conniving as I believe, she will make up things to titillate Mary. To keep her hooked.

"You vacationed recently," Sasha continues.

"No, I didn't. I haven't taken a vacation in—"

"You didn't actually travel anywhere," Sasha says, undaunted. "You stayed in your house and licked your wounds."

I open my eyes when Sasha's hands glide from mine. She's gazing at me steadily, but not into my eyes. She's gazing at the faded scars on my neck.

Sasha reaches for my right hand and turns it over so that it lies flat on the felt, palm up. She touches each fingertip in slow succession, then puts her hand to her neck. Her upper lip curls slightly, and she stares into my eyes, her fingers gently stroking the soft skin of her throat. I'm left only to imagine what she's thinking because she doesn't say another word. A few minutes later Mary and I are back up the stairs and out of Sasha's cave.

As I guide the Toyota out of its parking space and head back toward McLean, Mary puts her hand on mine as it rests on the stick shift. "Thanks for going with me," she says. "That was nice of you."

"Sure. It was interesting. I've never done anything like that." I sense that if I get to know Mary better, I'll be doing a lot of things I've never done before.

"Sasha's amazing, don't you think?"

"Yeah, amazing."

"She picks up on things so fast. She knew I had made that money on Teletekk, and she knew about your poor wife," Mary says, her voice dropping.

"I'm not sure she—"

"How long were you married, Augustus?"

"Eleven years."

"That's a long time to be with the same person."

"Yes, it is." I ease the Toyota to a stop at a red light and check my watch. It's quarter of nine. Mary was right. We'll be back to Bedford in plenty of time for the New York open. "How long were you married to your first husband?"

"You mean the man I was married to before Jacob?"

"Ah, I guess so." It never occurred to me that Mary might have been married more than twice.

"Five years, and none of it was very pleasant."

"Oh?"

"He cheated on me the week after our wedding."

"I'm sorry to hear that."

"The son of a bitch thought I wouldn't find out, but I did," she says, her voice suddenly trembling. "He gave me the old line about how the other woman didn't mean anything to him, and how being with her didn't change how he felt about me. How can men say that with a straight face?"

"Lots of practice in front of the mirror. Were you married before him?" I ask quickly, regretting my flippancy.

"I've been married three times and divorced twice."

"Really?"

"Is that a problem?" she asks, slipping her hand from mine when the light turns green and I start shifting gears.

"No. It's just that I don't think I've ever known anyone who was married more than twice."

"Come on, tell me what you think."

"No, really." I don't know why I reacted like I did. "It's unusual. That's all."

Mary lets out a heavy sigh. "I was married the first time when I was seventeen."

"Jesus."

"Right, big mistake," she admits. "But what you have to understand is that I lived in a trailer park outside of Lexington, Kentucky, with my stepfather." She swallows hard. "He—he wasn't . . . he wasn't very nice to me," she says, her voice choking up. "He did some terrible things to me after my mother died and I was all alone with him." She pauses. "He made me sleep with him."

"I'm sorry." I reach for her hand. "That's awful."

"The boy I married was willing to stand up to him. He took me away from that place. I was desperate to get out but I didn't know how. He did." She turns and looks out her window.

I swing the car to the side of the road and pull to a quick stop. "Come here."

"Don't worry about me," she says, tears now streaming down her face. "I'm all right."

"No, you aren't." I pull her toward me and suddenly she's wrapping her arms around me and crying loudly, burying her face in my shoulder. I hold her tightly as her body heaves. "I shouldn't have pried. It's none of my business."

"I started it. It's my fault."

"That's not true," I say compassionately.

"I hate being so weak," she says, pulling back and taking a tissue out of her purse.

She starts to wipe her face but I take the tissue from her trembling hand. "Let me do that."

Mary smiles and touches my cheek. "You're such a good man, Augustus."

"I don't know about that." I dab at the moisture beneath her eyes.

"Yes, you are. I bet you never cheated on your wife, did you?"

"No."

"See?"

"That doesn't necessarily make me a good man."

"It does in my book. Jacob was the only man who was never unfaithful to me." Mary caresses my face with the back of her fingers. "Sometimes I think maybe it was just because he was too old."

"Don't be so hard on yourself. I'm sure he loved you very much."

I have no idea whether or not that's true, but it seems like the thing to say.

Her eyes well up again and she hugs me tightly. "We've become friends so fast, Augustus."

"Yes, we have."

Mary pulls back and looks into my eyes. It's that same look she gave me at lunch yesterday, but I'm more comfortable with it this time. "Those green eyes of yours," she says, her voice hushed. "They're so beautiful."

Our faces are only inches apart.

She makes a subtle move closer, then the cell phone in her purse goes off with an obnoxious whistle. She pulls back, groans, and digs it out.

As she talks I guide the Toyota back into traffic and head for Bedford.

"I can't believe it," Mary says, replacing the cell phone in her purse when she's finished talking. Her voice has the same quality it did after Sasha told me I'd experienced a terrible loss.

"Believe what?"

"That was an old friend of mine from Kentucky whom I haven't talked to in years. She got my cell number from another friend."

"Really?" I ask slowly.

"Yes, and you want to know the really strange thing?"

"What?"

"She said she called me last week at home but didn't leave a message. Just like Sasha said. That's incredible, isn't it?"

I don't answer. I just stare straight ahead, thinking about Sasha's comment that Mary had found someone she cared for. And about convenient phone calls.

Mary considerately suggests that we walk back into Bedford separately, so I drop her off in front of the Ritz-Carlton Hotel, which is only a short distance from our building. She wants to use the hotel ladies' room to freshen up so no one on the trading floor will see that she's been crying, and I want to be by myself when I park the car. I don't want any rumors starting.

As I come through the firm's glass doors, Roger is waiting for me in the lobby.

"I'm glad you're here," he says, bolting up off the couch. He seems anxious.

I glance at Anna, but she's focused on a blizzard of papers spread out on her desk. "What's wrong?"

"I think I really screwed up. Come on! Hurry!"

We walk quickly onto the trading floor and head down the aisle toward his desk. He's a few steps ahead of me, waving me on. "I inputted a buy order on Trader One, but I entered the wrong stock ticker. Jesus Christ, I put ten thousand dollars into the wrong company," he says, trotting into his cubicle. "My wife's going to kill me."

Slammer is up to his usual thing—beating the hell out of his keyboard and shouting into his phone. He doesn't even look up as I move into Roger's cubicle. The young kid, Daniel, is staring at something on his screen. He gives me a nod but that's all.

"Sit in my chair." Roger guides me into his seat, then kneels down beside me, stroking his beard. Tiny beads of sweat dot his forehead.

"How do you know you entered the wrong ticker?"

"Like you showed me last night, Seaver's clearing firm in New York automatically returned an e-mail showing me that the order was received. I printed out the e-mail when it got to my computer, and that's when I noticed I had entered the wrong ticker."

"Where's the printout?"

While Roger scours his cluttered desk for the order, I notice that there are now several framed photos of a plain-looking woman and two children decorating his cubicle. "This company trades on the New York Stock Exchange," I point out, perusing the paper he thrusts at me. I can tell because there are only three letters in its ticker. NYSE tickers have three letters or less. All Nasdaq tickers have at least four. "So there's no problem," I say checking my watch.

"What do you mean?"

"It's only nine fifteen. The NYSE doesn't open until nine thirty. We'll cancel the order. We've got plenty of time." I watch Mary walk down the long aisle.

"But my damn computer is frozen up. That's my other problem. I've tried rebooting twice and nothing happens. What the hell am I going to do?"

"We'll send a fax to the broker. There's plenty of—"

"What is it?" Roger asks when I interrupt myself.

"You've got nothing to worry about," I say, scanning the paper once more, then tossing it on his desk.

"Why?"

"It's an invalid order."

"What do you mean?"

Over the cubicle partition I hear Anna calling me on the intercom. "You forgot to fill in the number of shares you wanted to purchase," I point out. "Seaver's clearing firm will automatically DQ this thing."

"DQ?"

"Disqualify. If he calls you, just cancel the order verbally. No sweat," I assure him, rising out of the seat and hurrying to my cubicle, passing Mary on the way. She gives me a pleasant smile. "Yes, Anna," I say into the intercom.

"Could you come up front, Augustus? Reggie Dorsey is here to see you again."

I freeze. What does he want this time? "I'll be there in a minute."

"He's waiting in the conference room," Anna says as I come into the lobby. "What's the deal with this guy?"

"It's no big thing," I say, trying to sound unconcerned.

Reggie's sitting in the same seat as yesterday—at the head of the table. He doesn't bother to shake my hand. "Sit down." He points at the chair beside his, but I leave one seat between us.

"What do you want, Reggie? I'm getting tired of this."

"Steady, Augustus. Don't get upset."

"I'm not upset, but you've got to understand. This is my place of business. I would appreciate you at least calling to let me know you're coming if there's a next time. People are starting to ask me questions about who you are."

"Does that bother you?"

I start to snap back at him but manage to control my temper in the nick of time. I know he's just trying to get under my skin so he can de-code my body language more easily. Human beings give away much more about themselves when they're under pressure, and he's trying to get me to that point quickly. A friend of mine from college is a Richmond cop, and he told me all about law enforcement's investigative methods one night when I was there on a business trip.

"You don't have anything to hide, do you, Augustus?" he asks, pulling out a cigarette and taking a whiff but not lighting it. The same way he did last time. "For my grandchildren," he mutters under his breath.

"No, I do not have anything to hide," I say strongly. Suddenly the thought of turning the tables on Reggie dawns on me. As our high school football coach said so many times, the best defense is a good offense. "Have you made any progress at all in the case yet? You don't seem to be accomplishing much."

Reggie glances up. "I'll tell you about any progress when I'm good and ready to—"

"Do you think Frank Taylor murdered Melanie?"

"Why do you ask that?"

I can see by the irritation on his face that Reggie doesn't appreciate being questioned. He likes to be the one calling the shots. "You went to see him again yesterday. That's twice that I know of."

"So what? Taylor was Melanie's boss. He knew a lot about her. And how do you know I went to see him twice?"

"He told me. He showed up at my house last night very drunk." Reggie and I stare at each other evenly for a few moments. "So, do you think he killed her?"

"I just had a few simple questions for him."

"Why did you go back to see him again?"

Reggie's eyes narrow. "Someone gave me another anonymous call, Augustus. The message was that we needed to investigate Frank Taylor very carefully."

"Do you think the call came from the same person as before?"

"I assume so. And I assume it was you," he says firmly.

"Me? That's crazy! The first message you got was to let you know that I was here at Bedford. Why would I call you anonymously to tell you that?"

"So I wouldn't think you were the source when the second call came concerning Taylor."

"Forget it, Reggie. Wrong tree. Stop barking."

"Would Frank Taylor have had a motive?" he asks.

"You tell me. You're the detective."

"Was Taylor having an affair with Melanie?" Reggie wants to know.

"You asked that last time you were here."

"Well?"

"Did you ask Taylor that question?"

"Yes."

"What did he say?"

Reggie looks at me thoughtfully. "He didn't. He said he wanted his lawyer present if I was going to continue interrogating him. I told him not to get so upset, but he refused to answer any more of my questions."

"I've never been uncooperative like that."

"No, you haven't." He pauses. "So tell me. Were Taylor and Melanie having an affair?"

I take a deep breath. "Yes, I think they were."

"Did you ever catch them in the act?"

"No, Taylor bragged about it to me." So did Melanie, in her own way, I think to myself, remembering how she slipped her arm into his so comfortably and how she let him touch her in front of me as she was walking away the afternoon before her death. "Taylor told me he had made love to her in my own bed," I say, gritting my teeth. It's still revolting for me to remember that.

"You think he was telling the truth?"

"I do."

Reggie hesitates. "I'm sorry, Augustus."

"Maybe that was his motive. Maybe she was ending the affair, and he killed her because he couldn't stand losing her."

"Maybe." Reggie loosens his tie and undoes the top button of his shirt. "Somebody else we both know would have had that same motive," he points out. His eyes narrow. "Do you know who killed your wife, Augustus?"

"No."

"I'm not asking if *you* killed her."

"Uh-huh."

"I'm asking if you *know* who killed her. Those are two very different questions."

"I understand and my answer is no to both," I say angrily. "Maybe *I* should have a lawyer present."

"There's no need for that." Reggie strokes his thin mustache with his thumb and forefinger a few times before speaking again. "Did your father ever mention having children by another woman? Did he ever tell you anything like that?"

What the hell is he talking about now? "Children by another woman?"

"Obviously not," he says, rising from his chair. "Well, I'll make a point of calling before I visit in the future. I promise."

"Wait a minute, Reggie! You can't ask me something like that, then just leave!" I shout, jumping up from my chair and moving in front of the conference room door to block his way. "What are you saying? Was he married to someone else before my mother?"

"I told you. I'm very thorough with my investigations."

"What did you find out? Please tell me, Reggie!"

He takes a deep breath. "Law enforcement's ability to track people down has been enhanced dramatically in the last few years thanks to technology. The ability to share fingerprints and DNA information with other police forces and federal agencies has taken investigative work to a much higher level. It's hard for anyone with a record to hide anymore."

"What does that mean?" I ask, my mouth running dry. "Do you know something about my father? Did he have a record?"

"Some things are better left in the dark," Reggie says.

As if I don't already know that. "Tell me, Reggie. Tell me what you found out."

For several moments he stays silent. Finally he motions toward the table. "Sit back down," he says softly. He sits too, this time in the chair next to mine. Then he begins. "I'm going to tell you a story. So far it isn't a very happy one, but who knows, maybe it'll end up okay."

I stare at him, wondering what in the world he is about to tell me.

"Forty years ago a young man goes to jail in a small town in southern Ohio for raping a fifteen-year-old girl. It's statutory rape because the girl admits that the sex was consensual and there's no evidence of a struggle. But it's still rape under the law. Seems like this young man was a real smooth talker. At least, that's what everybody around town says.

"The girl runs away from home a few months after the incident, when she starts to show. She's pregnant with the man's baby and the townspeople are being damn cruel. She won't give up the baby and she can't stay, so she runs."

"I don't follow," I say, my voice shaky.

"The young man is released from jail a year later for good behavior, and he leaves the area. Drops off the face of the earth as a matter of fact. For two years no one knows where he is." Reggie rests his elbows on the arms of the chair. "Then one day he turns up in Richmond, Virginia. Turns up at a police precinct charged with raping another young girl. This one's sixteen. Seems he likes them young."

The story is coming together and the blood is beginning to pound in my brain.

"But this time the young man has a stroke of good luck. He finds himself with a sharp lawyer doing pro bono work as a public defender, and all he gets is probation. Law enforcement wasn't nationally coordinated in those days so the Richmond court doesn't even know about the Ohio crime. Besides, once again the young woman admits that the sex was consensual, so it's statutory rape, and she pleads with the judge to show leniency. Turns out she's in love with the young man."

"Keep going," I urge.

"There's no pregnancy as a result of the rape this time, but they end up getting married," Reggie continues. "The young man gets a job at a local factory and the girl works as a maid for a family on the rich side of town. After a while they save enough for a down payment on a small house in a working-class section of the city. Then she does get pregnant and they have a baby boy. Everything's going along fine. They're in love and the young man seems to have gotten control of himself. But his past catches up to him. The girl from Ohio shows up on their doorstep with *her* child and suddenly the situation gets complicated again. Seems the young man had secretly been staying in touch with the Ohio girl the whole time."

"The young man in the story is my father," I whisper.

Reggie nods.

"But how did you find out all of that?" After so many years I'm finally learning who he is, and it isn't pretty. I don't see how this story could possibly have a happy ending. "Did you find old newspaper clippings from Ohio or something? Is that how you found my father?"

"No. He wasn't William McKnight when he lived in Ohio. He was George Wayne Franklin. He didn't change his name to William McKnight until he came to Richmond."

"George Wayne Franklin," I whisper to myself. "Then how did you find him?"

"Everything's digital these days, and when we entered William McKnight's fingerprints into the computer, Franklin's record came up too. I pieced things together by talking to people in Richmond and Ohio who were around when this all happened." Reggie puts a hand on my shoulder. "Are you all right, Augustus?"

"I don't know," I say, my voice raspy. Maybe it was good that I hadn't been close to my father. If I had been, this news might be hitting me even harder. Though it's hard to imagine how I could feel any worse right now.

"You sure? You want to talk?"

Down deep I think Reggie has a good heart. He can say all he wants to about staying cold and objective with regard to the people involved with cases he's working on, but he knows he might as well have just dropped a bomb on me with what he's said, and I can see that he's concerned. "I just need a few minutes by myself."

He nods. "Okay."

He gets up and starts to walk out. "Just one more thing. Sorry to bring this up right now," he says evenly, "but I still need a blood sample. Let's get that detail out of the way."

"Tell me again why you need a blood sample," I say quietly, still stunned.

"I told you. It's standard operating procedure. There's nothing to be worried about."

"If it was nothing to be worried about, Reggie, you wouldn't be bugging me about it." Augustus Franklin. It sounds strange. "Be honest with me, Reggie. What's going on?"

"There was dried blood under Melanie's fingernails when they brought her body into the morgue. I'm sure none of it was yours because you told me that you were never physically violent with her. Right?"

I nod slowly, as if in a trance.

"But our pathologists still need to check it out. It's just part of the process. You understand, don't you?"

I really don't, but this afternoon I'll give him what he wants, I decide, letting my face fall slowly into my hands.

"Good-bye, Augustus."

So that's why my father disappeared for a couple of days every few months. He was seeing his "other" family. And my mother was letting him. She had to have known what was going on if the other girl showed up in Richmond like Reggie said.

There's a soft knock on the door.

"Yes?" I take my hands from my face but don't look around. I assume it's Reggie at the door, back with more questions.

"I'm sorry to bother you, Augustus," Anna says quietly, moving to where I can see her.

"Oh, it's you."

"Are you all right?"

"I'm fine."

"That was a cop who just left, right?"

"Yes."

"What did he want?" she asks reluctantly, as if she knows she has no right to ask but can't stop herself.

I look into Anna's eyes and I swear I see fear. "It's a matter concerning an old family business. Money stuff. Nothing to worry about."

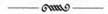

I sweat profusely as I slam the red Everlast punching bag hanging from the basement ceiling. I haven't even bothered to put on the eight-ounce gloves I usually wear when I work out. I just hit the bag harder and harder, faster and faster, making believe it's Frank Taylor. Or my father.

I may be in good shape, but hitting the bag is exhausting work no matter how fit you are. After a few minutes my hands feel like anchors, and I start to become light-headed. But I keep going, groaning louder each time my fist smashes the bag, until my head is spinning and I'm gasping for breath.

Failure. Ironically, that's my objective. Keeping my hands and arms going until I physically cannot do it anymore. That's how you increase strength when you train. Go to failure.

Finally it happens and my knees buckle. I try desperately to maintain my balance, but it's impossible and I stumble toward an old wooden wardrobe Melanie used when we were first married. My arms are so tired I can't even raise them to protect myself, and I have to take the brunt of the impact with my shoulder. I crash into the shabby piece of furniture so hard it almost falls over as I collapse on the cement floor in front of it.

For five minutes I'm flat on my back, chest heaving, while my body recuperates. As I'm lying there, I think about how I finally made the trip downtown this afternoon and gave the D.C. police department my blood. The whole procedure was over quickly and it seemed routine— Reggie wasn't even around. I haven't heard anything yet, but I suppose it's too soon to expect news. Not that I think there will be any news. Depending on how thoroughly Melanie washed her hands—or didn't—the lab people may find my blood beneath her fingernails because of the scratches to my neck. But that wasn't my fault, and if I have to explain the incident to Reggie, I think he'll understand.

Finally I raise myself onto one elbow, still drained from the exercise. Maybe the blood test has weakened me. The lab people took more than I thought they would.

Both wardrobe doors have swung wide open as a result of the impact. As I rise to my knees, I see it's full of Melanie's old clothes dangling from wire hangers. Blouses and dresses she used to wear but that went out of style a few years after we were married. I reach out and touch one of the dresses, thinking about how happy we were during our first years together. It was a time when simply having each other was enough. When the lack of money wasn't an issue. When eating hot dogs three nights a week didn't bother us.

As my fingers stroke the material, I feel something in one of the dress's pockets. It's a solid mass about the size of a baseball. I dig inside curiously and fall slowly back on the floor as I pull it out of the pocket and hold it up in front of my face. It's a thick roll of cash, held tightly together by a rubber band.

When I'm finished going through the rest of the clothes in the wardrobe I've found several more rolls. In total there's more than six thousand dollars hidden here.

CHAPTER

12

I'm not a gambling man. I'm not part of a neighborhood crew that meets regularly for Friday night poker marathons, I don't bet on sporting events, and I've been inside a casino only once in my life.

That was last February when Melanie and I drove to Atlantic City and stayed at the Taj Mahal on the boardwalk. I won the trip as a door prize at my company Christmas party in early December—the first time I had ever won anything like that. It was so cold when we got to New Jersey we stayed inside the casino the entire time. We never even made it to the boardwalk, let alone the beach.

The afternoon of our first day we bought two very expensive cocktails and wandered aimlessly through the cavernous, neon-lit rooms. I didn't have extra cash for the tables—the door prize included only the room and dinners—so we people-watched. Most of them appeared to be enjoying themselves. The whole gambling thing was simply an experience and the cash they were throwing away was funny money.

But a few people in the casino didn't take losing quite so easily. They slammed their fists on the green felt of the tables every time the house hit twenty-one. They yelled and cursed and shouted for a new dealer whenever they lost, unable to accept the simple fact that Lady Luck was laughing at them. One guy was even ejected by two huge uniformed guards after he banged the table so hard following a bad deal that other players' chips fell to the floor. There was a mad scramble as the crowd tried to grab a few.

I actually saw a woman try to snatch her chips off a craps table and make a run for it after a bad roll of the dice—she was nabbed quickly. And Melanie watched a man dissolve into tears standing in front of a slot machine, clasping an empty plastic change bucket with both hands. As soon as the man used his last quarter and stood up, another guy slipped onto the stool in front of the same one-armed bandit and on his fourth pull won a huge pot, filling *his* plastic bucket with the exact same quarters the first guy had lost. It was sad. For no apparent reason, one guy was a huge winner and the other guy was a total loser, but I suppose that's just the way life is.

Most Atlantic City blackjack tables have ten- or twenty-dollar perdeal minimums, so the few five-dollar tables are usually pretty crowded. Melanie and I camped out near one of the cheaper tables to watch, and when a player at the end closest to us left in disgust after the dealer scooped up his last chip, Melanie shocked me by stuffing two hundred dollars in my palm and pushing me toward the vacated seat. I slipped in front of a pudgy woman wearing a loud orange jumpsuit who was scrambling to get to it too. I gave the woman a quick wink as I claimed the seat just ahead of her, then got my two hundred dollars exchanged for chips.

Like I said, I'm not a regular gambler so I don't know the ins and outs of a complex game like craps, but blackjack is pretty straightforward. Get as close to twenty-one as you can, but don't go over. Go over, you lose. Beat the dealer without going over, you win. Aces count one or eleven—it's the player's choice—all face cards like kings and queens count ten, and every other card's value is its face amount. The key to blackjack is knowing the odds cold. Knowing when to hold and when to take a hit, and never deviating from the probabilities no matter how good or bad the cards are treating you.

I'm fairly disciplined, I've always been good with numbers, but I was still surprised when I walked away thirty minutes later with five hundred dollars in chips. As soon as I started to feel the cards going against me, I picked up and left. Which is almost as important as knowing the odds. Knowing when to walk away, and having the discipline to do it. Otherwise the casino will end up with everything.

As soon as I had exchanged my five hundred dollars' worth of chips for cash at the window, Melanie slipped both hands around my neck and kissed me deeply. Then she whispered in my ear that she was going upstairs to our room, and that I should follow in a few minutes. That if I did, she'd give me the fuck of my life. Then she tapped the money in my hand and told me that such a good time would cost me exactly five hundred dollars.

As I watched Melanie walk toward the elevators, turning heads as she always did, I remember trying to figure out where in the world she could have gotten the two hundred bucks. I kept the checkbook and I would have known if she was taking money from the account. There were never any ATM withdrawals or cash checks on the monthly statements other than mine. But sometimes there were crumpled tens or twenties lying on her bureau in the morning after one of her late nights. I figured Taylor had given it to her in case she had car trouble on the way home and needed to call a cab.

There were some winners at the casino, a few people with piles of chips that seemed to constantly grow. But they were few and far between, and they weren't at the center of a wild crowd and with a gorgeous woman on each arm like you see in the movies. They kept to themselves, most of them wore sunglasses so you couldn't see their eyes, and their expressions didn't change whether they won or lost.

I've been thinking about that weekend ever since it occurred to me that Bedford & Associates is exactly like that Atlantic City casino. It's government sanctioned, enables the general public to recklessly thrill-seek, and chews up and spits out inexperienced players in a heartbeat. Since I go there every day, maybe I'm a gambling man after all.

Of the hundred day traders who were at Bedford the day I started nearly two weeks ago, eleven are already gone because they couldn't pay off their debts to Michael Seaver. But they've been replaced quickly because there are always more people who believe they can beat the odds, who want in on this action that they think will make them rich.

I suppose I shouldn't be surprised that so many people in our society want to play the day trading game. Day trading defines us perfectly. We're a nation obsessed with risk in the pursuit of huge reward, and we have absolutely no patience. Things have to happen for us at light speed or we're bored to tears. Nowadays people day trade their *careers*, for crying out loud. Monday your neighbor is working for ABC-dot-com, Wednesday he's at MNO-dot-com, and by the end of the week it's XYZ-dot-com. No more forty years to a gold watch and a pension like it was for our fathers. We want it now, and if you can't give it to us, we'll find someone who can. If people are willing to day trade their careers, they'll sure as hell day trade stocks.

Once in a while a newspaper runs a story about somebody losing everything after investing their life savings in a dot-bomb like SweatersForRats.com or in plans for a south Texas ski resort, but you're more likely to hear about the original eBay investors who turned four million into four billion. The eleven day traders who left Bedford over the last two weeks without a dime aren't good PR for the machine, so we assume *they* screwed up, not the system.

I don't know for certain, but I think Daniel is about to become the twelfth person to disappear from the Bedford trading floor. He looked terrible this morning when he arrived—his eyes were bloodshot and his purple hair was a mess. I mean, even more of a mess than usual. He told me yesterday that he was having a bad run with his portfolio, and I caught him popping pills in the men's room a few minutes before noon today. I feel bad for him, but it's none of my business and I don't want to meddle where I'm not wanted. Sometimes people who need help the most will devote more energy to covering up their problems than to saving themselves. It's strange how that works, but I've seen it before. Mom tried to help my father so much, but every day he receded a little farther into his shell until at the end he barely even spoke to her. He was a broken man. Now I know why.

Up to now I haven't technically been day trading. Aside from Teletekk, I've been buying and holding my securities for at least a couple of days, whereas classic day traders are in and out of their positions in minutes, sometimes seconds. They use strategies with names like "hi-mom" as they search for identifiable high momentum—hence the name—in a particular stock or index like the S&P 500 or the Nasdaq 100. Day traders closely track trading ranges of a specific security or index over short time periods, and when they see an aberration or identify high momentum in either direction—up or down—they take advantage of it. Say XYZ Co.'s share price has traded in the range of $20 to $25 during the last month. A day trader may snap up XYZ Co. when the price nears $20 and sell as it approaches $25. In fact, he may buy at $20, sell at $20.25, buy at $20.50, sell at $20.75 and so on all the way up the range. He'll do the same thing as the price declines by shorting the stock. He'll do it on the way up and on the way down, over and over all day long. That's day trading. There are lots of unique strategies within that framework, but that's the basic idea.

A few years ago this kind of rapid-fire trading wouldn't have been possible. The creaky mainframes the stock exchanges used back then would have melted under the weight of today's volume. But now the supercomputers the American exchanges have installed can handle almost everything we throw at them. Which, ironically, isn't necessarily good because most of the individuals out there who are trading shouldn't be. But that's the double-edged sword of capitalism. We cheer those who take risks and make millions and mock the idiots who take risks and lose it all.

Day trading sounds simple, which is the problem. The average Joe figures he can easily identify a historical trading range in a security by himself and be an instant success. He figures he doesn't have to be able to understand a complex set of financial statements or be completely up to speed on all of XYZ Co.'s latest products. In fact, he figures it might hurt him if he were. Then he might think *too* much. All he's trying to do is stay on the alert for major announcements about the companies he's invested in that could propel his stocks violently in either direction. The challenge for the average Joe is that securities don't remain in the same trading range forever, even when there are no major announcements—which might seem obvious. But in the minute-by-minute chaos of the market, day traders can lose sight of the bigger picture. Then they lose their shirts.

The trader who buys XYZ Co. as the share price approaches $20—the bottom of the identified range—may be shocked when the shares suddenly plunge past $20 to $17 or $16. What he doesn't know is that some huge portfolio manager in Omaha, Nebraska, arbitrarily decided to dump a ton of shares, causing a sell-side imbalance—and there's no way the trader could have ever anticipated this. As a result there are many more shares trying to find a home than there are homes—more sellers than buyers—so the price drops below the $20 resistance point until enough buyers surface to stabilize the price. And the day trader may not see the cause of the imbalance on Trader One because the portfolio manager's dealer may be able to hide the transaction—if it's a Nasdaq-traded issue—until it's too late for the day trader to react.

The portfolio manager in Omaha may not have learned anything bad about XYZ Co. He may have dumped the shares simply because he had liquidity issues at his mutual fund—a decision unrelated to anything that's going on at XYZ. But it doesn't matter to the day trader. All that matters to him is that he's suddenly underwater. If he's used margin lending to increase his position and the stock price hasn't rebounded by the end of the day, he'll have to pay the piper at the closing bell. And if he doesn't voluntarily pay the piper, his Seaver equivalent will make him pay—or shut him down. The stock might pop right back into its range the next day, but it doesn't matter to the day trader. He's already shit out of luck.

The most important thing to understand is that the odds are stacked heavily against the individual in the stock market. But most people don't get that, or they choose to ignore it. It's exciting—for a while. Then reality sets in.

It's almost three o'clock and I'm heading for the men's room—only a couple of hours until Vincent stops by Bedford to pick me up and we head to the Oriole game in Baltimore to meet his high-roller buddies. When I enter, Daniel is standing in front of the mirror, staring at himself. He doesn't acknowledge me as I come through the door and move to a urinal. When I go to the sinks, he still hasn't moved. "You all right?" I ask.

No answer.

"Daniel?"

He turns his head slowly to look at me. His face is pale. "I never thought it would be like this, Augustus," he says. "I thought I could win. I got great grades at Georgetown, but I didn't see any point in sticking around. It wasn't getting me anywhere and I wanted to make some bucks in the real world."

"Sit down, Daniel," I say gently, leading him slowly by the arm to lean against a wall. He looks like he might need medical attention. "Take it easy."

"No," he says, flailing at me suddenly when he feels the wall against his back.

"Relax."

"Get off me!"

"All right, all right," I say quietly, not wanting to agitate him any further.

"I need money," he blurts out. "You've got to lend me some."

"Daniel, I—"

"Please."

"I—"

"I know you made a bunch of cash on that tip you gave Mary a few days ago. The one you wouldn't share with the rest of us."

"That was wrong," I say. But I don't really think so. Who I choose to give information to is my business. But if that's what Daniel needs to hear me say right now, I'll say it. "I should have told everyone in the group. If I ever have information like that again, I promise I'll share it with you."

"That's so nice of you," he says sarcastically, "but it doesn't help me right now."

"What do you want me to do?"

"Lend me ten grand," he replies, as if that amount of money is nothing to me. "That's all I need," he says, his voice desperate. "Just ten grand, Augustus. I'll pay you back in a few weeks. If I'm not back in the black by then, I'll call my parents and ask them for the money. They've got plenty of dough."

"Why don't you go to your parents now?" I'm standing very close to him, and I notice a small vial in his shirt pocket, but I can't see exactly what's inside it. Looks like white pills—probably the ones he was popping this morning—but I can't tell. "If you're in trouble, they'll help."

Daniel reaches for the ring protruding from his eyebrow, then pulls on it hard enough to make me cringe. "My father is my last resort. He's such an asshole."

"You should talk to him any—"

"Lend me the money, Augustus," Daniel interrupts. "I know you've got it. I saw the way Mary was jumping up and down in her cubicle the other day. That wasn't any ten percent pop. That was a big win."

"I can't lend you the money, Daniel."

It's strange. I'm willing to give Father Dale and ultimately someone I don't even know ten thousand dollars, but I won't lend this kid the same amount even though I can clearly see the desperation in his eyes. We haven't talked much since I've been at Bedford, but Daniel was helpful my first few days, showing me around and making me feel comfortable. So why won't I lend him the money? I was a kid not too long ago. I know how things are when your father takes about as much interest in you as he does in cleaning the garage. And it isn't that I don't believe Daniel when he says his parents will repay me. Beneath his purple-haired, body-pierced facade, he's got a silver spoon way about him, like he's always had a safety net when he really needed it. Georgetown University isn't exactly cheap either.

"Come on."

"No." Someone has to teach the kid a lesson. Someone has to teach him that life isn't always fair. That there won't always be someone around to pick up the pieces for him when he's in trouble.

"Please," Daniel begs. "Seaver's going to shut me down if I don't come up with rent. He told me that last night."

"Call home."

"You asshole!" Daniel shouts, clenching his fists. "You're as cheap as my father! I oughta kick your ass."

"Easy, Daniel," I snap, rising up to my full height as a warning. He's six inches shorter and seventy pounds lighter than I am, and I could knock him into next week with one blow to his purple head.

"You and Mary!" Tears of anger stream down his face. "You both have plenty of money, and you won't lend me a dollar. Goddamn it! That isn't right. Fuck both of you!"

"Shut up!" People out on the floor might hear him and I don't want to get involved in something ugly that everyone will be talking about for weeks. I'm trying to keep a low profile—without much success.

"How about *five* grand?" he pleads. "Just five, Augustus. That'll tide me over. It's only a temporary thing. Just a bad streak. That's my problem."

"Your problem is that you came here in the first place. Georgetown is a great school. You should have graduated and thanked God that your parents were willing to send you there."

"Don't judge me."

"Go back to school. Admit that this wasn't the right thing for you."

"Screw you!"

Out of nowhere he takes a swing at me, but whatever's in that vial has severely retarded his motor skills. I block his punch easily, then grab him by his collar and lift him off the ground until his feet are way off the bathroom tile. The whole thing takes no more than a split second, and I can tell by the terror in his eyes that he's never been in a real fight. Maybe it was the drugs that caused him to act so foolishly, but at this point I don't care.

"Let me go," he gasps.

"Stop struggling!"

I've never been trained to fight; it's just always come naturally to me. Go for the throat and they'll give up fast. And so he does.

"Here's what I'm going to do," I say, not even breathing hard as I set him down. He hunches over, hands on his knees. "I'm going to lend you the five thousand, but I want it back two weeks from today. If you don't repay me, I will get it from you." I push his shoulders against the wall and make sure he's looking me straight in the eye so he's absolutely certain of my conviction. "If you skip out on me, I'll find you and it won't be pretty when I do. Do you understand?"

He nods.

"All right. I'll give you a check in the morning. You can tell Seaver he'll have his money then."

"Okay," Daniel whispers. "Thanks." He lurches past me and heads for the door.

"Two weeks," I call after him, but he's already gone.

Daniel isn't anywhere on the trading floor when I emerge from the men's room a few moments later after splashing cold water on my face. I'm worried about him, but I don't have much time to think about it because it's almost three thirty. I've been researching companies all day in case Vincent's people grill me on my investing strategy, but I still want to review specifics on a few more stocks before he gets here.

Vincent said his pals might kick in as much as ten million, *if* I made that three hundred thousand dollars he gave me this past Monday hum. Fortunately, I have. Like a hive of pissed-off hornets. In three days I've turned three hundred grand into four hundred grand. That ought to impress them.

Monday afternoon I bought three hundred thousand dollars' worth of put options on a small pharmaceutical company that went public two months ago. Put options are a cheap way of betting that a company's stock price will fall. They enable you to force the seller of the options to buy shares of the underlying stock from you at some specific future date for a predetermined "strike" price. If the market price subsequently falls after you buy the puts from him, then you can purchase shares at the low market price and force him to buy them from you at the higher strike price—or "put" them to him—even though the market price is lower.

Which is exactly what I did.

I found out that the management team of the pharmaceutical company had done a great job of negotiating their "lock up" provision with the investment banking firm that took them public two months ago. A lock up provision is a standard requirement in an underwriting agreement that bars all employees and other insiders of a going-public company from selling any of their shares for a specific period of time after the IPO—almost always 180 days. The investment bankers make management sign the lock up provision because they don't want their preferred clients—the ones they sold the IPO shares to—to see insiders dumping shares right after the IPO. Insider selling isn't generally regarded as a good sign. After all, if management thought their company was so great, why would they be selling? That could cause the preferred clients to dump the stock—and the price to tank, And brokerage firms never want to see prices tank, especially right after the IPO.

This management team must have had a very sharp lawyer because they negotiated a ninety-day lock up provision—half as long as the normal 180-day period. After those ninety days, they and all the other employees would be free to trade. But the market wasn't widely aware of that. I found all this out by combing through the company's IPO document, called an S-1, and I knew there was an opportunity. The company was small and not well known, the lock up period was short, and most companies' stock prices take a hit as the normal 180-day lock up period comes close to ending. Investors figure the rank-and-file employees will want liquidity to buy homes and cars, so the price tends to drift down with about two weeks to go before the lock up expires.

I bought the puts on Monday, then started alerting the market to the unusually short lock up period by blasting that information out on the company's Yahoo! chat page. Sure enough, the price dropped eight bucks, and I made a hundred grand in two days. The Internet is fantastic—and Vincent's high rollers ought to be very happy.

"Up for a beer tonight?" Roger asks as I sit down in my cubicle.

"Can't," I say brusquely. As I've gotten closer to my self-imposed day trading launch date, I've become less chatty with everybody—even Mary.

"Why not?" he wants to know, leaning on the cubicle wall.

"Busy."

"Doing what?"

I take a deep breath and count to ten. As I feared, Roger has turned into my second shadow, constantly wanting to know what I'm doing with my portfolio, where I'm going for lunch, or if the insurance policy he thinks my mother left me has paid off yet. "I'm going to the Oriole game over in Baltimore."

"Great! You got an extra ticket?"

"Why don't you go home early and give your wife some attention?"

"Trust me, the game would be a lot more fun."

"Well, it's not my call. Someone's taking me." I'm sure Vincent will have at least one extra ticket, or would be able to get his hands on one by the time we made it to Baltimore. After all, he's Vinnie the Ticket Guy. But I don't want Roger screwing things up for me in front of the high rollers. I've gotten pretty juiced about managing other people's money. In fact, if tonight works out I'm going to look into buying that new car over the weekend. A BMW, I've decided. I can't believe I'm thinking about a car as expensive as that, but what the hell, you only go around once. "Sorry, Roger."

"Who's taking you?" he digs.

"An old friend." My voice is on edge. The clock's ticking, and I want to make certain I've nailed this research before Vincent gets here.

"Who?"

"His name's Vincent Carlucci."

"Carlucci?" Roger chuckles. "I'll bet he can get me a ticket. He'll just make somebody an offer they can't refuse."

This time I count to twenty. Roger's sarcasm is usually harmless, but this time he's aimed it at my best friend. "I've got work to do, Roger," I say coldly.

I start to turn away, but he calls after me. "Has the money come from your mom's insurance policy yet?"

"Roger!"

"Excuse me for taking an interest!"

Out of the corner of my eye I watch him head up the aisle toward the lobby. "Jesus," I curse under my breath, answering the telephone on its first ring. "Hello."

"Hi there."

The female voice is familiar, but I can't place it, and as the seconds tick by and I hesitate to respond, I can feel my blood pressure rising. I hate making people feel like they aren't important.

"Augustus?"

Relief. It's Mary. This is the first time we've ever spoken on the phone and her voice sounds different over a wire. "Hi, Mary." She hasn't been in today. I was wondering where she was.

"Did you miss me?" she asks in a sweet voice.

"Of course."

"What's the Nasdaq doing?"

"You mean you don't have all of that information at a push of a button on your cell phone?" I tease.

"I haven't gone that far yet, but maybe I should."

There's a horn in the background so I can tell she's on the road. "Tooling around in your Jag, huh?"

"Yup, making all the guys jealous." She laughs. "So what's the market doing?"

I glance at the thin ticker scrolling continuously across the top of my computer screen. "Up just fifteen and change. It's been a slow day. Everybody must be at the beach."

"Must be. Hey, I've got a favor to ask you. Let's have dinner tomorrow night. A man Jacob introduced me to a few months before he died just opened a new restaurant in Adams Morgan. He wants me to see the place, and I can't very well say no because he was a good friend of Jacob's. But I think he wants to date me, so I don't want to go alone because I'm not interested in him that way." She hesitates. "Will you come?"

I've noticed that when Mary talks about something that happened in her recent past, she almost always describes it in relation to the day Jacob died. She bought a kitten three months *after* Jacob died. She and Jacob went to Paris three months *before* he died. She's been seeing her psychic, Sasha, *since* Jacob died.

"Let's talk about it tomorrow morning," I suggest.

I don't want to be anybody's chaperone, and I'll probably want to go to bed early tomorrow night. Vincent called this morning to warn me that he'd rented a limousine for tonight, and that we'd be staying out late. He also said he was going to have a surprise for me at the end of the night. Something to celebrate my new career. I tried to pry out of him what he was talking about, but he wouldn't say. I told him about the quick profit on the put options—the hundred grand. He was pretty impressed and he said he thought that would cinch the deal with his investors. I hope he's right. I could make two hundred thousand a year managing ten million bucks for them.

"I'll be disappointed if you don't come," Mary says.

"We'll see tomorrow."

"Okay. Listen, I'm about to go into a bad reception area, and I know there's nothing more annoying than talking to people when their cell phones are fading in and out, so I'll save you the aggravation. See you in the morning."

"Bye," I say, but she's already gone.

"So how's our lovely Sassy? She can't go a day without talking to you, can she?" Slammer is staring down at me from his cubicle, sucking on a lollipop. "She hasn't called *me* today."

"Don't bother me right now, pal," I warn him. "I'm very busy."

"That woman certainly is sweet on you," he says. "She used to talk to me a lot, but not anymore. Now she only talks to you, *Gus*."

I look him squarely in the eye. "I warned you about calling me that."

Slammer chuckles and disappears. A moment later he's back at the partition, holding up his briefcase. "I'm going home a little early today. Got some errands I need to run," he announces, pointing at the briefcase. "See you tomorrow, Gus."

I roll my eyes. From now on I'm just going to ignore the idiot.

Forty minutes later Anna's voice crackles through the intercom speaker. "Vincent Carlucci is in the lobby for you."

"Okay, thanks. Be right there."

I notice that the message light on my telephone is blinking. I forwarded my calls to voice mail after Slammer left so I wouldn't be disturbed. Most likely it was Vincent trying to call me on his way over here. Glancing at my watch, I decide I'll listen to the message tomorrow.

I expect Vincent to be draped all over Anna's reception desk like he was last time I came out here to meet him, but he isn't. He's sitting on the couch, quietly leafing through a business magazine I know he's got no interest in, and Anna is staring down at a blank pad of paper. In the few seconds it took me to get out here he must have already insulted her. He can be pretty crude after a couple of drinks, and it wouldn't surprise me if he threw back a gin and tonic or two on the way over.

"Hello, Augustus," he says loudly, rising from the couch.

"Hey, pal." It's as I suspected. Vincent's been drinking. He's much louder than normal.

Roger emerges from the conference room just as Vincent and I shake hands. This is way too convenient.

"Hi, Augustus," Roger says politely. "Who's this?"

"I'm Vincent Carlucci." Vincent swings his hand from mine to Roger's. He's wearing a short-sleeve golf shirt so his massive biceps and forearms are on full display. "I'm this jerk's best friend," he says, laughing and pointing at me.

Roger pats me on the back. "Augustus is no jerk. I just started at Bedford, but he's already been a big help to me. Our cubicles are close together on the floor," he explains. "He's a good man."

Vincent smiles. "I've known Augustus for a long time and he's a *belluva* good man."

"Right." Roger puts a hand to his head as if he's trying hard to re-member something. "Vincent Carlucci, Vincent Carlucci." He snaps his fingers. "Hey, you're the one taking Augustus to the baseball game tonight."

"That's right," Vincent confirms. "We've got box seats about ten rows up on the first-base side. It'll be great."

"Sounds like those seats are almost as good as being on the field," Roger says wistfully.

Vincent smiles. "Just about."

"It's been a long time since I've been to a baseball game."

I try my best to catch Roger's eye. I want to give him the cut sign. I know what he's trying to do, and I'll kill him if Vincent takes the bait.

"The smell of the grass, the taste of a hot dog, the crack of the bat," Roger continues. "There's nothing like it on a summer evening."

"Let's get going," I say quickly, trying to usher Vincent to the door. But he doesn't budge.

"How long has it been?" Vincent asks.

Roger looks up. "How long has what been?"

"How long since you've been to a baseball game?"

I try to push Vincent toward the door again, but again he resists.

Roger looks down at the carpet sheepishly. "Actually, I've never been," he admits.

"*Never?*" Vincent asks, astonished. "Didn't your father ever take you?" He can't believe any red-blooded American male could possibly reach adulthood without going to a major league baseball game.

"My father wasn't around much when I was young."

"I'm sorry to hear that." Vincent glances over at me. "Let's take him with us, Augustus. I've got an extra ticket."

I knew it. Roger's plan has worked perfectly. He's probably laughing to himself. I never should have agreed to help him at all. I should have kept my distance. He's a leech, one of those people who's going to try to worm his way into my entire life. "I don't know, Vincent. I don't want the people you're introducing me to tonight to be uncomfortable because Roger shows up unexpectedly."

Vincent bows his head. "Sorry, pal," he says quietly. "Turns out they couldn't make it."

My heart sinks. I knew I shouldn't have gotten so excited about the high rollers. I should have known it was too good to be true. No reason to get the BMW now.

"That's all right," I say, my voice dropping.

Vincent nudges me. "They're not coming because they're already in, pal. They gave me the thumbs-up this afternoon," he says, leaning toward me and lowering his voice so Roger can't hear him. "I told them about the hundred grand profit you made on the other money. They want to start with ten million right away. Like we talked about. And if you do well, there might be even more."

I gaze at Vincent and suddenly I want a drink to celebrate. "You prick," I say, laughing loudly.

He smiles widely and points at me. "Gotcha."

We're going to have fun tonight and on Saturday morning I'll be the first damn person inside the BMW dealership. Suddenly I don't care that Roger has weaseled his way in. It doesn't matter anymore. The deal is done.

I've never ridden in a limousine so I didn't know what I was missing. Everybody should have the chance at least once. I feel like a rock

star. It's spacious inside and there's everything I could want right at
my fingertips. Stereo, TV, phone, food, drink—even a fax machine. All
the creature comforts as I lounge on soft, sweet-smelling leather seats.
As I sit in cool comfort, I look out from behind tinted windows at the
working-class stiffs sweating in their old wrecks, afraid to use their air-
conditioning for fear that their engines will overheat in the hundred-
degree heat of the slow-moving rush-hour traffic clogging the Capital
Beltway. They gnash their teeth and lean on their horns while I drink a
scotch and Vincent tosses back gin and tonics like water. I see them
wondering who's behind the tinted windows, and I know they're jealous. I would be.

The only creature comfort the limousine doesn't have is a bathroom, and halfway to Baltimore, Roger has to go. He's had only three
beers, but he's desperate, clutching his midsection as if he's been
shot. Vincent finds the situation amusing and won't have the driver
pull off the interstate into a rest area until Roger threatens to go out
the window. Roger bursts from the door before the limousine even
comes to a full stop, shoving people out of his way as he races up the
steps of the rest area toward the bathrooms.

Vincent turns his glass upside down to get to that last sip of gin
and a few ice cubes tumble past his mouth and onto the leather seat,
but he hardly notices because he's already half in the bag. "Roger's a
funny guy," he says, pouring himself another drink. "Sarcastic, but I
like him."

"He's all right."

Vincent chuckles as he stirs his fresh drink. "I don't like his
toupee, though. That thing's got to go. Men who wear rugs are kidding themselves if they think the rest of us don't notice."

It never even occurred to me that the mop on Roger's head might
not be real. I suppose I give people too much credit, or maybe I just
don't like to think they're so pitiful. A toupee. Jesus.

Vincent presses a button and the partition between the driver and
us rises. "I almost forgot," he says when it's all the way up. "You said
you were going to pay off that loan tonight. The five grand."

Before he's even finished I pull a check from my shirt pocket and hand it to him. "Here you go. I made it out this morning so I wouldn't forget. I really appreciate your arranging that for me, Vincent. That money helped Melanie and me through a tough stretch."

Vincent smiles as he stashes the check away. "No problem. I'm always willing to help my best friend."

A long silence follows. I feel like it's my turn to tell him he's my best friend too. I want to, but the words don't come right away and it becomes harder and harder to say anything.

I'm finally about to speak but then the door swings open and Roger tumbles inside the limousine, falling on the backseat in a heap against Vincent, laughing hysterically. Roger starts telling us about how there was a crazy woman chasing a runaway beagle through the men's bathroom, and the awkward moment passes. Vincent's laughing now too, the combination of alcohol and the image of a woman chasing a dog past a row of shocked men holding themselves causing tears to come to his eyes. As I watch, I can see he's right about Roger's toupee. It's not even a good one. How could I have missed that?

Forty-five minutes later we're in our seats at Camden Yards, watching the Orioles take the field in their home whites to a smattering of applause from the half-full stadium. The Birds aren't winning much this year and tonight they're playing the California Angels. Hardly a hot rival. Certainly not the Yankees or the Red Sox, so there isn't all that much for the home crowd to cheer about. Especially when the Angels score five runs in the top of the first.

Vincent was right about the seats. They're fantastic. Just ten rows up from the Orioles' dugout on the first base side. So close I can see the pained expression on the starting pitcher's face as he heads off the mound when the manager yanks him in disgust. But I'm not too concerned about the Orioles. I've always been an Atlanta Braves fan. The Braves' Triple A farm team played in Richmond, so I've always cheered for Atlanta because I recognize some of the guys who had been through Richmond.

Tonight I probably wouldn't care about how badly the Birds are getting beat even if I were a fan. It's a beautiful evening, I've had a few drinks, I've got a million dollars coming to me soon, and I'm going to

be managing ten million more. Life is good. And it'll be even better after I get my Beamer. As long as I don't let myself think about Melanie, I
can coast along in a state that feels like happiness.

In the second inning Vincent starts wagering on anything and
everything. He bets a buck that the next batter will get a hit or walk or
strike out. Batter after batter, dollar after dollar, and he's good at it. Before I know it, I'm into him for thirty bucks. Then he starts betting on
every pitch. This one will be a ball, a strike, or a foul. He bets an over
and under with me on the game's attendance right before it's an-
nounced on the public address system. He bets on how many minutes
an inning will take to complete.

I call it quits when I'm in the hole fifty dollars, and Roger does the
same a few minutes later. Vincent complains bitterly—it's only the
sixth inning and he doesn't want to stop. He tries to make us feel
guilty by reminding us of the fact that he's paid for everything tonight,
but neither of us cave in so he convinces two women sitting behind us
to take the other side of his wagers. By the end of the game he's gotten their money—and their telephone numbers.

The Orioles end up losing 12–1.

On the ride back to Washington, Vincent keeps guzzling gin. He's
wound up tighter than a rubber band on one of those old balsa wood
airplanes. It's been a while since I've seen him like this.

As we near the city, Vincent flicks on the limo's interior lights,
grabs the near-empty gin bottle, and pours what's left into his glass.
Then he points at Roger and chuckles. "Look at him."

Roger is curled up in one corner of the backseat, knees to his
chest, head on his hands, fast asleep. He had quite a few beers at the
game, buying rounds for the two women sitting behind us each time
he bought one for himself. He tried to get their attention, and I think
he was irritated that they kept accepting the drinks but showed no
other interest in him whatsoever. They were interested in Vincent, and
that was that. "He's sleeping like a baby," I say.

Vincent leans over and pulls up the back of Roger's toupee. "See?
Bald as a newborn baby under there."

"You were right," I agree, placing my glass of scotch down on the
console beside me and letting my head ease back against the seat. I

poured the drink as soon as we got in the limo after the game, but I haven't had a sip. I stopped drinking halfway through the game. I wasn't drunk, just tired. I've been working hard this week.

"What a loser," Vincent snickers. "I mean, why wear that thing? Is he trying to fool me?" Vincent asks, his tone turning surly. "Does he really think I'm that stupid? Does he think I won't notice?"

I shrug my shoulders, thinking about how *I* didn't notice. "I don't know. Maybe it's hard for us to understand what it's like to be Roger."

Vincent lets go of Roger's hairpiece and settles back onto the seat. "You're a good guy, Augustus," he says, the hard edge in his voice fading. "You know that?"

"What do you mean?"

"Me, I figure the guy's trying to get over by wearing that stupid thing, and it irritates me. I take it personally, but you try to see it from his perspective. You have compassion. That's why I like you so much."

There's another pause, just as there was on the way to the game when I didn't respond. "Do you ever think about that night we won the state championship?" I finally ask, avoiding the issue of our friendship a second time.

Vincent gazes out the window into the darkness. It's almost midnight and we've reached the Capital Beltway. "Sometimes," he says quietly.

"It was great, wasn't it? We were awesome."

"Yeah, sure we were," he agrees halfheartedly.

"That was one of the best nights of my life."

"Mmm."

I take a deep breath, frustrated at the way he won't reminisce about the game. "Why don't you like to talk about that night?"

He doesn't answer.

"Vincent?"

"You can't dwell on the past, Augustus. It doesn't do anyone any good."

"I'm not dwelling on it. It was a great night, that's all. I felt really good about myself for a few hours during a time when I wasn't happy a whole lot. A time when I didn't like myself much. Being a teenager was hard."

"It was just a damn high school football game," Vincent snaps. "You can't get caught up in those kind of trivial things."

I glance out the window and notice that, after a very short distance on the Beltway, we've exited the highway and are heading toward downtown Washington. I assumed Vincent was going to drop me off at Bedford so I could pick up my car. In that case we should have stayed on the Beltway around the city's north side and headed across the Potomac River to Virginia.

"What would be meaningful to you?" I ask.

"Not that."

"Well, it was to me."

"Maybe that's your problem. Maybe that's always been your problem."

I glance up. I have to remember that he's drunk and he might say things he'll regret in the morning—like we all do once in a while. "What's that supposed to mean?"

"You figure it out."

"No, tell me."

But Vincent doesn't have a chance because Roger wakes up with a start, complaining about his bladder, and we have to stop right away. We pull into a seedy-looking all-night gas station on New York Avenue so he can relieve himself. We sit in silence while he's gone, and then he's back and we're off again.

"Where are we going?" Roger asks, bleary-eyed.

"I have a surprise for you guys." Vincent grins at me, as if the uncomfortable exchange of a few minutes ago never took place. "I told you there was going to be a surprise at the end of the night, Augustus."

"Surprise? What do you mean?" Roger demands, suddenly wide awake.

"You'll find out," Vincent says mysteriously, sipping on what's left of his drink. "This is gonna be fun."

Roger nudges me and nods expectantly.

Fifteen minutes later our driver turns down a dark side street, then whips into what looks like an empty warehouse parking lot.

"We're here," Vincent announces, putting his drink down and rubbing his hands together. "Let's go." He's out of the limousine quickly and heading across the dark parking lot toward a door of the large building, Roger right on his heels.

I follow, reluctantly. It's late and I'm tired.

Vincent waits for me to catch up, then raps on the door of the building. It swings open and instantly I'm hit by pulsing music and blue light. Two guys bigger than Vincent stand on either side of the doorway, arms folded across their broad chests. They're dressed all in black and are wearing dark sunglasses, and I wonder how they can see anything at all. They nod respectfully to Vincent, like he's a big wheel around here.

He turns and motions us in. "Come on guys."

"Wait a minute," Roger says, peering hesitantly around the corner of the door. "What is this place?"

Vincent's grin widens. "Welcome to one of Washington, D.C.,'s finest gentlemen's clubs. I've arranged for us to enjoy first-class treatment tonight. Get ready to have some fun. This is the Two O'Clock Club."

Roger shrinks from the blue light like a vampire from dawn. "The Two O'Clock Club?"

"Yeah. The main entrance is around the other side of the building, but that's for the cattle. We're VIPs."

"I'm not going in," Roger says firmly. "I gotta get home to my wife."

"Come on," Vincent says, his voice turning testy. "Live a little. What your wife doesn't know won't hurt her." He chuckles. "I saw you trying to make time with those girls sitting behind us at the baseball game. I know what you wanted." He gestures toward the door. "I guarantee you the girls inside here are way better looking than those girls at the game, and you won't have to work anywhere near as hard to get their attention."

"I don't have much cash," Roger complains.

"That's all taken care of," Vincent explains smoothly. "You don't need any money tonight. We'll be in the Champagne Room, away from the riffraff. Everything in the Champagne Room is comped."

"No." Roger shakes his head like a child at the dinner table refusing to eat his vegetables. "I'm not going in."

Vincent shrugs. "Fine. You can wait in the damn limo for all I care."
He looks at me. "Come on, Augustus, let's go."

I don't know if it's the grinding music or the blue light or the momentary glimpse of a naked woman, but something draws me toward
the door. I've never been to a strip club before. Vincent has invited me
to join him several times. But I've always turned down the invitations,
which is probably why he made tonight a surprise. He didn't want me
to have the chance to back out.

I take a step toward the door, then stop as Melanie's image looms
in my mind. Am I betraying her memory by going into a place like this
so soon after her death? I can only imagine what her parents would say.

"Come on, Augustus," Vincent urges.

I've always wanted to go inside a club like this. I should probably
turn away like Roger and go home, but suddenly I really want to find
out about what goes on behind this door.

I feel Vincent's hand on my shoulder, tugging me along. "What
about Roger?" I ask.

"Screw him."

"I'm catching a cab," Roger mutters, turning and walking away.

"Roger," I call after him.

"I'll be fine," he yells back, breaking into a trot as if he's afraid we'll
chase after him.

I watch until he moves beneath the glow of an overhead streetlight and disappears around the corner of the building. I'm surprised
that he reacted the way he did. I thought he would have been leading
the charge inside.

"It's just you and me now, pal," Vincent says, pulling me toward the
door again, "and I'm kind of glad about that."

The Two O'Clock Club is incredible. The women are wearing almost nothing, and they're all gorgeous. I mean *gorgeous*. And they all
have these kind of bored expressions on their faces, like it's no big
deal to be walking around nude in front of all these men.

The large main room is furnished with plush chairs and tables and
has watercolors of nude women on the walls. There's a long bar on
one side of the place, and a wide stage on the other with several silver
poles a couple of inches in diameter rising twenty feet from the stage's

shiny black tiles all the way to the ceiling. There must be fifty men seated at the tables watching three women in various states of undress writhe around up there. As I'm watching, one of the women onstage jumps up and swings herself around and around on the pole to the far left, balancing herself with one foot and one hand while her long blond hair flows behind her.

The blue light makes everything white seem very bright. There's a guy standing at the long bar wearing a white shirt, dark pants, and white sneakers. When he picks up his drink and saunters back to his table I can't see his legs very well, but his shirt and shoes glow like neon.

When he sits down at his table there's a woman waiting for him and she's dressed in nothing but a skimpy bikini. She grabs the glass from him, takes a long drink, then raises the glass to his lips. Then she places the glass down on the table, drops to her knees, spreads his legs, moves in between them, and seductively removes the bikini top so her breasts spill out on his lap. She grinds them into him for a few moments, then stands, turns around, and sits back on his lap, grinding some more and steadying herself by clasping his thighs. When my eyes become accustomed to the dim light, I see that there are twenty or thirty girls giving these same kinds of private performances all around the place.

"This way," Vincent calls above the music, distracting me from what's going on in the main room. He waves toward a dark corridor. "We don't want to waste time out here. This is nothing. Wait 'til you see what goes on in the Champagne Room."

As I follow Vincent, I notice rows of pictures on the hallway wall—photographs of women performing onstage or at the tables, as well as signed black-and-white head shots of the dancers. They're all incredibly beautiful. There isn't an average-looking girl on the wall, and it's amazing to me. Why would they choose to do this? Isn't there a way to make a decent living without them having to compromise themselves in front of a pack of animals? It has to be about more than money.

Suddenly I stop short, and it's as if every ounce of breath has been sucked from my lungs. I stumble back, away from the wall of photographs, until I can go no farther because I hit the opposite wall. For a few moments I bend over, hands on my knees, trying to catch my breath, praying that this is a nightmare and I'm going to wake up. I shut my eyes tightly, hoping the grinding music and the catcalls from down the corridor will fade to nothing—but they don't.

Slowly I rise up and lurch toward one specific picture hanging on the wall. It's a woman onstage. She's grabbing one of the silver poles with both hands, nothing on her body but a gold chain belt that doesn't even hide her navel. I take another look and there can be no denying it. The woman in the photograph is Melanie.

In the picture, men around the stage are cheering and she's smiling that same gorgeous smile she gave me at our wedding right after college and said good-bye to only a few weeks ago. Melanie up on the stage for the animals to enjoy. This is where the crumpled tens and twenties on her bureau came from. And the rolls of bills in the basement. This is where she was at night when I thought she was working in Frank Taylor's law office.

I look slowly to my left and Vincent is staring at me, an anxious expression on his face. He must know what I've seen.

CHAPTER

13

Vincent and I sit next to each other in the back of the limousine, star-ing straight ahead into the darkness. He told the driver to get out and stay out until otherwise instructed, so we're alone. Through the tinted window I can see the guy leaning back against the brick wall next to the back entrance of the Two O'Clock Club, puffing on a cigarette, oblivious to the cesspool of emotion I'm drowning in. I thought I had been able to come to grips with Melanie's death. I thought I had been able to accept what had happened and go on with my life. But the de-spair is back, and it's worse than before.

"You all right, Augustus?"

We've been sitting here for five minutes in total silence. "No."

"I'm sorry you saw that photograph. *Really* sorry. I swear I didn't know it was there. I wouldn't have brought you here tonight if I had. You know that."

I don't respond. I don't know how to respond. For some period of time Melanie led a double life. She was an exotic dancer. A stripper. All along I thought it was Frank Taylor distracting her, but now I find out there was more. Much more. How am I *supposed* to respond?

"Talk to me, Augustus," Vincent pleads. "You've got to talk to me."

The worst part is that I'll never be able to ask Melanie about it. I'll never be able to find out why she'd want to hurt me like this. Maybe Vincent and the women Melanie worked with at the club will be able to shed some light on what was going on, but anything they tell me will be secondhand. I'll never know if they're telling me the truth, or just giving me some sugar-coated version they think will be less painful.

"You can't just sit there and say noth—"

"What do you know about all of this?" I snap, my voice shaking. It's Vincent's turn to go silent. "You're obviously a regular at this place."

"I don't come here that often. Once a month maybe."

"When those two guys opened the back door, they all but saluted you."

"I know the owner. They've been told to treat me right when I show up."

"So what else do you know?"

"I really don't—"

"Vincent!" If Melanie was willing to take her clothes off in front of men at a place like the Two O'Clock Club, she might have been willing to do other things. Worse things. "Tell me what you know!" The driver glances toward the limousine—he must have heard me yell even though all the windows are closed—but I don't give a rat's ass. "Tell me, dammit!"

It hits me that the Two O'Clock Club could somehow be related to Melanie's death. It isn't that far from the alley where her body was found. Maybe one of the club's regulars developed a fatal attraction to her as he watched her dance. The kind of monster you hear about on television. Maybe he finally got up the nerve to ask her out on a date after he paid her for a private dance, and when she turned him down he was so bitter he tracked her down and murdered her. I let my face fall into my hands. Or maybe she accepted the offer and when they were alone things got out of hand. Maybe being rough excited him, and he couldn't stop himself. When he was finished he dumped her body in the alley and disappeared into the night. It's horrible to have to consider these things.

"It's not what you think," Vincent says.

"How do you know what I think?"

"You think Melanie and I were having an affair," he says. "I know you do."

"Were you?"

"No," he answers firmly. "Melanie and I never slept together. That's the truth."

"Why should I believe you?"

"Because for twenty years I've always been loyal to you. I've always tried to help. What about the loan? What about the ten million you're gonna be managing soon? I've always had your best interests at heart. Down deep, you know that. You know I'd never do anything to hurt you."

I swallow hard. Reggie wanted to know if Melanie had ever performed for me. I thought it was an odd question but now I wonder. Reggie seemed to know a lot of things. Like my father's true story. He knew where I worked and I'm convinced he already knew about the insurance policy. Maybe somehow he knew she was working here too.

And maybe Vincent's more involved in everything than he's letting on.

"How did Melanie come to start working at the Two O'Clock Club?" I ask, my voice dropping to a whisper. "When did it happen?" I'm not convinced by Vincent's denial of anything. His sexual appetite is enormous, especially when he's been drinking, and I don't believe for a second he would have been able to resist Melanie if she had come on to him. No matter how much he tells me he'd never do anything to hurt me. "Tell me."

Vincent takes a deep breath. "One afternoon last fall, Melanie and I ran into each other on the Mall. She was taking a walk at lunch, and we bumped into each other in front of the Smithsonian."

"And?"

"And we got a bite to eat at an outdoor café on Seventeenth Street. It was all very innocent."

"Go on."

"We talked about normal stuff. You know, the weather, my job, her job. Then all of a sudden she starts telling me about how you guys are broke. How you're scraping to make ends meet, but it isn't working and you're falling further and further behind each month. But I already know that, right? I've already gotten the five grand for you, but I don't say anything to her about that because I know you don't want me to tell her." Vincent rubs his eyes, like he's got a headache and he wishes he could be anywhere else. "Then Mel says she's thinking about taking a second job at night. She's going to do word processing for a big law firm downtown to make nine bucks an hour. She says her boss knows a partner at the big firm and is arranging the whole thing." Vincent rubs his eyes again, harder, then exhales loudly.

I turn on the seat toward him. "And?"

He leans back and stretches his neck, as if it's stiff. He's stalling.

"Vincent."

"I told her I knew of a place where a woman with a body like hers could make a helluva lot more than nine bucks an hour."

"What? Jesus Christ!"

Vincent clenches his fists. "I was joking, for God's sake," he says quickly. "How could I have been so stupid?"

"Exactly."

"I didn't think she'd take me seriously, Augustus. I was just kidding with her because I could see how much she hated the thought of sitting at a desk, word processing until midnight. But she asked me what I meant. She wouldn't let it go."

"And?"

"And I told her."

"What did you tell her?"

"The truth. That some of the girls at this club make three to four hundred dollars on weekend nights. All cash."

"I can't believe you did this."

"She wanted me to bring her down here that night, but I

wouldn't," Vincent continues, as if that initial refusal somehow absolves him of any major guilt. "I mean, she wanted to do it right away. There was no hesitation on her part. In fact, she told me she'd always had a fantasy about being an exotic dancer." Vincent's chin drops slowly to his chest. "Like I said, I told her I was joking about the whole thing. She pestered me about it all through the rest of lunch, but I still wouldn't do it. And I didn't tell her the name of the place so she couldn't come down here on her own."

"Then how the hell did she end up here?"

"She kept calling me, Augustus. She begged me. She said Christmas was coming and she wanted to be able to buy nice things for her family and something very special for you, but she didn't have the money. She said it was tearing her apart. She swore to me that she'd only do it until she had the money she needed, and that would be it."

My "very special" gift from Melanie last Christmas was a plain sweater from JCPenney that was too small. She said she was going to return it when it didn't fit, but she never did. "So you brought her here?"

Vincent nods, regretfully. "Yes," he admits, his voice barely audible. "Like I told you, I know the guy who owns the club pretty well and he agreed to let her go onstage. He was skeptical when I told him she had no experience, but he owed me a favor." Vincent's eyes take on a distant look, and he shakes his head slowly. "It was a Tuesday night so there weren't many people here. They always start new girls on weeknights in case they get stage fright or aren't very good. But she had the guys drooling right away. I mean, they were in awe. She made two hundred bucks that night and she knew she could do even better." He clears his throat. "She enjoyed it. You could tell. She was a natural."

"You watched?"

"She asked me to come that first night because she was nervous."

"You watched her?" I ask again, incredulous. "You watched her perform?"

"I just wanted to make sure she was okay."

"My God."

"I tried to make her stop, Augustus. I swear to you. I reminded her in January that she had promised to quit after Christmas, but she wouldn't listen. She was addicted to the thrill and the money. She kept on coming. I threatened to tell you, but she didn't care."

"Why *didn't* you tell me?" I yell, ready to drag Vincent from the limo and beat him senseless. "Why?"

"I couldn't," he says. "I couldn't hurt you that way." He coughs, trying to hide his emotion. "I knew you'd think I had let you down, and I couldn't handle that. Please forgive me, Augustus. Please."

I look out the window at the driver who's still puffing on his cigarette, oblivious to my pain. I want to blame Vincent for everything, but I can't. And it isn't his plea for mercy that makes me change my mind about beating him to a bloody pulp. It's the horrible realization that the blame for all of this could just as easily be heaped on my shoulders. If I had been a success and made enough money, maybe Melanie would never have considered her double life. If I had been a better provider, then she wouldn't have needed the cash.

And no one forced Melanie up on that stage. Ultimately, it was her decision to show her body to men she didn't know. Maybe in the end it had little to do with the money anyway. Maybe it was about something else.

I feel Vincent's hand on my shoulder. "I'm sorry, buddy. I'm really sorry."

CHAPTER

14

I'm not a naive man, so how could I have gone so long without discovering what Melanie was doing? The clues were right there for me to see. Late nights two or three times a week. Crumpled cash on her bureau in the morning. Exotic perfumes. Lacy lingerie hidden deep in her bedroom closet.

I've always heard that if you're playing poker and you haven't figured out who the sucker at the table is after the first few hands, you're the sucker. I suppose Melanie, Vincent, Frank Taylor, and I were all playing a form of poker, and I turned out to be the sucker. But it feels more like we were playing Russian roulette, and I took the bullet. Of course, it was Melanie who paid the ultimate price.

I had rationalized her behavior by convincing myself that our relationship was just going through a stage that would eventually pass, but I didn't delude myself completely. In those dark moments late at night, when the phone at her office just rang and rang, I figured she must have been having an affair. But I was certain her lover was Frank Taylor. Like some jilted teenager who'd had his cheerleader girlfriend stolen away by a teammate, I did away with him dozens of times in my imagination to try to satisfy the rage, jealousy, and hatred that filled me. But of course the fantasies never satisfied me.

I should probably hate Vincent too. He's probably nothing but a damn liar and was having sex with Melanie all along. After all, he introduced her to a place where she took off her clothes for money. He probably watched her onstage lots of times, maybe even requested some of those same intimate performances I saw going on at the tables around the stage last night. But I'll never know for certain what went on between them because he'll never come clean with me. He'll swear to me until the day he dies that nothing was going on.

On nights Melanie was out late she would call most of the time to let me know when she was about to leave the office—usually around midnight. She'd call to tell me that she'd just about finished whatever menial tasks Taylor had assigned her that evening and that she'd see me in about an hour. She'd be sweet and say how much she missed me. Sometimes, especially at first, I'd mention the fact that I'd tried to call her several times during the evening. She'd explain that she had been away from her desk copying something or working in a file room, and that was why she hadn't been able to hear the phone. Now I know the truth.

When she finally made it home, she would head straight to the bathroom without a word and draw a hot bath. When she came out, she would crawl into bed, turn off the light, and roll away from me. I would caress her shoulder and try to talk to her about my unanswered calls to her office. She would tell me that she was just trying to do her part to help our financial situation, and ask how I could question her loyalty. Then she'd say she was dead tired and needed sleep, and she'd push my hand away from her warm skin. Toward the end, even on nights when she made it home at a normal time, she'd pick a fight about something trivial as soon as she walked in the door. She shut me out, until I felt completely isolated.

I thought about installing caller ID so I could check the number she was calling from on nights she was out late, but that was when my rationalization kicked in. I told myself we couldn't afford things that weren't absolutely necessary, including caller ID. Maybe down deep I didn't really want to know where she was.

Vincent and I said nothing at all to each other last night during the half-hour drive from the Two O'Clock Club to Bedford. Not even good-bye when the limousine pulled up alongside my car. An evening that had begun so well ended in disaster.

I didn't get home until after three, but I still couldn't sleep. So after two hours of tossing and turning, I got up, showered, and returned to Bedford, intent on losing myself in my work.

During the drive in I still couldn't get Melanie out of my mind. I couldn't stop imagining that scene at the Two O'Clock Club—her up on that stage with all those men watching. The absolute focus of their attention. The drunken applause as each piece of clothing came sliding slowly off her body. The wild cheers as she exposed everything.

It's a few minutes after seven in the morning as I reach for my third cup of coffee. Someone's coming down the aisle, and I look up from my computer screen and strain my neck to see who it is.

It's Daniel and he walks straight into my cubicle. He doesn't normally get in this early, but then he isn't usually trying to close on a five-thousand-dollar loan.

"Morning," he says quietly.

Without answering I take one more sip of coffee, then place the mug down and reach across the desk for my checkbook. It's a miracle I remembered to bring it with me this morning, but I try to honor my commitments.

"There's no need for that, Augustus."

I glance up curiously from the check I've already half scrawled. "I told you I'd lend you the money, Daniel. I won't back out of our agreement. My word's good."

"I appreciate that, but it's all right," he says, a resigned smile coming to his face. As if he's lost a battle, but defeat hasn't turned out to be so bad. "I don't need the loan anymore."

"What happened? Did Seaver cut you a break?"

"No, nothing like that. Seaver's a shark. He'll be coming to my cubicle sometime this morning for his money."

"Then how did you work things out?"

"I took your advice. I called my father last night after I got home and had a chance to sober up." Daniel sighs. "That's the hardest call I've ever had to make. I had to admit that maybe I wasn't as smart as I thought I was. Then I told him I needed the cash."

"And he agreed to give it to you?"

"He did when I told him I'd made a very bad mistake leaving Georgetown, and that if he were still willing to pay my tuition, I'd go back this fall and finish my degree. I started to tell him that I'd understand if he didn't want to shell out the cash, but he said not to worry. He didn't even make me beg like I thought he would. He went pretty easy on me."

"I'm glad."

"It's been a long time since he and I have talked like that," Daniel says quietly. "About things that matter. It feels good to know I have someone I can count on when I really need help."

I always wanted that kind of relationship with my father. Maybe I at least helped Daniel find it.

He shakes my hand. "I needed somebody to knock some sense into me, Augustus. I was acting like an idiot," he says. "Thanks."

"Sure." I can tell by the way he looks me straight in the eye that he's learned something important over the past twenty-four hours.

He's about to go but hesitates. "You okay, Augustus?"

"Yeah, why?"

"You look beat."

"Nah, I'm fine."

He hesitates by my desk a moment longer, then heads for his own cubicle.

I remember that my phone is still forwarded to voice mail, so I switch it back, then check for messages. There's only one—the one that came yesterday afternoon. As I listen to it, I forget everything. My despair, my exhaustion, my satisfaction over helping Daniel. My breath quickens, I grip the phone tightly, and I hunch over my desk. Suddenly I'm numb.

The message is from a man named Scott Snyder who says he's representing the Great Western Insurance Company and he's calling in regard to the death of Melanie McKnight. Snyder's got a deep voice and speaks with what sounds like a Brooklyn wiseguy accent. He says the insurance company won't send me the death benefit proceeds until he's had a chance to sit down with me and ask a few questions. He tries to use nonthreatening language while he goes into detail about slayer statutes and being unable to check appropriate boxes on the insurance claim until we meet. But the tone of his voice makes me think he might as well be telling me he's going to hack off my fingers with an ax if I don't tell him exactly what he wants to hear.

Snyder leaves a number for me to call at the end of his message, and I have to keep replaying the message to make certain I've written the numbers correctly because he races through the digits like he's double-parked. When I hang up the receiver, I'm sweating like mad. I've had too much caffeine this morning.

Mary arrives around nine and leans over the cubicle partition to talk as soon as she's put her pocketbook down. "I'm looking forward to dinner tonight," she says. "This restaurant is supposed to be very nice. It's been written up in the *Post* a few times and gotten great reviews."

I'd forgotten all about her invitation. I'm in no mood to chaperone her anywhere, and in fairness to both of us, I'd be terrible company. "Mary, I think I'm coming down with something, and I just want to go home tonight right after work and sleep it off. Would you mind if I took a rain check?"

"You'll be fine by this afternoon," she says confidently. "We'll have lots of fun." With that she's off to the ladies' room, giving me no chance to argue.

Just before the nine-thirty opening a number of large technology companies report lousy quarterly earnings and the markets crater at the bell. The Wall Street gurus have been predicting bad news for several days, and when it actually hits, the reaction is devastating. Within five minutes the Nasdaq is off two hundred points and the Bedford trading floor has turned to chaos. As if a switch has been flipped, people are suddenly screaming and cursing at the top of their lungs. The noise level is three times its normal volume.

Slammer didn't make it to his desk until just minutes before the opening bell—which is unusual—and he's totally unprepared for the disaster. Over the partition it sounds like a barroom brawl. He shouts and repeatedly kicks a metal trash can beneath his desk. He didn't close out all of his long positions last night, and the prices of those stocks have dropped off the table this morning with the negative earnings reports. The bid sides of his positions are falling at terminal velocity, and he can't find the rip cords on their parachutes.

"Jesus freaking Christ!" he shouts, hurling what sounds like a stapler across his desk. "This is a joke!"

"Having fun this morning, Slammer?" I ask through the partition.

I realize that my comment may spark a volcanic reaction, but I don't care. I'm in no mood for his attitude.

"Screw you, Gussie," comes the response. "You piece of shit."

Like a rocket, I'm out of my chair and on my feet. "I warned you, Slammer," I shout, bolting out of my cubicle toward his. Above the chaos on the trading floor, I hear Mary scream at me to stop, and in my peripheral vision I see Roger and Daniel leap up from their chairs. But I'm laser-locked on the short man with the crewcut who has been the bane of my Bedford existence, and everything else blurs around me as I sprint toward him.

My self-control has finally and completely evaporated. I've been trying to deal calmly with the fact that my murdered wife has turned out to be a total stranger, but I can't stop myself from erupting at this little prick who can't keep his damn mouth shut. No one could blame me for this, I think to myself as adrenaline pumps through me at the prospect of a fight I realize I've wanted since the beginning. We'll see what kind of Army Ranger training Slammer really has. I'm going to rip him limb from limb. I'm going to smash his face into his computer monitor. I'm going to make him pay for what Melanie has done to me.

As I race around the corner of his cubicle, I see Slammer reach into his briefcase and smoothly draw from it the huge .44 Magnum revolver that Mary was absolutely certain didn't exist. He points the barrel directly at my chest, and I freeze, six feet away from him. I've never had a gun aimed at me before, and it's an amazingly sobering experience. What impresses me most is how calmly he produces the shiny silver weapon with the black handle—like an experienced gunslinger drawing from his holster. He isn't fast or slow, just silky smooth. He times it so the weapon comes into view exactly as I enter his cubicle. As if he doesn't want me to realize what he's doing until I reach his cubicle because I might be able to turn away and escape if I see what's happening too soon. But now I can't move. My shoes are glued to the floor because the crazy-calm expression on his face tells me he's capable of anything.

"What are you going to do now, Gus?" Slammer cocks the .44, then waves it menacingly at Mary, Roger, and Daniel in turn. "Don't move," he warns each of them. Then the barrel is back on me.

I'm vaguely aware of people rushing for the trading floor exits. They're shrieking and shouting and climbing all over one another to get out. I glance over at Mary and she's sitting at her desk, back ramrod straight, hands over her mouth, unable to move. Roger and Daniel look like freeze-frames with their arms held oddly away from their bodies and their eyes wide.

"Put the gun down," I plead.

"Screw you!" comes his loud response.

"Nothing good can come of this if you keep going," I say. "But if you stop now, it's no big deal. We can forget it happened."

"How can I make certain you'll *never* forget it happened?"

For several seconds I say nothing, carefully considering my response. "I didn't mean that I won't remember," I answer respectfully. "I will. You've made your point."

Slammer's eyes dart quickly to the right, and he waves the gun at Roger, whose hands are dropping slowly to his sides. "Get 'em back up!" he shouts.

Immediately Roger raises his arms back to where they were. It's as if Slammer can see in all directions right now. Maybe I *have* underestimated him. Maybe he really does have extensive military training, and Mary was dead wrong about him exaggerating his capabilities. After all, she was dead wrong about the gun.

"What *did* you mean?" he asks me.

"I meant that there's been no real harm done yet. You've scared the crap out of us and made your point. I shouldn't have said what I said, and I shouldn't have come at you the way I did. I was wrong. I apologize. Now we can get on with our day as if nothing happened and make some money."

Slammer laughs loudly. "Do you really believe that?"

The trading floor has fallen strangely still. There's still a commotion coming from outside the swinging doors at the far end of the room, but other than the five of us, everyone else has made it into the lobby. "Believe what?"

"That at this point we could get on with our day as if nothing really happened."

"Yes," I reply, forcing conviction into my voice, "I do."

"Then you're delusional or, more likely, lying. You might be able to go on with *your* day, but they're going to cart me out of here in handcuffs. Or a straitjacket. Hell, I'll be lucky to ever get out of the psycho ward they commit me to." Slammer's eyes narrow. "I've been in a place like that before. It's no fun, and I ain't going back."

Mary lets out a muffled sob and Slammer levels the gun at her. She shrieks and I take a step toward him, but he turns the .44 back on me and once again I freeze.

"So what'll it be, Gus?" he demands.

My heart feels like it's going to explode, it's beating so fast. "What are you talking about?" I can't believe how calm Slammer is. It's as if he's been down this road before.

"What will leave a permanent impression of this day on your brain?"

"You showing mercy."

"Good answer," he says in a friendly voice, smiling as if we're playing a harmless board game, "but not good enough. I've lost fifty thousand dollars in the past two months. Everything I had. A few minutes ago I said good-bye to my last dime, so I think you can understand why I'm not feeling very merciful at this moment." His voice turns even tougher. "In fact, I'm feeling like I really want to hurt somebody. Like I want someone else to suffer too."

"Let's talk about it. I understand your pain."

"Don't give me that shit, Gus. You don't want to talk about anything with me, and you don't have any idea about my pain. You just want to get your sorry ass out of this situation in one piece. Once you've gotten this gun away from me you'll turn me over to the cops and that'll be that. I'm not stupid."

"No, you aren't," I agree quickly.

"Don't patronize me."

"Sorry."

"So, what'll it be?" he asks again, raising the weapon slightly so that it's pointed at my face.

Sweat is pouring from my body, and I wonder how a .44-caliber Magnum shell would feel ripping through my skull. I only hope his aim is good so I don't suffer too much. "I don't know."

"Then I'll have to make the decision myself." Slammer swings the gun away from me, points it directly at Daniel, and pulls the trigger without hesitation. Daniel doesn't even have a chance to react. The bullet hits him square in the middle of his chest with an awful thud, propelling him violently back against his cubicle wall, which collapses under his weight. He sprawls on the floor, grabbing his chest and struggling for breath. He makes a gurgling noise, then his body goes completely still. It's all over before any of us can even move.

I gaze at Daniel's body while Slammer scrambles over the wall into Mary's cubicle, grabs her roughly by the hair, and jerks her to her feet. Then he shoves the gun barrel against her ear. "Get to the conference room!" he shouts at Roger and me, motioning toward the room off the trading floor where less than a week ago I agreed to be Roger's mentor. In the wake of the gunshot Slammer's cool has vaporized, replaced by sheer panic.

"Don't do this, Max," I plead, avoiding the nickname he hates as I stare down at the horrible expression on Daniel's lifeless face. I hear shouts from the lobby outside the swinging doors at the far end of the aisle, but I can't take my gaze from Daniel's open, unseeing eyes. An expanding puddle of dark blood is spreading out on the carpet beneath him. The wound in his chest is massive. The bullet must have gone straight through him. "Let Mary go, Max. Please."

"Get in the conference room!" he yells wildly. "Get moving or I'll shoot her too! Right before I blow both of you away."

"My God," Roger whispers as he moves unsteadily out of his cubicle, his lip curling as he glances at Daniel's body. "He's going to kill us all."

"Shut up!" Slammer shouts, roughly pushing Mary ahead of him. He waves the gun at Roger, then me. "Move it!"

Roger and I stagger ahead of Mary. She's begging for her life. Slammer pulls her hair back tightly so she has to look up at the ceiling and can't see where she's going as he forces her ahead.

"Let her go, Max," I say over my shoulder. "Please."

"Shut the hell up! Now get in there!" he orders as we near the conference room doorway. "Get inside."

When the four of us are inside, Slammer pushes Mary farther ahead of him, then slams the door shut. Now we can't see what's happening out on the trading floor. We're totally cut off.

"Sit down over there," Slammer orders. He indicates exactly where he wants us to go as he trots quickly to the conference room windows and lowers the blinds. "Come on, move it! On the floor."

We sit side by side on the floor in the corner farthest from the door, as Slammer directs. He hustles back to the door, squats down, grabs a brown rubber jamb, and wedges it between the bottom of the door and the carpet. He stands up slowly, gun pointed at the door. "No one's coming in or leaving until I say so," he mutters.

"What are you going to do now?" I ask. "There's nowhere to run."

"Don't talk to him," Mary cries, grasping my arm tightly. I'm sitting in the corner and she's between Roger and me. "For God's sake, don't provoke him," she pleads. "He's lost his mind, can't you see that?"

Slammer's gaze snaps from the door to her. "You think I've lost my mind, huh, Sassy?"

Mary hunches down against the wall and shields her face, realizing that she's made a terrible mistake. "No, no, I don't. I'm sorry," she whimpers. I can hear sirens wailing in the background. "Please get me out of this alive," she whispers to me. "I don't want to die."

"If you don't shut up, you'll be the first one to go," Slammer warns her.

"Oh, God." She buries her face in my arm.

Slammer walks slowly around the table until he's standing directly in front of us. "Get up," he says to her.

"No, please."

"Don't do this to her!" I yell so loudly my vocal cords feel like they'll snap.

"Shut up!" he yells back, waving the gun wildly.

For fifteen seconds we stare at each other until finally he reaches down—gun pointed directly into my face—grabs Mary by her hair again, and brutally yanks her to her feet. She screams in pain as he hurls her against the far wall. As I instinctively scramble to stand up, he points the .44 at me and fires twice. Two searing blasts thunder past my left ear. For a moment I'm completely deaf and feel like I've been sent into a kind of suspended animation where everything is happening in slow motion. Then I tumble to the floor, hands over my ears, fearing the worst. But in the seconds after the gunshots I realize I'm not hit. There are two holes pocking the wall above me, but I have no pain other than a sharp ache in one ear, and I'm still conscious. For some reason, Slammer wasn't trying to hit me, just terrify me. He was five feet away when he fired, and I know he could easily have killed me.

I glance over at Roger. He has turned toward the wall on his knees and covered his face with his hands, cowering. He'll be no help if I see a chance to make a break for Slammer and try to wrestle the gun away. His true colors are shining through—as everyone's do when the chips are down.

Mary screams, and my eyes flash back to the far corner where Slammer has her pressed face first against the wall, the end of the .44's barrel moving slowly along her cheek toward her mouth.

"Why don't you like me, Sassy?" Slammer demands.

"I do like you," she sobs. "I do."

"No, you don't," he hisses, his upper lip quivering as he tries to pry her clenched teeth open with the gun. "Open your mouth," he orders.

"No, no, Max, please!" she begs, metal scraping her teeth. She turns her face away, but he forces her back to where he wants her. "Why are you doing this to me?" she asks pitifully. Still he slides the barrel roughly past her lips and down her throat.

"Stop it!" I yell, my voice sounding faraway because I haven't fully recovered my hearing. I know the violent reaction my shout may cause, but I can't help it. I can't watch this. "Max! Look at me!"

He pulls the silver barrel from Mary's lips, points the gun at me from across the room, and fires again. Another bullet blows past and I throw myself to the floor, hands over my head. Roger whimpers a few feet away, moaning that he just wants to see his wife and children again. Roger Junior and Alicia—he cries their names softly, over and over.

I peer between my fingers and see that Slammer has spun Mary around so that she's facing him now. Her back is pressed to the wall, the gun just a few inches from her mouth. She's sobbing uncontrollably and her cheeks are smeared with mascara.

"Why do you like Gus so much?" Slammer demands.

But Mary's sobs are so powerful she can't speak. She's fighting for air as tears rush down her face, and she just shakes her head.

"Goddamn it!" he roars. "Answer me!"

But she still can't produce words. Her chest is heaving too violently.

Slammer slowly pulls the hammer of the gun back and cocks it.

"Please," she's finally able to moan. "Please don't. I'm begging you."

Slammer's upper lip quivers, and he turns his head slightly to the side as he aims the .44 directly at her face.

I get ready for another deafening roar and the horror that will cover the wall behind Mary after the bullet tears through her head. Just as I'm sure Slammer is about to pull the trigger, his lip stops quivering and he slowly lowers the gun and uncocks the hammer. A moment later he turns and strides quickly to a phone on top of a credenza near the conference room door. "Come here, Gus," he orders.

I scramble up off the floor and hurry toward him so he doesn't have time to think about going back after Mary.

"Slow down," he warns, backing away from the credenza and training the gun on me as I approach. "Call the lobby and get Seaver on the phone," he demands.

"Right away, Max." I pick up the receiver and dial zero, not expecting anyone to answer. If they're smart, everyone at Bedford has gotten out of the building and they've warned people on the other floors to do the same thing.

But someone at the other end picks up the phone on the first ring. "Who is this?" a male voice demands.

"This is Augustus McKnight. I'm calling from the conference room at the back corner of the trading floor."

There's a slight pause. Whoever answered put his hand over the mouthpiece and is talking to someone else in the background. It occurs to me that the police may have already made it to the scene and taken up strategic positions in the Bedford lobby. Perhaps tactical units are crawling through the trading floor toward us right now, though that seems unlikely as I think about it. It's been only a few minutes since Slammer shot Daniel, and it seems more likely that the police would try to negotiate with a gunman before storming in. Especially when they know he has hostages.

"What was your name again?" the voice asks. The background noise grows louder when he removes his hand from the mouthpiece.

"Augustus McKnight," I repeat slowly. "Who is this?"

There's another muffled silence, but the man is back to me quickly this time. "This is Officer Grant of the Fairfax County police department. Is Maxwell Frasier with you?"

"Yes," I answer, not making eye contact with Slammer.

"What's going on back there?" the officer demands. "We've been advised that there were shots fired. Are you all right?"

"I'm fine. We're all fine." I don't want to say anything about Daniel because I don't want Slammer to hear me tell someone on the outside that there's been a killing. It might make him even more desperate if he realizes the police know he's a murderer.

"But there were gunshots," the officer says. "Confirm that for me."

"Yes there were, but—"

"Get Seaver," Slammer hisses.

"We need Michael Seaver on the line," I say, making certain not to address the man as "officer." "He's the owner of Bedford and Associates."

"How many people are in that room?" the officer asks, ignoring me. "Four."

"Get Seaver!" Slammer shouts at the top of his lungs.

"Please get Seaver," I urge.

"All right, all right," comes the response. The officer has heard Slammer's frantic tone.

There's a flurry of activity and shouting at the other end of the line, then the officer is back. "It's going to take a few minutes to patch Seaver in. The building's been evacuated, and we'll need to find him outside."

"They're looking for him," I tell Slammer. "The building has been evacuated."

"Who are you talking to?" he asks suspiciously.

"Fairfax police," I answer. I can't lie to him at this point.

"Let me talk to Mr. Frasier," the officer requests.

I hold the receiver out toward Slammer. "They want to talk to you."

"Not a chance," he says, pointing the gun at the receiver and taking a step back. "You talk."

"Mr. Frasier doesn't want to speak to you," I reply. "I'll be the spokesman during this, and he wants Mr. Seaver on the line now."

"I told you, we're looking for him," the officer says. "It's going to take time to find him. Mr. Frasier is going to have to be patient. Now tell me who else is back there with you and Mr. Frasier."

I look over at Slammer. "They want to know who's back here," I relay to him, trying to build a psychological bridge. "Should I tell them?"

"No!"

"I'm sorry, I can't give you that information."

"Has anyone been hurt?" Grant asks.

"Everyone in here is fine," I answer calmly.

Slammer nods his approval as he listens. I was right. He doesn't want them to know about Daniel, which may mean he's trying to get himself out of this thing alive. At least he isn't planning some murder-suicide situation where he's going to take all of us with him, then turn the gun on himself as the police are breaking down the door. Not yet, anyway.

A couple of minutes later Seaver comes onto the line. He's being connected from somewhere downstairs, the officer informs me.

"Hello."

"Seaver?"

"Yes?"

"This is Augustus McKnight." I can hear the officer breathing heavily into the phone.

"Are you all right?" he asks, his voice shaky.

"I'm fine."

"Is that Seaver?" Slammer demands.

I nod.

"Tell him I want all my money back in fifteen minutes or Mary takes a bullet to the head. It comes to fifty grand. All the money I've lost to this rip-off operation he runs. I swear I'll kill her if he doesn't do exactly what I say."

At Slammer's direction, Mary has taken a seat beside Roger on the floor, and I can hear her whimper at Slammer's threat. "Did you hear the demand, Seaver?" I ask.

"I heard it," he replies grimly. "But I can't get fifty thousand dollars together in fifteen minutes. That's simply impossible."

"He says it's going to take some time," I relay.

"Then the woman's going to die," Slammer shouts, leaning close to the mouthpiece so Seaver can hear. He raises the gun and shoots at the ceiling, and I dive to the floor, dropping the phone. "You motherfuckers!"

I grab the phone again as I lie prone on the floor, and Roger and Mary hold on tightly to each other. "Did you hear that?" I gasp.

"Is everyone all right?" the officer yells. "Jesus!"

"I can get some of the money quickly!" Seaver promises. "Maybe ten thousand."

"He says he can get ten thousand right away, Max."

"No! It's fifty right away or she dies." Slammer leans down and grabs the phone from me. "Listen to me, you slimy son of a bitch! You get me that money. You go to your bank and get me the money, or I'm going to kill this woman and throw her body out the window so all of those people down on the street can watch. You get me fifty thousand dollars. No, make it a hundred grand to make up for all the pain and suffering you and your damn day trading firm have put me through. Do you understand? A hundred thousand. Send one person in here with it in a bag. They knock on the conference room door, then they leave it outside and run! Got it? Fifteen minutes, Seaver, or you'll see her body come flying out the window!" With that, he holds the receiver out away from his body, aims the gun at it, and pulls the trigger. Instantly the phone disintegrates into a hundred tiny pieces. "Think he got the message?" Slammer asks, staring down at me wild-eyed with what's left of the phone still shaking in his hand.

"Yeah," I mutter. "I think he got it."

"Please don't kill me, Max," Mary whines. "Please."

Slammer pays no attention to her. "Get back over there with the others, Gus."

Slowly I pick myself up off the floor and move to Roger and Mary. I kneel down beside her, taking her shaking hand in mine. "It's all right. Calm down. Everything will be fine."

"He's going to kill me," Mary sobs. "I've never done anything to him. Why is he going to do this to me?"

I shake my head and smile. "He isn't going to do anything to you, Mary. He isn't going to do anything to anybody."

After I say this I stand up again. "What are you doing? Be careful, Augustus," she warns.

"Sit down!" Slammer shouts.

I turn toward him. "Give me the gun, Slammer."

He laughs incredulously. "Shut up."

"Give me the gun," I repeat calmly.

"Go to hell."

"It's over, Max."

"It's far from over," he snaps angrily. "In a few minutes they're going to bring me a hundred thousand dollars, and I'm going to walk out of here with a human shield around me."

"No," I say, taking a step toward him, "you're not."

He raises the gun and points it at my face. "Take one more step and I'll kill you."

"No, you won't."

"God help me, I will."

"Then do it," I dare him, taking another deliberate step toward him and holding my arms out to my sides. "Come on."

"Don't tempt me, Gus. I've already killed one man. I won't hesitate to kill you."

As I take another step forward, he aims the gun directly at my chest, but I keep going.

"No, Augustus!" Mary screams.

Slammer pulls the trigger and the hammer falls. But there's only a sharp metallic click. Nothing else.

I lunge the last few feet between us, grab him, and pull him to the ground, beating his wrist mercilessly against the floor until the gun flies from his hand. Instantly Mary scrambles to her feet and bolts for the door, followed a split second later by Roger.

Slammer lands a nice right cross to my jaw that stuns me momentarily and he's able to push me away. As he tries to make it to his feet, I grab his lower leg and trip him, sending him hard to the floor. Mary and Roger are racing toward the lobby and in seconds this place will be crawling with cops. He must realize it's over. He must realize that his freedom can now be measured in seconds.

Slammer makes it to his feet again, but instead of chasing after Mary and Roger, he turns and stares intently at me for several seconds. Then he spins to his left, runs toward the window at a full sprint, and leaps, crashing through the glass and plunging toward the cement nine floors down.

CHAPTER

15

It's been six hours and what seems like an ocean of scotch since Slammer committed suicide by crashing through the Bedford window. Nine stories down with nothing but unforgiving pavement below. I heard from another Bedford trader who saw the whole thing from the street that it was a gruesome sight when his body hit the sidewalk. The guy started to describe the bloody impact once more for one of several television crews who had flocked to the scene, but I turned away when the red light above the camera lit up and the reporter began firing questions. I couldn't listen to the horrible details.

Slammer was never my friend, but I couldn't help thinking that I was the one who had set him off. If I hadn't charged into his cubicle and challenged him the way I did, he wouldn't have pulled the gun, wouldn't have murdered Daniel, and wouldn't have taken his own life.

I can try to make myself feel better by thinking about how people have to accept accountability for their own actions. I know that Slammer was ultimately responsible for everything that happened this morning, but I was the match that lit the fuse. That single fact is indisputable, and it torments me.

After all these drinks it still seems like it was only minutes ago that Slammer took one last look at me—a look equal parts desperation and terror—and hurtled through the window. Desperation because he felt there was no other choice. Terror, I believe, not of the mind-numbing plunge and that momentary physical suffering he was about to endure, but of what lay beyond. As we locked eyes for that split second, it seemed to me that he was petrified of what he might find. He hadn't made peace with himself, which must be a terrible way to go.

The ice cubes in my glass rattle as I lift them to my lips. My hands are still shaking, and I plan on drinking until they stop. Maybe the police will pull me over on the way home and force me to spend the night behind bars, but I won't care. In fact, I may ask them to lock me up.

"You were so brave, Augustus," Mary says, sipping her fourth glass of white wine. She sits beside me in a comfortable booth at a dark bar a few miles from Bedford where she, Roger, and I have taken refuge to try to deal with what's happened. Mary and I are alone for the moment while Roger visits the men's room. "I couldn't believe it when you walked straight at Max while he was pointing the gun at you." One of her hands is resting on my leg. "For the first time in my life I really thought I was going to die. You saved my life, Augustus."

"I wasn't that brave," I mutter. "That was a six-shot revolver, and I knew when I approached him that he was out of bullets. He'd fired all six rounds. The one that killed Daniel, three at me, one into the ceiling, and one that blew up the phone." I recount the shots as if by rote, my voice a low monotone.

I must be in shock, or maybe I'm just exhausted, because I haven't been able to show much emotion—except for my trembling hands—since moving slowly to the window to gaze nine stories down at Slammer's body lying crumpled on the pavement. While I watched, the people on the ground rushed to where he lay, forming an ever-expanding circle around his body. As I stood there and looked down through the shattered window, its broken blind hanging limply by one bolt, a warm wind rushing past my face, I wondered what Melanie was thinking as she lay in that alley, her throat slashed wide open, her life ebbing away. She was probably conscious for twenty or thirty seconds after the attack, unable to move or speak as her blood pressure plummeted. I wondered if she experienced any kind of freedom as the physical pain subsided and the inevitable overtook her. Freedom from the day-to-day concerns and insecurities that rule us all, and sometimes make our lives hell, whether we admit it or not. I've often wondered whether there is that final freedom.

I actually placed one foot up on the windowsill as I looked down at Slammer's body so far below me. I was about to pull the other leg up, but then the police poured into the room, guns drawn, and they were all over me, guiding me to a chair to make certain I was unharmed.

I don't know why I stepped up onto the sill like that. I've never come close to committing suicide, never even considered it. But suddenly it seemed like I was standing in the middle of a railroad track in the dead of night as a speeding train bore down on me, whistle blaring and brakes shrieking as the engineer tried to stop it. I was frozen in its headlight until an unseen force pushed me out of the way at the last second, and the train raced past. That's what it was like this morning. I could feel the rush of wind as death swept right past me. Then there were cops all around me, asking me where the gun was, and I couldn't tell them.

I wonder if I would have taken that last step if they hadn't burst into the room when they did. For the first time in my life I was ready for that final freedom.

"And you didn't even go right at Slammer after he fired the last time," Mary continues.

"I knew I could get to him before he had a chance to reload," I explain. "There was no reason to rush."

"You are *so* brave," she says for the tenth time. "How in the world did you have the presence of mind to count the number of shots? I couldn't have even told you my name, I was so scared in there."

"I don't know," I answer honestly. It wasn't as if I was counting all along. The fact that Slammer was out of bullets hit me out of nowhere when the phone blew apart in his hand. Something snapped, and I realized it was over. "I just wish there could have been another way," I murmur.

The strange thing about the whole ordeal was that I never felt like I was in any real physical danger, even when Slammer first leveled the gun at me in his cubicle. I thought about how it might feel if the bullet tore into me, but I wasn't frightened.

"Max Frasier was an evil man," Mary says with conviction. "The world is better off without him. He murdered poor Daniel."

"Maybe we are better off without him," I agree, "but the thing is, if I hadn't reacted the way I did, going into his cubicle and confronting him, Daniel wouldn't be dead. He'd be sitting right here with us, looking forward to his senior year at Georgetown. Looking forward to the rest of his life."

"You can't blame yourself for that." Mary takes her hand off my thigh. "Slammer was a time bomb. Anything could have set him off. I feel bad for Daniel, but on another day it could have been any one of us. Next week Slammer might have walked into Bedford and tried to kill everyone on the entire floor. You just don't know."

I finish what's left of my scotch. "Maybe," I agree quietly, wiping my mouth with the back of my hand. "But that doesn't make what happened any easier to deal with."

Roger returns from the men's room and slides onto the bench seat across from Mary and me. For a few moments he says nothing, silently contemplating his glass, then he looks up. "I still can't believe what happened this morning, can you? I mean, we could all be dead right now."

I found out during the ordeal that Roger is a complete coward. He's a spineless jellyfish, which, I suppose, a lot of sarcastic people are. I learned something else too. He's a liar. Maybe there's nothing significant to the fact that the life he's portrayed is a sham, but I'm going to find out just to be on the safe side.

"Without Augustus, who knows what would have happened?" Mary says. "We might all be dead. He's our hero."

"Yeah, right." Roger rolls his eyes and picks up his glass of beer. "Sure he is," he scoffs.

"What's your problem?" she asks.

"Augustus said it himself," Roger answers, glancing at me. "He knew Slammer was out of bullets. Augustus wasn't looking death in the eye when he went for the gun."

The waitress appears at the table with our next round of drinks. Before she has a chance to serve us, I grab my fresh glass from her tray and bring it straight to my lips. Roger's acting like what I did in the conference room was nothing, and I know why. All cowards act that way. They try to convince themselves after the fact that they weren't scared, and that what another person did wasn't any big deal. I'm not upset that Roger isn't kissing my ass for saving him. That's not it at all. I just hate it when people try to fool themselves. Even more than when they try to fool others.

"Did you know that the gun was empty, Roger?" Mary asks.

"Sure I did. Augustus just got to him first." Roger glances at me. "You know, I've been thinking. We should sue Michael Seaver," he says, changing the subject. "He has some liability for what happened today."

"How's that?" I ask.

"He should have known Slammer was dangerous."

"How could he have known that?"

"Hell, I don't know," Roger says, frustrated with me for not jumping on his bandwagon. "Maybe he should have been out on the trading floor more often to oversee what was going on, not holed up in his office figuring out who was late on their monthly payments. Maybe he should have offered a training program before letting anyone trade. I'm sure an attorney could tell us more about that. I, for one, plan to explore my legal options. Even if it's a quick settlement of fifty or a hundred thousand bucks, I'm going to pursue it."

"Don't stoop to that level," I say. "Maybe Seaver ought to be more diligent about what happens on the trading floor, but let it go. Be glad you're alive, and give Roger Junior and Alexis an extra special hug when you get home."

"I agree," Mary chimes in. "Let it go."

"Oh, I'll hug them all right," he says, "but I'm not going to miss a golden opportunity to make some money either."

"Write a book about what happened or sell TV movie rights."

At my suggestion his long neck all but disappears as his head sinks down between his shoulders. "Nah."

"Why not?"

"I'm not the Hollywood type," he says, sliding out of the booth and standing up. "I'm getting out of here. See you two later."

"Roger," I call after him.

He's already a few unsteady strides from the table. He had seven beers while we sat here. "What is it?" he asks, seemingly irritated that he's had to stop and turn around.

"What year did you graduate from the University of Maryland?"

"Pardon me?" he asks after a few seconds.

I know he heard me. He's trying to figure out why I asked the question. "You told me you went to the University of Maryland and I was just curious about what year you graduated. Like I told you before, I have some friends who went there. If it turns out they were there around the same time, I want to see if they remember you."

"Maryland's a big school," he answers. "I'm sure I wouldn't have known any of your friends."

"You never know."

"I do," Roger says flatly, turning to go.

"One more thing."

"What?" he snaps.

"You told me you worked at the Department of Energy before coming to Bedford, right?"

"Yeah. So what?"

"What area did you say you worked in again?"

Roger forces a thin smile. "Look, I'm tired and I'm going home. It's been a terrible day. I'll see you both later." He stalks off without another word.

"What was that all about?" Mary asks when he's gone.

"Just curious about a few things," I answer, guzzling scotch as I look into her eyes. It's four o'clock in the afternoon, the world is spinning, and she's looking better and better to me. The last time Melanie and I had sex there was snow on the ground, and I'm desperate to feel that wonderful sensation of a woman wrapped around me again.

"Those questions were kind of out of nowhere."

"I guess, but given how much I've had to drink in the past couple of hours," I say, holding up my glass and smiling, "I don't think I can be held responsible for my words or my actions." I give her a long look.

"I love those green eyes of yours," she says softly, gazing back at me the same way. "I've always wanted eyes like that. Can I have them?"

"It'll cost you."

She inches closer to me on the seat and puts her hand on my thigh again. "How much? I have a lot more to spend thanks to you and Teletekk." She squeezes my leg seductively.

"I wasn't thinking money." The alcohol is leading me toward a slippery slope.

"What *were* you thinking?" Mary takes her hand from my leg, turns toward me, and puts her elbow on my shoulder so that our faces are very close. "Hmm?"

Suddenly I get the feeling that Mary is a tigress in bed. I don't have much experience to back up my hunch, but I've listened to Vincent tell me for years how every once in a while he'll coax a divorcée of a certain age into bed. Divorced women know what men want, he claims, and they'll do whatever it takes to please you, as opposed to the twenty-two-year-old with the perfect body who knows every man in the place wants her. Vincent says divorcées are more willing to look at sex like men do—like an amusement park ride. A wild time with no commitment. As I look at Mary, I try hard to convince myself that she falls into that category.

"Tell me," she whispers.

"I don't know," I say, taking a deep breath and looking down into my drink. Suddenly I feel the same way I did at lunch when I told her about Teletekk. Even though the tip turned out very well for her, I didn't know it would at the time. I was telling her about it just to make myself feel better. And I know that's why I'd have sex with her.

She runs her fingers through my hair, gives me a little smile, then backs off. She must have glimpsed the telltale reluctance in my expression. Or maybe it was guilt. "So why the fascination with Roger? Why all the questions?"

I take another sip of scotch before answering, carefully considering how much I should tell her. "I don't think Roger is who he says he is."

"I beg your pardon?"

I'm going to take a calculated risk—though, given how drunk I am, I don't know how *well* calculated. "I don't think he's really married and I don't think he has any children. I doubt he ever attended the University of Maryland," I continue, "and I'm certain he didn't work at the Department of Energy before showing up at Bedford."

Mary raises her eyebrows. "I didn't even know he claimed to have been at the Department of Energy before he came to Bedford. I saw the pictures of his wife and children in his cubicle, but—"

"Those aren't his children."

"How do you know?"

"He told me his daughter's name was Alice a few days ago. When he thought Slammer was going to kill him in the conference room he moaned about never seeing Alicia again. You just heard me call her Alexis a minute ago."

"I think you're reading too much into that," Mary says firmly. "Roger probably had no idea what he was even saying in the conference room. And maybe Alicia is his daughter's nickname. For all his talk about being ready to go at Slammer himself, I don't think Roger is a very brave man." She moves close again. "And maybe he didn't hear you when you said Alexis," she adds.

"His name isn't Roger either." This gets her attention.

"Really? How do you know?"

"I saw his driver's license."

"When?"

"He and I went to dinner last Monday, after his first day at Bedford. After the markets closed I helped him set up his Trader One, then we went over a few of the basics. He took me to dinner as thanks."

"And he told you his name wasn't Roger at dinner?"

"No."

"Then how did you find out?"

I hesitate. "While we were there, he got up to go to the men's room, and his wallet fell out of his pocket. I picked it up, and while he was gone I looked at his driver's license. I just wanted to see what he looked like in his picture." I laugh, trying to convince her that my intent wasn't to pry. "Those pictures never turn out well, you know?"

She nods. "I know. Mine's terrible."

"Well, he looked a little different in the picture. His hair was different and he didn't have a beard. He looked a lot younger too, but I could still tell it was him. Anyway, the name on the license wasn't Roger Smith."

"What was it?"

"John Embry." I take a deep breath. "It was an Ohio license that had expired ten years ago."

"How strange."

"And neither name shows up on the University of Maryland's computer list of past students. I called and asked."

"Really?"

I lean forward and run my finger around the rim of my glass. "Roger keeps asking me for details about an inheritance I told him I'm about to come into. He's asked me about it five times if he's asked me once."

"Maybe he's just trying to be friendly. He's not the most gifted conversationalist. . . ."

"I don't know," I answer as her voice trails off.

I look away, trying hard to resist the temptation of asking Mary to come home with me. I can only imagine how awkward it could be when she realizes I have no long-term interest in her, and we still have to work side by side. For all I know Vincent's theory about divorced women being more casual about sex is totally wrong. It seems to me they ought to be even *more* careful.

"Have you ever noticed that Roger wears a toupee?" I ask.

"Sure. It's so obvious."

"Really?"

"Yup."

"I didn't notice until somebody pointed it out to me."

"That's probably why his hair looked different in the picture on his license. It was probably thinner, right?"

"That's right."

"Women pick up on things like that more quickly than men. I think we're more observant about our surroundings." She smiles coyly. "So, how big is that inheritance of yours?"

"Just a token from a distant relative."

"Oh."

"You want to know something else? Roger hasn't executed a single trade since he came to Bedford. It's been an entire week, and he hasn't bought or sold one share."

"I wonder why."

"Probably because the five-thousand-dollar check he wrote to open his brokerage account bounced."

"How did you find that out?"

"Did you know that Anna keeps the books for Seaver?"

Mary's eyes narrow. "Anna told you about Roger bouncing a check? That doesn't seem like the kind of information she ought to be disclosing," she snaps.

"I didn't say she did."

"Anna's a little tramp," Mary says spitefully. "Those skimpy outfits she wears are outrageous. Seaver ought to do something about that. After all, Bedford is a place of business, not an escort service."

"Whoa, what's she ever done to you?"

"If she's willing to give out confidential information about Roger, I'm sure she'd say things about me too."

"I never said she gave out any information."

"You said—"

"I asked if you knew that she kept the books. I happened to see a notice about Roger's bounced check on her desk one day. Anna never showed me anything."

"Oh." Mary crosses her arms over her chest, embarrassed. "You seem to dig up a lot of things on people, don't you?"

I try to catch her eye, but she won't look at me. "You're jealous of Anna."

"I am not!"

"Yes, you are."

"Well, what woman my age wouldn't be?" she asks, finally turning to look at me. "She thinks she's God's gift to men. I've seen you ogle her just like all the rest of the guys on the trading floor."

"Of course you have. That's only natural. We're programmed to do that when we drop out of the womb," I say, stealing Roger's line. "Anna's a gorgeous woman. There's no denying that. But she's not my type." Anna's everybody's type, but I know what Mary wants to hear.

Mary looks up. "She's not?"

"No. I like blondes." I reach up and push her hair back over her ear, caressing her neck for a moment before taking my hand away. "And I like you."

"I like you too," she says, her voice low. She takes my hand in hers and kisses it. "Very much."

We're silent for a long time. "Will you walk me to my car?" she finally asks.

"You're leaving?" I glance at my watch. "It's only a little after four."

"I've had enough to drink. Any more and I won't be able to walk, let alone drive," she says, pushing me gently out of the booth.

When we get to the front door the sky is black. Another thunderstorm is bearing down on northern Virginia, and rain is already starting to sprinkle the parking lot. As we stand there a jagged flash splits the sky, followed by a blast of thunder. Mary clutches my arm and pulls herself tightly against me.

"Should we chance it?" I ask. The clouds look like they could let loose at any moment. "Or do you want to go back inside and wait out the storm?"

"Let's take a chance," she says, grabbing my hand.

"My car is over that way," I shout above another rumble of thunder, pointing in the opposite direction from the way she's pulling me. All three of us drove to the bar in our own cars. I got here after Mary and Roger because the police had a few last questions for me.

"I'll give you a lift to your car," she says, dragging me along.

Suddenly the clouds open up and the rain comes pouring down. I follow her, sprinting as best I can with all of the alcohol in my system.

By the time we reach her car and fall inside, we're drenched.

The rain beats a deafening rhythm on the roof and hood of the aging hatchback. Then it starts to hail. Marble-sized balls of ice pelt the car, and the combination of rain and hail obscures everything around us. Even the cars on either side of Mary's are difficult to see through the downpour.

"I thought Jacob left you a Jaguar," I say, pushing wet hair from my eyes. This car reminds me a lot of my own. It's old and the seat fabric is wearing thin.

"He did. It's still in the shop," she explains, wiping moisture from her face as she looks at herself in the rearview mirror.

"But you told me yesterday on the phone it was fixed and that you had picked it up."

"I had to take it right back again," she says distractedly, still looking at herself in the mirror as the rain pours down. "God, I look awful."

She's arching her back as she looks in the mirror, pushing her chest out against the thin cotton of her drenched white blouse. "I would have to disagree," I murmur. "You look wonderful." I glance up and she's gazing back at me. "You really do," I whisper.

She looks deeply into my eyes and reaches out to caress my cheek, then brings her fingers to the top button of her blouse and undoes it. Then she undoes the second and the third buttons and spreads the blouse, so now I can see the outline of her nipples beneath her bra. Slowly she slips her hands around my neck, leans forward, and kisses me deeply.

I haven't passionately kissed a woman other than Melanie since high school. That was a girl named Cathy, and as I feel Mary's lips press against mine, I remember what I had forgotten after so much time. That every woman has her own taste. It's completely different with Mary than it was with Melanie.

"Let's go to your place," she suggests, pulling back.

"I live way down on the south side," I say. "The rush-hour traffic will be terrible on the Beltway right now. It'll take us at least an hour to get there, especially with this rain. Don't you live right here in McLean? Isn't that what you told me?"

"I'm having the kitchen remodeled," she says, kissing my neck and sliding her hand up my thigh. "The workmen are there. We wouldn't have any privacy. Come on, let's go to your place."

"Father Dale, it's Augustus McKnight."

He squints against a bright light streaming down from above, peering at me from behind the rectory door that is slightly ajar. It's almost midnight, and I hope I haven't awakened him.

"I was here a few mornings ago," I continue. "I was out on the front steps of your church," I mutter, not proud of the condition I was in when he found me. "We talked for a while, and—"

"And you gave me a very generous contribution for Betty's shelter," he says, opening the door all the way and coming out to shake my hand. "I'm sorry I didn't recognize you right away, Augustus. It's just that it's very late and I had a long day."

"No need to apologize, Father. I shouldn't be coming by at this hour."

"Nonsense. I'm here for everyone at any hour of the day. It comes with the turf." He tilts his head and smiles warmly, still clasping my hand in both of his. "I want you to know how much your gift meant to Betty. She was able to begin a remodeling program on the shelter that will allow her to double the number of women and children she can accommodate. She'd like very much to meet you so she can thank you in person."

"Oh, no, that's all right. Hearing about it from you is enough."

He hesitates. "What can I do for you? Would you like to come in and talk? I could make us some coffee."

"Thank you, Father, but that's all right."

"It wouldn't be any trouble."

He must realize that there's more to these visits than I'm letting on, but I'm not ready to open up yet. I thought I was on the drive over, but I'm still not. "That's very kind, and I may take you up on your offer at some point. But the reason I stopped by tonight was to give you something." I press a large envelope into his hands.

"What's this?"

"More money for the shelter, Father. I told you there would be more." He peers inside and it makes me feel good to see his expression. Inside the envelope is most of the cash Melanie made performing at the Two O'Clock Club.

"How much is in here?" he asks in amazement.

"About six thousand dollars. The guys down at the club wanted Betty to have it. I'm just the messenger."

CHAPTER

16

The rich leather aroma permeating the inside of this new BMW 330i sports car is even more intoxicating than the one in the limousine I rode in the other night. It's like holding a pair of calf-skin gloves to your face and inhaling deeply. For the first time in my life I feel like a wealthy man.

Nestled behind the steering wheel of this sleek black showroom model, listening to a needle-nose salesman describe what this incredible machine can do while he kneels beside me, I know I'm going to buy the car. It's simply a matter of time. Through the spotless windshield I catch the eye of another guy checking out my black beauty. I stare him down, silently but surely letting him know that he might as well forget what he's thinking.

"I don't care what anyone says about the Porsche or the Mercedes," the salesman is saying as I tune back into him. "The BMW isn't just the ultimate driving machine, it's the ultimate driving experience. Everything else is just a means of transportation. After you own one of these babies, Mr. McKnight, you'll never want anything else."

"I'm sure I won't."

The salesman can see how much I want this car, and he turns suddenly from my pal to a negotiator. "Now, with the sports package and all the other extras on this particular car," he says solemnly, "the price will be forty-three thousand even. And I'm telling you, that's a great deal. These puppies are so popular, we're having a hard time keeping them in stock. In fact, this car came in late last night on the truck, and if you hadn't been the first one in the door this morning, there'd be someone else sitting where you are right now. Yup, forty-three grand and you've got yourself one of the best cars money can buy. You hand me a down payment of, say, ten thousand dollars, and I'll have this car prepped and ready for you by one o'clock this afternoon."

I glance over at him as he kneels beside me, one hand on the inside of the open door, anticipation written all over his face. He's a small man who reminds me a little bit of my old boss Russell Lake. "Let's not get ahead of ourselves, Harry." I can't remember what he said his name was, but he looks like a Harry to me, and letting him know I don't remember his name will put him back on his heels and wipe that smug expression off his face. "Tell you what. Let's you and me take this car out on the road for a spin before we talk price. Let's see what it can do, Harry."

"Of course," he says quickly, motioning for a man in dark blue overalls to open one of the large showroom doors. "By the way, Mr. McKnight, my name's Bill. Bill Morris."

"Whatever you say, Harry."

A few minutes later Harry and I are on the Beltway doing ninety and it feels like the engine is hardly working. It's purring, begging to go faster, and the RPM needle is nowhere near the red zone. My Toyota would be disintegrating at this speed, I'd be smelling hot oil leaking from something, and it would be all I could do to keep the Toyota on the road. But the Beamer is whipping and weaving around other vehicles on the four-lane highway like they're in reverse and I'm on rails. Harry's in the passenger seat babbling about torque and tight suspension and how these cars are built to handle the autobahns in Germany as he sinks lower and lower behind the dashboard, hoping to God he makes it back to the dealership alive.

I've been thinking about buying this car for a week, but yesterday's insanity at Bedford pushed me to do it. Something clicked while I was sitting at the bar with Mary, and I realized that life is too short not to go for what you want all the time. From now on I'm going to do what I want, when I want, as long as it doesn't hurt someone else. I immediately think of Mary. God, what a mess I almost got myself into.

"Why don't you get off here?" Harry shouts as a large green exit sign looms on the right. I've got the sunroof open and the windows down so it's loud inside the car with the wind whipping around us.

"Relax," I say calmly, feeding the car more gas and blowing past the off-ramp.

"I don't recommend this," he says, gritting his teeth as we narrowly avoid the back end of an eighteen-wheeler. "There are lots of cops on this part of the Beltway. Let's go back to the dealership."

"Let's talk price instead."

"I can't do that. Our policy is that we only discuss terms on the dealership premises."

"Don't give me that. I didn't fall off the turnip truck yesterday, Harry. Now, what did you say the price was again?"

"Look out!" he yells, bracing himself.

A pickup is little more than a red blur as we flash past it. "The price," I say again. "What is it?"

"Forty-three thousand dollars."

"No way. I've checked around on the Internet. I can buy this exact same car from a dealer up in Philadelphia for forty grand, but I don't feel like hoofing it all the way up there. You're screwing me at forty-three," I say calmly as we come within inches of a blue Ford sedan. "The speedometer tops out at one-seventy. Let's see if we can get there."

"Jeeeesus Christ! All right, all right. Forty-one, Mr. McKnight, but that's as low as I can go without my manager's permission."

"Thirty-nine. That's a very fair price for this car."

As I dart into the far left lane to avoid several slower cars, we race across a short bridge. On the other side of the span, tucked in behind an abutment, is a Virginia state trooper. I glance into the rearview mirror as we race past. He's already flicked on his emergency lights.

"Now you've got a problem," Harry announces triumphantly, looking back over his left shoulder. "These guys don't screw around. The speed limit here is fifty-five. Twenty miles an hour over the limit is reckless in Virginia, and you're doing almost *forty* over. This guy is going to take your license away. You'll be lucky not to go to jail. Looks like I'll be driving back to the dealership." He settles back into his seat, not even trying to hide an I-told-you-so grin.

"Hold on, Harry." I pump the accelerator twice, then drop the clutch, shifting the car into a higher gear and pushing the speedometer needle over a hundred.

"Oh, my God," Harry mutters, like he's seen the grim reaper pointing at him in the lane ahead. "Please don't do this."

"Thirty-nine thousand," I say firmly, swerving to the far right across four lanes. "Did you hear me?"

"I hear you!" he shouts, covering his eyes as I race up an exit ramp, lean on the brakes, and make a right turn at the top of the incline doing forty miles an hour.

This car handles like a dream. In seconds I'm back up to seventy on a winding two-lane road. "I can make all of this end." I give him a sly smile. "One way or the other."

"Forty even!" he yells. "That's as low as I can go."

"You're really disappointing me, Harry."

"Please!" he yells, burying his face in his hands.

A yellow-and-black SHARP TURN AHEAD sign looms in front of us. "Harry."

He peeks through his fingers. "Jesus. All right, thirty-nine!"

I nod. "Good boy."

The thing about going a hundred miles an hour past an object at rest is that within fifteen seconds you're half a mile past it. We were out of sight before Johnny Law even had a chance to get his blue-and-gray cruiser out into traffic. I knew it wasn't going to be that hard to lose him—unless he had friends ahead he could radio. Which was why we got off the Beltway so fast. I'm not a thrill-seeker, but damn, it felt good to outrun that trooper.

Harry doesn't utter a word during the entire drive back to the dealership across the back roads, and I laugh as I ease the car to a stop in the lot, cut the ignition, and hand him the keys. "Now that wasn't so bad, was it?"

"It sure as hell—"

The hundred-dollar bill I'm holding out cuts off his tirade. That and my friendly, confident smile. "This is for you, Harry. Now, do we have a deal?" He wants to be angry, but he can't be. I simply won't allow it.

He nods and finally smiles along with me when I let go of the bill and it falls into his lap. "You're crazy," he says.

The credit check on me doesn't go well, but there's always a solution to any problem. This time it's called "more cash." Instead of a ten-thousand-dollar down payment, I suggest twenty, and we have ourselves a deal. It turns out that there's a branch of my bank within a half mile of the dealership and it's open until noon on Saturdays. When I return with a certified check for the agreed upon amount—I don't think Harry and his manager seriously thought I'd be coming back—there's no more discussion about my credit. I sign on the dotted line and that beautiful black car is mine.

While the mechanics tune and spit-shine my new machine, I take a swan song in the Toyota to an AT&T store to purchase a cell phone. I spend a half hour with a young salesman determining which cell phone and which long distance plan best fit my specific needs. When I've made my choice of hardware and service, I spend another half hour going over exactly how all of the options on the phone work. The young guy becomes completely frustrated because he's on commission and spending a full hour with one customer isn't going to do much for his paycheck, but I don't give a damn. This is *my* purchase, and I'm not going to walk out of the store until I'm a hundred percent satisfied. There are others waiting to be served and I catch them giving me dirty looks, but I don't care.

The first thing I do when I come out of the store is call Vincent. He left several messages last night on my answering machine at home, asking me to call him because he'd heard about what happened at Bedford. News of the hostage crisis was on the front page of the *Post* this morning. It's dominated airtime on the local television and radio newscasts too.

Vincent answers on the first ring. "Hello."

"Vincent, it's Augustus."

"Augustus!" he thunders. "God, it's good to hear your voice. I was worried about you. I heard about that hostage thing over at Bedford. Are you all right?"

"I'm fine," I assure him. I purchased a headset for the phone and I'm getting used to the way the foam-covered plastic piece fits snugly into my ear. "How are you?"

"I'm okay," he says, sounding calmer. "Hey, I'm really sorry about the other night. I feel terrible. I should have told you about what happened with Melanie a long time ago, but I really didn't know how."

"It's all right." I've thought a lot about how he took Melanie to the Two O'Clock Club, but I've decided to forgive him. It won't be easy, but I've made the decision to believe him when he said nothing happened between them, and that *she* pushed *him* about working at the club. "I hate what Melanie did, but the truth is I can't hold you responsible. Not entirely anyway. She was the one who got up on that stage and took her clothes off. It's terrible for me to think about, but there's nothing I can do about it now. And I don't want it to ruin our friendship."

"Thanks," he mumbles in a low voice. "Hey, my investors were asking about you," he pipes up, his mood brightening.

"Oh?"

"Yeah, they're ready to go."

"Still? I thought maybe what happened over at Bedford yesterday might have scared them off."

"Nope. I spoke to them this morning and they're ready to roll. That hundred grand you made has them licking their chops."

"Good."

"The lawyers need to draft some paperwork. Partnership documents or something, I think they said, but we ought to be ready to go by next Friday."

"Okay."

"They want to pay you two percent a year. Two hundred grand. They'll pay you a hundred up front every six months. If you do well, you can keep five percent of the profits too. How about it?"

"Make it six and we have a deal."

There's a momentary silence at the other end of the phone, then Vincent's laugh comes booming into my ear. "Negotiating with me, huh?"

"Hey, I'm going to make these people lots of money," I say. "They need to understand that. I've already shown what I can do."

"All right," he agrees, still chuckling. "Six percent."

"We should get together to talk about details," I suggest. "About setting up accounts and all."

"How about dinner tomorrow night?"

"Good. I'll call you tomorrow afternoon. We'll figure out a place then."

"Sounds good."

I give Vincent my cell number, then clip the phone to my belt before heading out into the bright sunshine from beneath the roof that spans the length of the strip mall. As I approach my Toyota, I notice a man standing beside the driver-side door. "Can I help you?" I ask as I near him. He's a burly man, almost as tall as me, with a gut and thinning hair.

"Augustus McKnight?"

"Yes," I answer, turning cautious at the sound of my name.

"I'm Scott Snyder," he says in that tough Brooklyn accent I heard on my voice mail yesterday morning. "I left a message for you Thursday at your office but didn't hear back, so I figured I'd track you down. I'm representing Great Western Insurance Company in the matter of the death benefit claim you made. I hope you don't mind meeting like this, but I know we all want to get this matter cleaned up as quickly as possible. Great Western certainly does."

"I'm not sure what you mean by 'matter.' "

"There's still a few i's to dot and t's to cross."

"How did you find me?" I ask uncomfortably, putting the plastic bag with the cell phone box and the owner's manual down on the Toyota's trunk. I hold one hand over my eyes to shield them from the glare of the bright sunshine.

"I stopped by your house this morning just as you were leaving, so I followed you to the BMW dealership," Snyder explains, moving to the back of the Toyota so we're standing face-to-face. He holds out his hand and we shake. "That's quite a nice car you're buying. I wish I had that kind of money. What do those 330s run nowadays? Forty grand or so?"

"Around that."

"Well, I didn't want to interrupt the deal. That's why I waited until now to talk." He points down at the new cell phone clipped to my belt. "Did you just buy that too?"

"Uh-huh."

"That's AT&T's new top-of-the-line product, isn't it?"

"Yep."

"I hear they have lots of features. That's got to be another expensive toy."

"What can I do for you, Mr. Snyder?"

"As I said on my voice mail message, I have a few questions I want to ask you."

"What about?"

Snyder's gaze drops to the pavement as he does a terrible impression of a man who cares. "About your wife's murder," he explains, lifting his eyes back up in time to catch my reaction.

"Let me get this straight. You work for the insurance company?"

He shakes his head. "No, I work for an investigative firm. We're located downtown. We specialize in workmen's comp claims, but we take on other work as well. Surveillance. Loss recovery. Insurance companies hire us to make sure people aren't defrauding them."

"What do you want to know about my wife's murder?"

He shoves his hands in his pockets and his shoulders slump as he tries to strike a nonaggressive pose. "Look, I know how difficult this is, but when someone dies under questionable circumstances, the insurance company has to investigate the incident to protect itself. I'm sorry to dredge up bad memories but this just has to be done."

"The police are already investigating my wife's death. Why does the insurance company have to do it too?"

"That's just the way it is. Especially with a million bucks on the line."

"Okay." I try to smile politely, but I'm sure he can see my aggravation. "What can I tell you?"

"You want to go to a coffee shop or something and sit down?" he asks, scanning the strip mall. "Maybe get something to eat?"

"Nope."

"Okay." He nods, probably annoyed that I won't buy him lunch. "Where were you the night your wife was murdered?"

I stare at Snyder for several moments before answering, rage building inside me. "Does the insurance company actually think for one minute that I might have killed my wife?" I ask, my jaw tight. "Is that what this is all about?"

"Settle down, Mr. McKnight," Snyder advises, his manner turning tough for the first time.

"I didn't kill my wife."

"Uh-huh."

I take a deep breath. "I don't really understand what you're after, Snyder. The facts are that my wife is dead and she had a valid policy with Great Western. She was murdered. The police have confirmed that. She didn't commit suicide. Great Western can't wriggle out of their obligation on that technicality. So no matter what lies the insurance company might try to invent, they owe me the money."

"Actually that's not true," Snyder says, smiling the same smug smile Harry gave me when he realized I had been snagged by a state trooper as we tore over that bridge doing ninety.

"What do you mean?"

"There are laws in Washington, D.C., and Virginia called slayer statutes. Slayer statutes prevent anyone who has caused bodily harm to another individual from benefiting monetarily. So a person can't collect the proceeds of a life insurance policy if they were directly responsible for the death of the insured."

I blink several times. The sun is really bright today. "I didn't kill Melanie. I've told the police that several times."

"How many times?" he asks, pulling a small notepad from his pocket.

"Several," I repeat tersely.

"Reggie Dorsey is the lead detective on this case, right?" Snyder asks.

"Yes. Do you know Reggie?"

Snyder smiles as he opens the notepad. "Reggie and I go way back. He's a good man. He'll find your wife's killer, Mr. McKnight. I'm sure of that."

"Have you spoken to him?"

"Yes, we're in contact." Snyder flips back several pages, checks something, then looks up at me. "Where were you the night your wife was killed?"

"At home."

"Did you go anywhere after work?"

"No."

"You went straight home?"

"Yes, well . . . well, no, not exactly straight home."

"What do you mean, not exactly straight home?" he asks.

"It was a terrible day at work so I went for a drive."

"A drive?"

"Yes, a drive. Is that all right with you?"

"Sure it is." Snyder pulls a pen from his shirt pocket and starts scribbling. "Where did you drive?"

"Out to the country. Out to Winchester."

"Why Winchester?"

"Why not?" I ask angrily.

"There's no reason to be defensive, Mr. McKnight."

"I'm not being defensive. I just don't appreciate these questions."

"Uh-huh," he agrees, not really listening to me. "Winchester is about seventy miles west of the city. Over the mountains, correct?"

"Yes."

Snyder flips a couple of pages farther back and studies his notes for a moment before beginning again. "It says here that you were fired from your job the same day your wife was murdered. Is that why you took the drive? To cool down after being fired?"

"Fired? I wasn't fired. I quit."

"That's not what a man named Russell Lake told me. I believe he's your ex-boss," Snyder says. "Mr. Lake said you physically assaulted him and he was forced to terminate you on the spot."

"He's lying! I resigned—"

"He also informed me that your wife had asked you for a divorce the night before, and that you were understandably disturbed about that. He said that you told him you"—Snyder looks at the pad again—" 'weren't doing well.' Is that true? Is that what you said?"

I stare at Snyder for several moments without responding. Russell Lake is taking revenge for not getting a cut of the Unicom profits.

"A man named Frank Taylor also informed me that your wife had asked for a divorce the evening before you were fired," Snyder continues. "He was your wife's boss."

A burst of red flashes before my eyes at the sound of Taylor's name. "All right! Yes, Melanie said she was going to leave me that night! But we would have worked things out."

"You must have been very upset," he says, showing no reaction to my outburst.

"Of course I was."

"At the time of her murder, was your wife having an affair with a man named Vincent Carlucci?"

My eyes snap to Snyder's. "No! Who in the hell told you that?"

"It doesn't matter," Snyder says with a wave of his hand.

"It does to me."

"Forget it. Now, did you stop anywhere while you were on this drive to Winchester?" Snyder continues. "Can anyone confirm your whereabouts that night? If someone could, that would be really helpful. Otherwise, while I may believe that you were tooling around the countryside working off steam, the executives at Great Western may not. They tend to be pretty skeptical about these things."

"I wanted to be alone. That was the whole point."

"Right. Alone."

For several moments we stare at each other, then he slowly closes his notepad and nods. "Thank you for your time, Mr. McKnight. I'll be in touch."

"Snyder!" I call as he walks away.

"What?"

"If Great Western doesn't pay the life insurance proceeds to me, who gets it?"

"The secondary beneficiary," he says, opening his pad once more and glancing at it. "That would be Frank Taylor."

CHAPTER

17

I'm not a self-centered man. I care deeply about the feelings of others, so I try very hard never to be arrogant. But the few times in my life I have been, when I've made the mistake of getting even the slightest bit cocky, it seems like I've been punished for it right away.

I remember tackling the other team's quarterback near the end of a rainy game in high school, and after I'd picked myself up off the soggy turf, I raised my arms in celebration and did one of those victory dances over him, screaming and pounding my chest. I even ran my hand across my throat with the slash sign to show that the game was over because we were so far ahead. We were crushing those poor bastards. On the next play I got hit so hard by one of the opposing linemen on a crack-back block, I had to be carried off the field on a stretcher. Or so I was told. I didn't remember the hit. I didn't even remember my name for two days.

Now it's happened again. This morning I sped away from a state trooper at a hundred miles an hour, bought a flashy sports car, and thought I was a big shot while I negotiated with Vincent on my new cell phone about my fee to manage his investors' money. Then thirty seconds later, boom, I'm confronted by Scott Snyder, who's going to do everything he can to keep me from getting the million dollars out of Melanie's insurance policy. He didn't say that, but I could see it in his eyes.

It isn't as if Snyder has a good reason for wanting to keep me from getting the money either. We'd never even met before this morning. In fact, I bet if Snyder got to know Taylor at all, he'd want *me* to have the cash because he'd realize that Taylor is one of the most contemptible human beings on earth. So the only explanation for what happened in the parking lot must be that some greater power sent Snyder to cut me back down to size as I was congratulating myself on how far and I'd come so fast. It's just like what happened on the football field with the crack-back block. If there is anything that might turn me to religion, it's that pattern of arrogance and setback. Maybe someday I'll learn.

After my run-in with Snyder, picking up the BMW turns into a chore. I try to concentrate as Harry sits with me for an hour and takes me through the car's options, explaining every detail about my new machine. But my excitement of a few hours ago is gone, replaced by an eerie sense of dread. I can't focus on what he's saying because I'm wondering what I'll do if the insurance company denies my claim and gives the money to Taylor. I'm wondering how Reggie would interpret that outcome too.

And I'm trying to figure out why Taylor is the second beneficiary on Melanie's policy. I vaguely remember Melanie saying something about her mother being second the night she was filling out the applications last spring. But I wasn't listening very hard because I thought the whole damn thing was so ridiculous. Melanie had to actually place the application down directly in front of me, put a pen in my hand, and force me to sign my name on the bottom line that night.

From the dealership I drive my new car directly to Bedford. There are several more companies I want to analyze so that when I get the ten million dollars from Vincent's investors, I'll be ready to go. More important, I'm finding myself drawn back to the scene of yesterday's events, though I'm not sure why. Perhaps it's because once the police were certain I was unharmed, they ushered me right out of the conference room and didn't give me a chance to really reflect on what had happened. I have to see the spot where Slammer pulled the gun on me, the spot where Daniel fell, what's left of the window Slammer crashed through, and I have to look down those nine stories from the conference room to the hard pavement below.

I learned a lot about myself yesterday. I learned that I wouldn't cower in fear when a gun was pointed at me, that I would act to save others even in the face of grave danger to myself, and that I could still feel compassion for a man who had threatened to kill me only moments before.

Bedford's lobby door is propped open by a two-by-four so I don't need my swipe card to get inside. When I push through the swinging doors and walk onto the trading floor, I see that there's a cleaning crew hard at work scrubbing the place where Daniel died. They're using a big industrial carpet cleaner, and over the loud hum of the machine, I hear the banging of hammers and the whining of a circular saw coming from the conference room. The smell of sawdust hangs heavy in the air and the carpet is marked by dusty footprints. Michael Seaver is determined to be back up and running first thing Monday morning as if nothing happened, but all of this activity seems kind of disrespectful. Maybe Roger was right. Maybe Seaver should pay for what happened.

From my cubicle I gaze at the dark stain that's fading quickly as the crew works. One minute Daniel thought he had solved all of his problems. He had reconnected with his father and he was headed back to Georgetown. He was happy and relieved. The next minute Slammer pointed a gun at him and pulled the trigger. It was surreal watching Daniel tumble backward, grab his chest for a few horrible seconds, then go absolutely still.

That was the part I remember most clearly. His frantic death struggle suddenly stopped as his heart and his brain quit working and he just didn't move anymore. A life can end so quickly.

One of the workers shoots me an odd look. Like I'm crazy or something. He probably can't believe I'd want to be inside an office building on a beautiful summer Saturday afternoon. Especially an office where a hostage situation and a murder occurred little more than twenty-four hours ago. Maybe he's right. Maybe I am crazy. But I needed closure. I needed to see all of this again right away.

And I have some serious work to do. Vincent's friends are going to expect the same kind of results with the ten million dollars they're about to hand me as they got with their test-case three hundred thousand. The pressure will be immense, and there's no way I'll be able to return thirty-three percent in a few days with the ten million the way I did with the three hundred grand. But I'm confident I can do well.

Some people might be satisfied with the money I've already made in the stock market and the proceeds from the insurance policy I'm still assuming I'll ultimately collect. They wouldn't want the stress of managing someone else's money. They wouldn't want the stress of those weeks or months when the portfolio doesn't perform well—which there will inevitably be. But I've come to realize in the last few days that a million bucks isn't exactly retire-to-Tahiti dough either.

Don't get me wrong. It's a sizeable amount. But I'll still have to work for a living because if I put that million in the bank, it would earn me only about fifty thousand dollars of interest a year—about four grand a month. After taxes, four grand a month would just about cover the rent on a nice apartment and my new car payment, but there wouldn't be much left over.

Besides, I'm not going to put that money in the bank. I'm going to day trade with it. I'm going to try to turn it into two million or three million, but you never know. The same thing that happened to Mary could happen to me, so I want to have other income.

I grab a pad of paper off my desk. I want to understand my financial situation in detail and figure out what kind of trouble I'll be in if the insurance money doesn't come through.

I made seventy-seven thousand dollars on my Unicom investment, thirty-five thousand on the Teletekk play, and I started with the ten grand my mother saved for me. That's a hundred and twenty-two thousand dollars on the good side of the ledger, but I've had some major cash outflows as well. I gave Father Dale ten grand—not including the cash I found in Melanie's dresser—put five thousand down as my deposit and first month's rent at Bedford, repaid the five-thousand-dollar loan Vincent arranged for me, paid off the stack of bills on the kitchen table to the tune of another ten grand, and just stroked a twenty-thousand-dollar check to the BMW dealership—not to mention locking myself into a six-hundred-dollar payment for each of the next forty-eight months. So net-net I'm back down to seventy-seven thousand, which sounds okay, but I haven't yet accounted for the fact that next April I'll have to pay short-term capital gains taxes on the Unicom and Teletekk profits. That will put about another thirty-five thousand or so in the negative column, leaving me a real net of somewhere around forty thousand dollars.

And I almost forgot. I still owe the funeral home five thousand dollars for Melanie's ceremony and cremation. Which really leaves me less than thirty grand. Jesus, a couple of bad days on the trading floor and I could be in trouble.

To make certain I've figured everything accurately I reach inside my top right-hand desk drawer for my calculator. As the drawer glides open, my hand snaps back as if I've touched red-hot coals. Someone's rifled through my desk. I quickly check the other three drawers and they're in the same wrecked condition.

I go back through each drawer, carefully taking inventory. The only thing missing seems to be the letter from Great Western Insurance Company confirming the amount of money they'll pay me after finishing their investigation—the letter Anna delivered last Monday as I sat in the conference room. I had stashed it in my lower right-hand drawer along with some research material, where I thought it would be safe.

I stand up and move deliberately into Roger's cubicle. The guy has asked me several times about that insurance policy I told him I got from my mother. At first I didn't think much of it. I figured he was asking because he was taking a friendly interest in me, not because he might have some other agenda. The same friendly interest I thought he was taking that night I helped him with his computer. But now I'm not so sure. Now I'm wondering if all of his questions have something to do with the lies he's told me about going to the University of Maryland and working at the Department of Energy.

I glance at the cleaning crew, worried that they might wonder why

I'm going from cubicle to cubicle, but they aren't interested in me at all. They just want to get finished and get out of here. I scan the trading floor, but other than the cleaners, I'm still the only one here.

My letter from the insurance company isn't in Roger's desk. The drawers are mostly empty except for pencils, pens, and pads of paper.

The cleaning crew finishes and begins wheeling the large machine down the aisle. When they've disappeared through the swinging doors, I glance into Mary's cubicle. Mary asked me about the inheritance too. She tried to make light of it in the bar yesterday, but I could tell she was interested. So I walk into her cubicle and scan her desktop, rummaging through papers and files and notebooks, but nothing catches my eye. Then I reach for the top right-hand drawer and pull, but it's locked tight. I sit down in her chair and lean back, contemplating the drawer for a moment. Then I reach for it again and give it a savage yank. There's a loud snap and I'm in.

Stuffed inside the drawer is a pile of yellow tickets—Bedford buy and sell orders—and I grab a handful of them, place them on her desk, and begin to go through them. The third one is her Teletekk purchase, and as I glance at it, I'm puzzled. I scan it three times to make certain I'm reading the printed gibberish correctly, but I've read enough order tickets over the past two weeks to know how to decipher the code.

Mary told me she had purchased one hundred thousand dollars' worth of Teletekk stock, but this ticket is for only *one* thousand. I pick up the next ticket and the next, thinking maybe she bought a number of small-order lots to disguise what she was doing. But they're all for purchases or sales of other stocks—not Teletekk—and they're all for small amounts, two to three hundred dollars each. Not the big-buck trades a woman who supposedly inherited two million dollars from a real estate mogul ought to be executing.

"What are you doing?"

I spin around and there she is, standing behind me, her face twisted by rage. "Mary, I—"

"What are you doing?" she demands again, louder this time.

"I was just, just . . ." My voice trails off.

"Tell me!"

"Why are you here on Saturday?" I ask lamely, unable to come up with a response. Usually I'm quick with a comeback in these situations, but not this time.

"You're going through my desk!" she screams.

"I don't know what to tell you," I say apologetically, rising up and taking a small step toward her, hoping she'll move out of my way. But she doesn't. "I'm sorry."

"What is with you? What do you have against me?"

"What are you talking about?"

"I thought we were getting along so well yesterday at the bar, then out of nowhere you blew me off. Now you break into my desk. I should tell Seaver what you've done and have you barred from this place Monday morning."

"It'll be your word against mine."

"Why do you hate me?"

Mary and I kissed in her car yesterday afternoon until the rain let up. Then she drove me to where my car was parked, ready to follow me home. As I was about to get out, I turned back and told her I couldn't go through with it. One moment I couldn't wait to have her body wrapped around me, the next it was the last thing in the world I wanted.

"I don't hate you," I say gently. "Just the opposite. I like you very much."

"Don't give me that." Her voice trembles as she turns her back on me. "Everything was fine one minute yesterday, then the next you told me you didn't find me attractive. Now you're breaking into my desk. What am I supposed to believe?"

"I never said I didn't find you attractive." I move to where she stands and try to caress her shoulders, but she steps away, her back still to me.

"You didn't have to say it. It was obvious when you told me I couldn't come home with you. That was terrible, Augustus."

I take a deep breath. I don't want her going to Seaver to tell him I've broken into her desk, but I want to understand why she lied to me about the size of her Teletekk purchase, learn the real reason she didn't want to go to her house in McLean yesterday, and try to find out why she's come onto me like a hurricane. "Mary, I thought you told me you had purchased a hundred thousand dollars of Teletekk." I want to know why I haven't seen that Jag of hers either.

She turns around slowly, an irritated expression on her face. "Excuse me?"

I hold up the Teletekk order I found in her desk. "This purchase order is for a thousand dollars, not a hundred thousand."

"What's your point?" she snaps.

"Is this all you bought? A thousand dollars' worth?"

"Maybe."

"Why did you tell me you bought a hundred grand?"

"None of your business."

"Mary, how much did you lose when MicroPlan's stock crashed this past spring?"

"None of your business," she says again.

"How much did Jacob really leave you when he died?" I ask. Now I know how Reggie feels when he's interrogating someone.

"I told you, two million dollars."

"Why didn't you want to go to your house in McLean yesterday after we left the bar?" I press.

"What?"

"You were willing to drive all the way to my place in Springfield. That would have taken us an hour in rush-hour traffic. But your house is five minutes away."

"Why am I being made to feel like a criminal?"

"Answer me!"

"I told you," she says, seething. "There were men at the house working on the living room."

"You said it was the kitchen yesterday." I pause. "And I have yet to see that Jaguar. What kind did you say it was?"

Her eyes turn to slits. "I didn't."

"Where did you tell me you were from?" I ask.

"I didn't."

"Yes, you did. It was Kentucky."

"Is that why you don't like me all of the sudden?" she asks angrily. "Because I opened up and told you that I'm nothing but trailer trash? Because you can't be with a woman who grew up dressing in rags and eating leftover meatloaf for Christmas dinner? Is that what this is all about?"

"That's ridiculous, Mary, and you know it. We haven't been friends for that long, but by now you know I wouldn't let—"

"Then why wouldn't you let me come home with you yesterday?" she sobs, her eyes tearing up.

My gaze drops to the carpet. "I'm not over my wife yet. I didn't feel right about it."

"The man who kissed me yesterday wasn't missing his wife."

"You don't understand."

"Oh, I think I do," she says, her voice chilling. "Slammer warned me about you right from the start. He told me he thought you had killed your wife, and that I needed to be careful. That we all needed to be careful. I guess he had you pegged."

"That's absurd."

"He checked out the stories about your wife's murder on the Internet, and he said he had you all figured out."

"Slammer was a lunatic. Yesterday should have proved that to you. Besides, what could he possibly find out on the Internet? He was just jealous. He didn't like how quickly we got close."

"Which is exactly what I told him, but now I'm not so sure."

"What's that supposed to mean?"

"Exactly what you think it means."

It's my turn to stare her down. I can feel my anger building. Mary has no right to accuse me of these awful things. "If you're so worried, why don't you go ask your psychic about me?"

"Maybe I will."

"Sure, Sasha will have *all* the answers. She did one helluva job warning you about yesterday. What a load of crap all that is. I don't know how you can delude yourself that way."

Mary swallows a sob. "I hate you."

"Is there anything you want to tell me about that call you got while we were driving back to Bedford from seeing Sasha?" I ask.

"What are you talking about?"

"You told me it was an old friend from home. You sure you want to stick to that story?"

"Why shouldn't I?"

"Why did you go through *my* desk?" I ask.

"What! *You* were the one going through *mine*."

"What were you looking for?" I push. She's not answering anything, but if I press, maybe I'll break through. "Was it just the letter from the insurance company, or was there something else you were hoping to find?"

"You're crazy!" she shouts at the top of her lungs.

The sound of the circular saw in the conference room fades, like it's been turned off and the blade is slowing down. "You've been lying to me all along, haven't you? There was no two-million-dollar inheritance, no house, and no Jag. Probably no marriage either. Were you his mistress? Was that the real deal? Did the guy's wife find out about you and threaten him with divorce if he didn't stop seeing you?"

"You bastard! You goddamn bastard!"

Two guys with tool belts hanging low around their waists appear at the conference room doorway. "You all right, miss?" one of them calls.

Mary doesn't answer. She just stares at me, shaking.

"Miss?"

I step past her and head straight for the door, hoping she won't come after me. Or tell the workmen that I went through her desk and have them try to stop me.

Thankfully, she doesn't do either. But as I open one of the glass doors leading out of the Bedford lobby, I almost run smack into Roger coming in. We stare at each other silently for several moments.

"What was all of that about yesterday at the bar?" he finally asks. "Why the Perry Mason routine?"

"I wanted to know why you lied about going to Maryland and working at the DOE," I answer evenly, glancing back over my shoulder at the swinging doors leading to the trading floor, expecting to see Mary emerge. I ought to blow past him, but I can't resist asking one more time.

"Listen to me, Augustus. I don't like people digging into my past.

Not that I have anything to hide," he adds quickly. "I'm warning you," he says, pointing a bony finger at me, "stay away from me from now on. There'll be trouble if you don't."

We both know he can't threaten me. He probably couldn't punch a hole through a wet paper towel. "You didn't work at the DOE, did you?"

"What difference does it make?" he asks.

"Maybe none, but I want to know."

"Ten years. Doing budgets, like I told you."

"No way. I called over there. They have no record of a Roger Smith ever having worked there."

"Oh, yes, and we all know how good the federal government is at keeping records."

"There was no John Embry either."

His face goes pale. "Huh?"

"Are you really married?"

Roger shakes his head, trying to regain his composure. "You can't quit, can you, Augustus? You can't accept the fact that I'm an average guy, and that this day trading gig is just me trying to save myself from a grind of a life before I end up doing what Slammer did."

"Then why all the lies?"

"You're—"

One of the swinging doors opens suddenly and Mary appears. She stops short, her eyes flickering from Roger to me. "Better check your desk, Roger," she says fiercely. "Augustus doesn't seem to have much respect for personal privacy."

Sticking around right now isn't going to do me any good. Neither one of them is going to answer my questions, and I'll just end up taking a verbal ass-beating. So I push past Roger, and instead of waiting for an elevator, I take the stairs. Nine stories down, and with each step all I can think about is how far it is and how desperate Slammer must have been to jump. How there must have been so much more going on in his life than I knew about. And then there's Mary . . .

It doesn't make sense to me that a woman who seems to have so little, and, by her own admission, grew up poor, would waste money on a psychic. Before I can reconsider, I decide I'm going to the source to find out what's really going on. I make the fifteen-minute drive to the small side street where Mary took me the other morning.

"Hello, Sasha," I say calmly, standing in the open doorway beneath the tarot sign.

Her eyes widen as she looks up from her desk. She hadn't heard me coming down the steps to her substreet lair. I close the door behind me, and now the room turns quiet and the street noise fades.

"What do you want?"

"I want to know about your relationship with Mary Segal."

"I'm her psychic," Sasha answers, standing up. "That's all."

"Don't screw with me!" I shout, slamming my hand on the round table in the middle of the room where we all sat a few days ago. "I'm tired of these damn lies."

"Get out of here," she orders, her voice cracking. "Or I'll call the cops."

When I don't react she reaches for the phone on her desk, but I step across the room and rip the cord from the wall before she can finish dialing. "Tell me what's going on!"

"Get away from me," she hisses, backing up until her body meets the wall.

I take several steps around her desk and now we're only a few feet apart. "Talk to me."

"Get away," she pleads again, turning toward the wall and shutting her eyes. "Please don't hurt me."

"Why would I hurt you? What have you done that would make me want to do that?"

"Nothing, I swear."

"Why did you call Mary on her cell phone a few minutes after we left here the other day? She said it was an old friend from Kentucky, but we both know the truth, don't we?"

Sasha's eyes open and she slowly turns her head back to look at me.

It was a gamble, but I've definitely hit a nerve. "I got a quick look at the inbound number on the screen of Mary's cell phone," I continue. "I didn't catch it all, but I saw the 703 area code. I have no idea what Kentucky's is, but it isn't 703 because that's right here in northern Virginia." I take another step toward her. We're only inches apart. Her back is flat against the wall, and I can see she's terrified. "How long have you been offering your services as a psychic?"

"Ten years."

"But you're not in the Yellow Pages. I checked. All good psychics advertise in the Yellow Pages because they, better than anyone, know that copper and glass phone lines are the only real transmitters."

"I . . . I put the ad in there last month," she stammers. "The new book hasn't come out yet."

"Why did you wait ten years to advertise?"

"I came to this area only recently."

"Where did you come from?"

"Florida."

"Problems with the law down there?"

"No, nothing like that."

She swallows hard as I reach up and wrap my fingers around her thin neck. This is crazy, I think. This isn't me.

"What are you going to do?" she gasps.

"You're the psychic," I say, gently squeezing the soft skin of her throat. There's no escape, and she knows it. I'm so much stronger than she is. "You tell me."

"I have an appointment coming," she whimpers. "He'll be here any minute."

"I doubt that. It's Saturday, it's summer, and it's a beautiful day. Most men are playing golf or cutting their lawns right now, not visiting psychics. If you had said *she* was going to be here any minute, I might have believed you." I play her game—the game of probability. There's no appointment coming. I move my hand up her throat until my thumb and forefinger rest tightly beneath her ears, then I squeeze even harder and push her chin toward the ceiling. A strange excitement overtakes me.

"Mary told me she had been coming to you once a week since her husband died. That was last Christmas. Seven months ago. But when I drove her over here a couple of days ago she was paying very close attention to where we were. She was checking landmarks off as if she wasn't sure where she was going. A woman who had been coming to see you for seven months wouldn't do that."

Sasha's eyes flash from side to side. She puts one hand on my wrist, but doesn't attempt to pull my fingers from her throat as she struggles to breathe.

"When did you move here from Florida?"

I ease the pressure on her throat so she can reply. "Two months ago."

"Mary hasn't been seeing you since Christmas like she told me she has."

"No, she hasn't," Sasha admits. "Please stop," she begs.

"Keep answering the questions and everything will be fine." Should I be enjoying this? Shouldn't this just be about getting the facts? "When did Mary come to see you for the first time?"

She coughs and winces.

"Tell me!"

"About two weeks ago."

"*Exactly* when."

"I'd have to look at my date book," she says, gripping my wrist with both hands now. "I don't know exactly."

"Think!"

"It was a week ago this past Wednesday," she says. "I remember now. I exercised at a gym around the corner for the first time that morning, and Mary came in after that. She was my first appointment after my workout."

A week ago Wednesday. My third full day at Bedford. "What did she want?"

Now Sasha is trying to pry my fingers off her neck, but she can't. "She said she was going to bring you over to see me on her next visit, and she wanted me to say that I envisioned you and her together. That was all we talked about during her entire visit."

"Why did she want you to see us that way?"

"She thought it would help make you feel about her the way she feels about you. She's very attracted to you, Augustus. Is that so terrible?"

"You called Mary on her cell phone after we left to give your vision credibility," I say, squeezing a little more tightly. "If your prediction about the call from Kentucky came true, then I'd be more inclined to believe your vision about us, right?"

"Mary's just a lonely soul, like so many others. She told me it was love at first sight when she saw you."

I'm about to tell Sasha that there is no such thing as love at first sight when I think back on how I felt in that high school hallway the first time I saw Melanie. I don't know if it was love, but it was a powerful emotion. "She told you about my wife too, didn't she? That was the terrible loss. She primed you, right?"

"Yes, yes!" Sasha whines. "You're hurting me. I've told you everything I know. I swear! God, I can't breathe!"

I grit my teeth and squeeze Sasha's throat even harder, gazing into her terrified eyes. I'm enjoying this. I can't believe it.

Suddenly the door creaks on its hinges and I whip around, releasing my grip on Sasha's neck. Standing in the doorway is a young man who reminds me of Daniel. He has wild, multicolored hair and a ring in his nose. The probabilities have failed me.

"Get out of here!" I roar.

He stumbles backward, then turns and scrambles up the stairs. I take one quick look back at Sasha, who has dropped to her knees and is gasping for air, then race for the stairs myself.

Inside of five minutes I'm back in the BMW, heading for home around the Beltway. I try to call Reggie at his office, but he doesn't pick up so I try him on his cell phone. He scrawled that number on a scrap piece of paper at the morgue and told me to use if I ever really needed him.

"Detective Dorsey."

"Reggie, it's Augustus."

There's a slight pause. "Hello."

I hesitate, wondering if it was a mistake to have called. "What's going on with the investigation? I hadn't heard from you in a few days, and I'm getting worried that you're losing steam." I want to put him on the defensive. I want to establish who's in charge of this call.

"Not at all. I'm working on several promising leads."

"What are they?"

"I'd rather not go into them right now," he says, "especially on an unsecured line like this. Why did you call me on my cell number? Something wrong?"

"No," I answer defensively.

"Is there anything else? I'm very busy."

"I have a favor to ask."

"What?"

"I need you to check someone out for me."

"Why?"

"I think a woman I know has figured out that I'm going to be coming into some money."

"So?"

"She's been following me. Stalking me."

"Stalking you?"

"Yeah, she's showed up a couple of times out of the blue," I say, trying to say something that will spark Reggie's interest.

"What do you mean?"

"I stopped by the office today and all of a sudden she showed up. She works at Bedford too, but it's Saturday. Why would she show up right after me on the weekend?"

"That's not exactly—"

"I think I saw her in the parking lot of a store near my house a couple of nights ago too, and I could have sworn I saw her car go by my house this morning. But she doesn't live anywhere near me." I've got to get him to investigate her. Suddenly I've got a bad feeling about Mary.

"I can't check anyone out based on that. Do you know—"

"She claims she was married to a real estate wheeler-dealer here in northern Virginia," I continue. "A man named Jacob who she says left her two million dollars, a Jaguar, and a big house in McLean. She never told me his last name." There's no response from the other end of the line, and I'm worried I've lost the connection. "Reggie?"

"I'm here," he says.

"She says the guy died last Christmas. He was older. In his sixties or seventies. He had kids who weren't happy about him leaving her the money."

"What's her name?"

"Mary Segal."

No response.

"Does any of that sound familiar, Reggie? A northern Virginia real estate mogul dying last Christmas Eve?"

"No," he says indifferently. "Augustus, you let me do the investigating."

"Check her out, Reggie. Again, her name's Mary Segal. Do you hear me?"

"I hear you, Augustus, but now you listen to me. If you know what's good for you, you'll stay away from Vincent Carlucci."

I hesitate. "Why?"

"He's organized crime."

For a moment all sounds fade to nothing. This is Vincent he's talking about. Someone I've known for more than twenty years. Reggie's crazy. "Organized crime? That can't be."

"Believe me. He's with the mob. He hangs with some very nasty characters."

"How do you know?"

"Scott Snyder told me. He's ex-FBI and he's known about Vincent for some time." Reggie pauses. "I believe you and Scott met this morning after you bought the cell phone you're talking on right now. And the BMW you're driving."

I have to jerk the steering wheel to the left to avoid a slower car, and I glance down at the speedometer. I'm doing eighty. "You're wrong about Vincent," I say firmly, easing my foot off the accelerator.

"No, I'm not. Snyder called his buddies over at the Bureau, Augustus. Carlucci's been under surveillance for the last few months. I'm not at liberty to tell you why, but if you're smart, you'll stay away from him."

The money. The ten million dollars. I still haven't met his investors.

"Call me tomorrow, Augustus," Reggie says. "I want you to stay in very close communication with me from now on."

"Why?" I ask shakily.

"I just do."

Then he's gone, the connection cut.

Twenty minutes later I ease to a stop in front of my house, walk up the path, and open the front door. For several moments I stand in the foyer in disbelief. The living room is a disaster area. Furniture is ripped apart and turned upside down, cabinets are turned over, and dishes and glasses lie shattered on the floor.

I stumble to the bedroom and find the same awful sight. The bed is a shambles, covers are on the floor, and the mattress is sliced down the middle. Clothes have been pulled from closet hangers and are tossed about. Dresser drawers lie overturned on the floor, contents strewn everywhere.

I move slowly into the room, dazed, and ease myself down onto the shredded mattress, allowing my face to fall into my hands. When I finally lift my head, I notice the half-dozen photographs spread out all around me on the bed. More horrible pictures of Melanie performing at the Two O'Clock Club.

CHAPTER

18

It's Saturday night at the Two O'Clock Club and the place is in high gear. It's packed with half-drunk men, their eyes fixed on the beautiful women performing up onstage or at the tables. Thursday night—the night Vincent brought Roger and me here—was tame by comparison. It was crowded, but not like this. Tonight there aren't any empty seats around the stage and the smoke-filled bar is standing room only. The other night the men were reasonably well behaved. Tonight they're rowdy, almost unruly, straining to stuff money into garter belts and shouting for more alcohol—and more skin.

Now I understand why Melanie had to "work late" more and more on weekends. It had nothing to do with "the load of new cases" she claimed Taylor had taken on, and everything to do with this target-rich environment. Money's flowing like beer at a fraternity party, and money was what she wanted. Money and power.

Admission at the front door tonight was fifty bucks, which didn't even include a complimentary drink or a lap dance, but I don't care. I'm not here to get drunk or leer. I'm here to preserve a memory.

I make my way slowly along the bar through the tightly packed crowd of men watching the stage. They're mesmerized by a dark-haired woman writhing against one of the shiny silver poles. She's making them believe she's actually enjoying herself, moving her hips faster and faster while she grabs the pole tightly with both hands and throws her head back, her expression a combination of intense sexual pleasure and excruciating pain as she grinds herself against the metal. The men around me are buying into her act completely, pointing at the stage and yelling to one another about how she couldn't possibly be faking her pleasure. We're so damn gullible, especially after a few drinks.

Suddenly there's a commotion. The woman has dropped to all fours in front of a guy sitting close to the stage. She's giving him a close-up view, intent upon getting paid. The guy stands up unsteadily, a drunken grin on his face as the crowd cheers him on, and the woman puts her hands on his shoulders and allows him to smell and briefly touch her. He looks back over his shoulders at his buddies and rolls his eyes as if he's in heaven, then the woman slides one hand to his face and brings his eyes back to where she wants them.

It's all over quickly. He shoves his hand into his pocket, pulls out a crumpled bill, and holds it up. With a move a magician would be proud of the woman slips the bill from his fingers. She keeps her eyes locked on his the whole time, and he never even realizes the money is gone. She stays in front of him a few seconds more, then moves on to her next victim after giving him a sly smile and a kiss on the cheek. When he looks at his hand, he can't believe the money's disappeared. I can see it in his face as he slowly blinks at his empty fingers.

The guy's a sucker, like the idiot who pays retail at the factory's back door. The woman probably whispered something seductive in his ear while she was draped all over him. Something about how beautiful she thought his eyes were and how she wanted to take him home, and, of course, he turned to putty in her hands because in his drunken state he actually believed her. He'll wake up tomorrow morning with an empty wallet and wonder how he could have been so stupid. He'll realize that there was never any chance she was coming home with him, and that the alcohol was in total control. Then he'll come right back here again next weekend and do it all over again.

Once more I start moving through the crowd, excusing myself as I elbow people aside. Then there's another commotion. The man who just lost his money has hauled himself up onstage and is crawling across it to where the woman's putting on another intimate show. The guy's so boozed up he can't stand seeing his prize perform for someone else. He can't handle the thought that she could turn her back on him so easily, and he's going to do something about it. In a flash three huge security guards scoop him up and haul him away to a loud cheer from the crowd. His visit to the Two O'Clock Club is over.

If he's got anything left in his wallet, the bouncers are doing him a favor. If he had stayed much longer, he'd have lost everything.

Finally I make it to the far end of the bar, near the VIP entrance that Vincent brought me through Thursday night. Scantily clad waitresses breeze past me on their way to deliver drinks to men in the Champagne Room down the corridor, and I'm careful to stay out of their way while I inspect the wall of photographs, searching for the one of Melanie.

I decided after I found the photos of Melanie in my house this afternoon that I couldn't allow that picture to stay on the wall for other men to gape at. Despite everything Melanie did to me, I can't have her memorialized this way, I think to myself as I finally locate the photograph. She'll always be the innocent girl I first laid eyes on in that high school hallway so many years ago. Not a woman who stripped for money.

"Hey, what the hell are you doing?"

It's one of those huge bouncer guys who nodded so respectfully to Vincent Thursday night. He's dressed all in black again tonight, but he's lost the sunglasses. "Nothing." Actually, I was trying to pry the picture from the wall, but not surprisingly, it's bolted on tightly in case of someone like me. "This woman is amazing," I say, pointing at Melanie, trying to distract the guy from the fact that I was trying to take the picture. "But I haven't seen her in here tonight."

The bouncer sidles over to me, a toothpick protruding from his mouth. He glances at the picture. "And you won't," he says. "She moved away from the area a month ago."

"Oh?"

"She was incredibly popular," he says. "Somebody told me her real name was Melanie, but her stage name was the Vamp. She did this routine every once in a while. When she did, the place would go wild."

I look over at him. "A routine?" There I go again, asking a question I probably don't want the answer to.

He smiles and tugs at the collar of his shirt like it's suddenly become too tight. "She had this soft-core bondage act. She'd have another girl tie her to a pole on stage, or tie her hands together in front of her and lead her out into the audience. It was nothing real bad because we don't allow that kind of stuff to go on here at the Two O'Clock Club," he says, like he's proud to be associated with such an upstanding place. "But, man, it drove the guys crazy. She made some serious cash with that act."

I swallow hard, remembering the purple bruises on Melanie's wrists the night she asked me for a divorce. Remembering Reggie's comment about the marks on her wrists and ankles the coroner had identified. How the coroner was confident that the marks had been inflicted well before her murder. How Reggie tried to dig into the darkest corners of our most private affairs during the first interview at Bedford.

A chill crawls up my spine. Melanie always knew how to bring out the animal in me. It was her special gift, and I always thought I was the only one who would ever get to enjoy it. But I was wrong, and I can understand why she would want to come here so much. Sure she wanted the money, but there was more to it than that. Much more.

"Have you ever been to the Champagne Room?" the bouncer asks over the music, gesturing down the corridor after a waitress who just flashed past with a tray full of drinks.

"No, I don't—"

"Of course, if you really want to have some fun, you've got to try the Kitten Closet all the way down at the end of the hall."

"The what?"

"The Kitten Closet," he says. "That's where we keep the hottest girls at the Two O'Clock Club. They never actually come out onstage. It'll cost you two hundred bucks to go in," he says, leaning close and grinning, "but it's worth every penny."

A few minutes later one of the cocktail waitresses leads me down the corridor toward the Kitten Closet. As we move past the Champagne Room I try to peer inside, but the double doors are tightly closed. Anyway, the bouncer assured me that the Kitten Closet is what I really want. A moment later we're standing in front of another door.

"You get half an hour," the waitress explains, like I'm going into a tanning booth or something. "Anything you and the girl arrange for later is strictly between the two of you. The girl will let you know when your time is up. And don't get rough," she warns, her demeanor turning tough, like she's had that happen to her. "We do prosecute."

"I understand," I say, handing the girl a twenty.

She smiles at me, then opens the door and gently pushes me ahead. It's pitch black inside except for these tiny bulbs in the floor that remind me of runway lights. It's quiet too. The music fades to almost nothing when the door closes behind me.

Another woman appears out of the darkness. She takes my hand and leads me down a narrow corridor to another door, where she shows me into a room not much bigger than my Bedford cubicle. On one wall of the room there's a small window—a foot by a foot square, I guess—and the woman leads me right to it. I follow her hesitantly as my eyes are still adjusting to the gloom.

"Choose," she instructs, pointing at the window.

The window would be at eye level for a man of average height, but I have to stoop slightly to see through it. I take a deep breath, then lean down. It's exactly as I anticipated. Everything is finally falling into place. "Second from the left," I murmur, my emotions swirling. It's much darker here in this room than where the girls are standing, so I know they can't see me.

"Stay here," she instructs.

I step back into a corner when the woman leaves. Back into the darkness.

A moment later a seductive form slips into the room and the door closes behind her. She's wearing a short lacy slip that barely covers anything, as I saw when I peered through the glass and selected her over two other women who stood before me a few feet away.

Kitten. That was what Vincent called her the day he came by Bedford. Now I understand why.

As I move out of the corner, she recognizes me. Her eyes widen and she steps back as I come forward. "Augustus!" she says in her Spanish accent.

"Hello, Anna." I make certain my voice is calm. I don't want any trouble. All I want is answers.

She slides along one wall until she's trapped in a corner. "What are you doing here?"

"I came to get my wife's picture off that wall out there."

She gazes at me for a few moments, trying to act as if she doesn't understand.

"I know everything, Anna. I know Vincent brought Melanie here, and I know she was working a couple of nights a week." I move closer. "I know they called her the Vamp, and I know about the routine. I know everything," I repeat. "There's no need to act like you don't."

Anna's chin slowly drops. "I'm sorry," she says softly. "I know how you must feel."

"No, you don't."

She shakes her head. "No, I guess I don't," she agrees.

"Vincent told you about Melanie's connection to me, didn't he?"

"Yes," Anna admits, looking back up at me. "He said he wanted me to be aware of what was going on so I wouldn't screw it up. He was worried you might put a picture of her on your desk at Bedford, and that I'd recognize her and say something that would give it all away."

My vision has grown accustomed to the faint light. Now I can fully appreciate how little her lacy slip conceals. I can't help myself and for a moment my eyes flash down. "Vincent had you send me all of that promotional material on Bedford, didn't he? He told you to offer me the discount that kept getting higher and higher."

"Yes," she whispers.

"Seaver never knew. That's why he was so surprised when I told him about it the morning I came to rent the desk."

Anna puts a hand on my chest, thinking that I'm going to get angry, maybe even violent. "Don't try anything, Augustus," she warns, her voice trembling. "If I yell, they'll be in here right away. They monitor these rooms very carefully."

"Just keep talking, Anna."

"Vincent swore he'd have me fired if I didn't help him," she says, shaking her head. Her long black hair tumbles about her bare shoulders. "And he could have. He knows the people who run this place. They don't screw around. I need the money. What I earn at Bedford isn't nearly enough. I have to send money home to my family in Colombia. I have many brothers and sisters. They depend on me." She eases her head back against the wall.

I look down again. My God, she is beautiful.

"I'm sorry," she apologizes, her voice turning hoarse. "I didn't want to hurt you, especially after I got to know you a little. You seem like a nice man, but Vincent made me do it. He wanted you at Bedford so bad."

"I know he did, and I know why."

"I'm so sorry," she apologizes again, starting to sob. "Now Vincent will kill me. He said that if I ever told anyone about this, I'd end up like Melanie."

"Vincent, let me in! Wake up. Come on, Vincent! Push the button. Open up!"

Vincent's drowsy voice finally filters through the lobby intercom of his apartment complex. "Augustus, is that you?" Vincent lives in Alexandria, a suburb across the Potomac on the southeast side of Washington.

"Yes! Now let me in. I have to talk to you."

He clears his throat. "What are you doing here so late?"

"Just let me in," I say, trying to keep my voice calm to hide my anger. If he understands how furious I am, he may not push the button. "Please."

The buzzer finally sounds and I yank the lobby door open.

Moments later I'm out of the elevator and rushing down the bright red carpet of the sixth-floor hallway toward his apartment at the end of the corridor. Vincent's waiting for me at the door.

"What the hell is going on?" he asks, wearing a white T-shirt and light blue boxers. He's bleary-eyed, obviously just awakened from a sound sleep.

If Reggie is shooting straight with me about Vincent being under FBI surveillance, the place could be bugged. But I don't care. "I went back to the Two O'Clock Club tonight," I say, gritting my teeth.

"Atta boy." Vincent smiles and gives me a big-brother slap on the upper arm. "Now we're talking. Now you're getting back in the game."

"Anna was there."

Vincent stiffens. "Anna?"

"Bedford's receptionist. She was back past the Champagne Room, working in something called the Kitten Closet."

"No shit? That's unbelievable."

I'm so pissed off I'm shaking. "Don't do this, Vincent."

"Don't do what?"

"Don't act like you don't know what I'm talking about. Like you don't know Anna works at the club."

He holds his arms out, fingers spread wide, and gives me a baffled expression. "I *don't* know that. Now, if you don't mind, I've got a new acquaintance in the bedroom who's getting lonely." He steps back into his apartment and starts to shut the door.

"Anna told me everything!" I say, wedging my shoe into the doorway before he can shut it. "While she was dancing at the club, you found out that during the day she was the receptionist at Bedford. And you found out that she ran Seaver's books. She told me you got her to send me the Bedford promotional material. You had her keep sending it to me, offering me a higher and higher discount. That's why Seaver was so surprised the first day I went to Bedford to rent my desk because she was the one who had sent the material offering the old incentives without his knowledge. You told her you'd have her fired from the club if she didn't do what you said. She was scared, Vincent, and not just for her job."

"You're out of your mind, Augustus."

"You called her Kitten that day in the Bedford lobby." I groan, pushing against the door with my shoulder. "You always find out a woman's first name, but you didn't that day because you already knew it."

"Anna's full of shit."

My temper nears the breaking point. Vincent and I have never really fought. We had a couple of scraps on the practice field in high school, but nothing of any consequence. I point at him. "You wanted me at Bedford so you could keep your eye on me while you fed me inside information on stocks. You kept pushing me into day trading because you wanted to use me, not because you thought it would be good for me. You don't give a damn about me. After all these years, you were using me like somebody you didn't even know."

He grabs me by the arm and pulls me inside the apartment, then takes a quick look up and down the hallway, before shutting the door. "Keep your voice down," he hisses, then pads over to his stereo and turns on some music.

"Worried about what the Feds will hear?"

Vincent's eyes narrow. "What did you say?"

"Reggie Dorsey told me about you and your connections. Now it all makes sense."

Vincent walks slowly toward me. "What are you talking about?"

"Your Mafia connections."

He stops a few feet away and points at me. "I think Melanie's death has pushed you over the edge."

"Bullshit, Vincent! I was going to be your pigeon and don't deny it. You had a network of people who were going to slide me hot tips on companies, like Jack Trainer did with Teletekk. At a bar here or a ballgame there until I was in so deep I couldn't get myself out even if I did figure it out. Maybe you were even going to throw me bad information once in a while to keep it all feeling normal. Or maybe you figured I'd pick enough losers on my own to cover the trail. That was the plan, wasn't it? I would make all the trades and manage the money so you could keep your people protected in case there was ever a problem. If the Feds ever figured out what was going on, I would take the fall and do the time. Not you and your pals. That's why I never met the investors. That's why you made me prove myself with that first three hundred grand. So I wouldn't suspect. So I would think everything was on the up and up. Hell, they would have given me the ten million even if I'd made nothing on the three hundred grand. I knew it was all too neatly packaged, but I let you talk me into it anyway."

"You wanted to be talked into it."

"I thought you were my friend, Vincent. But no one would treat a dog the way you've treated me." I hesitate, breathing hard. "You don't have any real friends, do you?"

For several moments Vincent glares at me. But then, unexpectedly, he breaks into his most engaging smile. The smile he uses when he's trying to convince a woman he's just met to come home with him, or when he's trying to talk his way out of a speeding ticket. I've seen that smile many times—and it usually works.

"So what's the big deal, Augustus? What are you so uptight about? You'll make a nice fat fee and share in the profits. And the Feds will never figure out what's going on here. Believe me."

"That's where you're wrong. I told you, the Feds are already on to you, Vincent. They have you under surveillance. Reggie found out from an ex-Bureau buddy of his."

Vincent chuckles. "FBI guys are always talking that kind of crap, Augustus. It's just an intimidation game. Forget about it. Besides, we have friends downtown who can take care of anything if some young turk decides to make a name for himself. Everything's cool."

Adrenaline is surging through me. It's all I can do not to take a swing at him. "You lured Melanie to the Two O'Clock Club."

"I didn't lure her anywhere," he snaps, his smile disappearing.

"Yeah, you did," I answer evenly. "You wanted me at Bedford so badly. You probably pitched the idea of using me as an insider trading front to your bosses a long time ago, and they ate it up like chocolate. But you knew I could never execute the transaction volume you wanted unless I was trading full time. And you knew I'd never quit my sales job to trade full time until I had capital. So when I told you about the insurance policies, you lured her into that hellhole downtown so you could make her conveniently dead and get me the capital I needed to make the leap. It was perfect, wasn't it? Did she tell you about her fantasy of dancing at a club during that weekend in the mountains?"

Vincent makes a subtle fist. "Careful where you go with this, buddy." Then he relaxes as if he's just had a helpful thought. "Besides, you and Melanie didn't take out those policies until a couple of months ago," he points out. "She was dancing at the Two O'Clock Club way before that."

He thinks he's just scored, but when it really comes down to it, Vincent isn't very bright. "Melanie first raised the idea of the insurance policies that weekend we went to the mountains. In the car as we were following you and your date up there. She could have told you what she was thinking on your little 'walk.' "

"Didn't happen," he says matter-of-factly. "You're going to have to control your imagination. I know it's been a tough time but—"

"You knew there would be so many people for the police to go after if you got her onstage, including all the animals who watched her." I clench my teeth. "It was so easy. I had the insurance money and you had your pigeon."

"You actually think I murdered Melanie?" he asks, his eyes flashing. "You think I'm capable of that?"

"You could have *had* her murdered. I'm sure the people you associate with wouldn't have thought twice about slitting a woman's throat if it meant making millions without any risk at all."

"Get out of here, Augustus, or so help me, I'll—"

"You'll what, Vincent? Anna said you told her she could end up like Melanie if she didn't watch out." I grit my teeth. "You gonna do the same thing to me you did to Mel?"

"Augustus!"

"You know how Melanie died, don't you? Did you kill her yourself, Vincent? Did you rip that blade across her throat and leave her to die in that alley yourself?" I shout, leaning close to him. "Did you?"

He lunges at me, but I easily avoid the punch, grab his arm, and slam my foot into the side of his knee—the same knee he tore up years ago playing pro football. He's told me many times how it's never completely healed, and sure enough, he crumples instantly to the floor, clutching his leg and howling in pain. I'm on him right away, rolling him onto his stomach and pulling one wrist up to the back of his neck, and he's begging for mercy. In a matter of seconds we've resolved a question that has simmered between us for years—who's physically superior. I like the answer.

"Did you kill her?" I shout as I keep him pinned to the floor. "Tell me the truth." I force his wrist another inch higher up his back. "Tell me!"

"I swear I didn't."

"Tell me!" He groans loudly and struggles, but he's surprisingly easy to control. The pain must be intense. Another inch and his shoulder will snap. "Talk, Vincent."

"You need to have the cops check out that Taylor guy very thoroughly," he mutters. "The guy who showed up at the Grand that night two weeks ago. The guy you decked."

I ease off slightly. "Why?"

"Taylor was at the club almost every night Melanie danced. At least that's what the guy who owns the place told me. He sat right up front every time where he could get the best view. He was even there that first night Melanie danced. I saw that myself. I asked Melanie about him and she told me he was her boss. She said he was harmless, but I don't know that she was right."

"What do you mean?" He doesn't answer and I pull his wrist up his back again. "Vincent!"

"Aw, shit!"

"Tell me."

"One of the girls told the manager she had seen them arguing out in the street right before Melanie was murdered," he yells, his face contorted into an awful expression. "On a side street where Melanie had parked away from the club. That's all I know, Augustus. I swear."

I look down at him and I don't recognize him anymore. He was such a good friend for so long, and now he might as well be a perfect stranger—or the devil. "Did you and Melanie sleep together?" I ask, my voice suddenly ice cold. He doesn't answer right away and I send another jolt of searing pain through his body. "Vincent."

"Yes," he finally mumbles.

"Did you have her that weekend in the mountains?"

"Yes."

"On your walk?"

"Yes."

"When was the first time?" I have to know.

"Please let me go, Augustus. My shoulder's killing me."

"When!"

"High school," he gasps. "After the championship game."

I gaze down at him, suddenly sick to my stomach. No wonder he never wanted to talk about that night. The night I considered one of my happiest memories. Now he's ruined that for me too. "What's the name of the girl at the Two O'Clock Club who saw Taylor and Melanie arguing?"

"Erin," he says. "She's the woman who showed up at Melanie's memorial service. The one I was talking to in the parking lot afterward. I guess she and Melanie got to be pretty good friends at the club."

CHAPTER

19

Reggie's message on my cell phone's voice mail is disturbing, to say the least. He warns me to watch out for Mary Segal. As it turns out, a wealthy real estate developer was murdered in his home last Christmas. He didn't live in McLean. He lived on the other side of Washington, east of the city in a wealthy area of Maryland's Montgomery County. He and his wife were found dead by their son in their home on Christmas Day after they didn't respond to the son's repeated telephone calls. Each was a victim of a single gunshot wound to the head. According to Reggie, the man was having an affair with his blond female assistant. The woman was his bookkeeper, and the police found out that she was being paid an unusually high salary for her job—almost two hundred grand a year. Her name is Connie Harper, but she didn't show up for work after the holidays, has disappeared, and has no criminal record anywhere. The case remains unsolved, which is why Reggie is so concerned. The circumstances are too similar. The only difference is the location.

Reggie lets me know that he got my cell number off of caller ID when I phoned him from my car yesterday afternoon. He tells me to get in touch with him as soon as possible, and finishes the message by saying that it might not be a bad idea to stay in a motel tonight on the off chance Mary Segal is involved in the Montgomery County slayings. He says he thinks the odds are slight that she would show up at my door, but admits that the police are looking for her and, at some point, will want to question me about exactly what she might have said. I press the End button on the cell phone and continue to sit in the BMW, gazing through the darkness at the back entrance of the Two O'Clock Club.

I left Vincent sprawled on the floor of his apartment. I don't think I've ever been more disappointed in a person in all my life. Not even my father. I was almost sure the first day Vincent dropped by Bedford that he had been with Melanie. I could see it in his eyes when he swore they hadn't done anything that weekend we went to the Shenandoah Mountains. He kept avoiding eye contact with me. I could hear it in his voice too, but I denied it because I didn't want to face the truth. I won't ever do that again, as much as it may hurt.

I check my watch in the glow of a streetlight that filters down through the heat and the darkness. It's exactly four in the morning. Closing time for the club.

As if on cue, the door opens and a group of about ten women stream out of the place, laughing, chattering, and lighting up cigarettes. I'm out of the car and heading toward them right away, aware that they'll probably be uneasy about a man approaching them as they leave the club at this hour of the morning.

I'm right. They stop and huddle together when they see me.

"I didn't mean to startle you," I call out, halting a safe distance away. "Nothing to be worried about."

One of them hustles back toward the door and pounds on it frantically, unimpressed by my reassuring words.

"I'm looking for a woman named Erin," I say, coming a few feet closer. When I first got back here from Vincent's apartment, I checked at the front door to make certain she was working tonight. She was. "Is she here?" I ask, scanning their faces. But it's difficult to see much in the dim light, and no one answers.

"What's the problem?" The bouncer I was talking to earlier pokes his head out of the door, obviously annoyed about being bothered.

"There's a guy out here looking for Erin," the woman at the door explains, pointing at me.

I move past the huddled women toward the door, hoping Erin is still inside. "I talked to you earlier tonight, boss," I say in a friendly tone.

The bouncer squints into the darkness as I come close, but he shows no signs of recognition.

"You got me into the Kitten Closet," I remind him quietly. I don't know why I care whether these women hear that I went to the Kitten Closet, but I do.

"Oh, yeah," he says, nodding. "What do you want?"

The woman who banged on the door skirts around me back toward the group, and they head off. "Is a woman named Erin inside?"

"The club is closed for the night."

"I realize that. I waited until closing time because I didn't want to bother her while she was performing. If I could just speak to her for a minute, I'd be very grateful," I say. "This isn't about a date or anything like that." I can see he's suspicious. He's probably heard that one a million times. "It's about something else."

"What?"

"Just something," I mumble. "Please tell her I'm here. I only need to speak to her for a moment." It occurs to me that he's probably looking for a handout, so I reach in my pocket and pull out a twenty-dollar bill. "This is for you."

He grabs it. "Wait here and I'll see what I can do."

A few minutes later the bouncer pokes his head out of the door again and motions for me to come inside. "Give me another twenty bucks," he demands as I near the door.

As I slip inside the club I dig into my pocket and produce the cash.

"Stay right where you are," he orders, pointing at me authoritatively while he walks away. "Don't move."

The Two O'Clock Club is empty except for a couple of tired-looking old guys sweeping the floor with big push brooms. The chairs are upside down on the tables and the lights are bright. It's totally different in here without the women onstage, the music blaring, and men shouting for skin. But it's no less disgusting.

I recognize Erin when she appears at the far end of the bar, an apprehensive expression on her face. She looks exactly as she did at Melanie's memorial service. Her face is classic Irish—blue eyes, fair skin, and freckles all framed by dark red hair—and she seems innocent to me in her loose-fitting dress.

"What do you want?" she asks timidly from fifteen feet away, moving hesitantly along the bar.

The bouncer leans against the bar behind her and pretends to read a magazine, but I can tell he's keeping close tabs on me. "Do you recognize me?" I ask quietly.

Erin looks over her shoulder at the bouncer to make certain he's there, then back at me. "I'm sorry, I—" She moves a step closer, and suddenly I see recognition in her eyes.

"I'm Augustus McKnight, Melanie's husband. You came to her memorial service a few weeks ago."

"Oh, yeah," she agrees with a heartfelt sigh. "That whole thing was so sad."

"I wanted to thank you for coming. That was very nice of you."

"You're welcome." She has a high-pitched voice.

"I didn't have a chance to say that after the service."

"That must have been very difficult for you." She moves a little closer. We're only a few feet apart now.

"It was."

"Is that what you came here to say?" she asks curiously. "At four o'clock in the morning?"

I shake my head. "No."

"Then what do you want? I'd like to go home. I'm kinda tired, you know."

I hesitate, still unsure about the best way to approach this.

"Mister, I—"

"I hear you and Melanie were friends."

Erin's eyes flash to mine. "How did you hear that?"

"I asked around after I found out she was working here." I don't want her to know I got my information from Vincent. She'd probably clam right up. He seems to scare the hell out of people who work here. "That's what people told me."

"Yeah, so?"

"I'm trying to find out what happened to her. I understand there was one particular man who was here a lot when she was performing."

"Are you working with the cops?"

"No, I'm just a husband trying to find out what happened to his wife." I look into Erin's eyes and I see compassion. I think anyone who heard my tone just now couldn't help but feel bad for me. "I just want closure, you know?"

She nods.

"So you were friends?"

"Yeah. I liked her. She was different from the other girls." Erin shakes her head. "Which is why she never should have come here in the first place. She wasn't ready for it. She thought she was, but she wasn't."

I look down at the cigarette butts and spilled beer on the sticky floor. "I wish she had never come here too." I glance up quickly. "I don't mean that as an—"

"It's all right," Erin says, allowing herself a sad smile. "I know what you mean."

"I also heard that Melanie was known as the Vamp," I say. "And that she had a routine."

"*We* had a routine."

I look up. "You?"

"She never did it with anybody but me," Erin says, almost proudly. "But it wasn't my idea," she adds quickly. "She was the one who thought it up. The one who wanted me to do it to her. And it wasn't anything really out of control either. I mean, I never tied her real tight. She could have gotten out by herself anytime she wanted to. That was all there was to it," Erin says. "The Two O'Clock Club isn't that kind of place."

"What kind of place?"

"The kind of place that gets into all of that underground stuff. You know, the live sex shows. We dance here, but that's it."

"Uh-huh."

"She suggested it on the spur of the moment one night a few months ago," Erin continues, lighting up a cigarette and inhaling deeply. "The people who run the place weren't real happy about it at first, but it was a weeknight and there weren't too many people around. And this one guy sitting right up front was tipping us really well. The other guys went wild too, so management let us keep doing it as long as we promised not to get too crazy and not to do it too often. They didn't want trouble from the cops. I guess there are guidelines about that stuff."

"You said that this one guy up front tipped you really well?"

"Yeah, he did."

"Was he a regular?"

Erin frowns as she props her elbow against her side and holds the cigarette out away from her body. "He was here almost every night Melanie was," she finally says, smoke trailing away from her fingers toward the ceiling. "I think Melanie knew him before she came to the club. That was the impression I got from the way she talked, but I don't know for sure. Like I said, he tipped real well at first. After a while he didn't throw his cash around as much, but Melanie still gave him special attention. One night she even let him tie her wrists while she stood in front of him, but management freaked out about that and they made her promise never to do it again."

I feel the fine hairs on the back of my neck beginning to stand up. She let him tie her wrists. "Do you know anything about the guy? Did Melanie ever mention his name?" I'm not going to prompt Erin. Vincent might have been making up everything about Taylor just to get me off him. He saw me go after Taylor at the Grand. He knows how much I hate him.

"She called him David."

"David?" I ask, disappointed.

"Yeah, but I don't think that was his real name. She always kind of laughed when she called him that. Like it was a joke or something."

"Anything else?" I ask.

She takes another drag from the cigarette, thinking. "Stay here," she finally says. "I'll be back in a minute."

The bouncer flashes me a nasty look, like he wants me out of here soon. Fortunately, Erin is back quickly.

"Here," she says, handing me a blue backpack. "This was Melanie's." She opens a flap while I hold it and reaches inside. "This is the guy," she says, pulling out a Polaroid.

I let the backpack fall slowly to the floor as I take the photograph. It's a picture of Frank Taylor and Melanie standing alongside a silver Mercedes. A big sleek Mercedes that looks a lot like the one that almost ran me down in the parking garage a few weeks ago. I can't believe it.

"Melanie asked me to take that picture of them a couple of months ago." Her lip curls as she glances at the photograph. "I never trusted him."

"Me neither," I whisper.

"He and the bald guy were her biggest fans." She shakes her head sadly. "I told her they were both bad news, but she wouldn't listen."

"Who was the bald guy?"

"Just some other guy who was here a lot of the nights Melanie performed too, but he always sat in the back, seemed kind of shy. David was always right up front." She smiles. "For a while there the bald guy tipped me pretty good too, but he hasn't been back in a month or so. Come to think of it, neither has the other guy. Not since Melanie was—" Erin interrupts herself and looks away.

"What did the bald one look like?"

"Tall and thin." She grimaces. "He had bad acne scars on his face too. Real bad."

"Did he have a beard?"

"No. I wouldn't have noticed the scars on his face if he did."

"Did you ever get his name?"

Erin shakes her head. "I never ask nobody's name. The only reason I knew David's name was because Melanie told me. Better not to know. That kind of intimacy can get you in a lot of trouble." She hesitates. "Like it did Melanie. I warned her, but she didn't listen. Like I said, she wasn't ready for this place."

I check the bouncer. He's finished with his magazine. My time's running out. "You've been very helpful, Erin." I hand her a twenty-dollar bill and she takes it automatically. "I want to thank you for your time."

"Sure." She puts her hand on mine. "Melanie was a good person."

"Is there anything else you can tell me?"

I expect an immediate no, but that's not what I get. "You may not want to hear this, mister. I don't want to hurt your feelings. You seem like a good person too."

"Tell me. Please."

"I think Melanie was real sweet on that guy in the picture," she says, nodding in the direction of the pocket in which I placed the photograph. "At least in the beginning."

"I think she was too," I agree, my voice hoarse.

"See, I knew it would—"

"It's all right," I assure her.

"But it wasn't like that in the end."

"What do you mean?"

"In the last few weeks she was here they were arguing a lot. I saw them a couple of times late at night on the street near where she had parked her car."

For once, Vincent might have been telling me the truth. "Go on."

"David was yelling and shouting at her. I mean, going crazy. Finally she ran to her car and peeled off. It was the same both times. She didn't know I was watching either time, but I was worried about her. I told the manager about it," she recounts sadly, "but he didn't do anything."

"What were they arguing about? Were you close enough to hear?"

Erin looks around. "I don't want to get in trouble," she says, lowering her voice even though the bouncer and the guys sweeping the floor couldn't possibly hear her. "I don't want to have to talk to the cops. Some detective was here asking a lot of questions after Melanie died, but I was able to avoid him."

"What did the detective look like?" I ask quickly.

"He was a black guy. Big," she says, making a sweeping gesture with her arms. "I didn't talk to him. I've got a record," she admits quietly.

"I understand," I say. "But did you hear anything? It's very important for you to tell me if you did."

She nods. "There was some kind of deal Melanie had agreed to go into with David. Like a business transaction or something, and when it was done, they were going to collect some big money. It didn't sound like it was on the up-and-up, but I don't know much about that stuff."

Erin's voice fades. Frank Taylor admitted the night he came to my house that he was broke, and I never did get an honest answer from Melanie about why we were taking out the insurance policies on each other. If I had died, Melanie would have received a million dollars, which would have been one helluva dowry if Melanie and Taylor were planning all along to get married.

I'm suddenly struck by another thought. An ironic one. If I don't get the proceeds from her policy because of those slayer statutes, Frank Taylor will. As Scott Snyder told me yesterday, Taylor was secondary beneficiary on Melanie's policy. So, in effect, Taylor always had a pretty good chance of getting his hands on a million dollars of insurance proceeds no matter who died—Melanie or me.

CHAPTER

20

After giving Erin an extra hundred bucks left over from Melanie's secret stash, I check into a motel a couple of miles from my house. I'm
not that worried about Mary, but Reggie seemed pretty concerned so
I'll listen to his advice. After all, he's a cop and he doesn't strike me as
the type to get worked up over nothing. It'll be interesting to see if
Mary shows up at Bedford tomorrow and, if she does, how she acts. If
I go in, that is. I'm not sure I will.

I haven't returned Reggie's call yet. I'm worried about what he
wants. I'm not certain, but I have a hunch. That's the real reason I
check into a motel.

It's four o'clock in the afternoon, and though I'm dead tired and
crawled into bed immediately after checking into the motel at six this
morning, I haven't been able to fall into that deep sleep that restores
your energy. I keep rolling around on the bed, trying to get the pillows

256

right, but it isn't working. It's not a bad motel, as motels go. It's quiet and the mattress is pretty comfortable, even if the sheets smell like smoke in what's supposed to be a nonsmoking room. I just can't stop thinking about how Vincent lied to me about Melanie all these years, and how he was so willing to use me as a front for his insider trading scheme. How Melanie lied to me about what she was doing at night, and with whom she was doing it. How Frank Taylor could smile and shake my hand at an office party while he was screwing my wife every chance he got. How people have been lying to me and manipulating me all my life. And it all started with my father.

I can't stop trying to figure out who tore up my house too. Maybe Taylor was looking for the cash he must have known Melanie made at the club. Maybe Reggie sent his people to look for some piece of evidence they'll never find. Or maybe it was Mary who went through my possessions, just like I think she did at Bedford. I don't know. There just aren't any answers.

Around six I get dressed and leave the motel room to get dinner. I haven't had food since yesterday morning, so I drive to a diner near the motel and sit in a booth by myself, reading a *People* magazine while a kind, older lady serves me a breakfast dinner of scrambled eggs, bacon, sausage gravy, hash browns, and pancakes. It's delicious—like my mother used to fix on Sunday nights—and I take my time with the meal, savoring each bite. With a full stomach, I'm asleep five minutes after returning to my room.

The next thing I know it's seven o'clock Monday morning. The television is still on and the remote is poking me in the cheek. I sit up and rub my eyes. It's time to get on with what I need to do.

At ten o'clock I walk straight into the reception area of Frank Taylor's law firm. It's a small firm and I remember the office layout from the Christmas parties he threw. There are about ten offices beyond this reception area off of two corridors, and a few cubicles for the assistants in an open area in between the corridors. Where Melanie used to sit.

"Good morning, sir." The receptionist is a prim woman with a high, starched white collar reaching almost to her chin. "Can I help you?"

"I'm here to see Frank Taylor."

"Do you have an appointment?" she sniffs, reaching for a leather-bound book on one side of her desk. "I don't remember Mr. Taylor having any appointments this morning."

"His office is all the way down the left corridor, isn't it?" I ask as I move past her desk. "All the way in the back, yes?"

"Wait a minute," she pipes up. "You can't go in there like that. Stop!" she orders shrilly as I stride into the corridor.

Out of the corner of my eye I see her reach for the phone, but I keep going, intent on what I'm about to do.

"Hello, Frank."

Taylor's eyes flash up from a thick casebook as I move into his doorway. His feet are up on his desk, and he drops them heavily to the floor as soon as he recognizes me, then tosses the book on his cluttered desk and stands up. "What are you doing here?" he snaps, wincing and touching his ribs as he rises. He must still be hurting from that knee I dropped onto his chest a few nights ago. And his face doesn't look so good either. I beat the crap out of him, that's for sure. Felt good too.

"We need to talk, Frank." The receptionist appears behind me, and I turn toward her for a moment, giving her a fierce look. "Get out of here," I order. She stumbles away, petrified, and I close and lock the office door behind her.

"My receptionist will call the police," Taylor tells me, sitting back down in his desk chair with a muffled groan. "She has orders to do that if anyone barges past her desk. When you're in the divorce business, you have to anticipate that passions may run high. You have no more than three minutes before the cops get here, so you better tell me quickly what's on your mind."

I stare at him for a moment before I speak, thinking about the knife slicing through Melanie's soft skin. "You killed her, didn't you, Frank?"

Taylor laughs loudly, then grimaces as pain ripples through his chest. "Do you *really* think that, Augustus? Are you that stupid?"

"You told me yourself that your law practice is in a shambles." I motion at the door behind me. "There were a lot of vacant offices along the corridor. It's a ghost town in here."

His eyes narrow. "So?" he asks, crossing his arms over his chest.

I could always sense when we talked at his Christmas parties that Taylor didn't believe I was a very intelligent man. He always had a vaguely condescending manner, like he considered himself well above me on the IQ ladder. But suddenly I can see in his expression that he's worried I've figured a few things out and that maybe I'm not as average as he thought. "I never understood why Melanie wanted us to take out those life insurance policies, but now I know."

Taylor pulls his arms tighter across his chest but says nothing.

"Remember at the Grand that night you 'happened' to show up?" I continue. "You accused me in front of a woman I was talking to of killing Melanie. You accused me of killing Melanie before she could sign her will, and that as a result her parents wouldn't get the money as she would have wanted. But that was all crap, Frank. Just legal mumbo jumbo you thought a guy like me wouldn't understand."

"You let me worry about the legal issues."

"You're the secondary beneficiary on Melanie's policy. Who gets the life insurance proceeds has nothing to do with a will, even if she had signed one. Somehow you got her to name you as the second before she died, which is all the insurance company really cares about."

"Someone has been feeding you bad information—"

"Don't lie to me, Taylor," I warn, raising my voice and taking a step toward him. He straightens up in the chair quickly and makes a subtle move for one of his desk drawers, but stops when I stop. "I know you're the second on the policy. A guy named Scott Snyder dropped that bomb on me. Seems he's been taking quite an interest in my life lately. He's a private investigator here in Washington, and though he didn't come right out and say it, he thinks I killed my wife."

"Well, it's good to know people like him are on the ball. Good to know it won't be long before you're where you belong. Behind bars."

I want to throw Taylor out of the fifth-story window behind his desk so he can feel the same pain Slammer did, but I keep my anger under control—for now. "Snyder told me all about slayer statutes too, Frank." I'm seething and my voice is starting to shake. "About laws that bar a person who causes bodily harm to another in the course of a crime from benefiting. So if I'm implicated in Melanie's death, you'll get the money because you're the second. You'll get the million dollars."

"That's news to me, Augustus," Taylor says, trying his best to seem surprised. But it's a terrible performance.

"Your original plan was to kill me."

Taylor points at the door. "Get out of here, Augustus. I've had enough of this."

"Then you were going to marry Melanie so you could get your hands on the insurance money to save your law practice."

Surprisingly, he nods. "I won't deny that I wanted to marry her. I loved her very much."

"Sure you did," I reply sarcastically. "A million dollars' worth." His hands squeeze tightly into fists, but he won't challenge me. He knows better than to try something after that night on my lawn. "But Melanie wouldn't agree to all that, would she?" I continue. "She was willing to divorce me for you, but ultimately she wasn't willing to help you kill me. She went as far as to convince me to take out the policies, but when you pressed, she wouldn't go through with it. Down deep, Melanie wasn't the monster you are."

Taylor laughs as if to say that he finds my accusations ludicrous. "You have quite an imagination, Augustus."

"Is that what you and Melanie fought about outside the Two O'Clock Club the night of her murder? Killing me?"

Taylor's eyes flash to mine, and I see that I've gotten his attention. "We never fought," he says, his voice cold.

"I have a witness who saw you two arguing that night. She's a woman Melanie danced with. Erin would pick you out of a lineup with no trouble. You watched that routine so many times. Participated once too, didn't you?"

Taylor licks his lips nervously but remains silent.

I take another step forward, and now I'm right in front of his desk. This time he makes no move for the drawer. "You were worried Melanie might go to the police, and you were desperate for cash, so you hatched a different plan right there on the street while you argued. One that would end up getting you the same amount of money as long as you could hang the murder on me. A million dollars tax free. You knew she had demanded a divorce from me the night before. You knew the cops would latch on to that as the motive for the murder. That and the insurance money, because I was the primary beneficiary. It was perfect, wasn't it? You couldn't have scripted it better."

"You're so far off. You're desperate because you know the police are closing in on you."

He's saying all the right things, but I can tell he's rattled. I've figured everything out, and suddenly he understands that his perfect plan wasn't so perfect after all. "You almost screwed up," I continue. "You almost let your temper get the best of you. After I popped you at the Grand, you got your silver Mercedes and tried to run me down in the parking garage. You were drunk and pissed off and you wanted the money right away."

"I told you before, I don't have a Mercedes!"

I reach into my pocket and pull out the photograph of Melanie and him alongside the car. "You may not now, but you did." The picture trembles with my fingers.

Suddenly there's a commotion in the hallway. The police have arrived quickly, as Taylor predicted they would. "I know everything, Frank," I say quietly, aware that I have only a few moments of freedom remaining. But this is the way I want it. I'm not going to run from Reggie. I'm going to face him like a man. "I know what Melanie did for you, at the club and in private. I know how she performed. She used to do the same thing for me." I hesitate, then point at him. "I'll convince the Washington police that you are guilty of Melanie's murder if it's the last thing I do. I promise you that."

"It'll be the last thing you *try* to do before they send a couple of thousand volts screaming through your body," he says. "But you won't convince them, because I didn't do it. You did!"

"Mr. Taylor!' comes a loud voice from the corridor.

The police are right outside, probably with their guns drawn. I'm almost out of time.

"Mr. Taylor, are you in there?"

"Yes, help me!" he shouts suddenly. "He's going to kill me!" He struggles to stand, holding one hand out in front of his face, clutching his ribs with the other. I watch in amazement as he tumbles backward over his chair just before uniformed policemen break down the door and spill into the room. His timing is impeccable. What a showman. Moments later my hands are cuffed tightly behind my back, and I'm being hustled down the corridor toward reception by five officers.

21

Reggie is subdued as he sits on the opposite side of a scratched wooden table in this sweltering, sparsely furnished interrogation room. He's slouched down, chin on his chest, hands thrust deeply into his pockets, and he seems to be contemplating the toes of his cordovan loafers while he thinks about how he wants to proceed. A few beads of sweat glisten on his forehead.

"You must have known I'd find out about you going after Frank Taylor in his office this morning," he says quietly.

Standing behind Reggie is another man. It's the same guy who accompanied Reggie to my house the night he stood on my stoop and informed me of Melanie's murder. The guy stands in front of the door to the hall like a sentry, arms crossed defiantly, his sports coat off so I can see the handle of a 9-mm pistol protruding menacingly from his leather shoulder holster. As if I'd even think about trying to escape. This dimly lit room is buried in the bowels of the precinct, and I wouldn't stand a chance of making it out of here, even if I could get past Reggie and the other guy.

"Did you hear me, Augustus?"

"I heard you."

"What do you have to say for yourself?"

As near as I can tell, it's been about three hours since the cops brought me to the precinct. Most of that time I've been confined to a cell down the hall with a couple of guys who looked like hardened criminals. Two uniformed officers brought me in here a few minutes ago to meet with Reggie. "I wanted to look Taylor in the eye."

"Why?"

I shoot another quick glance in the direction of the man standing in front of the door. "You know why."

"Is Lewis bothering you?" Reggie asks.

"He isn't making me real comfortable with that gun sticking out of his holster," I admit.

"Take a cigarette break," Reggie orders.

"You sure?" Lewis asks. "This guy's pretty big."

"I'll be fine."

"Okay. I'll be right outside if you need me," Lewis says before closing the door. I see him peering at me through the door's small window for a moment, then he disappears.

"Now tell me why it was so all-fired important for you to be able to look Taylor in the eye," Reggie says.

"I wanted to make certain he was the one who murdered Melanie."

Reggie pulls a pack of cigarettes out and offers one to me, but I decline. "And?"

"And now I'm certain he did it."

"Tell me why you're so certain." Reggie removes a cigarette from the pack and taps the filter end on the table several times, then places it in his mouth. But he doesn't light it. He's trying so hard to be good.

I take a deep breath. "He had a clear motive."

"Which was?"

"His law practice was failing, and he was broke. He needed the money from Melanie's insurance policy to save himself financially."

"But Melanie's mother was second on the policy. You told me that yourself."

"Somehow Taylor must have convinced Melanie to make him second. Maybe he asked her to marry him and that's when she agreed to make the change." I run my hands through my hair and realize that it's gotten long over the last few weeks. "But I'm sure you already knew that." He strokes his thin mustache and looks away. "Don't play games with me, Reggie," I say. "You're much too thorough not to have already uncovered that piece of information."

"So you think Taylor was banking on the fact that we'd arrest you," Reggie continues, "and that he would get the money from the insurance policy on account of the slayer statute."

"Yes."

Reggie puts the cigarette under his nose and takes a long whiff, then pulls out a pack of matches and drops them on the table. "Let's not forget that you had a very compelling motive too. Melanie was demanding a divorce and she was having an affair with Taylor. You needed the money as well." Reggie's fingers crawl across the table toward the matches.

"I've been with Melanie since we were in high school. I couldn't have killed her. My God, she was my wife."

"Like no husband has ever killed his wife," Reggie scoffs, rolling his eyes. "People kill out of revenge and passion much more often than they do for money. I can tell you that from experience. The odds aren't in your favor on that one, Augustus. A capable prosecutor will easily convince a jury of that." Reggie frowns. "And it would be very difficult for that same prosecutor to convince a jury that Taylor would kill a woman for insurance proceeds when he wasn't the primary beneficiary on her policy. Prosecutors play the odds like anyone else, Augustus. After a while it becomes just a job for them. They indict the person they think they can convict. They lose sight of the human aspect. It's too bad, but you can't blame them."

Reggie is a hard man, but I've always felt that down deep he liked me. Despite all of that tough talk about being able to remain objective and never being surprised at what people are capable of.

"What do you mean, you can't blame them?"

"I mean that prosecutors in this city are judged by their conviction rate. They get raises for putting people in prison, not for letting them back on the street. Prosecutors want cases they know they can win, not ones they think they have a good chance of losing."

"Frank Taylor is guilty," I say firmly. "He had motive, he had opportunity, and he argued with Melanie the night of her murder. There was a witness."

Reggie looks up. "Who? What was her name?"

"A woman named Erin who dances at a place here in D.C. called the Two O'Clock Club." I hesitate. "I know you've been there. Erin said you showed up a couple of times asking questions, but that she was able to avoid you." I pause again. "She and Melanie had a routine they did at the club. A bondage routine." Reggie stares at me but says nothing. "That's why you asked me if Melanie had ever performed for me when you came by Bedford that day. That's why you tried to dig into our sex life. You already knew about Melanie and the club."

"Yes, I did," Reggie agrees quietly.

"How did you find out?"

"I checked Melanie's social security records. We always do that in a murder case just to see if there's concealed income that could lead to another life that people close to the victim might not have known about. In this case, that's exactly what we found. Even places like the Two O'Clock Club have to pay the women who work there a small per-hour amount. It's required by law. Consequently they have to withhold taxes and social security. Like waiters and waitresses, the women make most of their money in cash tips, but they still get that tiny weekly paycheck, part of which has to go to the Social Security Administration. That's how I found out." He folds his arms across his chest. "Now, go on."

I take a deep breath. "Erin saw Melanie and Frank Taylor arguing outside the club on a couple of occasions," I say, not wanting to think about Vincent. "She saw Taylor shouting at Melanie a few blocks from the club the night of Melanie's murder."

"I'll check into that," Reggie promises, his fingers an inch from the matches.

I lean forward and snatch the matches away just in the nick of time. "One more thing."

"What?" Reggie asks quickly, eyeing the matches longingly.

I close my eyes tightly. "The night Melanie told me she wanted a divorce . . ."

"Yes?"

"The night before her murder."

"Yes?" he asks again impatiently.

"Melanie had bruises on her wrists, as though she'd been tied up. I saw them right after she asked me for the divorce. The ones the coroner identified."

Reggie stares at me intently. "So?"

"Taylor was the one tying her up. She probably even asked him to do it the first time," I say, remembering a night long ago when she first suggested that I bind her wrists with my necktie and take what I wanted. "She liked it." I'm thinking on the irony of how she partly satisfied her need for power over men by being restrained. "Taylor was enjoying it," I continue. "He even did it at the club once. You can ask Erin. He thought he was the one who had the power in their relationship, but he was wrong. Ultimately it was the other way round. Melanie had all the power. Until he decided he couldn't take it anymore." I look away. "It all blew up on him that night she asked me for the divorce. He needed the money desperately, but when he asked, she wouldn't help him kill me. So he killed her instead."

"Whoa, kill you?" Reggie asks incredulously. "What are you talking about?"

"That was Taylor's initial plan."

"Do you have proof of that?"

"He was going to kill me," I say adamantly, even though I know I don't have anything at all that would stand up in court. "Then he was going to marry Melanie so he could get the money to save his practice. But ultimately she wouldn't help him kill me so he killed her instead, betting that you would come after me as the murderer. Just as you have."

"You're reaching, Augustus."

"His plan was ingenious, and you're doing exactly as he knew you would. Frank Taylor is a monster, Reggie.

Reggie's eyes narrow. "It was your blood beneath Melanie's fingernails, Augustus, not Frank Taylor's. Our lab people confirmed that yesterday."

"That's no surprise," I reply calmly. "The night before her murder, the night she asked me for the divorce, she became violent, beating my chest over and over. I tried to restrain her without hurting her, but at one point she was able to wrench her hands free. It was then that she scratched my neck," I say, pointing to the faint scars below my left ear. "That happened the night *before* her murder."

"Remember what I said about prosecutors," Reggie reminds me. "About how they want to win. That kind of physical evidence makes their mouths water. Blood beneath the victim's fingernails is the kind of thing that sticks in a jury's mind." He takes a deep breath. "That and the fact that you have a recent history of violence."

"What are you talking about?"

"Today was the third time in the last few weeks that you've assaulted Frank Taylor. The third time you've tracked him down and beaten him silly. He logged in the other two assaults a couple of days ago and said he was going to get a restraining order against you. Said he had plenty of witnesses." Reggie's expression turns grim. "You just couldn't leave him alone."

"Nope."

"Well, it's another nail in your coffin. It proves you hated him. And it will prove to a jury that you thought he was having an affair with Melanie, and that you couldn't handle it. It will make them believe that you are a man capable of cutting your wife's throat. As will the fact that you assaulted a woman named Sasha in Vienna. There's a witness on that one too."

I was about to explain to Reggie how Taylor had searched me out on the previous two occasions and that I hadn't touched him today, but I'm momentarily stunned by the news that Sasha has filed a complaint against me for what happened on Saturday. I try to say something, but I can't.

Reggie watches me struggle. "You jacked her up against the wall of her place," he says. "You choked her and she has a witness. A young man who swears you looked like you were going to kill her when he came down the steps. By herself, I don't believe the woman would be convincing. She's a psychic, for Christ's sake. Even a cut-rate defense attorney could shred her on the stand. But with an additional witness, you're as good as convicted, my man."

"The witness looks like a druggie."

"He might now, but when the DA's office gets through with him, he'll look like a choirboy. They'll get him a haircut and buy him a suit, and before you know it, Augustus is a dead man."

I realize what Reggie's saying is right. If I were a prosecutor I'd want me at the defense table too. I look up when I hear his chair scratch across the linoleum floor.

"I'm sorry, Augustus, but you leave me no choice," he says, standing up. "I'm going to book you on a charge of first-degree murder." He tosses his unlit cigarette into a trash can by the door. "Lew will be in to read you your rights, and if you don't know a good criminal lawyer, I can help." He starts to turn the doorknob, then stops. "Augustus?"

I was staring down at the floor again, wondering if this nightmare will ever end. "Yes?" I ask, my voice gravelly.

"One of the first times we talked, I asked where you were the night of Melanie's death."

"And I told you. I took a drive. I'd quit my job, and Melanie had demanded a divorce. I needed some time alone."

"Winchester, right?"

"Yes," I mumble, wondering why he's asking. "I wanted to go to the mountains. I love the mountains."

"How did you come back to the city? What road did you take?"

I think for a second. "Route 50. I took it out and back."

"Do you remember what time you started back from Winchester?"

"Around ten, maybe even a little later than that."

"Okay," he says, turning to go.

"Reggie?" I call as he's about to walk out the doorway.

"What is it?"

"Did the Montgomery police ever find Mary Segal?"

He shakes his head. "Not as of ten this morning."

"One more thing."

"What?"

"Does Washington, D.C., have the death penalty?"

CHAPTER

22

A few moments after Reggie leaves the interrogation room, Lewis returns to read me my Miranda rights in a fast-forward monotone I can barely understand because he's speaking so quickly. I'm not paying much attention either.

During the entire time Lewis "processes" me into the penal system, I don't sense that he cares one way or the other about me. It's just his way of making a living, and I can tell he can't wait until his shift is over. He isn't passionate about his job, or life, the way Reggie is. He'll never be the cop—or the man—Reggie is.

It's interesting the way Reggie markets himself as a cold, hard man, when down deep he's really a good guy who's just driven to do the right thing. To find the truth. It's strange what you think about when you're being fingerprinted for the first time in your life.

When Lewis has a clear imprint of each of my fingertips, he hands me a roll of paper towels to wipe off the ink while he completes my paperwork. Then he leads me back down the hall to the holding cell where I sit for a few hours until they're ready to transport me to the city jail with the rest of the hoodlums they've rounded up overnight. It's a short ride and it isn't pleasant. The whole time I feel like the other guys in the van are sizing me up. I can only imagine what for.

A few hours after being locked in my cell, I'm sitting on the lower bunk, staring at a cold gray wall two feet away. A feeling of despair sinks in as someone down the hall calls lights-out. I thought I was lonely in the motel room, but last night was nothing compared to this. I almost wish there was somebody else in here just so I'd have some-one to talk to. Even if he was a hard case with a violent record. Any-thing would be better than this.

I remember the first time I spent the night at a friend's house as a child. I was seven years old and I woke up in the middle of the night in that strange, dark house feeling completely alone. My first night in jail, I wake up the same way, shivering even though it isn't cold, wishing I could go home. Knowing I can't. Knowing that this time there's no one who will magically appear to rescue me.

I manage to keep my emotions in check, though I feel the heat in my eyes and the pit in my stomach more than once during the night. But two other men can't. They sob uncontrollably in their cells while the hard cases laugh, then finally yell for them to shut up. If they don't, the tough guys warn, they'll pay. It's a helluva first night, and more than once I second-guess my decision to go to Frank Taylor's of-fice. But I had to bring everything to this. There was no other choice.

The thing about jail is that you can hear everything. There's noth-ing but rock and metal inside these walls—nothing to absorb sound the way there is on the outside. It's like being on the water, the way sound travels in here. As I lie awake and stare through the darkness at the wall, I can hear all of the whimpers, the whispers, the obscenities, the snores, the guttural coughs, and the guy in the cell next to mine who masturbates repeatedly—at least once an hour—without any at-tempt to conceal what he's doing from the rest of us. I close my eyes, and for the first time in years I pray, hands folded on my chest as I lie on my back on the lower bunk. I pray that someday I'll see the mountains again.

Reggie comes through on his promise to help me find a defense attorney. The guy's name is Walter Cox, and I can tell the first time we meet that he's as competent as they come. He's a sharp dresser with a deep tan and authoritative good looks. He speaks as quickly as Lewis did while reading me my rights, but I can understand Walter. He's incredibly articulate, and I can see how a jury would fall in love with him right away. He has a knockout smile and there's something about him that makes you want to believe what he's saying, whether it makes sense or not. He tells me he's defended several famous people and that he has an excellent track record. Then we get down to business.

At the end of the last of our three meetings over the next week, Walter raises one dark eyebrow and levels with me. He says I'm in a tight spot, and that it will take a minor miracle to convince a jury of my innocence. He doesn't actually say it in those words, but I think I'm translating accurately. As he's leaving, he pats me on the back and tells me to keep my chin up. He says he's been on a roll lately and he doesn't want me ending that winning streak. Then, with a nod to the guard, he's gone and I'm led back to my cell from the visitors' room, the shackles on my ankles forcing me to take short, awkward steps.

I just want my life back. That's all I want.

"Augustus."

I look up from the wall of my cell and a guard named Randy is standing outside the bars. He's taken pity on me since I was brought in, slipping me newspapers and magazines so I won't go crazy. He even smuggled me in a shot of scotch the other night. I just hope there isn't a quid pro quo in all of this somewhere.

"There's someone here to see you," Randy announces.

I'm not expecting anyone. Cox said he wouldn't be back for a couple of weeks. He said he had everything he needed for now, and that he was going to Nantucket on vacation. "Who is it?"

Randy smiles slyly. "You'll see," he answers, nodding for the guard down the hall to unlock my cage.

When he opens the door of the cell, I stand up with my feet close together and hold my hands side by side in front of me so he can put the cuffs on my wrists, then the shackles on my ankles. I follow him down the cell-lined corridor in my prison grays, struggling to keep pace in the clumsy gait the shackles impose, wondering.

The visitors' room is a large open area surrounded by bars and furnished with large tables and benches. It's Monday afternoon so it isn't crowded. There's only one family over in the near corner. A mother and her two children—one of whom is a just a baby—visiting a tattoo-covered convict. The man cradles the little girl in his arms while the young boy hugs him.

"Wait a minute," Randy says as we come to the door. He unlocks my handcuffs, then squats down and unchains the shackles. During my visits with Walter Cox I was forced to remain in chains, but once again, Randy's taking pity on me. As he rises up, chains dangling from his hands, he points to the far corner of the large room. "Over there."

I walk slowly through the open area toward a woman with long dark hair who sits with her back to me. As she hears me coming she turns around and I'm overcome by her beauty. "Anna."

Anna smiles the most gorgeous smile I've seen in a long time as I sit down across the table from her. "Hello, Augustus." Surprisingly, she leans across the table and kisses me on the cheek.

"What are you doing here?" I ask. "I mean, I appreciate your coming, but I'm kind of shocked to see you."

"I heard what happened and I couldn't believe it." She pats my hand. "I just wanted to make certain you were all right."

"I'm fine," I say bravely, not at all certain that I am.

We're silent for a few moments, then she speaks up. "I have something for you," she says, picking up a manila envelope off the bench beside her and placing it on the table. She motions toward Randy, who stands by the room's lone door. "It's all right for you to look. The guards have already inspected it."

I pick up the envelope and peer inside. And there is the black-and-white photograph of Melanie that was affixed to the wall of the Two O'Clock Club. Now the animals can no longer gawk at her. "Thank you," I whisper. I can't believe she's done this for me.

She squeezes my hand. "It's the least I could do. You were so nice to me that night at the club. You could have been furious. You had every right to be. It's so hard to believe they've arrested you for mur—" She glances into my eyes, then quickly away.

"I didn't kill Melanie," I assure her. Anna has to believe that, even though I know there will always be doubt in her mind—in everyone's mind—unless somehow I'm let out of here *and* the real killer is brought to justice.

"I believe you."

"Thanks." Even if she doesn't, it's nice to hear her say that.

"It must be so hard in here."

"It is. It's—" I interrupt myself at the sight of Reggie standing behind Anna. I didn't see him come in. I was so focused on Anna's beauty. There is no beauty in prison.

"Hello, Augustus," he says, staring down at me over Anna's shoulder.

"Hello."

"I'm Detective Reggie Dorsey," he says, extending his hand to Anna, who has turned around.

"Hello," she says stiffly, shaking his hand.

"I'm sorry to be rude," he says, "but there's something I need to discuss in private with Augustus."

"Oh, of course." She gives me a quick parting smile, then stands up and heads toward Randy and the door.

"Sorry about that," Reggie says, noting the disappointment in my expression, "but I think what I have to tell you will make you forget everything else."

I catch my breath. "What?"

"One hour ago we arrested Frank Taylor for the murder of your wife. You're a free man." Reggie says this as directly as the way he told me Melanie was dead. "You were right about everything."

"My God," is all I can murmur. The relief is overpowering. I can't even begin to describe it.

"We found the murder weapon in his garage. It was a hunting knife and it had Melanie's blood on it. He said he'd never seen it, but he's lying." Reggie begins ticking off the evidence. "We tracked down the silver Mercedes, which he had sold a few weeks ago. There were several drops of Melanie's blood on one of the back wheel rims, and we found her hair inside the car too. You were right about his practice. He owed five hundred grand to a bank in town and he had no way to pay it off. He'd been counting on a big payoff from a case he took on a contingency basis last year, but the plaintiff ended up settling for almost nothing three months ago. Taylor was on the brink with nowhere to turn." Reggie shakes his head. "We think he killed Erin too. That woman you spoke to at the club. She was found yesterday, strangled to death in her apartment."

"Oh, no."

"Yeah," he says, grimacing. "There were fibers from Taylor's carpet in her apartment. He must have figured she would talk." Reggie hesitates and lowers his voice. "You must have told Taylor that you had spoken to Erin."

"Yes, I did," I say, stunned. Erin seemed like a nice person, and she was one of the few people willing to help me. Now she's dead. I've caused more pain. "Has Taylor admitted to Melanie's murder?" I ask quietly.

"No, but he will. The evidence is overwhelming." Reggie smiles again. "By the way, you've got an alibi."

I look at him curiously. "How is that possible? I told you, I didn't talk to anyone when I took the drive."

"I got your tag number from the DMV and ran a check for any traffic monitoring systems the Fairfax County police might have set up on Route 50. They do that a lot these days. You know, cameras at bad intersections to catch people who run red lights."

"Yeah?"

"You got lucky," he says, his smile widening. "A few months ago the county boys set up one of those systems at an intersection just east of the bridge where Route 28 crosses over Route 50 coming south from Dulles Airport. There had been several fatal accidents at that intersection within a couple of weeks. It's a long light for people trying to turn onto Route 50 from the side road, and people were running it. It took some time, and I had to call in a lot of favors, but the county people went through tapes of that day and, sure enough, they tracked your Toyota heading east through that intersection at 11:12 P.M. The coroner confirmed that, based upon the coagulation of Melanie's blood, she died before eleven o'clock that night, so there's no way you could have killed her."

I stand up slowly and reach across the table to shake Reggie's hand. His constant search for the truth has saved me. I can't begin to explain what I'm feeling right now. It's as if I've been given a second chance at life.

"There's one thing I don't understand, though," Reggie says.

"What is it?"

"Nothing, I'm sure."

"Tell me."

Reggie purses his lips and strokes his mustache. "I still have an anonymous source. Someone who told me to go to Erin's apartment. Otherwise it might have been days before we found her."

I stare into Reggie's brown eyes, thinking. Then suddenly it hits me. Now it's up to me to make things right.

CHAPTER

23

Two hours south-southwest of Washington, D.C., in rural Rappahannock County, Virginia, a winding Route 211 passes over the most eastward line of the ancient Appalachian Mountains at almost four thousand feet above sea level, near a point called The Pinnacle. Here you can turn off 211 onto Skyline Drive—a sliver of road that snakes along mountaintops—and pick up the Appalachian Trail, a lonely and demanding hiking path that stretches all the way from Georgia to Maine. Points on the trail provide breathtaking views of the lush Shenandoah Valley to the west and the rolling hills of Virginia's horse country extending back toward Washington to the east. On summer weekends, Skyline Drive and the Appalachian Trail can be crowded with tourists, but from Monday to Friday, the thickly forested slopes provide a rare measure of solitude.

During times of emotional intensity—whether it's joy or sorrow—

I'm drawn to these mountains so strongly it's difficult for me to describe. I came here the day after we won our high school football championship; the day before I asked Melanie to marry me; and a couple of days after she died—each time alone. And here I am—alone again—only a few hours after having gotten out of jail.

I don't know why I'm drawn so intensely to this place, but I am. If I were religious, I'd say it's because I feel closer to heaven and because up here I can truly appreciate the vastness and beauty of God's world. But I'm not a religious man, and my stay in jail hasn't caused me any sort of stunning epiphany, though I thought a great deal about hell while I gazed at my cell wall.

I'm headed toward a lonely cliff popular with rock climbers on weekends and a favorite destination of mine. It's a strenuous hike from a remote parking area off Skyline Drive to get here, but it's worth it. The panoramic view of the valley stretching out far below is incredible. You can see the thin blue line of the Shenandoah River flowing north, picturesque farms dotting its banks for miles. You have to walk for over an hour to get here, even at a brisk pace, following a steep rocky path as it rises through the dense forest. Then suddenly you break through the foliage and move out onto twenty feet of flat rock. You have to be careful not to rush ahead too quickly because at the end of the shelf the cliff falls straight down several hundred feet. I always get a nervous thrill as I inch toward the edge and crane my neck to look over the side.

For several minutes I stare out over the valley, standing only a foot from the drop-off, basking in the warm sunshine, the solitude, and my regained freedom.

When I turn back around, Roger is standing at the tree line where the earth meets the rock, pointing a revolver directly at me.

"Hello, Augustus," he says calmly. His toupee is gone, as is his beard. He looks very different, but I still recognize him. "I was kind of hoping you'd still have on your prison grays," he says, smirking. "I wanted to see what you looked like on the inside."

"Is that Slammer's revolver?" I ask, nodding at the gun.

He hesitates, surprised by the question. "Yeah."

He should have known I'd figure out everything. There was so much time to do nothing but think in jail. "The police were looking for it after Slammer jumped. They searched the trading floor but couldn't find it. I knew you or Mary had taken it."

"Good for you," he retorts sarcastically, glancing around. "What else did you know?"

"I knew you were never married. Hell, I've seen that picture you put up in your Bedford cubicle of your 'wife and kids' in a Hallmark store near my house. I had a feeling from the start that you weren't really married. The odds of a guy being able to quit his job to day trade without telling his wife or having her find out are pretty damn small. And that night you came to the baseball game with Vincent and me, I had to remind you to call home. A man married to the kind of woman you described would have been calling home to make excuses. And you kept changing the name of your daughter. It just didn't add up."

"Yeah, well—"

"And it occurred to me that you'd been to the Two O'Clock Club before Vincent took us there last Thursday. You were so excited about the prospect of going to a strip club, but when you found out it was the Two O'Clock Club, you practically set an Olympic record for the hundred-yard dash getting out of there. At first I couldn't figure out what had happened. I thought maybe you'd just gotten cold feet. But then something Erin told me made me realize it was the Two O'Clock Club in particular you wanted to stay away from, especially with me. She told me how much you liked that routine she and Melanie did." I take a step toward him.

"Hold it right there," he warns, raising the gun.

"That's why you ran that night, wasn't it?" He doesn't answer. "You'd seen Erin dancing at the club before and you were worried she might recognize you when we walked in. Or any of the other girls for that matter. That if they did, and said hello, I might start to wonder. You weren't ready for me to wonder at that point, were you?" I pause. "And of course that's why you wore that pathetic toupee and grew a beard before you came to Bedford. Just in case you ran into Vincent or Taylor or anybody else who might have noticed you in the shadows of the Two O'Clock Club." I pause again. "You'd always had to come through the front door of the club, but we were coming in through the back. You didn't recognize the place. If you had, you would have been gone as soon as the limo stopped."

He pulls the hammer of the gun back and it clicks menacingly in the quiet of the mountaintop.

"You saw Melanie dancing there too," I continue. "Erin told me that. She didn't actually mention your name," I say, "but when she said there was a bald guy with bad acne in the back of the club almost every night Melanie danced, I figured it had to be you. I looked for you in the pictures on the wall near the back entrance. I was hoping the cameras might have caught you in the crowd, but you must have been careful about that." My anger starts to burn. "Did you enjoy that show Melanie and Erin put on? Erin said you tipped her very well, at least in the beginning."

"I enjoyed the hell out of it, Augustus. I enjoyed getting a real good look at your wife."

"You killed her," I whisper, now absolutely convinced of the revelation that struck me this morning in the visitors' area of the jail. I was wrong about Vincent. Taylor too, as much as I wanted it to be him. It was Roger all along. "You were the one."

"Yes, I was," Roger confirms. "She had a habit of stopping at a convenience store a few blocks from the club. And so I followed her. When she came out of the store, I surprised her and dragged her around the side of the building. I sliced her neck wide open, then carried her back into the alley where the cops found her. It was over in a few seconds. No one ever saw a thing."

"Jesus," I murmur. It's exactly as I imagined.

Roger raises the gun and points it straight at my head. "Thirty-five years ago our father raped my mother in southern Ohio. Statutory rape, but still rape."

I stare at Roger, all else around us except his face fading to nothing. "I know."

"George Wayne Franklin stayed in touch with my mother, Regina Embry, over the years. He visited her every few months. He knew where she was living, and she knew where he was. She knew he had a wife and a child too, another son. And she knew when he died last fall. She told me he was rich while I was growing up, but I found out how wrong she was when I got here ten months ago. I guess he bragged to her to make her think he was better than he was." He shakes his head. "I got here thinking I was going to find a half brother who'd just inherited a boatload of money. Instead, I found a man as poor as me, with a wife who was cheating on him. I was going to turn around and go home, but then I decided to stay. Now I'm glad I did because I'm going to be rich.

"I spent months learning about you and Melanie," he continues. "I'd follow you to work, and I'd follow Melanie when she'd meet that Carlucci guy at his apartment to fuck him. I was there the very first night she danced at the Two O'Clock Club too. That's how I found out about her affair with Frank Taylor. Then I found out about the insurance policies from that woman she did the routine with. Erin. I kept tipping her real well and she mentioned it. When I saw Melanie and Taylor get into it one night outside the club, I knew I could frame him. The only thing left would be to do away with you, and I'd have the money when I showed up at the table as your only living relative. The law is pretty straightforward there.

"But the cops went right for you as the murderer, Augustus, so I had to 'help' them see the error of their ways. I had to throw them another more believable suspect. So I murdered Erin and planted evidence on Taylor. I guided them toward that silver Mercedes as well. Made them see Taylor had plenty of motive to kill Melanie too." He smiles proudly.

"You were Reggie's anonymous informant," I say quietly.

"Yes, I was very helpful to him."

"Were you the one who went through my desk and my house?"

"Yup. Left those nude pictures of Melanie for you to see too. I wanted you to get a load of what a slut your wife was," he snarls.

"Why? What did I ever do to deserve that from you?"

"You got our father all those years. I always hated you for that. I figured you deserved a little suffering too."

"Having our father around was no bonus, let me tell you."

We're silent for several minutes, staring at each other. Both of us looking for the similarities—and the differences.

Finally Roger waves the gun at me and smiles. "I'm sorry to see you so depressed, Augustus."

I don't say anything. I was waiting for this.

"You've come here all alone to do something rash," Roger continues. "Something terrible. Your grief has finally caught up with you, hasn't it? You hid Slammer's gun after he jumped, then went back to Bedford the next day to retrieve it. That's what you were doing there that Saturday," he says, taking a long look at the revolver he's pointing at me. "Getting the gun so you could end it all." He looks around. "Such a beautiful spot too. The cops will call it a horrible suicide after I've wiped my prints from the gun and wrapped your dead fingers around it. And they'll just be glad to be finished with the case so quickly." His eyes narrow. "In a couple of months, when things have calmed down, I'll claim your estate. In Virginia all estate proceeds automatically flow to the closest living relative if there isn't a will. Which there isn't. I'll receive the insurance proceeds and the money you've made day trading. And Reggie Dorsey will continue to think Frank Taylor killed Melanie and Erin," he says confidently.

"How did you make the cops think Taylor had killed Erin?"

"I murdered her while wearing a pair of Taylor's shoes with carpet fibers from his house all over the soles. Fibers that the D.C. police have probably already discovered on Erin's apartment floor. It was tight squeezing my feet into his shoes. He's a size eleven, and I'm a twelve, just like you, but I managed. I dropped a couple of his dog's hairs around her place as well, just for good measure. Just to make certain those idiots made the connection."

"And Melanie?"

"I planted the knife I killed her with in Taylor's garage. Spattered a little of her blood on the Mercedes wheel as well. I had to make certain the police couldn't convict you as the killer. Because of the—"

"Slayer statutes," I finish for him.

"That's right."

"You were the one who went through my desk and took the letter."

"Yes," he says. "And those million bucks are almost mine."

"You could kill me that easily? Your own blood?"

A cruel smile comes to his face. "Absolutely," he says simply.

I smile right back. "But didn't you ever wonder *why* I made this so easy?"

He turns his head slightly to the side as he aims the revolver at me. "What are you talking about?"

"Didn't you wonder while you were following me out Route 211 why I would come to such a remote place right after being released from jail?"

Roger stares down the shiny barrel at me, eyes focused on mine for a long time. Suddenly he swings the gun to his left, but it's too late and the stillness of the summer afternoon is shattered by the loud report of a gunshot. Roger tumbles backward toward the edge of the cliff, teetering on the brink for a moment. Then his body disappears, plunging down toward the treetops below.

EPILOGUE

I may not be a religious man, but autumn in New England makes me stop and think about a higher power. The colors are incredible and I have to wonder if all of this beauty could really be just a random result of the massive explosion that occurred billions of years ago to form the universe. I'll never know the answer as long as I'm alive, which is the most frustrating aspect of being human.

Not that I'm complaining. It's thanks to Reggie that I'm still around to have such thoughts. Reggie was the one who stepped out of the forest and shot Roger dead before he could shoot me. We stood in silence at the edge of the cliff for a long time, long after the gunshot had echoed away, gazing down into the treetops cradling Roger's body.

Two weeks later Great Western Insurance Company sent me a million dollars. I'll never forget the expression on the bank teller's face when he saw the amount on the check. I would think they'd be trained to show no emotion, but he actually gasped out loud and raised both eyebrows, then smiled at me and tried to start up a conversation. In eleven years of using the branch, I've never received so much as a hello from that old guy. The other tellers were nice, but this guy was always a jerk. I just picked up my deposit slip, smiled back at him, and left. Money has a strange effect on some people.

Vincent called me out of the blue the same day I accepted an offer on my house. It was about a week after the insurance check showed up, and I was shocked to hear from him. I figured we'd never talk again after I left him sprawled on the floor of his apartment with a separated shoulder and his flavor of the evening cowering in the bedroom doorway, looking at me like I was the Boston Strangler as she held a towel around herself.

I was apprehensive when Vincent asked if he could come over and talk. After all, my supposed friend of more than twenty years had turned out to be full of secrets. And venom. I wondered what else I didn't know about him, and I was tempted to call Reggie, who has come to be a great friend, and ask his advice. But there was no reason to worry. Vincent didn't come over to threaten me. He just wanted to talk. He was more subdued than I'd ever seen him as he sat in a chair at the kitchen table, his arm in a sling. He apologized to me over and over for everything. For trying to use me to make money for his friends. For never telling me that he and Melanie had been sleeping together since high school. And for taking her to the Two O'Clock Club. I pointed out to him that maybe deep down he had been trying to come clean with me by taking me to the club that Thursday night after the baseball game. After all, I could have easily recognized Anna or Erin and started putting things together, and he knew that. He shook his head at my amateur psychology and told me that Anna never appeared in the main room and that Erin had switched to working only weekend nights a few weeks before. He had actually called the manager that afternoon to make certain neither of them would be there, just in case. But he had no explanation for Melanie's photograph in the hallway, which he admitted he knew was there. We shook hands and smiled at each other when he left, but I'll never see him again. I know that for sure.

Frank Taylor's law practice crashed and burned, and I was happy about that. After all, I'm only human. But Taylor will grow a new skin and come back to the jungle. Snakes like him always do. It's not right, but it happens.

Mary wasn't a double murderer. She really had been married to a real estate developer named Jacob, and he really had left her two million dollars, a huge house, and a Jaguar. The only thing she'd lied to me about was the size of her MicroPlan purchase. She hadn't bought one million dollars' worth of its stock, she'd actually put everything she had into it. All two million. When the IRS came looking for its share of estate taxes, which she didn't even understand that she had to pay, she was forced to sell the house and the car to cover the debt because by then her portfolio was worth less than fifty grand. She'd lost almost everything in six months. Reggie told me she ended up going back to Kentucky. Go figure.

After I sold my house in Springfield, I packed a bag with a week's worth of clothes, threw the bag in the trunk, put everything else in storage, and headed north on I-95. I'd always heard that New England was beautiful, so I put Van Morrison on the CD player and just started driving. There was nothing keeping me where I was.

I ended up near a little town called Massey in northeastern New Hampshire. It's on a small river called the Androscoggin very close to the Maine border. For two hundred thousand dollars I bought a three-bedroom cabin on top of a mountain a few miles from town, and I have my own little piece of heaven. From my porch I look out over a picturesque valley and the mountains on the other side. The closest house is a mile away, and I can see only two other homes far below me from the rocking chair I bought for the porch. I got a dog too. A golden retriever I named Drexel Burnham. Drex to his friends. He's more loyal than any human being I've ever known.

I gaze out over the landscape with its splashes of red, orange, yellow, and green, brilliant before me in the noon sun, taking it all in for the tenth time today. Then I ease myself into my black beauty and head carefully down the winding dirt drive toward the valley floor and the thin ribbon of pavement that leads to Massey.

But I don't stop in Massey because I can't get the access I need there. Fortunately there are still some places that refuse to be touched by fat pipes.

So I keep going a few miles farther to a bigger town named Berlin and a bar there called the White Mountain Bar and Grill, known simply as "the Grill" by locals. For a few hundred dollars a month I was able to get a T-1 line brought in. It's kind of expensive, but in the end it worked out great. I get to go to my regular booth in the back of the bar overlooking the Androscoggin, plug in my laptop, and day trade for a few hours almost every afternoon while I sip single-malt scotch. In a month I've made another twenty-five grand. Not a huge profit, but I paid cash for the cabin and prepaid what was left on the car. In return for letting the locals use my T-1 access when I'm not, I eat free anytime I want from the Grill's kitchen, which serves surprisingly good food. The Internet access has quickly become a big attraction, and business at the Grill has never been better. So my only real monetary responsibility is Drex's food. But he eats free at the Grill too, so come to think of it, that's not a problem either.

"Mr. Augustus?"

I look over from my laptop screen, which is just firing up. "Yes, Claire?"

Claire is the ten-year-old daughter of the Grill's owner, a stout woman named Eunice whose husband left for California a few years ago and hasn't come back. Claire is a cute little thing who hardly knew what a computer was a couple of weeks ago and could now probably hack into the CIA's mainframe.

"Can I use the computer?" she asks, a sly grin on her face.

"Claire, don't bother Mr. Augustus while he's working," Eunice calls from behind the bar as she changes a keg.

"Hey, it's Monday. Shouldn't you be in school?" I ask, grinning back at her.

"Teacher meetings," she replies in a tone that suggests I should have known about such a momentous day.

I chuckle as I stand up. "All right, but what are you going to do?"

"Going to a couple of Beanie Baby Web pages," she says as she hops up onto the bench seat and settles down on her knees in front of the computer. "Mom bought me a couple when she went to Boston last week, and I think I can sell them for a lot more than she paid."

I shake my head and move to the bar. Claire is ten years old, and she's already learning how to trade. In fifteen years she'll make a fortune on Wall Street.

"Sorry about that," Eunice says, handing me a cold glass of club soda. "She loves that computer."

"It's okay," I say, smiling as I take a seat on the stool. People have started to straggle in for lunch but the place is still pretty empty. "Just club soda for me today?" I ask, raising the glass to my lips.

"Well," she says in a drawn out voice, "the last thing I figure you need is another scotch after Saturday night. Why don't you take it a little easy today?"

A band from Manchester was playing at the Grill Saturday night, and we all had a pretty good time. I met a pretty young woman who lives down on Lake Winnipesaukee—about an hour south of here—and we ended up going back to my cabin. She was nice, and she likes the mountains. I think I'll drive down there to see her next weekend.

"Okay," I agree, taking another sip of soda. It's funny. People have taken to me right away up here. They look out for me. "Thanks."

"Mr. McKnight?"

There's a young man sitting on the stool next to mine. I didn't see him sit down. "Yes." I study his face, but I don't recognize him. I don't know how he knows my name. Maybe we were introduced Saturday night and I just don't remember. "But call me Augustus."

He holds out his hand and we shake. "Tim Price. I live over in St. Johnsbury."

"What can I do for you?"

"I heard that you're a day trader."

I chuckle. "How did you hear that?"

"Friend of mine talked to a guy in town who knows about you. Said he's watched you on the computer back there," Tim says, nodding toward Claire. "Says you're pretty successful, and I was just wondering if you could show me some of the basics."

I stare at Tim for a few moments. I can't help but think about the last time I agreed to teach the basics of day trading to a virtual stranger. Roger. My brother.

"Sure, why not. Meet me here tomorrow afternoon and we'll see how it goes." I guess I'm still a sucker for somebody who wants my help.